"You deserve to know what it is like to be wholly seduced," Jack said roughly.

"You deserve to know what it feels like to be aroused to the point of weeping, to be released from that arousal in a manner that leaves you weak and short of breath. You deserve to know the raw intimacy that only a man and a woman can share," he said, and let his hand drift down her shoulder to the swell of her breast.

Lizzie could hardly seem to catch her breath. "I think you are mad," she whispered breathlessly.

"Aye, if I'm mad, then half the world is mad with me," he said softly.

Critical acclaim for the captivating novels of Julia London

"A triumph of wit and passion."

—*BookPage*

"Singular, outstanding."

—*Publishers Weekly* (starred review)

JULIA LONDON

HIGHLAND SCANDAL

POCKET BOOKS

New York   London   Toronto   Sydney

Pocket Books
A Division of Simon & Schuster, Inc.
1230 Avenue of the Americas
New York, NY 10020

This book is a work of fiction. Names, characters, places, and incidents either are products of the author's imagination or are used fictitiously. Any resemblance to actual events or locales or persons, living or dead, is entirely coincidental.

First Pocket Books paperback edition May 2009

POCKET and colophon are registered trademarks of Simon & Schuster, Inc.

For information about special discounts for bulk purchases, please contact Simon & Schuster Special Sales at 1-866-506-1949 or business@simonandschuster.com.

The Simon & Schuster Speakers Bureau can bring authors to your live event. For more information or to book an event contact the Simon & Schuster Speakers Bureau at 866-248-3049 or visit our website at www.simonspeakers.com.

Cover design by Min Choi.
Cover art by Jon Paul.
Hand lettering by John Stevens.

Manufactured in the United States of America

10   9   8   7   6   5   4   3   2   1

ISBN-13: 978-1-4165-4710-5

ISBN-10:   1-4165-4710-X

For Jameson

HIGHLAND SCANDAL

Chapter One
∽

From his vantage point in the middle of a brambly thicket—which, Jack noted gloomily, had torn his best buckskins—he could see the road through the branches. He'd ridden hard the last hour, pushing his horse to stay a mile ahead of the two men. He gulped down air as he watched them trot by, their hats pulled low over their eyes, their greatcoats draped over the rumps of their Highland ponies and wearing scarves about their necks that were definitely plaid.

Diah, they *were* Scots! The old man in Crieff had been right—the prince's men had hired Scots bounty hunters to help find him.

Bloody, *bloody* hell. He'd put himself in quite a quagmire this time, hadn't he?

Jack waited until he was certain they'd passed and moved down the road a piece before picking his way out of the thicket, cursing beneath his breath when another thorn caught his buckskins. He untethered his horse and tossed the reins over the mare's neck and swung up onto the saddle.

And sat.

Jack really didn't know where to go from here. He'd been running from the prince's men for more than a month, fleeing England the moment he'd learned he'd been accused of adultery with the Princess of Wales, running deep into the Highlands.

Adultery. Jack snorted as he rubbed the mare's neck. Imagine, taking the Princess of Wales to his bed! It was preposterous to believe he'd do such a thing! Yet Jack couldn't help the wry smile that curved his lips as he spurred the mare up onto the road.

He'd never taken the princess to his bed, to be sure— but he was guilty of participating in more than one vulgar activity at her residence.

In spite of his innocence, when Jack had been warned that men accused of bedding the princess were being rounded up for questioning and would likely face charges of high treason—a hanging offense—he'd decided to decamp to his native Scotland. That sort of accusation flung about in the midst of a royal scandal rarely played out well for a Scot in England, and Jack Haines, the Earl of Lambourne, who was no stranger to moral transgressions and shocking behavior, knew a bad scandal when he saw one.

On the road again, he paused to look up at the tops of the Scots pines that seemed to scrape a stretch of sky the color of blue China silk, and inhaled deeply. It was clean, crisp air that swept down the glens and hills that made up the Highland landscape . . . glens and hills that seemed endless and exasperatingly uninhabited.

Jack reined his horse north, in the opposite direction of the bounty hunters. He had four, maybe five hours of daylight left and would need to find a place to bed down for the night. *Diah,* he dreaded the thought of another night in a bloody cold barn. But a barn was a good sight better than the frigid forest floor.

The air was so still—he could hear the breathing of his mount above the clopping of her hooves.

The only thing he could recall this far north was Castle Beal, and that was several miles away across some questionable terrain, two days' hard ride from Lambourne Castle, just south of here. He was trying to recall the best route—it had been eleven years since he'd spent any time in Scotland other than the obligatory annual fortnight at Lambourne—when he heard the faint but unmistakable *clop clop* of another horse's hooves on the road . . . or worse, a pair of horses.

Jack reined up and listened. Damn their eyes—the bounty hunters had turned back. There wasn't a moment to spare. Jack dug his spurs into his mare, but she was fatigued and he spurred her too hard; he winced when she whinnied as loudly as if he'd stuck her with a hot poker and broke into a run. The bounty hunters had surely heard it and would realize they were on Jack's heels.

Indeed, they had gained ground on him throughout the day in spite of wretched terrain and the prime horseflesh he rode. Christ Almighty, where had the prince found these men?

Jack sent the mare crashing into the woods and its thick undergrowth, leaping recklessly over the trunk of a downed tree. A deer path led off to the right; Jack reined her in that direction. The mare careered up the path, splashed through a running stream, but balked at a steep embankment. Jack quickly wheeled her around, pointed her toward the embankment again. "Move on, then—*move!*" he urged her, bending low over her neck and digging his spurs into her flanks.

The horse gave it all she had; she crested the top of the embankment—and reared at the sight of two men on horseback. Jack hung on and managed to yank her around with the intention of going back down the embankment, but saw the bounty hunters crashing through the stream and heaving up behind him.

He reined his horse tightly as four men encircled him. He quickly looked around for an escape, any escape, but saw only a pair of shotguns leveled at him. The mare's spittle was foaming and her breathing labored—she'd not sprint, and even if she did, she'd not get far.

Jack looked again at the shotguns leveled at him as his heart began to pound in his chest. There was no out—he'd been caught. "*Mary, Queen of Scots,*" he uttered irritably as he eyed the one with the largest gun. "I donna suppose we might have a chat, then? I am a wealthy man."

His answer was the cock of the gun's trigger.

"All right, all right," he said, slowly lifting his hands. "You have me, lads." And he braced himself as they closed in, entirely uncertain if today would be his last.

Chapter Two

If it was possible, Castle Beal was even drearier than Lambourne Castle.

When Jack realized where the men were taking him, and caught sight of the imposing, drab, gray structure, he mentioned, in a rather flimsy bid for better accommodations than might be given to a fugitive, that his great-grandmother had been born a Beal.

That clearly gave the four men pause.

He hastily added that she was of the Strathmore Beals, and hoped that was true—he was hard pressed to remember the tedious details of the family tree; his sister, Fiona, was the one who could recite it precisely—but it seemed to have the desired effect. Instead of a room in the dungeon, into which Jack knew very well he would have been tossed like a sack of tubers, he was put into a suite like a proper guest.

And there he'd been left to rot, apparently, divested of his gun and hunting knife. But Jack cheerfully reasoned that though he'd been in London quite a long time, he'd been born and bred a Highlander, and he knew how to fight his way out of a scrap.

The door was left unlocked. They considered him a gentleman, above escape. He debated whether or not he was, indeed, that sort of gentleman as he walked the length of the room, counting his steps for the breadth and depth, again and again. The room was approximately sixteen by fourteen feet, give or take an inch. There was a faint odor, too, a rather acrid smell that led him to believe something was rotting beneath the wood flooring.

Jack had no idea how long he'd have to wait, as they were a wee bit reluctant to discuss their plans with him. But they'd brought him something that passed as gruel, and had thrown a block of peat on the hearth when the sun slipped below the horizon.

By then, Jack was tired of pacing and lay on the bed fully clothed, including his greatcoat, on the chance an opportunity for escape should arise. He fell into a shallow sleep in which he envisioned himself floating on a cool green river near Lambourne Castle. The sunlight was dappled on the stern of his little boat, and a woman in a very large-brimmed hat was rowing. She had slender arms and elegant hands. She possessed a fine figure, but Jack could not see her face. . . .

Something awakened him abruptly. He came up with a start and looked right into the eyes of a boy whose dark golden hair stuck out from beneath his cap.

Jack relaxed and idly scratched his chest as he observed the lad. "Who are you?"

The boy did not respond.

"You're a page, I'd wager, sent to attend me, aye?"

Again, the boy did not respond.

"No' a page? A spy, then?" Jack swung his legs off the side of the bed and stood, hands on hips, eyeing the boy. "The blackguards sent you to ascertain my mood and whether or not I have any nefarious plans, is that it?"

"Who are you?" the boy asked.

"Ah! I asked you first. Who are *you*?"

"Lachlan," he said shyly.

"Sir Lachlan," Jack said, with a bow of his head. "I am Lord Lambourne."

Lachlan blinked.

Jack's brows rose. "What? You've no' heard of me? I am the Earl of Lambourne! I own a big, gloomy castle— no' as gloomy as this one, aye, but gloomy nonetheless— a wee bit south of here. Does that spark any recognition whatsoever?" he asked as he walked around to the basin.

The child shook his head.

"Then I would say," Jack said, pausing to dip his hands into the ice-cold basin to splash water on his face, "that your education has been sorely lacking." He glanced over his shoulder at the boy, who was studying him closely. He was wearing trousers that were too short by an inch or more, and his face was stained with the remnants of his last meal.

Jack calmly continued his toilette, aware of his audience. When he was done, he turned to the child once more. "Here we are, then," he said with a formal bow. "You may take me to your king."

"We donna have a king," Lachlan gravely informed him.

Jack shrugged. "Then take me to your squire. Everyone has a squire."

Lachlan pondered that for a moment. "I think it is me uncle Carson."

"He'll do," Jack said, and gestured toward the door. "Off we go, then."

They got as far as the threshold, where a pair of rather large Highlanders who'd most inconveniently just arrived, pushed Jack firmly back into the room. Behind them a dignified, silver-haired gentleman strolled into the room and eyed Jack appraisingly.

"Might I have the pleasure of knowing who is ogling me?" Jack asked.

"Carson Beal," the man answered. "I am laird here."

"Ah. So young Lachlan guessed correctly."

"Pardon?"

Jack smiled. "A private jest."

Carson Beal's brows knitted; he clasped his hands behind his back and walked deeper into the room as he continued to study Jack. "Who are you?"

"Jankin MacLeary Haines of Lambourne Castle," Jack said with a curt nod of his head. "Close acquaintances call me Jack. You may call me my Lord Lambourne." He gave Beal a bit of a smirk.

Carson Beal frowned. "Rather flippant for a man wanted by the Prince of Wales for high treason, are you no'?"

Jack's smile broadened—he was not one to let his true feelings be known, and he would never let this Beal fellow know how that pained him. "My good friend the prince has been woefully misinformed."

"Oh?" Carson asked, arching one dubious brow. "Is that why you ran like a coward from my men?"

That certainly got Jack's back up, but he said pleasantly, "Your men did no' identify themselves. As far as I knew they were bloodthirsty thieves, and I but one man."

"Mmm . . . be that as it may, milord Lambourne," Beal said with contempt, "I think you find yourself in a spot of trouble, aye?"

Jack laughed and said honestly, "I am in the devil's own scrape, that I am. But I rather think my loss is your gain."

"What might *I* possibly gain?" Beal scoffed.

"I'd no' even hazard a guess," Jack said congenially. "But you have no' yet turned me over for what is, I assume, knowing His Highness as I do, a generous bounty. Therefore, you must stand to gain."

Beal's eyes narrowed. "As it happens, I have a proposition for you."

Aha . . . they *were* thieves. They would give Jack the option of paying his way out of their clutches. Bloody good of them, and he, fortunately, was a man of means. "I'm listening," he said, folding his arms across his chest.

"You have one of two choices," Beal said. "We can hand you over to the prince's men—who, incidentally, have arrived to escort you to London."

That was a mildly alarming bit of news.

"Or, we can tell the prince's men you've escaped and point them away. To Lambourne Castle, perhaps. Insinuate that you had help, aye?"

An appealing alternative but one fraught with questions. "And why would you do that, Laird?" Jack asked casually.

Beal paused, tilted his head back to look up at Jack. "Because you would agree to a handfasting with one of our women."

Jack almost choked. "A *handfasting*?"

"Aye," Beal said calmly, as if it were perfectly normal to suggest that Jack engage in an ancient pagan ceremony with a complete stranger. "You will agree to a trial marriage of a year and a day. If, at the end of that year and a day, you and the woman do no' suit . . ." He shrugged. "You are free to go."

Jack gaped at him. "That's insanity!" he blustered. "Handfasting is no'—well, it's hardly legal, I'd wager, and it is certainly no longer a custom, sir! It is obsolete, passé, backward—"

"We have a vicar who will perform the ceremony."

"*Why*? Why would you ask this of me? Who is this woman? She must have the face of a horse and the body of a sow to warrant this!" he said bluntly.

"She's rather handsome, I'd say," Beal said casually.

Jack knew the man lied, of course. This was too drastic, too fantastic—there had to be something entirely odious about her. "Why me?" Jack demanded. "Surely you can command one of your henchmen to it."

"Ah, but I have something with which to persuade you, aye?" he said with a cold smile. "The prince seems rather determined to find you, he does. His men are combing every glen in search of you."

George was that angry, was he?

"In addition to his own men, he's hired teams of hunters to help them search the Scottish wilds for you, milord. I suppose I donna need to tell you that a royal bounty is quite attractive to a Highlander."

"Is it no' to you as well?" Jack asked.

Beal paused a moment, his eyes narrowing on Jack. "If you agree to the handfasting, you will have a place to remain out of sight for a time until the prince has lost interest in seeing you hang."

"He does no' really intend to hang me," Jack said unconvincingly. "And how will I be certain that one of your clan does no' find the bounty as attractive as the rest of Scotland?"

"Because Beals are fiercely loyal," Beal said smoothly. "And I will match the prince's bounty if one finds he canna live without it, aye?"

"Would you, indeed?" Jack said distrustfully. "This scheme means that much to you?"

"I have my reasons, Lambourne. But you need no' fear a Beal. We will keep you safe in Glenalmond."

Jack considered him. As much as he mistrusted this laird, and as much as the suggestion of a handfasting repulsed Jack, Beal had a point: if he agreed to this insanity, he'd be tucked away until the scandal in London had passed like a bad winter storm. And he'd have the luxury of time to plot a proper escape. It was, surprisingly, the perfect situation for him in his present predicament. The woman might be as ugly as an old sow, but she might also be his saving grace. "A handfasting, is it?" he asked, studying Beal shrewdly. "A year and a day, and I may cry off?"

Beal nodded.

"Suppose I canna endure a year and a day."

"If you repudiate our woman and your troth, the Beals will act accordingly to avenge her honor."

An old clan threat to cut his throat, but a threat that would be difficult to carry out on a Mayfair street in London, where they'd have to go to find him.

"Once the ceremony is done, am I to be locked away?"

Carson Beal chuckled. "We are no' heathens, milord. Of course no'. We will depend on your word as a gentleman and an earl that you will remain on Beal lands for a year and a day and honor your vow. It will behoove you to do so, what with the prince so determined to find you, aye? But naturally, within our little glen, you shall be free."

Not bloody likely. The proposition was too outlandish to be true. Jack studied the gray-haired man, trying to think through all the angles.

"The prince's men are in the dining hall just now. I suspect they'll stay for a day or so unless I give them the unpleasant news that you've escaped and are headed for Lambourne Castle," the laird added far too casually.

That was enough. As mad as a handfasting sounded, Jack would take his chances. "Well, Laird, I suppose we both gain something this day."

Beal's smile was slow and cold. "Take him," he ordered his men, and the two brutes grabbed Jack before he could change his fool mind.

Chapter Three

They kept him locked away in a dark and dank room, where he could hear what sounded like a herd of cattle being driven on the floor above. Beal said it was to keep him out of sight until the prince's men had left, but Jack was beginning to despair he'd ever see the light of day again.

At last a pair of large Highland men appeared wearing the Beal plaid. They roughly escorted him upstairs, dragging him into the bitterly cold night air.

A crowd had gathered in the upper bailey, Jack was chagrinned to see. He was paraded through it like a fat Christmas goose to a cacophony of cheers and jeers. The laird had seen to it that the assembled throng had plenty of ale; the smell of it filled his nostrils, and his boots sloshed through more than one spill.

He was ushered through small wooden doors that deceptively marked a grand hall. Dozens of candles blazed inside and the hall was teeming with people. Frankly, Jack marveled that there were this many Beals and Beal tenants living in Glenalmond.

"Felicitations, milord!" someone shouted happily, holding a tankard aloft.

Felicitations, indeed.

Jack was practically dragged across the great hall toward a raised platform at the far end of the room, where musicians would sit during a ball. Tonight the platform was empty save the laird and a man of the cloth. Jack was deposited on that platform directly in front of Carson Beal. "You did no' make clear all the bloody Highlands would be on hand to witness," Jack complained.

"You'll be grateful to know that a small army assembled by the prince's men are riding hard to the south to Lambourne just now," Beal retorted, and leaned forward. "But a single word from me will bring them back."

Jack's reply was lost when a raucous cry went up. He turned to see what the shouting was about and saw a woman in a gray, homespun wool gown being dragged by two men to the dais. She was not dressed for a handfasting. She wore a plaid shawl around her shoulders, and her dark, auburn hair was tied up in a thin, long ribbon she'd wrapped around her head. As they reached the dais, one of the men grabbed her around the waist and bodily carried her up, putting her down next to Jack.

Jack was surprised—she was comely. Her eyes were blue, her lashes thick and black, and she looked at Carson Beal with what Jack instantly recognized as a woman's white-hot fury.

She was so furious, in fact, that she scarcely seemed to notice Jack or the vicar, who took her arm and held it out from her body, the palm of her hand turned up.

"Good evening, Lizzie," Beal said, as if she'd come for tea.

"Uncle, donna do this!" she said angrily. "I'll think of something, on my word I shall, but this . . . *this* is madness!"

Beal held up a thin strip of red ribbon. She tried to pull her hand away, but the vicar held it steady.

"It's no' legal!" she insisted as Beal quickly wrapped the ribbon around her slender wrist.

"I argued the same. Apparently it is," Jack said.

She snapped that stormy blue gaze at him, and Jack had the uneasy sense that she would have kicked him square in the knees if she could have managed it.

"Lass," Beal said as he knotted the ribbon, "the constable is here now. He's come to speak with you about your debts. I can send him away, or I can send him to Thorntree to speak with Charlotte."

The young woman froze.

"Sir," Beal said to Jack, indicating his hand. "Take her hand in your right hand."

Jack did not move as quickly as Beal liked; he was struck with a fist in his back at the same moment someone grabbed his arm and pushed his hand onto hers. There was no point in fighting it—he'd given his word, and Highland mercenaries surrounded him. He folded his fingers around the young woman's. Her hand felt delicate but rough, and if he weren't mistaken, there was a callus on her palm.

Beal tied the knot, binding them together. Satisfied with his handiwork, he stepped back, gesturing impatiently to the vicar. "Make it quick," he ordered.

"We stand here today to witness the handfasting of Miss Elizabeth Drummond Beal," the vicar said, "to Jankin MacLeary Haines, the Earl of Lambourne."

Jack heard the lass's small gasp of surprise as the man droned on, but she did not look at him. She was looking up, staring helplessly at a pair of ancient shields hanging above them. He could feel her pulse in her fingers—her heart was beating at a rapid clip. He hoped to high heaven she didn't swoon. He'd have this over as soon as possible and a dramatic swoon would only prolong it.

The vicar asked her if she agreed to the handfasting for a year and a day. Elizabeth Drummond Beal did not respond. Jack glanced down, arched a curious brow at the same moment Beal hissed, *"Lizzie! The constable?"*

She glared at him. *"Aye,"* she muttered.

The vicar looked at Jack. "Milord?"

"Aye," he growled.

It was done. A paper of some sort was thrust at them, and they were forced to put their names to it, at which point the vicar announced their troth plighted for a year and a day. They were turned about and their bound wrists lifted for the crowd to see. Cheers went up; tankards clashed, and from somewhere—the corridor, perhaps?—a pair of fiddles began to play.

The Highland brigade Carson Beal had assembled to enforce the handfasting pushed Jack and Lizzie off the platform and made them walk along at a rapid clip, causing Lizzie to stumble. Jack caught her elbow and held her up; she slapped his hand from her arm.

They were propelled through the crowd. "Well done, Lizzie!" one man shouted. "Who'd have thought it, Lizzie?" another called out with a laugh. "Is the hunting so bad in London, milord?" someone else shouted, earning the guffaws of several.

They were steered into a narrow corridor, and when Lizzie faltered, Beal barked, *"Keep on, keep on!"* from somewhere behind them. Several of the witnesses followed along behind them as well, breaking into a bawdy Gaelic wedding song. The men who swept Jack and Lizzie along picked up their pace when they reached a flight of stairs that spiraled upward, filling the narrow passageway with the sound of belts and boots scraping against the stone walls.

At the top of the stairs they came to an abrupt halt at

a closed door. They were at the top of one of four turrets, Jack realized.

Beal pushed past Jack and stood on the top step, facing the revelers. "Join me, lads," he said, motioning for his men to turn Jack and Lizzie around to face the crowd, "in wishing the Earl of Lambourne and my lovely niece many happy nights in complete conjugal felicity!"

"Uncle, *no!*" Lizzie moaned at the very same moment Beal opened the door at their back. The crowd, facing the open door, let out a cry of glee. Jack glanced over his shoulder, as did his bound companion.

"*Diah,*" she muttered.

Even Jack felt a flicker of surprise. The small, circular room was basking in soft candlelight. The brocade bed curtains had been pulled and belted around the bedposts and the bedlinens turned down. On a table in front of the hearth sat a dome-covered platter and decanted wine. Winter rose blooms were scattered on the floor and across the bed.

"There you are, milord!" someone shouted from the back. "A bit of romance to put her in a proper mood!"

"And a bit of wine if the romance does no' help!" someone else shouted to much raucous laughter.

"Oh, ye of little faith," Jack drawled, earning another round of laughter.

Lizzie closed her eyes.

"Go on, then," Beal said sternly, and pushed Lizzie into the room, and by doing so, forced Jack to follow her. He shut the door quickly behind them; a bolt on the outside slid into a lock. Jack could hear Beal tell the revelers that there was more ale and food in the banquet hall. More helpful and lewder suggestions were called through the door as the happy crowd began the trek downstairs.

It wasn't until he heard their voices far down the spiraling staircase that Jack looked at Lizzie.

"Get it off," she said, jerking their bound wrists up and holding them up under his nose.

"I thought perhaps we might at least introduce ourselves," he said lightly.

"Get it *off*!"

"What shall I call you?" he asked as he pulled her to the table and removed the silver dome on the platter. Mutton stew, by the smell of it. Not a single knife to be had. "Lover?"

"Rest assured you'll never need to call me anything at all!" she said with admirable conviction.

"You may reduce your rancor and save it for when you might need it," he said calmly. "I am as enchanted by this arrangement as you are. May I remove your brooch?"

"Pardon?"

"Your brooch," he said, looking at the small gold ring-shaped brooch that held her shawl on her shoulder.

Her eyes narrowed.

Jack knew that look and gestured to their wrists. "Rein in your thoughts, lass. I need something to *get it off*."

"*I'll* do it," she said tersely, and lifted her hands. Naturally, his went along with hers, and his fingers brushed against her breast. It was encased in thick wool, but it was a breast nonetheless, and little Miss Lizzie blushed furiously.

She quickly unfastened the pin and pushed it into his hand, managing to spear his palm in the process.

With a slight grimace, Jack took the pin and began to scrape at the sliver of red ribbon between their wrists. "Lizzie, is it?" he asked as he worked.

"Please hurry," she said.

"Perhaps you prefer Miss Beal," he said. "Although

that seems rather formal, given that we've just been bound to each other for a year and a day."

"Here then, shall I do it?" she demanded, trying to take the pin from his hand.

"*Patience*," he urged her, and lightly pushed her hand away with the back of his. He continued scraping until the fabric of the ribbon was threadbare. He then put his hand on hers and jerked their hands apart, ripping the last bits of ribbon and freeing them.

Lizzie Beal instantly rubbed her wrist, then put her hand out, palm up.

Jack looked at her hand, then at her. She really had remarkable blue eyes. The color of a Caribbean sea.

"My *brooch*, if you please."

He bowed unnecessarily low and placed it carefully in her palm.

Lizzie Beal spared him not as much as a glance. She marched to the single window in the room, shoved aside the heavy drapery, and then pushed the window open. She braced her hands against the casing and leaned over, looking out.

As it was black as ink outside, Jack couldn't imagine what she might possibly see. "It's quite cold," he said, and turned to the table. "Come and have some mutton stew. We may as well relax, for it looks to be a long night, aye?"

He expected a maidenly protest, but he heard what sounded like the scrape of a shoe against the wall. When he turned round, he started at the sight of Lizzie Beal crouched on the casing and fitting her body through the narrow window. "*Diah*, have you lost your mind?" he exclaimed. "Come down from there before you hurt yourself!" He surged forward to stop her, but Lizzie Beal never even looked at him—she just jumped.

Horrified, Jack lunged for the window and thrust his

head through, expecting to see her crumpled form in the bailey below.

She was not the least bit crumpled; thankfully, she was crawling off a terrace below the turret's window. As with his own castle, additions and restructuring through the years had added a room just below the turret's window. From the roof of that room, it was but a short distance to the parapet walk, onto which Lizzie lowered herself like a wood nymph, disappearing from view.

"Foolish chit," he muttered, and straightened up. He had no idea where she was going, but it was hardly his concern. He'd held up his end of the bargain. Jack pulled the window closed and divested himself of his greatcoat. He was ravenous—he sat down at the table and ladled a generous helping of mutton stew into a bowl. "No doubt she's taken a stable boy as a lover and got herself into this predicament," he uttered aloud. "That's what is wrong with Highlanders. They've no respect for the natural order of things."

He ate quickly, and when he'd finished the meal, he stoked the fire, then propped himself on the bed, his legs crossed at the ankles, and folded his hands behind his head.

His belly was full, he was warm, and while he found himself in yet another unwelcome situation, he believed that he might at least have a proper night's sleep.

He'd think what to do on the morrow.

Unfortunately, Jack never managed to sleep. A commotion in the hall brought him to his feet. The door was thrown open before he could reach it, and the barrel of a shotgun was pointed at his head.

He sighed, put his hands on his hips. "*Diah,* what is it now?" he demanded of whoever held the shotgun.

In response, someone shoved a disheveled Lizzie Beal

into the room. She stumbled headlong into him; Jack caught her and quickly put her behind him as Carson Beal strolled into the room along with the very large fellow who held the shotgun. Beal's nostrils were flared, his jaw clenched. He glared at Lizzie, then at Jack, and pointed a long, menacing finger at her head, which, Jack realized, was peeking out around him. "If she escapes again, Lambourne, you will hang," he said tightly. "It is as simple as that."

All this talk of hanging tossed about willy-nilly was beginning to grate. And this wretched handfasting! Not an hour old and already a bloody nuisance!

Jack felt the lass move, and had an inkling she meant to make matters worse. He clamped a hand on her arm behind his back, squeezing just enough to warn her not to speak. He clicked his heels, said, "Aye, aye, Captain," and flippantly saluted Beal.

Beal's expression darkened. He stared at Jack, assessing him, but at last lifted one hand. His bear of a companion stepped out of the room. "Mind you keep her close, milord," Beal said ominously, and quit the room, slamming the door behind him and then sliding the bolt into the latch and locking them in once more.

Chapter Four

Lizzie still could not believe this was happening. She could not believe Carson had abducted her from her home, forced her into this ludicrous and undoubtedly illegal handfasting ceremony, and then, in all the hubbub, remembered her childhood trick of climbing down from the turret.

Standing behind the broad-shouldered, tall man, Lizzie was struck by another disbelief—that Carson had bound her to the *Earl* of *Lambourne*.

Not that she had any idea who he was, really, but she rather supposed that in any event, an earl was quite a lofty title with whom to be handfasted. What madness had prompted him to agree to this? What debt did he owe Carson to warrant it?

When Lizzie had first seen him standing on the platform, she'd noticed that he hadn't bothered to shed his greatcoat, which gave her the impression he'd been ambushed and dragged inside, just like her. But then he'd been so bloody cheerful and had smiled so charmingly that she couldn't help but believe that he'd agreed to it.

Sir Charm continued to hold her arm as Carson and his enormous Highlander locked them in the room again. When she heard the bolt slide into the lock, Lizzie jerked her arm up, intending to break free of the earl's tight grip, but he startled her by suddenly wheeling about. In one swift movement, he pushed her up against the bed. Lizzie was so startled that she lost her footing and slipped, landing on the bed.

Suddenly he was looming over her, forcing her onto her back and bracing himself with one knee and his hands. "If you do *anything* so foolish again, Lizzie Beal, I shall no' hesitate to exact a proper punishment! I do no' intend to hang!"

The ominous sounding *proper punishment* notwithstanding, Lizzie snapped, "You obviously *deserve* to hang, you scoundrel, or you'd no' be here, aye?"

For some reason that made him smile roguishly, and honestly, he seemed almost an apparition with his handsome, chiseled face, his square chin, his black hair, and dove gray eyes. In fact, his smile was astonishingly captivating, and for a moment, one slender moment, Lizzie didn't mind that he was holding her down on a bed.

"I'll no' deny that I'm a scoundrel . . . but I've done nothing to deserve the likes of *you*." His eyes wandered from hers, drifting lazily down to her lips, to the skin of her bosom, which was, Lizzie realized with horror, revealed to him, as her shawl had slipped. "Although I will freely admit that I had imagined someone far less comely."

"Let me up!" she cried, pushing against his chest.

Lambourne caught her hand and held it tightly against his breast. "Let us no' be so hasty, lass. First, I will have your word that you'll no' try something as foolish as leaping from windows."

"I'll no' promise anything!"

"Then prepare for your punishment."

"All right, all right!" she cried.

"All right, all right *what*?"

She took a breath, chiding herself to *think*. "I *promise*," she said testily as she slyly moved her free hand down her side, to her knee, where she gathered the fabric of her gown.

He cocked his head and frowned. "As easy as that?" he asked suspiciously. His gaze was drawn to her bosom again, making Lizzie feel hot beneath his perusal. "I pray you are true, for I need you to be easy now."

Easy! Lizzie gasped and tried to shove him off her body, but Lambourne planted the hand he held high above her head and placed his other hand on her shoulder, holding her down. "Try to listen, will you, for there is more than one way to skin a cat," he said, and Lizzie frantically gathered more of her gown until she could touch her bare knee. "It has been my experience that if one fights, the chains that bind will only tighten," he said. "But if one is easy, the chains will slacken."

"I will *never* be easy for you!" Lizzie cried as she raised her leg and touched the polished handle of the small dirk she'd managed to put in her stocking before Carson's men could drag her away from her home. "I will *die* before I am easy for you!"

"*Ach*, now, a stubborn, willful lass is bound only for trouble," he added, and without as much as a glance at her free hand, he caught her wrist and twisted her arm. Lizzie cried out and dropped the dirk.

The earl grabbed it off the bed and held it up between them. "This might have been handy to have when you demanded I undo the binding, aye?" he snapped angrily. "Why did you no' tell me you had it? Because you intended to use it on *me*?" He hurled the dirk across the room.

"How *dare*—" Lizzie started, but he grabbed her arms and pulled her up at almost the same moment he twisted her about and tossed her facedown on the bed. Lizzie barely managed to get her hands beneath her before he crawled over her, his legs locking her in on either side, his body on hers.

He pressed close, his mouth next to her ear. He was heavy. Solid. "You sorely try my patience, lass," he said gruffly. "Are you mad? Do you truly think you can harm me with that wee knife? You only vex me with it! Now *listen* to me! You are no' the only one in this room who would be free of this bloody rotten predicament! If you will be easy and have a bit of patience, you and I might achieve our mutual goal, eh? Eventually, the scoundrel will free us, and when he does, we may free ourselves! But until that moment comes, you best learn to play a clever game to get what you want—no more throwing yourself out windows or pulling wee knives, aye?"

"Get *off* me," she hissed.

"I will, and gladly. But allow me to offer a piece of advice, will you? A lady should *never* physically engage a man, for invariably, his thoughts will turn to another sort of tussle entirely."

Lizzie cried out with alarm, but the earl had already lifted himself off of her. Stunned, she rolled onto her back. Lambourne was standing beside the bed, his hand outstretched in a silent offer to help her up. Lizzie ignored him and rose from the bed, her mind whirling as she methodically straightened out her rumpled skirts. When she glanced up, Lambourne's gray eyes were shining with amusement . . . and interest.

Lord, but it was suddenly warm in this room. Heat swelled inside her, licking at her seams, looking for an escape. A little air might help things, and she glanced at the window.

"Donna even think it," he warned her.

She frowned and carelessly tossed her shawl onto the bed.

"Whom do you mourn?" the earl asked, his gaze flicking the length of her gray gown.

"Why do they seek to hang you?" she retorted.

He lifted his gaze; one corner of his mouth curved up in a wry smile. "It is naugh' but a rather unfortunate misunderstanding," he said. "Now it is your turn—whom do you mourn?"

"My father," she said, and slyly glanced toward the wall where he'd tossed her dirk.

He followed her gaze, then nonchalantly walked to where the dirk lay, picked it up, and held it out to her.

The gesture surprised her; she quickly snatched it from his palm, lest he think to take it back, and put her back to him. She bent over, gathered up her skirt, and slid the knife into her stocking again. When she turned round, he was smiling. He walked to the table and held up a decanter of wine. "Madam?"

Lizzie shook her head. He poured a glass for himself and took a healthy drink before settling into one of the chairs at the table. "There is mutton stew if you're of a mind," he said, gesturing to the dishes.

"I could no' possibly eat," she said, folding her arms implacably. She didn't understand how he could remain so calm. He was more than calm—he was insouciant as he broke a chunk of bread from the fresh-baked loaf and ate it. He smiled.

Lizzie looked anywhere but at him. His gaze was too intimate somehow, and it had the very disturbing effect of muddling her thoughts. She had no patience for muddling—she was worried to death about her sister, Charlotte, and she couldn't imagine how she and Lambourne might possibly pass this night in the same room without giving rise to all sorts of harmful speculation. What would her intended, Gavin Gordon, think when he heard the news she'd been *handfasted* of all things?

He'd probably already heard of it, for that was precisely what Carson hoped to achieve—ruining her chances with Mr. Gordon.

"My grandmother believed that a frown would become permanent if one indulged in it too long," Lambourne opined.

Lizzie glared at him. "I've quite a lot on my mind just now, aye? Really, milord, how can you be so . . . so *jolly*?"

"I am hardly jolly," he said cavalierly, and propped his feet up on the empty chair. "But I see no point in fretting overmuch."

With his bread and wine, he'd made himself quite at home, and it riled Lizzie. "Who are you, really, then? There is no hangman, is there? My uncle *paid* you to do this!"

He laughed. "I assure you, there is no' enough money in all of Scotland to entice me to this," he said, gesturing to the two of them.

"Then why would you agree to a handfasting?" she demanded. "You donna even know my name."

"That is no' true—your name is Elizabeth Drummond Beal, otherwise known as Lizzie," he said with an incline of his head. "And I did no' *agree* to a handfasting, I was coerced just as you were."

Lizzie snorted. "Coerced is hardly an appropriate description." Abducted, kidnapped, and dragged from her house while her horrified sister and servants looked on was more apt.

"What I can no' understand," he continued, "is why Beal would feel the need to handfast you to anyone.

You're a handsome woman, aye? Surely your prospects are no' so dim."

The offhanded compliment inexplicably made Lizzie blush. " 'Tis none of your concern," she said, and abruptly walked around the bed, as far away from him as she could possibly get in this small room, and pretended to examine a painting of an elk hunt.

"Dimmer prospects than one might imagine, apparently," he added with a snort.

"I *have* prospects." At least she hoped she still did.

"Then I take it your uncle Beal does not approve of them."

She was not going to have this conversation with this man. She glanced over her shoulder at him. He gave her a slight but cocky smile. "How did he coerce *you* into this handfasting, milord? Who wants to see you hanged?"

"*Ach,*" he said, and waved a hand before helping himself to more bread.

" '*Ach*?' " she echoed. "That's all you will say? What have you done, then—murder someone?"

"The thought has recently crossed my mind, aye, but no, I did no' murder anyone. I had a . . . a wee falling out with the Prince of Wales."

Lizzie blinked. "The *Prince* of *Wales*?"

"A trifling matter," he said with a dismissive flick of his wrist. He lifted his wineglass. "It will resolve itself." He sipped.

Lizzie turned round fully now, eyeing him curiously. "I've no' seen you in these parts. Did I err in thinking you a Scot?"

"Oh, *is mise Albannach,*" he said, assuring her he was a Scot. "But I've lived many years in London."

His Gaelic, she noted, was roughly spoken. Lizzie studied him. He was obviously a man of wealth. He was dressed in fine clothing, albeit rather rumpled. His boots were the finest leather she'd ever seen. "Perhaps you would have done well to remain in London, milord."

He smiled; his fingers toyed absently with the stem of his wineglass. "Perhaps. I think we are too intimate for titles, aye? You may call me Jack." He flashed a deliberately seductive grin. "That is what all my intimate female acquaintances call me."

"The ones who would cause you to be hanged?" she asked sweetly. "Please make no mistake, milord—I am no' an intimate female acquaintance of yours."

"No?" he asked, slowly gaining his feet. "As long as we are locked in this bloody awful room, we might at least consider the possibility."

When a man so strongly built and pleasing to the eye uttered those words, the possibility flitted dangerously across Lizzie's mind. But she abruptly turned her back to him. "I'll be lying cold in my grave before I'll consider it."

That didn't stop him; he walked a slow circle around her, studying her from the top of her head to the tips of her boots. "A pity, that." He spoke low, shifting even closer to her. "I'd think lying cold in one's grave is no' as enjoyable as lying warm in one's bed."

Her pulse was beginning to race. "This is a hideous circumstance in which to attempt a seduction."

"Seduction?" He straightened up and gave her another smile that left her feeling a little light-headed. "I am not attempting a seduction, I am making an observation. I will have you know that I would never attempt to seduce a woman who did no' desire to be *completely*"—he paused, letting his words hang a moment as he admired her décolletage—"and thoroughly seduced."

"I assure you, I have no such desire," she insisted.

He smiled knowingly. "No' yet, at least."

Lizzie gasped. "You are unconscionably bold! And you flatter yourself, milord!" She abruptly pushed past him and fled to the foot of the bed, where she looked about the small room for any sort of escape from his dancing gray eyes.

"Well, then!" he said cheerfully. "If you're no' inclined to make this confinement at least a wee bit more enjoyable, I believe I shall retire. I've had a rather long day." He gestured to the bed. "For you, madam."

She looked at it. So did he. "Y-you take it," she said. "I'll sleep by the door."

"The *door*?"

"Aye, the door!"

"You'll protect us, will you, with your wee knife?"

"Please! When my fiancé comes, he shall find me by the door and know that nothing transpired here that could possibly raise alarm."

"Oh?" Lambourne asked, looking interested. "So the mysterious suitor is coming, then?"

"If my fiancé hears of it, I am certain he shall," Lizzie said, lifting her chin.

"Well, well . . . a *fiancé* rides into the midst of this madness to straighten things out," he said. "That ought to liven things up a bit." He winked playfully at her and began to unwind his neckcloth.

"He's . . . he's no' precisely my fiancé," she absently amended as she watched him remove the neckcloth and lay it across the back of a chair. "But we have a very firm understanding," she said as he laid his collar there too.

"I admire that you'll no' allow a wee thing like a handfasting vow to stop you, lass. My compliments on your impending nuptials," he said as he started on the buttons of his waistcoat. "And you must have the bed. I've no' yet lost all sense of decency—I canna allow a lady to sleep on the floor."

She realized Lambourne intended to remove his clothing to sleep. "No," Lizzie said, shaking her head. "I will sleep on the floor."

"Ach, now, Lizzie, donna be so stubborn!" he playfully chided her as he shrugged out of the waistcoat and draped it over the chair. "Take the bed—"

"I will no' take it!" she insisted. "I will no' allow him to believe I've taken one step near that bed!"

"Sleeping on the floor will make for a miserable night, you may trust me."

She shrugged.

Jack sighed. "Very well, then. Suit yourself." He pulled his lawn shirt from his trousers.

"Stop, *stop!*" Lizzie cried, throwing up a hand and turning her head.

"What now?" Jack demanded. "Can a man no' sleep unencumbered?"

Her face was blazing; she could feel it. "No! *No!* Of course no'!"

"I was no' intending to sleep naked, if that is what you think," he said irritably. He took one of the pillows and a blanket from the bed, then strode to where Lizzie stood and handed them to her. "Good night, lover," he said, and flashed that dashing, rakish smile.

Lizzie grabbed the pillow and blanket and whirled away from him. She made a place to sleep near the door and pretended to be fastidious about it so she'd not have to look at him. She heard him at the basin, then heard the creak of the bedsprings. That was followed by the sound of his boots dropping, one by one, onto the floor.

She did not want to look, she *would* not look—

She looked. He was on top of the counterpane,

propped against the headboard, watching her. "This," she said primly, gesturing to her pallet, "is the only acceptable solution under the circumstances."

"Then it would seem there is nothing left to say but good night." And with that, he snuffed the candle.

Only the coals of a dying fire at the hearth illuminated the room. Lizzie eased herself down on her pallet and tried to make herself comfortable, using her wool shawl as cover. To be safe, she withdrew her dirk and held it in her hand.

Minutes later—maybe as much as an hour later, who knew?—Lizzie heard Lambourne's breathing deepen. At least one of them was sleeping soundly. He was right about the floor—it was hard and cold, but at least Lizzie had the small and admittedly foolish hope that Mr. Gordon could not possibly believe anything devastatingly improper had happened.

She slept poorly, the cold seeping into her marrow. Her back hurt and her limbs felt numb. At some point, something startled her out of her shallow sleep. The fire had been stoked and, moreover, Lizzie felt a presence near her. With a gasp of fright, she jerked her hand up, waving the dirk in the air as she rolled onto her back.

"*Diah*, put that away!" Lambourne exclaimed.

He was crouching next to her. Lizzie quickly pushed herself up and pushed her hair from her eyes with one hand as she pointed the dirk at him with the other. "Blackguard! If you touch me I will no' hesitate to use this!" she exclaimed, and took another swipe in the air for good measure.

The Earl of Lambourne sighed wearily and held up the greatcoat that he'd obviously been holding in his hands the whole time. "Lie down," he commanded her. When Lizzie did not react immediately, he groaned. "I only mean to cover you! I could hear your teeth chattering across the room. If you'd prefer no' to shiver all night, then *lie down*."

The greatcoat did look warm. Lizzie reluctantly did as she was told.

He spread the greatcoat over her, taking care to tuck it in close to her body. When he was satisfied, he inched closer and smiled at her with the lazy confidence of a roué. "Do allow me to make one thing perfectly clear, Lizzie Beal," he said softly. "I am no' a man who forces his affection on any woman—do you quite understand me? Furthermore, when the time comes that you *want* my affection, you will bloody well beg me for it."

Lizzie swallowed. "I'll no' want it."

"Then you may stop acting as if you expect me to snatch your maidenly virtue," he said coolly, and disappeared from her side. When she heard the creak of the bed, she rolled onto her side and burrowed in under his greatcoat. It was heavy and warm and, she thought drowsily, it smelled quite nice—spicy and leathery, just like a man.

She drifted back to sleep with the words *you will bloody well beg me for it* echoing in her mind.

At Thorntree, Lizzie's sister, Charlotte, sat at the front window in the drawing room, staring morosely at the top of the gray, imposing structure of Castle Beal visible above the tree tops, high up on the hill. Castle Beal dominated everything in this part of the Highlands, including Thorntree, the modest family estate on the banks of the River Almond, down the way in Glenalmond, in Castle Beal's long shadow.

Three miles separated the two structures, yet sometimes it felt as if Thorntree was in the castle's upper bailey, so closely did Uncle Carson keep Lizzie and Charlotte to him.

Since their father, Carson's brother, had died several months ago, Charlotte and her sister rarely passed a day in which Uncle Carson did not call on them at Thorntree. He did not care that they were grown women—Charlotte was five and twenty, Lizzie three and twenty—and did not need or want his protection. To Carson's way of thinking, they were Beal women, part of his clan and little more than inferior property, and he insisted on interfering.

Of late he'd tried to keep Lizzie from accepting the attentions of Gavin Gordon, a Highlander who resided with his family in Glencochill, just a few miles over the hills from Thorntree. He was well regarded around Aberfeldy and Crieff. He was rebuilding the Gordon estate—they'd lost quite a lot during the Clearances several years ago, but Mr. Gordon was slowly bringing it to life again. Charlotte understood he'd been buying sheep and adding to his flock. He had plans to begin exporting wool when he had enough sheep to produce it.

Lizzie had been introduced to Mr. Gordon at a harvest dance last year and had instantly taken a liking to him. So had Charlotte. He seemed the perfect choice for her sister. He seemed to genuinely adore her and, moreover, he'd made it quite clear that Charlotte was more than welcome in his house.

Carson's objections to Mr. Gordon were vague at best and seemed to center on old clan rivalries that the Gordons insisted no longer existed. Lizzie believed Carson's objection had to do with Thorntree, but as she and Charlotte were the surviving heirs, Carson had no claim to it . . . other than as collateral against the debts their father had left when he died. Carson had paid a few of the larger debts and, in doing so, had essentially put Lizzie and Charlotte in debt to him. The only way they might repay that debt was with Thorntree. They had no money.

Before their father had died, Lizzie and Charlotte had perhaps known, but not appreciated, that Thorntree was so small it could not support sheep or cattle, and because of the terrain it could not be properly farmed. When Papa died they discovered that not only did it cost more to manage the estate than the estate brought in, they had less than five hundred pounds in their coffers to support the estate, the two of them, and the Kincades, longtime servants who depended upon them for their livelihood. They'd been forced to let go the daily servants.

Aye, Lizzie and Charlotte had been beholden to Carson before they'd even known it. Yet it perplexed them nonetheless—Thorntree was essentially useless to Carson. Although it was useless to him, it was the only thing the Gordon family might accept in dowry.

Charlotte couldn't comprehend why Carson would deny them that one spot of happiness. They'd argued with him and he had threatened them. Charlotte was proud of Lizzie—she'd refused to give in to Carson's demands to stop seeing Mr. Gordon.

And then, yesterday evening, Carson had arrived with his little Highland army, dragging Lizzie from Thorntree for God knew what purpose—other than to ruin any chance she might have of marrying Mr. Gordon—and left Charlotte alone in the company of his minion, an oafish brute he called Newton.

The valley's mist was beginning to lift with the dawn of a new day; Charlotte idly drummed a knitting needle against the arm of her chair, pondering the question of *why* Carson was so determined to keep them at Thorntree.

"Shall I take ye in to breakfast, Miss Beal?"

Charlotte didn't as much as glance in the brute's direction. He was as tall as a Scots pine and as broad as any Highland mountain, with hands as big as the round loaves of bread Mrs. Kincade made each day. His legs, peeking out from beneath the kilt he wore, were huge. Almost as huge as the knife he wore, in his belt. He had a rough beard, flecked with bits of red. Tiny crevices in his skin fanned out from the corner of his eyes, as if he'd been born squinting. He was the sort of Highlander who lived alone high in the hills, and Charlotte did not like him.

"Ye've been up most the night," he said. "Ye must have a hunger."

"I have a hunger for some privacy, but you do no' seem inclined to provide it."

"Ye must eat, Miss Beal."

Who *was* this man? Charlotte slowly turned her head to look at him. He stared back at her with brown eyes, his expression unreadable, his enormous hands on his knees. "Are you addlepated, Mr. Newton? Do you no' understand what I have been trying to tell you? I donna *want* your assistance! Have I no' made that plainly clear? I would that you go and do whatever it is oafs do," she said, wiggling her fingers at the door. "But *leave* me." She turned away again, staring out the window at the castle.

She heard him moving, but it wasn't until he was standing beside her that she realized he'd come even closer. "Out!" she cried, pointing at the door with her needle. "Go away from me!"

He ignored her. With a grunt of impatience, he took the knitting needle from her hand before she speared him in the eye with it, then bent over and scooped her up into his arms.

"Stop!" Charlotte shrieked. "Put me down!"

He did not put her down but carried her to the breakfast room as if she weighed nothing. And there was nothing Charlotte could do to stop him, nothing in the world that could make her legs and pelvis work. She'd lost the use of her lower body six years ago when she'd fallen from a galloping Highland pony.

She was at the mercy of this wretched beast of a man. She was at Carson's mercy, Lizzie's mercy—the mercy of the whole bloody world.

Chapter Five

The pounding on the door of the turret room the next morning was loud enough to wake all the dead buried in the Highlands.

From his seat at the table, Jack watched Lizzie almost kill herself trying to untangle herself from his greatcoat and the blanket to stand in her wrinkled gown and mess of wavy auburn hair that just reached her shoulders.

"Lambourne!" a man shouted at them from the other side of the door.

"What a gentle good morning he offers," Jack muttered. "*Aye!*" he called back as he gave Lizzie a once-over. She frowned at his perusal and put a hand to her hair. She must not have liked the feel of it, for she winced and hurried to the basin.

"The laird requests ye to break yer fast with him this morn!" the man said as Jack gained his feet and strolled the few feet to the closed door. "The lass as well—I'm to wait and bring ye, milord!"

"No!" Lizzie whispered loudly as her fingers worked frantically to comb her hair. "That's exactly what Carson wants, to parade us before everyone in this glen! I'll no' sit at a table with him! I'll no' so much as speak to him after what he's done!"

Her eyes—even more remarkably blue in the light of

day, Jack noticed—were flashing with ire. While he could not disagree with her—Beal's tactics thus far had bordered on barbaric—he'd be damned if he'd stay in this room any longer than necessary. However, his ersatz wife had a wild look in her eyes, and if he was to be freed from this room, he thought it best to proceed carefully. "As I see it, you have two choices, Lizzie. You may remain penned in this small room with me, giving rise to salacious gossip and innuendo that will spread throughout the glen"—he paused long enough to allow that to sink in—"or you may play along with your uncle's little game and attend breakfast and discern for yourself what he means to do next."

Lizzie opened her mouth . . . then quickly closed it. He could almost see a herd of thoughts stampeding through her head. He imagined her agreeing and even flinging herself at his feet, thanking him for his calm and reasoned judgment in a time of great trial, but she—unsurprisingly—disagreed and shook her head. "It's no' wise to be seen. The more we are seen, the more untoward the speculation grows."

"Perhaps your fiancé has come," Jack quickly suggested. "But you'll never know if he has come for you if you remain tucked away up here, will you?" Frankly, Jack thought if the fiancé were half a man, he'd come for her, and if he were a real man, he would be dismantling the door of this room just now.

The mention of the fiancé seemed to do the trick. Lizzie froze for a moment, then looked down. "I look a fright," she said, trying to shake the wrinkles from her gray gown.

She didn't exactly look a fright to him. Her gown was wrinkled and soiled, but her skin was flawless, her eyes little seas of blue, and her hair a very appealing mass of curls.

Naturally, Lizzie misinterpreted his look. She frowned. "You needn't look so aghast," she said curtly as she gathered up from her little bed her shawl and the ribbon she'd worn as a bandeau.

"I am hardly aghast—"

"Just a bit of privacy, if you please," she interrupted, motioning for him to turn his back.

Jack unenthusiastically turned his back to her.

"Very well," she said crisply. "I will go along, milord—"

"Jack."

"*Milord*. But only on the promise that you will no' do anything to imply or otherwise suggest that *anything* happened in this room last night. I must have your word!"

"*Jack*. Really, I think you are making far too much of this. The whole clan must recognize it for the scheme that it is."

"Please?" she said, her voice directly behind him and startling him. He abruptly turned and looked down into a most wistful expression. "Will you give me your word?"

"Yes," he said, so quickly that he surprised himself. "You have my word as an earl and a gentleman. I will let it be known that a veritable ocean of chastity lay between us last night."

She snorted at that. "You are in the Highlands, no' London. A simple *no* will suffice."

She'd wrapped the bandeau ribbon around her hair, but she'd missed one long curl that draped her neck. An insane urge to touch that curl overcame Jack; he was certain he would have if she'd not bent just then to pick up her shawl and wrap it loosely around her arms, draping the ends just so to hide the wrinkles in her gown.

Not that any man would have noticed the wrinkles in

the slightest, for Lizzie Beal had one of the most pleasing décolletages Jack had ever had the pleasure to observe. In fact, Lizzie Beal had a freshness about her, the healthy glow of clean Highland air, and a pair of dark plum lips that could, were a man to gaze too long, be quite dangerously arousing.

"What is it?" she asked uncertainly, her eyes narrowing at his perusal. "Is something amiss?"

"Only a desire to break my fast," Jack lied, and offered his arm. "If you please, Miss Beal."

With a roll of her eyes, Lizzie ignored his arm and walked to the door, banging a fist on it. "Open!" she shouted.

"That's subtle," he said wryly.

A moment later the bolt slid from the lock and the door swung open, narrowly missing Lizzie. Two rather large Highlanders stood on the other side and peered curiously inside, their gaze straying to the bed.

Jack stepped forward, blocking their view. "Mind your manners, gentlemen." And, with his hand on the small of Lizzie's back, he ushered her out.

Carson was waiting in a small room on the ground floor of the castle that some enterprising Beal had managed to convert into a breakfast room. A single window overlooked the meadow where horses grazed. As he waited for the unhappy couple to make their appearance, Carson was reminded that Lizzie and Charlotte used to stand at this very window when they were girls, longing to be on the horses' backs. Charlotte in particular would gaze wistfully at them, giving them all fancy pretend names such as Hyacinth and Miranda.

Who could have guessed they would grow up to be such intractable women?

The scent of a Highland breakfast—fresh eggs, kippers, brown bread, porridge, and black pudding—filled the room, but Carson was too impatient to eat. He wanted this over and done. There were many pressing issues that required his attention, and he blamed Lizzie for this inconvenience.

When the pair at last entered, Carson gestured to a footman, who instantly set about preparing the plates. "Do please sit," he said, as if they were proper guests.

Lambourne gallantly helped Lizzie into a chair. The rogue looked quite well rested, but Lizzie looked weary. And she was staring daggers at Carson.

Carson did not sit; he preferred to stand with his hands clasped behind his back, his dark brown eyes boring through his niece. His brother had raised two very headstrong women. He'd often warned Alpin that their independent ways would lead to trouble; certainly no self-respecting Highland man would want a woman who followed the flawed counsel of her own mind. There were already whispers about the two spinsters down the glen, and indeed they were both passing the marrying age. Charlotte would never marry, and Lizzie, well . . . she'd never marry if she did not learn to subordinate herself to the rule of men.

But Alpin never listened to him about much of anything.

"I trust you found the accommodations suitable?" he asked idly.

"Are you mad?" Lizzie shot back.

"They were quite comfortable, Laird," Lambourne said. "But a wee bit close, perhaps, for strangers."

Lizzie looked askance at Lambourne; he gave her a pointed look in return.

"Your niece was no' as pleased as me," Lambourne

added, still looking at Lizzie, "for she passed the night on the floor."

"The floor, eh?" Carson said. He was hardly surprised. Stubborn chit.

"Aye. It would seem my charms were no' enough to persuade her differently."

Carson snorted at that, and noticed that the footman glanced at Lambourne over his shoulder. That sort of news would carry through the household within the hour.

"I have learned," Lambourne continued amicably, "that a Highland lass does no' part so readily with her virtue. Miss Beal was rather adamant that she'd no' agreed to the handfasting or anything else."

Bloody scoundrel was intentionally speaking so frankly in front of the servant—he knew, too, that what he said would carry throughout the glen. Carson looked at the footman and gave him a curt nod, sending him instantly from the room. Ignoring Lambourne's smug smile, he picked up the plates the footman had prepared and laid them on the table himself before the pair. "My niece can be rather difficult at times, milord," he said. "She takes her own counsel."

"Why, Uncle, you say that as if it's undesirable," Lizzie said with false sweetness as she speared a kipper and put it in her mouth.

"In my day, women did as they were told."

"In your day, women were sheep."

"Ah, the kippers are excellent," Lambourne interjected. "Quite fresh."

Carson paid him no heed but continued to glare at Lizzie as she ate her breakfast, sliding into a seat directly across from her. "Alpin was too soft with your upbringing, lassie. He did you no service. You and Charlotte are as stubborn as any pair of braying donkeys! Why do you continue to fight me in this?"

"Charlotte?" Lambourne asked, lifting his head.

"My sister," Lizzie said curtly; and to Carson, "We *bray* because we are free to make our choices. You canna control us, Uncle. We are *grown women*."

"It would seem that I *have* controlled you," he snapped. "You are handfasted, are you no'?"

Her expression darkened. "When Mr. Gordon hears of this—"

"*Ach*," Carson cried, throwing up a hand. "Mr. Gordon, Mr. Gordon!" he shouted. How he hated that name! "Have you no pride in your heritage, Lizzie? Can you no' understand that a Beal despises a Gordon with all of his being?" he said, dramatically thumping a fist to his chest.

"I understand that *you* despise a Gordon, but that old clan rivalry is nothing but a tale for the history books! Mr. Gordon and I—"

"Are what?" Carson sneered. "*Engaged?*"

His niece lost her footing momentarily with that question—they were not formally engaged, owing chiefly to Carson's deliberate interference. "We have an understanding, and you know it perfectly well," she said tightly. "Does he know of this . . . this disaster?" she asked, gesturing toward Lambourne, who looked slightly offended. "Did you send your henchmen running to tell him straightaway?"

"Why would I do that?" Carson hissed. "Why should I care what that bloody Gordon knows?"

"It is the reason you stooped to this!" Lizzie cried disbelievingly. "The insanity of this handfasting was done precisely to make it impossible for him to offer for me!"

"It was done to keep Lambourne out of the hands of the English," Carson snapped.

"My, how that warms the cockles of my heart," Lambourne drawled.

"What a simpleton you must think me!" Lizzie exclaimed. "Yet it hardly matters, Uncle—your scheme did no' work as you'd hoped. When Mr. Gordon comes for me—"

"He'll no' come for you!" Carson said disdainfully. "He does no' know of it. He *will* no' know of it until several days have passed and the whole glen has heard the news and seen the two of you together. He is in Crieff, Lizzie! By the time word reaches him, he canna possibly save you."

Lizzie all but came out of her chair. Only the firm clamp of Lambourne's hand kept her from lunging. "It would seem," Lambourne said evenly, despite the grip he held on her arm, "that your plan has already worked beautifully, Laird. A handfasting witnessed by such a large party surely has tongues wagging up and down this lovely little glen. I'd no' be the least surprised if Mr. Gordon hears of the happy news posthaste. Therefore, your niece's chance at an engagement has been ruined, and she and I should be free to go."

"Donna take me for a fool, Lambourne," Carson said angrily. "You made your agreement with *diabhal*."

"I made no agreement with the devil!" Lizzie cried, wrenching free of Lambourne's grip by kicking him beneath the table.

Lambourne's breath came out in a grunt of pain as Lizzie found her feet.

"You will remain at Castle Beal!" Carson said sternly, pointing a finger at her. "You will participate in the events I have planned to celebrate your handfasting! I'll no' have questions as to whether or no' this handfasting is real, and *you*, sir," he said, swinging the pointed finger to Lambourne, "will do quite well to keep this one in hand, do you understand? The prince's men search for you yet and the bounty goes unclaimed. Any number of them can be here within a few hours."

"I beg your pardon, but I am no' a gamekeeper," Lambourne said. "You did no' tell me that the lass was a hellion."

"What?" Lizzie cried, affronted.

Carson stood up and slammed his cup on the table. "You will not defy me, either of you, if you value your lives as you know them!" He pushed his chair back and stalked to the door. "I've some clothing for you to don. I'll no' have you dragging about in mourning clothes that should have been put away two months ago. I shall expect you both in the great hall to receive those who have come to offer their felicitations!"

"What of Charlotte?" Lizzie exclaimed as he opened the door. "You know I canna leave her alone, Uncle!"

"She's no' alone! She has Newton to watch over her and Mrs. Kincade to see to her needs. She will do well enough without you, Lizzie!" And with that, Carson walked out the door, letting it slam shut behind him. His pulse was pounding; his jaw clenched so tightly that it ached. There was not a more willful woman in all of Scotland, and by God, he intended to break her!

He had to—everything depended on it.

Chapter Six

B ehind the breakfast room door, Lizzie glared at Jack. "No' a *gamekeeper*?" she repeated tetchily.

"The shoe fits your cheeky foot perfectly."

"*Ach!* I canna suffer you now—I must get word to my sister," she said, and pressed the heel of her palm to her forehead. Her head was reeling. She had to think. "She will fear something too horrible to speak of has befallen me."

"I've no doubt that if the laird had hanged you, bells would be tolling far and wide in this glen," Jack said, gesturing to the far and wide.

She gave him a withering look. "You are incapable of understanding, but my sister will be frantic with worry! I *must* get word to her!"

He leaned back in his chair and sighed heavenward. "Is she far from here?"

"Three miles down the glen."

"Three miles?" he echoed incredulously, looking at her again. "Then she could bloody well walk up the hill and see for herself, aye?"

"*No,*" Lizzie said smartly, "for she has lost the use of her legs. She is an invalid, if you must know, and there is no one to look after her save Mr. and Mrs. Kincade, and they are quite elderly and lack the capacity to lift her properly, no' to mention see that all her needs are met."

At least Lambourne had the decency to look properly contrite. "I beg your pardon. I had no idea."

But Lizzie waved a hand at him. She hardly cared what he said or did—she could think only of Charlotte, imagining her fear . . . *particularly* with Newton, or whoever he was. She stood from the table and walked to the window.

After a moment, Jack said, "All right, then. What foolhardy schemes are galloping through your head?"

She chafed at that, for she had just thought of climbing out the turret window again. "You hardly care," she said. Perhaps she could bribe someone. But with what? It wasn't as if she'd come with a purse to this little ceremony.

"Oh, but that is where you are wrong," he said. "I *do* care, and very much, for my neck depends on it. Just tell me—"

The door opened, interrupting him. Lizzie turned around to see the same henchman who had come for them this morning. "The laird says you are to dress for the day," he said to her. "You're to come with me."

"I will no'!"

Jack grinned at her obvious displeasure until the man said, "And you, milord."

"Pardon—*me*?" he said, his grin fading as he twisted around to look at the Highlander. The man nodded. Jack groaned, dropped his head back, and closed his eyes a moment. "Am I in hell, sir? Tell me true—am I, then?"

Predictably, the Highlander did not answer.

"I'll no' be ordered about," Lizzie said with great indignation.

Jack leveled a gaze on her. "This has all the markings

of a *very* vexing day," he warned her, as if it were some- how *her* fault, and came to his feet. "Come then, Lizzie. Let us no' fall on our swords at every opportunity."

He was infuriatingly right. Lizzie reluctantly followed him.

They were escorted to their little room in the turret. On their way up, they encountered a chambermaid. The lass stepped aside, her head lowered, but as they passed, she coyly glanced up and smiled at Jack. And *he*, Lizzie further noticed, quickly returned her smile with one so warm that it certainly melted the girl's stockings right off her legs.

A thought occurred to Lizzie—suddenly, she had an idea how to get word to Charlotte.

Not only did the hellion seem bound and determined to make trouble, but she now took issue with the cloth- ing that Beal wanted her to wear. What *was* it about the feminine mind that failed to see the reasonable course in most matters? Why did they always make things more complicated than necessary?

Not that he was terribly pleased with the idea that he must don a Beal plaid, but he didn't take issue with the kilt itself.

Lizzie, however, held out the offending garment to Jack, who was lounging on the bed now, having recalled, with some difficulty, the proper way to wear a kilt. "My uncle can no' expect me to wear this!" she insisted.

It was dark ruby red with long sleeves, which, he thought, given the bitter cold outside, was appropriate. He looked at her blue eyes, glittering with her anger. "Seems perfectly fine."

She gaped at him as if he were an imbecile. "It is *red*, milord. *Red!* Entirely unsuitable for day wear in the *best* of circumstances, and hardly *ever* suitable for evening wear! But be that as it may, it is *quite* impossible that it be worn by a woman who is still mourning the death of her father!"

"*Mi Diah*," Jack muttered.

"*Ach!*" she cried, and whirled away from him. She marched to the door and banged loudly. The Highland beast whose name they had learned was Dougal opened it, and Lizzie thrust the gown in his face. "Do please tell the laird that this will no' do!" she said firmly. "Do please remind him that I am mourning the passing of my father, his brother!"

A startled Dougal took the gown. "Aye, mu'um." He shut the door and locked it again.

"Well. This should all be speedily resolved, aye?" Jack asked, pillowing his hands behind his head. "Did you heed *anything* I said in suggesting we take Dougal under our wing and befriend him? We might have at least convinced him to keep the door unlocked."

"I will not befriend a troll," Lizzie said snippily, crossing her arms and pacing the small room.

"Madam," Jack said wearily, "you're no' helping matters in the least."

"Oh, and *you* are making astonishing progress in freeing us, is that it?"

"Perhaps if I just had a *wee* bit of help."

"Help! I've only tried to help in every imaginable way, yet you seem to enjoy all this lounging about. It's neither here nor there, really, for I've thought of a way you may atone for your lack of decisive action by helping me get word to my sister," she suggested as she paced.

"I beg your pardon, my *what*?"

"I was thinking," she continued, gliding past her little cut, "that perhaps you might seduce a chambermaid . . ."

"Now see here," Jack said sternly, coming up off the bed. "I'm no' loose in the haft."

Lizzie snorted and continued to pace. "Do no' pretend that you are a defender of propriety and virtue, sir. And I donna mean to suggest you take the poor lass to . . . to . . ." Her face pinkened; she couldn't bring herself to say it.

"My *bed*?" he said for her.

"Precisely," she said, flicking her wrist as she stole a look at his legs beneath his kilt, "but perhaps if you just smiled in that way you have she might be inclined to do you a favor."

Jack put his hands on his hips, trying to understand her. "Pardon?"

Lizzie sighed impatiently. "Ask a certain favor of her—the favor being, of course, that she take word to my sister that I am well."

"No' *that*," Jack said. "*Before* that," he added, making a circular motion with his hand. "After the pretending to defend propriety and virtue and before asking a favor."

Lizzie paused. Recognition dawned on her pretty face and she seemed thrown by what she'd said. "You know very well what I meant," she tried.

"No," he said, shaking his head. "No, I donna know what you meant at all. Please explain."

"Just . . . just persuade her in any way you can to take a message to my sister!"

But Jack wasn't letting it go so easily. He smiled at Lizzie—*that* smile—and watched the blush in her cheeks begin to spread to her neck.

He stepped closer; she turned awkwardly from him and put a hand to her nape. "It is very important that Charlotte know I am all right." She glanced back at Jack, and he saw something in her eyes that gave him pause. "*Please*, milord."

Bloody hell, the hellion was truly worried about her sister. And he could hardly deny her request, given that he had a weakness for big blue eyes, particularly when they were imploring him to help. "All right," he agreed, but pointed a finger at her. "With one condition."

She nodded fervently.

"You must call me Jack. I canna abide the *milords* and *sirs* when we are practically forced to live as man and wife."

"Agreed," she said, holding out her hand.

Jack glanced at her hand.

"We should shake on it. A man's word is sealed with his handshake."

"Where do you hear these things?" he asked irritably, but he took her hand nonetheless, her small, fine-boned hand with the callus on the palm. He looked in her eyes as he shook it, and the lass actually smiled at him.

Ach, that smile, that *smile*. It disturbed Jack, for it was terribly alluring. On a barmy Highland lass that smile and those eyes were a dangerous combination when used in such close quarters, and Jack quickly withdrew his hand from hers and stuffed it into his pocket. All he needed was that smile cast upon him throughout the day to make his blood run hot with want. "Where do you suggest I find this chambermaid?" he asked, turning round, walking to the table.

"Oh, I'll be happy to point you in the right direction when the time comes. Once we've sent word to Charlotte, then we might get on with the task of escaping, aye?"

"Yes, well, in *that* regard, do try and be kind to Dougal, will you?" Jack asked, and glanced over his shoulder at her. She was nodding vigorously and had succeeded in knocking another curl loose from her bandeau.

Yes, danger abounded in this room.

∽

Lizzie took Jack's advice to heart, for when Dougal returned—this time carrying an ancient dark blue bombazine lacking only the panniers—she smiled and thanked him and even apologized for being short earlier, but she'd been mortified to think of wearing red while in mourning.

Dougal nodded dumbly and pulled the door shut.

The moment it was shut, Lizzie whirled around to Jack and held up the old garment. "Will you look?" she demanded, wrinkling her nose at the musty smell. "I know this gown well—it belonged to my aunt Una—she wore it for two years after my uncle Robert died. She was a *wee* woman," she said, holding her forefinger and thumb up to show just how wee.

Jack looked at the gown, then at her. He seemed perplexed. "It's no' red," he said.

"Aye, but it is *old*," Lizzie said, trying to explain it to him.

He stared blankly at the gown.

"*Ach*," she said, with a dismissive flick of her wrist. "Uncle Carson means to shame me. But I donna shame so easily as that," she said, and stalked to the other side of the bed. Jack was still looking at her. She motioned for him to turn around. He sighed, took a seat at the table with his back to her. She began to unbutton her gown, but Jack turned his head slightly.

Lizzie paused to let down the bed curtains, putting them between her and his curious gaze. It was ridiculous, but just a glance from him was enough to make her insides swirl, particularly since he'd donned a kilt. A kilt! Of course Lizzie had seen men wear them all her life, but she'd never realized how a blasted kilt could make a heart beat faster. His legs, muscular and shapely beneath it, and the breadth of his shoulders in the short-cropped, tightly fitting coat, all of it—it was enough to give a woman vapors if she were inclined to them.

She changed quickly and, as she'd feared, the gown was too small. The hem reached the top of her boots, and the skirt—the skirt was far too large for today's fashion and made her look as if she were all hip. That wasn't the worst of it—the worst was the bodice. *Lord,* it was tight! Lizzie could scarcely breathe. She struggled to fasten the old buttons without a hook, but she could not manage the last two.

There was nothing to be done for it. She'd exhausted herself trying to button the bloody thing, and in a fit of frustration she stepped out behind the curtain. Jack had turned his chair around and was watching the curtains. He took one look at the gown and burst out laughing.

"Stop that!" she cried, which only served to make his laughter worse. "Stop this instant! You must help me, Jack."

"I canna help you, Lizzie. *No* one can help you. You need a seamstress. Were we in London, I'd march you to Bond Street and demand that someone—*anyone*—repair . . . *that,*" he said, gesturing to her gown. "Are you certain the red won't suit?"

"No' another word!" she cried, mortified. "I will wear my mourning gown—"

"Which is hardly an improvement. It looks as if the last woman who wore it crawled out of a turret window. The hem is muddied, there is a mysterious streak of black on the back, and it is badly wrinkled."

Lizzie glanced at her gown, draped across the end of the bed. It was indeed in worse shape than the one she was wearing. But *this* one—to be paraded about in front of God and everyone in this old thing? It was almost more than she could bear. Abduction, handfasting, a night spent in a room with a strange man . . . in a kilt. . . . The gown was the last straw, and she was mortified when tears suddenly filled her eyes.

"No, no, here now," Jack said soothingly. "You are far too spirited to be brought down by a gown, aye? And besides, you look radiant, *leannan*, as beautiful in mourning as a woman dares to be."

His compliment was false, and the endearment was absurd . . . but it warmed her nonetheless. "It's hideous," she moaned.

He did not disagree. "No one will ever see the gown, for your smile is far too bright and captivating."

She looked at him suspiciously, but Jack nodded firmly. "Would I lie?" he asked with a lopsided grin.

She couldn't help but smile, too. "I am certain you would *never* lie," she said with mock sincerity. She glanced down at the gown. At least it was clean. She sighed and peeked up at Jack. "I need your help," she admitted.

"Aye, they all come round eventually," he said, arching a devilish brow. "What may I do for you?"

"The buttons," she said, gesturing vaguely at her back. "I could no' reach them all."

"Ah. Allow me. Turn round, then."

Lizzie warily did so. He stepped behind her. She could feel Jack at her back, but when he laid his hands on her shoulders, she gasped.

"It *is* rather tight," he agreed, and deliberately traced his fingers over the bare skin of her upper back, to the top of the gown. Her skin tingled beneath his fingers; she pressed her hand to her abdomen and drew a deep breath. His knuckles brushed against her as the tugged the gown together. "*Diah*," he muttered.

"What? What is it?"

He responded by putting his hands on her shoulder, his fingers on her neck, and gently pressed his palms against her back, forcing her to stand straighter. "Take a deep breath," he instructed her, "and hold it."

Lizzie put her hands on her hips and took another deep breath.

He managed to get one of the buttons fastened. "I'd consider a corset, were I you."

She gasped. "I am *wearing* a corset," she snapped. "And—*ouch!*"

"Pardon." He paused in his work on the button to put his hands on her shoulder once more, pulling them back slightly so that she would stand even straighter, then went to work on the button again.

She was keenly aware of his body so close to hers, his hands on her skin. The sensation was surprisingly provocative. "What do *you* know of corsets?" she asked peevishly, trying to put *something* between them—indignation at the very least.

"Corsets? I've done quite a study of them," he said idly as he succeeded in fastening the button. "They've lain about most of the boudoirs I've had the pleasure of occupying."

Her pulse leapt; she could kick herself for asking. The image of him lying in a woman's bed, completely bare— as bare as he surely was beneath the kilt—suddenly towered before her in her mind's eye. "There you are," he said at last. "You are fitted as tight as a sausage in casing."

Lizzie stepped away from him, her hand to her abdomen once more. The gown was stifling. She could not *breathe*.

"What, no thank you?"

"*Thank you,*" she managed to get out.

He bent his head to one side to peer in her face. "Are you all right, Lizzie Beal? You are flushed."

She *was* flushed, but it had less to do with the gown than with the image of him that would not leave her now, no matter how hard she tried to erase it.

Out.

Out of this room was her only salvation, and she whirled around to the door, banging on it with her palm as if there was a fire at her back. "*Dougal!*" she cried.

"That wasn't precisely what I had in mind when I said *kind,*" Jack drawled as the bolt slid from the lock and the door swung open.

On the other side of it, Dougal's eyes widened as he looked at Lizzie's gown.

"*Diah,* donna stand there gaping!" Lizzie cried, and pushed past him, into the narrow stairwell, thankful to have put at least a few feet between her and Jack.

"You must no' mind her, lad," Jack said as he followed her out. "She's been in a state of high dudgeon all morning." And with that, he calmly caught her hand, gave it a bit of a yank to slow her step, and pulled her back, forcing her to behave like a lady and allow him to escort her down the stairs.

Chapter Seven

G iven that it was only eleven o'clock in the morning, Jack was surprised to see the number of people milling about the great hall . . . until he got a closer look at some of them. Judging by their bleary gazes, he assumed they hadn't yet been to bed.

Nevertheless, the mood was just as festive now as it had been last night, which was hardly surprising given the strong stench of ale that pervaded the room.

"Oh *no*," Lizzie muttered to the ceiling.

Jack looked at her inquiringly.

" 'Tis a *wedding* feast," she whispered angrily. "It's customary to celebrate a wedding with a feast and a race and silly games."

At the far end of the hall a long table had been set. Two large bowls graced the table, filled with fruit, which was a luxury at this time of year. At the center of the table sat Carson Beal in a chair that was fit for a king, and as they approached—hurried along by Dougal and two of his companions—Carson looked at Lizzie's gown and rolled his eyes.

"You are your mother's child, as contrary as the rose that blooms in winter," he said when they reached the table.

"You'd no' have me look the harlot, would you?"

Lizzie asked. "And besides, I am in mourning still, which makes this gown perfectly appropriate."

"No' for a celebration."

"I'm no' celebrating."

Carson grunted at that; Lizzie looked around them and asked, "This is a wedding feast, is it no'? What would you force us to do now, Uncle? Dance around like marionettes?"

"*Sit*," Carson said, his eyes narrowing on his niece. " 'Tis no' a wedding feast, you foolish lass! Your clan has come from as far away as Aberdeen to wish you well."

"Aberdeen?" Lizzie echoed, clearly surprised. Her brows knit as she glared at her uncle. "Just how long have you been planning this?"

Carson stood and pulled out a chair for her. "I am still your laird and your uncle. Now *sit*, Lizzie."

With a snort of disdain, Lizzie sat.

Jack took a seat next to her.

"Now then," Carson said. "When we've received the felicitations of your clansmen, we shall join the games in the lower bailey."

"Aha!" Lizzie cried. "It *is* a wedding feast!"

"*Diah*," Jack said, with a wave of sympathy for all the Beal grooms who were forced to endure three days of *this*.

Beal caught Lizzie's hand and forced her attention to a young couple who stood across the table, beaming at her.

Jack settled back for what he thought would be a long, drawn-out affair of greeting the clan members. He was not wrong. A steady stream of them approached the table, offering traditional good wishes, as well as a few ribald ones, to the happy couple. Almost all of them assured Jack and Lizzie that they would find conjugal bliss and would want to make their union official in a year and a day.

It was the height of insanity, Jack thought. Who among these fools actually believed that he and Lizzie would be anywhere near each other in a year's time? Even if Jack could not find his way out of this mess, he would cry off—marriage was not for him. His parents had had a rotten marriage, and he would not subject himself to such unhappiness.

Lizzie endeavored—earnestly—to assure anyone who would listen that this ridiculous and illegal handfasting would never last, and that she'd never agreed to it.

Jack, on the other hand, smiled and spoke when spoken to but spent his time fantasizing about his return to civilization. *London.* Necessity would dictate he begin with a call to the prince to disabuse him of any lingering doubts about Jack's innocence. Better yet, he'd have his good friend the Duke of Darlington go and make his case beforehand—and then he'd perhaps host a ball to announce this return to society. Ah yes, he thought idly as he peeled an apple with the little dirk he'd managed to coax from Lizzie in between her impassioned speeches, there would be a new crop of lovely debutantes—

"Ouch," he said, the moment her heel made contact with his ankle under the table. He turned a murderous gaze to Lizzie, who smiled sweetly and nodded to her right.

Jack looked to his right. The chambermaid was at a sideboard, refilling pitchers of water.

"Milord, would you be so kind as to bring me a cup of water?" she purred.

"There is water at your elbow," Jack said, nodding to the cup.

Lizzie's lovely winged brows dipped into a frown. "But I should like *fresh* water. From *that* pitcher," she added, looking pointedly at the chambermaid.

"Ah," Jack said, remembering his task. "Very well then." He gained his feet. "You will excuse me, Laird," he said over Lizzie's head, "if I fetch my lovely bride-to-be a cup of *fresh* water?" He did not wait for Carson's permission, merely smiled at Lizzie's glare, and began striding in the direction of the chambermaid.

The maid gave him a tremulous smile as he joined her at the sideboard. He stole a sidelong glimpse of Lizzie; she was speaking to another woman, but her eyes were on him. He smiled charmingly at Lizzie, then turned that smile to the chambermaid. "*Madainn mhath,*" he said, greeting her.

"*Madainn mhath,*" she muttered as a blush spread from her neck to her cheek.

Jack glanced around at the people milling about. "Quite a crowd, aye?"

"Aye, milord," she said shyly.

"A man can work up quite a thirst," he sighed, and glanced at the water. Would that there were something a bit stronger, such as whisky. He guessed Carson Beal had a store of fine whisky stashed somewhere in this drafty old heap of stones.

"Shall I pour you a cup?"

"Two, please," Jack said.

The chambermaid picked up the pitcher. It slipped in her hand; Jack caught it with one hand on her elbow, the other beneath the pitcher. The maid looked up at him with widened brown eyes.

"Thank you . . . what is your name?"

"Brigit, milord."

"*Brigit,*" he said, nodding as if he found that much to

his liking. "Brigit . . . may I make a personal inquiry of you?"

Brigit nodded, her gaze locked on his.

"Do you," he said softly, pausing to caress her elbow with the pad of his thumb, "perchance know the lad Lachlan?"

She nodded again.

Jack smiled and gave her elbow a gentle squeeze. "Lovely. Could you send him round to me, then?"

She swallowed; her gaze flitted to Carson Beal.

"Donna fret about him," Jack said reassuringly. "You'll send the lad round, aye?"

"*Aye*," she murmured.

"There's a good lass," he said, and took his hand from her elbow, picked up two glasses, and nodded, indicating she should pour. When she'd filled the cups, he winked at her and turned back to the dais.

He hoped he was correct in assuming that Lachlan would run a small errand for a half pence. Contrary to what little Miss Lizzie might believe, Jack was not in the habit of seducing young maids for nefarious purposes. And, as luck would have it, Carson had taken his weapons, but he'd not taken his purse.

"We came down from the hills to the village ye ken, on a pair of mules me old father had borrowed from the Camerons. Ach, but ye've no' seen a sight such as that, lass. . . . '"

Old Mr. Mungo Beattie was chatting up Lizzie about his own handfasting, which, Lizzie could only surmise, given his ancient age, had occurred five hundred years ago when perhaps handfastings were legal.

" 'Twas a Wednesday, it was . . . No, no, now, I've misspoke. A *Tuesday*, it was." He paused and pressed a finger thoughtfully alongside his nose. "Now, there I've mis-spoke again. 'Twas a Wednesday, for Tuesday we'd had a spot of rain. . . ."

As Mr. Beattie nattered on, Lizzie watched Jack from the corner of her eye. *He is standing awfully close to the maid, is he no'?* she thought. *The hand on the elbow might be the way things are done in London, but here it is too bold. . . . Really, look at how she smiles at him! Ah, but she's a blessed fool if she is charmed as easily as that! It's no' but a wee bit of flirting, for heaven's sake! Can she no' see him for what he is? He's a roué, wanted for something so awful that he might very well be hanged! Will you be looking at him so moon-eyed when he swings on the end of a hangman's noose?*

"Wednesday," Mr. Beattie said emphatically. "And I recall to this day the color. It was dove gray—nay, nay, it was *blue*. Aye, blue, it was," he said, scratching his chin. "A blue blanket beneath her saddle, a gift from our laird. . . ."

How long does one need to send a chambermaid on an errand? Perhaps he might handfast himself to her when I've rid myself of him. Aye, bind yourself to her, then!

". . . and the vicar was a wee little man, no more than knee high, on me honor. Smallest man I ever did lay eyes on, that he was. But he knew the ceremony well enough, I suppose, for he bound us together like the feet of a dead hen left to drain. . . ."

Lord help me! Had I known he'd intended to court the maid, I'd no' sent him, would I? I'd have gone myself! I could walk to Thorntree and back by the time he finishes his bit of flirting— oh, dear. Lizzie! What in heaven's name is the matter with you, then? Why should you give a fig what he's about? In a few days' time you'll never see him again or remember his name.

She turned back to Mungo Beattie and smiled. *Let him marry the wench if he so desires.*

"Did I already say that?" Mungo said, looking confused. "I canna rightly recall now."

"You did," Lizzie said kindly, having lost track of his tale completely.

"Ah. Well," he said with a shrug, "no point in repeating myself, then, aye? The point is this, lass, that if yer marriage prospects are whittled down to the point a lowly handfasting is the best ye might hope for, ye must no' despair, for a handfasting might well lead ye to the best years of yer life. I'll tell you a wee secret—love comes from the most unlikely places when ye are least expecting it."

Lizzie smiled thinly and clasped her hands together, squeezing them tightly in her lap to keep from saying anything that might alarm the old Highlander. "Thank you for your kind thoughts, Mr. Beattie."

"Me pleasure," he said with a flick of his wrist. "Here's one last piece of advice I'll offer ye. If ye want him to treat ye like a man ought to treat the woman he loves, then keep him well fed, and well loved, but above all, let a man be a man, aye?"

She had no idea what that meant but smiled and nodded all the same. As Lizzie watched him wander off, a touch to her arm startled her. Jack reclaimed his seat beside her.

"Well?" she demanded.

"Do you honestly expect me to divulge my intimate conversation?" he asked with a lopsided smile.

Oh, how he vexed her! "Did you do it?" she whispered impatiently.

"Aye."

"You're quite certain?"

"Lizzie," he said with an exceedingly warm laugh, and leaned forward, so that his face was only inches from hers, his lips only a breath from hers. He casually stroked her arm with his finger. "I am Jack Haines, no? The *deed*," he said, his gaze drifting down to her mouth, "is bloody well done."

There it was, that indescribably strange warmth flowing through her. She looked away and said pertly, "Well, then! You've proven yourself useful after all, milord."

"*Jack*. Aye, but that was child's play, lass. I look forward to demonstrating my particular use the day you ask for it politely," he said, and grinned in a way that made Lizzie feel light-headed.

"I would no' hold my breath, were I you," she murmured.

"I regret that I must interrupt your private conversation, lovebirds," Carson said, startling them both by suddenly leaning over Lizzie's shoulder, "but it is time that the games begin."

"Games?" Lizzie echoed absently, her gaze still on Jack's mouth.

"Aye, the games to celebrate your handfasting. Stand up now." He stood and announced that the earl would take challenges, which, judging by Jack's dark frown, was not the sort of game he was expecting.

Charlotte saw Lachlan walking toward the house through the field where they grazed the dairy cows, his hands shoved in his pockets, his hat pulled low over his eyes. The lad did not look as if he even noticed where he was stepping. When she realized he meant to come to the front door, Charlotte twisted in her seat as far as her useless body would allow. "Mr. Kincade!" she cried. "Do no' let the ragamuffin in the door! He's up to his ankles in . . . in mud!"

Mr. Kincade did not answer. She heard voices and

watched the door. When it opened, Newton strode through.

With a groan of exasperation, Charlotte gestured for him to move away from the door.

"What is it, lass?"

"Please move away, if you can manage it," she snapped, just as Mr. Kincade entered the room. Behind him was Lachlan. "Oh, for heaven's sake!" Charlotte cried.

"Master Lachlan to see you, mu'um," Mr. Kincade said, coming to a halt and assuming his perpetual bend to the right at the waist, the result of a particularly bad back.

"Master Lachlan," Charlotte said sternly, "look at your feet! You've tracked mud into the room, have you no'?"

Lachlan looked curiously at his feet. "Aye," he agreed. "Beg your pardon, Miss Charlotte."

That did not appease her. "What has Carson done with my sister?" she demanded.

"Woman, curb your tongue. He's but a lad," Newton said gruffly.

"I am aware he is a lad, Highlander, but he is also Carson's ward." She shifted a narrowed gaze to Lachlan. "What has he done with her?"

Lachlan shrugged. "I donna know, Miss Charlotte."

"Then why are you here?"

"Because the earl give me a halfpence to deliver a message to you," Lachlan said, moving around to stand where Charlotte could see him without twisting about.

"*Who?*" Charlotte asked, confused.

"The earl," Lachlan repeated.

The earl! Such nonsense! Charlotte looked him up and down. Behind Lachlan, Newton rolled his eyes. "Take off your hat," she commanded.

Lachlan quickly doffed his hat.

"Now then, let us begin again. Who is this earl?"

"Donna remember his name," Lachlan said. "But he's the one that married Miss Lizzie."

Charlotte gasped. And then she couldn't draw a breath, and instantly put a hand to her heart to see if it was still beating.

"He said I'm to tell you that Miss Lizzie is quite all right and you're no' to worry," Lachlan continued, undisturbed by her dramatic reaction.

"What?" Charlotte cried. "Are you deranged, lad? Do you think it is somehow humorous—"

"Miss Beal," Newton said firmly.

But Charlotte was outraged. It was obviously some sort of cruel joke, Carson's idea of intimidation.

And it was working brilliantly. Charlotte felt as impotent as she'd ever felt since the accident. She was exposed and helpless, and she wasn't even aware that she was beginning to breathe strangely until Newton put his hand on her shoulder and squeezed it.

"Thank you, lad. You might be on your way, then," he said in an authoritative voice that riled Charlotte even further.

"Aye," he said, already moving for the door.

"Wait!" Charlotte exclaimed. *"Where is Lizzie?"*

But Lachlan was already at the door.

"Come back here, young man!" Charlotte shouted, but the mountain that was Newton blocked her view of the door.

She collapsed against her chair as tears filled her eyes. What would she do? What *could* she do?

Newton eased himself into a chair near her, and Charlotte cried out in anger. She waved her hand at him. "Leave me!"

"She is no' officially married," he said calmly. "She was handfasted to him."

It took a moment or two for the meaning of that word to penetrate Charlotte's anxiety. "A *handfasting*?" she repeated slowly.

Newton nodded.

She impatiently motioned that he should continue, and quickly. And Charlotte sat in silent disbelief as the bear explained that Lizzie had been handfasted to the Earl of Lambourne when he had become . . . available.

When Newton finished, Charlotte had a single, overriding thought—if she had a gun, she would shoot Carson first, Newton second.

Diah help her and Lizzie—they were ruined. Irrevocably ruined.

Chapter Eight

At the end of a very long day, Jack and Lizzie were escorted back to the their little room at the top of the turret.

Jack was still very angry. When Carson had suggested he display his fencing ability that afternoon in one of their so-called games, Jack had been almost relieved to have something to do other than sit about and watch members of the Beal clan drink more ale. He'd never dreamed that his opponent would wield a claymore, the traditional broadsword of the Highlander. Jack knew of claymores—his grandfather had one hanging in his great room that was almost as long as Jack was tall.

But Jack had never actually *held* a claymore, much less tried to parry with one. He realized, when the broadsword was presented to him, that Carson had done it as a sort of jest. He'd purposely put Jack at a distinct disadvantage against a Highlander and he'd been beaten quite soundly, to the delight of all the Beals in the lower bailey.

It was really not very sporting of Carson.

"Your uncle," he said sourly as he tossed his coat onto a chair, "lacks the true qualities of a gentleman. I donna care for a man who makes sport of an uneven match." He yanked impatiently at the ends of his neckcloth, undoing the knot. "I should like him to meet me in the lower bailey with a pair of épées, I would. Then I would see how he laughs." He began to unwind the neckcloth.

A moment passed before Jack realized that he was being met with silence, which, in the short time he and Lizzie had been thrust together, he'd learned was highly unusual.

He glanced curiously over his shoulder.

Lizzie was standing with her back to the door, her arms folded across her middle, staring morosely at the floor.

"Aye?" he said impatiently. "*Now* what has you upset?"

Lizzie bit her lower lip and shook her head. Jack squinted at her. She did not meet his eye, but her chin began to tremble. "*Diah*," he muttered. "Come now, lass—"

"You are fretting over a silly game, while I am ruined," she said, and abruptly turned around, putting her back to him and her face to the door. "There was no' a person in the glen who did no' see me paraded about in this *awful* gown and with *you!*" she said, as if he were a troll. "Is there no way out of this nightmare? Even if Mr. Gordon were so inclined to ignore Carson's attempt to ruin me, his family can no' possibly ignore it, and he will never offer now!" A strange sound, sort of a sob and a hiccup at once, escaped her.

"Lizzie," Jack said, trying to soothe her. It had been a trying day for her. "You are no' ruined," he insisted, despite knowing full well that she was quite ruined. "Your Mr. Gordon is in Crieff, aye? He'll no' hear of it." For a few days, anyway.

"Now you're only being kind to a poor spinster," she said weakly. "I know very well what this has done. Charlotte and I shall never leave Thorntree, and it hardly matters that I esteem Mr. Gordon, for it is quite likely he shall never speak to me again." She made the sound again.

Jack winced. He was not very good at this sort of thing, feminine tears and whatnot. He'd never been able to comfort his mother and the Lord knew she'd cried rivers of tears. He started toward Lizzie once, then hesitated. But when he saw her shoulders sag, he briefly looked heavenward for strength, then crossed the room and very carefully put his hands on her shoulders. "Lizzie, you must no' fret—"

"I am *ruined*!" she exclaimed. "I have no idea of what I shall do now!"

Jack fished a handkerchief out of the pocket of his waistcoat, turned her around, and handed it to her.

Lizzie took it, dabbed at her eyes, blew her nose, then thrust it back at him. "Thank you," she said, as Jack gingerly took the handkerchief and tossed it aside. "What distresses me most is that I donna know how I will tell Charlotte. She's been so worried, and she feels she is such a burden as it is." She looked up at Jack with crystal blue eyes swimming in tears of worry. "And I canna bear to disappoint her."

"I donna think you could possibly disappoint her," he said sincerely, but Lizzie was not listening.

"There is nothing that can be done for it, for here I am with *you*, locked in this wretched room." She rubbed her hands vigorously on her arms as if she were rubbing herself back to life, and walked to the small window.

"I'd like a wee bit of warning if you intend to jump," Jack said.

She smiled weakly. "I'll no' jump . . . but I intend to escape at the first opportunity."

"Donna do anything rash, Lizzie," Jack said. "In a day or two, this will all be over."

"That's rather easy for *you* to say," Lizzie said angrily, the tears gone now. "*You* may walk away when Carson has done what he will, but *I* must return to Thorntree and attempt to make some sort of life for myself and my sister. *You* will no' be marked by this, but I certainly will!"

Frankly, he could not argue that. It was true. He remained wisely silent . . . or so he thought. Lizzie shot him a look over her shoulder; Jack shrugged a little sheepishly. But his tacit agreement annoyed her, and she snapped, "There is no *end* to the burdens men put upon women!"

He hardly knew what she meant by that.

With a groan of exasperation, Lizzie looked down at the old blue gown she wore. She squirmed as if the gown was chafing her. With a glare at Jack, she abruptly yanked the bed curtains down so that his view was blocked. He heard her rummaging about, heard what he thought were skirts rustling, and then some very loud and impatient sighs.

He clasped his hands behind his back. "May I help you?"

"No! You've helped me quite enough already, have you no'?"

"Now just a moment, Lizzie," he said sternly. "It was no' *I* who put you in this predicament."

"Perhaps no', but you've hardly endeavored to improve the situation in the least, have you!"

"I beg your pardon?" he exclaimed, throwing his arms wide in disbelief. "Pray tell, what might I *possibly* have done to improve this debacle? You may have noticed that things are scarcely within my control either!"

"Aye, but you might have at *least* pretended to find the whole thing entirely insupportable! But no, you lolled about half the day looking as if you rather enjoyed the games and the feast and eyeing all the women!"

"Oh, now, I am to be damned if I do and damned if I do no'," Jack groused irritably. "Had I shown my true feelings about this situation, you would have faulted me for making it seem as if you were unworthy of being handfasted to me!"

"*Me* unworthy?" She laughed wildly. "I think the whole of Glenalmond must at least own that if either of us is unworthy, it is *you*, Jack! You are a wanted man, and you are a . . . a *rake*!"

All right, there was only so much Jack would take. He'd done nothing but try to cooperate for both their sakes, and he was to be maligned for it? Incensed, he grabbed a hold of the curtain and yanked it back. Behind it, in the middle of removing the offensive blue bombazine, Lizzie squealed with surprise and hastily wrapped her arms around her body to keep the bodice from falling.

"And how would *you*, Elizabeth Drummond Beal, perfect lass that you are, know a *rake* if you were to see one?" he demanded roughly.

She swallowed. "I . . . I . . . I just know. There is an air about you," she said. "And I saw you with the chambermaid."

"At your behest!" he cried incredulously.

"I merely meant for you to inquire! *No'* to seduce her!"

"What is it, Lizzie?" he asked as he impatiently gestured for her to turn around. Her eyes widened even more, as if she expected him to throw her on the bed and take her there—an idea that was not entirely without merit. "Were you envious of Brigit?" he asked and put his hand on her bare shoulder . . . the smooth, pale skin of her bare shoulder . . . and forced her around.

"What are you doing?" she cried.

"*Helping* you!" he exclaimed brusquely, and began to

unbutton the gown. "I believe I have made myself *quite* plain: I will no' ravish you until you beg for it, and I hardly care that you are envious of a chambermaid."

"I am *no'* envious! Oh my, it is *entirely* clear why the prince wants to see you hanged!"

"He doesna want to *hang* me," Jack scoffed, although not with complete conviction. "He's merely confused."

Lizzie snorted. "Is that what you call it?"

"Hush now, woman," he said gruffly and finished unbuttoning her, letting his gaze wander her bare back as he did, and focusing, without intention, on the tantalizing gap where the bodice of the gown met the skirt, just where her back curved into her hip. "Before you go round calling a man a rake, you'd best know of what you speak."

He could see her skin through the gauzy shift she wore, and in a moment that he could not himself understand, he touched her back with a finger through the gap of her gown.

Lizzie cried out and whirled around, backing up so quickly that she banged into the nightstand. "Get out," she said, clinging to her gown with one hand, pointing to the end of the bed with the other. The gown was slipping off her shoulder.

"*Leave me!*" she cried. "If you donna want to be thought the rake, then you should no' act like one!"

"I am no' a rake," he said low. "But if I were a rake, I'd no' allow this moment to pass without . . ." He paused there, his gaze flicking over her body. Myriad ideas rushed through his mind, all of them carnal. He was just beginning to appreciate how lush Lizzie's body was beneath that awful blue bombazine, and his mind wandered to those things that men are physically incapable of ignoring when viewing a woman.

Lizzie's thoughts were likewise wandering to the unthinkable. When a man as physically appealing as Lambourne—eyes the color of smoke, and full, dark lips—looked at her as if she were something to be devoured, her heart raced at an unnatural clip. She did not permit herself to fully acknowledge that perhaps a small part of her wanted to be devoured, and grabbed up the candlestick on the bedside table, ignoring the unlit candle that toppled to the floor. She raised it above her head, prepared to strike if it came to that.

Jack responded with a sultry smile and stepped back, to the foot of the bed. With one more leisurely look at her, he stepped around the end of the bed, so that the bed curtain obstructed his view of her once more.

Lizzie lowered the candlestick and swallowed hard. Her heart was still racing. *"Bloody rooster,"* she muttered breathlessly.

"I can hear you, Lizzie," he said calmly from somewhere nearby, startling her. She clamped her mouth shut and quickly dropped the awful bombazine. Standing there in her chemise, she turned to the chair where she'd left her own soiled gown—and found it empty.

Lizzie gasped. "No," she whispered.

"Pardon?"

She whirled around to face the curtain, her arms crossed over her body. "Where is my gown?" she demanded. "I left it just here! Where is it, what have you done with it?"

"I've no' touched it," he insisted. "Shall I help you look?"

"No!" she cried. "No, no stay where you are!"

"I suppose that means I'll no' be treated to the sight of you *en déshabillé*, aye?" he said, his disembodied voice somewhere near the table.

Diah! She looked at the bombazine and slowly sank to her knees next to the bed, her arms braced on the bed. They'd taken her gown. Carson, a maid, she had no idea, but someone had taken her gown. "I . . . I've no' a thing to wear but this blue gown," she said, her voice betraying her dismay.

There was a long pause on the other side of the curtain. Lizzie sighed and stood back up, dragging the bombazine with her. "All right, then, donna panic," Jack said.

Lizzie froze; she heard him moving around, chairs scraping the floor, something being dragged. A moment later, the sound of his confident footfall moved toward the bed. Lizzie grabbed up the bombazine and held it up against her.

The first thing that appeared around the end of the curtain was a pair of wool trousers. That was followed by a lawn shirt, which slid on the floor until it hit Lizzie's feet. Still clutching the bombazine to her chest, Lizzie slowly crouched down and picked up the lawn shirt. "I donna understand," she said. "These are *your* clothes."

"Aye, it is my clothing—but I assure you the garments are no' the least bit contagious."

"I canna wear these!"

"Suit yourself, then. You may wear the blue gown and look the part of the spinster while you suffocate, or you might continue to titillate the glen by donning *my* clothes . . . at least until the morrow, when we might persuade Dougal to return your gown, aye?"

He had a point. And honestly, Lizzie had a pair of old buckskins that had belonged to her father. She wore them to fish. Trying to pull a carp from the loch in a gown was impractical at best, and generally impossible, and, well . . . She slipped the lawn shirt over her head.

It fell to her knees. The trousers were worse, the cuffs dragging on the ground. Lizzie stuffed the bottom of her chemise into the trousers and held them gathered at her waist with one hand.

"You'll no' keep me in suspense, will you?" Jack said, his voice jovial.

He found it all so amusing, while she, on the other hand, was beginning to feel the weight of the last twenty-four hours, and it was almost impossible to bear. She'd been humiliated in every way.

She must have sighed very loudly, for he said, a bit more gently, "Come on, then, Lizzie."

"Donna laugh," she said weakly.

"You have my word."

She self-consciously stepped out from behind the bed curtain and peeked up at Jack.

He'd discarded the kilt in favor of buckskins. His shirttail was out and the neck open; his feet were bare. He was looking at her, but he did not laugh. No, his reaction was something quite the opposite of a laugh. His eyes were darkly alive, as if something inside him had been awakened. His gaze was so intense, so penetrating, that Lizzie felt a rapid flush spreading through her as he slowly rose from his seat at the table. She nervously pushed a thick lock of hair from her face; his gaze followed her movement, then settled on the bit of flesh he could see through the open neck of the shirt she wore.

"No' a perfect fit, I'll grant you," he said, "but it seems more comfortable than the alternative, aye?" In two casual strides, he closed the distance between them.

His gaze wandered down her frame, his body seemingly as tense as Lizzie felt. He was standing too close, too *close*—she drew a startled breath when he laid his hand on her waist.

Jack looked up, his eyes the deepest gray color of a winter sky. But the cool color belied the heat she saw in them. "I—I need a belt," she stammered.

He slid his hand around to her back and pushed her forward, closer to him, but Lizzie resisted. "What are you doing?"

He did not answer at first but continued to look at her with that thing burning in his eyes. "Determining the size of your waist," he said tightly.

She cocked a brow.

"You need a belt," he reminded her as he continued to caress her waist with his hand.

"Anything will do," she said quickly, trying hard to ignore the feel of his hand on her waist. "A neckcloth, a piece of twine. Something, for I fear they might fall."

"Ah. We canna have that, can we?" he asked in a manner that suggested they could have precisely that. He reached behind her at the same moment Lizzie tried to lean away from him. He caught her with his arm, locking it around her waist, and held up the sash from the bed curtain. "Will this do?"

Lizzie grabbed for it, but he yanked it out of her reach. When she turned back to him, her gaze landed on his mouth, and for a moment, one long, terrifyingly hopeful moment, she thought he would kiss her, would press his mouth to hers, would put his hands on her skin.

Before she could want it, before she could do something that she would regret the rest of her life, Lizzie grabbed the sash. But he was quick, and rolled it up in his fist, so that their fingers tangled for an electrifying moment.

Lizzie's heart was skipping wildly about in her chest. "*Let go*," she whispered.

Jack smiled like a wolf and deliberately let the sash go,

holding it loosely in his hand as she yanked it free. She whirled away from him, gulped for air at the same time she lifted the shirt a bit and threaded the sash around the waist of the trousers and belted them to her. She knotted the hem of the lawn shirt just below her waist and turned round, her hands on her hips.

Jack had seated himself and was sipping wine. He gestured to the chair across from him. With a pointedly wary look at him, Lizzie took the chair. He watched her pull one leg up to her chest and roll up the leg of his trousers, then the other. When she'd finished, she sat with her legs crossed, her arms folded self-consciously around her. "You're staring."

"No' at all," he said, shaking his head. "I'm . . . admiring." He poured wine and slid it across the table to her. "I will insist that Dougal return your gown on the morrow."

The very thought of another day spent in this circus sobered her. "On the morrow," Lizzie repeated with a weary sigh. "I donna think I can bear the morrow."

Jack absently fingered the stem of his wineglass as he studied her. "I can no' begin to guess why your uncle has gone to such lengths, but you've endured quite a lot of ill treatment at his hand. Why would he do this to you?"

If only she knew. Certainly Carson did not care for the way she and Charlotte made their own decisions, but this . . . this was indescribably cruel. Lizzie glanced down at her attire and felt the tears of exhaustion and frustration filling in behind her eyes. "I want to go home," she said softly.

Jack nodded.

"On the grave of my father, I donna deserve this. He's ruined me. I canna imagine how we shall survive. I want to go home," she repeated tearfully.

Jack slowly sat up and put his hand on her knee. "Drink the wine. It will help you rest. You'll need your strength on the morrow."

"Will I?" she asked wearily. "Are you privy to what Carson will subject us to on the morrow?"

He squeezed her knee. "No. I know only that we are leaving Castle Beal," he said, and removed his hand from her knee, clinked his glass to hers, and settled back in his chair.

Lizzie wanted to believe him, she desperately wanted to believe him. "Really?"

"Really."

"How?"

He smiled warmly. "You leave that to me, Lizzie Beal."

Frankly, Lizzie was so exhausted she could do nothing else but leave it to him.

Chapter Nine

In spite of Lizzie's apparent exhaustion, there was, not surprisingly, an argument over who would take the bed, and in the end Jack had grown so agitated with her that he'd swept her up in his arms and dumped her on top of the counterpane with a warning that if she got up, he'd take matters in hand.

He was only moments, if not inches, from taking matters in hand as it was. He had to force himself to turn away from that bed.

Fortunately, his warning was enough to convince Lizzie that she ought to have the bed, and she quickly fell into a deep sleep. He could tell from her occasional soft snoring.

He, on the other hand, sat at the table and finished off the wine, hoping it would rid him of all the libidinous thoughts roaming about his head like dogs on the hunt. Jack needed to quit Castle Beal as much as or even more than Lizzie did, for he could not bear any more time alone in this small room with her and not touch her.

He was appalled by his body's reaction to the sight of her dressed in his clothing. In spite of the fact that his clothes were much too big for her, he could see her figure in a way he'd never seen it in a gown, and through the neck of the shirt, he'd been able to see the pale skin and the rise of her breasts. Breasts the size of plump oranges . . . the palms of his hands had itched with the urge to touch her.

He'd been as aroused as a lad experiencing the first pangs of lust.

Aye, he'd think of something to get her and him out of here just as he'd promised her. And if Lizzie's look of gratitude and hope had been money, he would have left Castle Beal a very wealthy man indeed.

Jack made do with the chair that night but slept badly, while Lizzie slept like the dead. The sound of early birds finally convinced him that his attempts at sleep were for naught. He abandoned the chair, stretched his aching back, and made his way to the basin.

He was in the midst of shaving when he heard her move, and glanced over his shoulder. Lizzie was propped up on her elbows, staring at him as if she could not quite place him. "Good morning," he said. "You look a fright."

Recognition dawned and she fell back into the pillows and rolled onto her side. "How very kind of you to remark."

He smiled as he rinsed the razor in the basin. " 'Tis early yet. Go back to sleep. I'll see if I might entice Dougal to bring a bit of food for the sleeping beauty, aye?"

"Aye," she said sleepily. Her eyes were already closed.

A half hour later, after Jack had convinced a weary Dougal to accompany him down to the see the laird, he was shown into a small dining room. He'd figured Carson Beal for an early riser, and he was not disappointed. The laird was breaking his fast in solitude.

He hardly spared Jack a glance as he entered the room. "A wee bit early for you, is it no', milord?" he asked before stuffing a forkful of black pudding into his mouth.

"Were I in London enjoying the pleasures of the evening, I'd only be finding my bed about now. But as society here seems to center on no more than a few games in the bailey, I found my bed rather early."

"And I suppose now I'll be forced to have the dubious pleasure of your company, is that it?" Beal asked as he sopped up the grease of the pudding with bread.

"I would no' impose," Jack said, but took a seat anyway. Beal squinted at him, then nodded at a young girl who'd appeared from nowhere. She poured a cup of coffee and placed it before Jack, then stepped to the sideboard and began to fill a plate with food.

"That's no' necessary," Jack said, nodding in her direction. "I'll no' be long."

"You speak as if you are in control of the situation, sir," Beal said with a self-satisfied smirk.

Jack bristled but managed to maintain his easy smile. "Now, now, sir. I'd no' dream of challenging your authority in your home," he said, leaving the lingering suggestion that in another setting he would. "But we are gentlemen, and as a gentleman, I must ask that you let the lass go home now." At Beal's scowl, Jack said, "You've done what you set out to do, aye? There is no' a man in Glenalmond who will touch her now. You canna bring her lower."

"What do you care?" Carson scoffed.

Jack leaned forward, pushing aside the plate the girl tried to place in front of him. "I donna know why you'd do what you've done to your own blood, Beal," he said, "but what is done is done. Show a bit of decency and let her go."

Beal flicked his wrist at the girl, sending her from the room. He leaned back in his seat and eyed Jack thoughtfully. "Have you fallen in love with her?"

Jack almost choked at that ridiculous notion. "Donna be absurd."

"Your concern for her humiliation is noble, I suppose." Carson said it as easily as he might remark he preferred brown bread to scones. "But she is naugh' to you."

Jack was beginning to appreciate that Beal was no more than an animal in gentleman's clothing. "I suppose I donna care to see anyone humiliated," Jack responded coldly, his chest tightening. "Particularly the fairer sex."

Beal laughed. He eyed Jack curiously for a moment, then shrugged as he picked up his fork again. "All right, then, Lambourne, you may have your gentlemanly wish. I shall send the two of you to Thorntree, where my niece can lick her wounds. But you'll go with her, and you will stay close, and no one"—he paused to lean forward—"*no one* will think you are anything but entirely devoted to her. No one will see you apart, no one will have cause to believe this is anything but true affection between a man and a woman, aye? The Gordons have eyes and ears up and down this glen, and if you give anyone the slightest pause, I shall hand your head to the prince myself. And if you think to escape?" He stabbed the black pudding on his plate. "You'll no' get far. The prince's men have redoubled their efforts to find you, milord, and have hired the canny Highland Scots to help them. They are slowly working their way north, traversing every glen, questioning every man. Unless you are familiar with the rugged terrain and can outfox a Highlander born and reared in these hills, you have nowhere to run but north. I'll give you a bit of Highland geography—there is naugh' north of here but more hills. You'd perish ere you reached safety, and perish you would, for I would hunt you down like a wounded fox, I would. Let us be clear: from this point forward, I *am* the prince's man, and I'll no' hesitate to send you off to the prince and collect the generous bounty he's put on your head. I'll even attend your hanging and cheer."

Jack grinned as nonchalantly as he could manage. "A *generous* bounty, eh? I shall endeavor no' to be too proud of it."

"This is no laughing matter to me, Lambourne. You'd best make sure it is no laughing matter to you. Keep her from that bloody Gordon, and see to it that no' a soul believes you are anything less than lovers, and you might live yet."

"Horses?" Jack asked, his patience all but evaporated.

"Aye. Send Dougal in when you've broken your fast," Beal said, and resumed his meal. "I'll send him to the stables."

But Jack pushed back and stood. "Thank you, but I've lost my appetite." When he reached the door, his curiosity got the better of his anger, and he looked back. *"Why?"* he demanded. "Why this charade? Could you no' just forbid a match with this Gordon?"

"You've known my niece for two days. Do you think I could forbid her a bloody thing?"

His point was well taken, yet it wasn't enough. "It seems rather harsh . . . even for you, Laird."

Carson snorted. "You've got a bit of Beal blood in you, aye?" At Jack's curt nod, he said, "Would you want to see as much of an inch of Beal land in the hands of a Gordon?"

"Perhaps not, but surely there are ways of preventing it other than the public humiliation of your niece."

"This is no' London, sir. We do no' sit about our parlors and sip our tea here. Perhaps you have forgotten the ways of the Highlands, eh? Go on with you, then, go to Thorntree. Send Dougal to me." Beal looked down at his plate. The conversation was over.

Jack was happy to leave the room—the less he had to look at Carson Beal the better, for his anger was beginning to heat inside him and he could not trust himself to keep his hands from the old man's neck. He didn't trust Carson in the least, and believed without a doubt Beal would hand him to the bloodthirsty bounty hunters the moment Jack was less than entirely useful to him.

Beal reminded him of his father, and that made Jack's disgust of him run even deeper.

With Dougal's help, Jack arranged for his horse and two additional mounts to carry Lizzie and Dougal. When he was satisfied that things were at the ready, he walked out into the upper bailey with Dougal, bound for the small room at the top of the turret, where he planned to wake Lizzie and give her the happy news. But the sight of a small figure moving awkwardly toward the gate distracted him.

Perhaps it was Jack's own clothing that caught his eye, or his hat, which was too big for her head and sank down to her eyes. Jack paused mid-stride, as did Dougal. Lizzie had not noticed them, but she had noticed a pair of maids carrying pails to the well. She turned sharply to her right, kept her head down, and picked up her pace. She was headed directly for Jack and Dougal.

Surely she did not believe for a moment she would go undetected.

"She's no' to be about without escort," Dougal said absently, confirming Jack's thought.

With her head down and her hat obscuring her sight, Lizzie did not see the fellow who carried chickens lashed by their feet to a pole that he balanced across his shoulders. "Pardon!" he said to Lizzie before she could walk headlong into his chickens.

"Why don't I fetch her while you bring the horses

round," Jack suggested lazily as Lizzie, recovered from her near collision with the chickens, adjusted her hat and struck out once more.

"Aye, milord," Dougal said, and lumbered off in the direction of the stables.

Jack moved a bit to his right and intercepted her just as she was about to sail by. *"Lizzie."*

With a cry of alarm, Lizzie jerked around like a guilty felon, but her wide-eyed gaze quickly narrowed when she saw him. "You *scoundrel!*" she whispered heatedly. "You tried to escape and leave me behind!"

"That's preposterous," he said calmly. "I did no such thing. If I had planned to escape, I would no' be standing in the middle of the bailey."

"Oh?" she said, her brows dipping into a frown. "Then why did you leave me?"

"To speak to—"

She suddenly gasped and grabbed his lapel in her fist, giving it a hearty tug. *"Dougal!"* she exclaimed excitedly. "You gained Dougal's cooperation, just as you said you would!" Before he could answer, her hopeful gaze melted into a dubious frown. "No, no, that canna be! Dougal would no' defy his laird! Then you *did* mean to escape? But you seem too . . . too *fresh*," she added, her gaze skimming over him. "And you are clean-shaven," she added, her gaze on his face, peering closely. "And you are wearing a fresh shirt and waistcoat." She cocked her head to one side like a curious little bird. "You took the time to dress properly to escape?"

"I—"

"Diah," she cried, and let go his lapel at the same time she shoved against his chest. "You didna mean to escape, because you are *one* of them—"

"All right, then, stop now before your imagination

takes flight and you are unwittingly whisked away to the moon," he warned her.

"Are you one of Carson's men?" she demanded hotly as she took a step backward.

"Mary, Queen of Scots, that is the most absurd thing you've said yet! I am no' one of Carson's men, for God's sake! For once, please do as I say, will you, and come along—we're leaving."

"*We*? How?" she demanded, taking another small step backward.

"By horse."

"Horse! If you are no' one of them, how can you possibly put your hands on a horse, then? Do you expect me to believe that Carson will allow us to ride out of here?" she exclaimed, gesturing wildly to the gate.

"Aye," he said simply, and pointed grandly to his left. Lizzie followed his gaze and saw the three mounts being led into the bailey, Dougal leading Jack's dapple gray mare. The horse was tossing her head, chafing to be out of her stable, just like Jack.

Lizzie gaped at the horses. "How did you manage it?" she demanded of Jack. "How could you *possibly* have managed it?"

"I am not without a few powers of persuasion," he said, a little irritably, annoyed by her disbelief in him.

"But . . ."

"Lizzie. I suggest that if you really want to be free of Castle Beal, you will take advantage of the laird's largesse and ride. You do know how to ride, do you no'?"

"Oh, for the love of Scotland!" she snapped, and marched forward, meeting Dougal and putting herself into a saddle before anyone could help her—and quite expertly at that. She wheeled the horse about and looked at Jack. "Do *you* know how to ride?"

Jack momentarily forgot his exasperation with her and admired the line of her slender leg in his trousers . . . not to mention the perfectly enticing way she sat a horse. He gave her a slow smile as debauched thoughts of riding her drifted aimlessly through his mind. "Oh, I *ride*, lass. I ride very well, indeed."

Lizzie returned his lazy smile with a murderous look, but not before she'd turned a telling shade of pink. She yanked the horse away from Jack and spurred it forward, riding recklessly for the gates.

Jack sighed and exchanged a look with Dougal as he took the mare's reins from him. "How far to Thorntree?"

"Three miles, milord, but the road is pitted and hard."

"*Good,*" he said as he swung up on his mount and set out after Lizzie Beal, hoping that the road would unseat her. It would serve her right, the headstrong little heathen.

Chapter Ten

The scoundrel tried to catch her, but Lizzie was too good a horsewoman to allow it—and she knew the shortcut to Thorntree.

She rode across a portion of the one hundred some odd acres that made up Thorntree, acres of unspoiled hills and woodlands, of towering pines and juniper, of cowberry and ling. She rode past the deep crevices that marked the highland terrain, past the waterfalls and streams and small glades where roe deer grazed. Papa had tried to teach Lizzie and Charlotte to hunt, but neither of them could bring themselves to shoot.

The day was crisp. Lizzie loved the winters at Thorntree. The air was still, the landscape starkly beautiful. In the spring and summer, the forests came alive with birds and rushing waters, and in the autumn bright, vivid colors burst across the hills as leaves changed seemingly overnight. It was an idyllic setting, and Lizzie had never realized until recently how tentative their situation here was, how they dangled off a precipice.

As she rode to the front of the house where she and Charlotte lived, she thought it looked very small after two days at the monstrously large Castle Beal. Thorntree was no great mansion, to be sure, but it was a lovely little manor, with six bedrooms and four chimneys. The east end was covered with ivy that Lizzie had long ago ceased trying to keep at bay. Mr. Kincade, their butler-groundskeeper-factotum was quite bothered that she'd let the ivy grow wild, but there were only herself and Mr. and Mrs. Kincade to keep the place up, and there were much more pressing chores than trimming the ivy.

Lizzie reined the horse to a sharp halt and practically threw herself off it, tossing the reins loosely around a hitching pole. She swept the hat off her head as she bounded up the steps to the door, shoved it open, and marched through. "Charlotte!" she shouted, striding down the main corridor. "Mrs. Kincade!"

Nothing but dogs rushed out to greet her, and those four lively mutts only served to get in her way.

She reached the drawing room where Charlotte spent a lot of time and pushed the door open with such force that it hit the wall with a bang. Seated at the window, Charlotte was twisted about in her chair, gripping the arms, pushing herself up as high as she could as Lizzie strode across the threshold.

"*Lizzie!*" Charlotte cried as Lizzie leaned over and hugged her older sister. "Lizzie, I have been so worried! Why are you dressed in such an appalling manner? What has happened to you? You did no' marry that man! You did no' handfast with him as Newton would have me believe, for heaven's sake!"

"No, I—are you well, Charlotte?" Lizzie asked breathlessly. "Where is Mrs. Kincade? And Mr. Newton?"

"Mrs. Kincade is in the kitchen. And the monstrous tree thing Carson sent to guard me is helping Mr. Kincade," she said with disgust.

"*Ahem.*"

Lizzie whirled around to the door, where the monstrous tree thing stood. He was a huge man, much larger than Lizzie had realized the night they'd taken her up to Castle Beal. He towered over her much like Jack towered over her, and his expression was one of displeasure. "Newton. We meet again," she said tersely.

He nodded, folded his arms, and braced his legs apart before the open door, as if to block her exit.

"You may *go* now, my sister is returned to me," Charlotte said angrily. "Tell him, Lizzie, for I've told that ogre as plainly as I might, and still he willna leave me be."

"Ye only make yerself ill when ye become so angry, lass," Mr. Newton said stoically.

Lizzie looked with surprise at Charlotte. But Charlotte was waving a hand at him dismissively, her eyes on Lizzie. "Tell me, Lizzie. Tell me everything. What has Carson done?"

Lizzie had not even opened her mouth when she heard the sound of a loud commotion in the corridor. There were raised voices, two of the dogs were barking, and the unmistakable sound of Jack's boots striding down the hall followed that.

"Elizabeth Beal, you'd best show yourself *now!*" he shouted.

Charlotte gasped.

The moment Jack crossed the threshold, Newton caught him and held him back with such force that the dogs scattered to the corners of the room, their tails between their legs.

"Bloody hell, remove your hands from me!" Jack snapped.

Newton shoved him up against the wall, pinning him there. Jack looked over the big Highlander's shoulder and leveled a gaze so heated on Lizzie that she felt her belly flip with fear. "This would all be a damn sight easier if you'd no' run off like you did, Lizzie!"

"Who do you think you are," Charlotte cried, "to come in here without announcement or invitation and speak to my sister in such an ungentlemanly manner?"

Understanding dawned on Jack's face the moment he looked at Charlotte, and Lizzie would be forever grateful to him that he did not make any outward sign of noticing Charlotte's useless legs. He shoved hard against Newton, who let him go, but kept himself between Jack and Charlotte.

"I beg your pardon, Miss Beal," he said with a murderous gaze for Newton as he yanked on the ends of his waistcoat, "but my freedom, and perhaps my very life, depends on your sister's cooperation, and she bloody well knows it!"

"Mind yer tongue, lad," Newton warned him.

"*Diah*, I did no' mean to speak disrespectfully, sir, but Miss Elizabeth Beal and I have something of an unresolved and ongoing contretemps—"

"And you think that allows you entry into our home? Your troubles are no' ours. Please leave!" Charlotte said.

"*Lizzie*," Jack said sternly, but the Highlander was moving toward him, gesturing to the door. Jack glanced at the large man, then at Lizzie. "*Ach*, for the love of Christ," he muttered, and with a look of great exasperation, he quickly dipped down and retrieved Lizzie's dirk from his boot.

"That's mine!" she cried.

He held it up to the Highlander, his eyes on that man. "Aye, that it is, but I rather thought—rightly, it would seem—that I might need it more than you. As for *you*, sir," he said to Newton, "I've no dispute with you. I mean no harm. I mean only to keep my neck at its present length. The laird has sent Mr. Dougal along to ensure I am no' parted from Lizzie."

"Dougal?" Newton said.

"A relative of yours?" Jack asked wryly.

"Newton, I donna want this man here!" Charlotte insisted. "I donna care what he wants, I should like him gone!"

Amazingly, Newton moved to do just that. Jack lashed out with the knife, and from where Lizzie stood, it looked as if he nicked Newton. But Newton was a massive man, and even though Jack was big too, he was no match for the Highlander. They struggled, but in one swift movement, Newton swept a knife from his waist and shoved Jack against the door, his arm across his gullet, the knife under his chin.

Lizzie cried out with alarm, but Jack was not cowed. If anything, it made him angrier. Pinned against the wall, it became apparent to him that he was about to be tossed out of Thorntree, and he pointed a finger around Newton at Lizzie. "Donna think you are done with this, madam! I do no' intend to hang on your account!" he shouted as Newton struggled to take him out.

Lizzie stood completely still; neither she nor Charlotte nor even the dogs so much as breathed as they listened to the shouting and scuffling in the hallway. When they heard the front door slam closed, Lizzie turned slowly and looked at Charlotte. She moved to her side, sank to her knees beside Charlotte's chair, and laid her head on her lap.

"Lizzie, what happened?" Charlotte put her hand on her sister's head.

"On my word, you'd no' believe what I've endured," she said, and the tension and every last detail of the last two days began to pour out of her in words and tears.

Newton would have tossed Jack in the river and been done with him had Dougal not stopped him. The two

Highlanders talked in Gaelic. Jack's Gaelic, which had never been more than rudimentary at best, was very rusty. The only thing he managed to ascertain was that the women did not want him at Thorntree.

He did not know the Gaelic word for *shed*, or he would have protested quite vigorously. As it was, he was dragged to a small structure that had been built against the barn. For reasons that Jack could not begin to guess, the shed contained a small brazier, a cot, and chamber pot, as well as some gardening implements. "You canna mean to put me here!" he protested as they tossed him inside like a bag of seed. "This is no' what I agreed to with your laird!"

Dougal, at least, seemed a wee bit perplexed by the arrangements—but not enough to actually change them, Jack noted. "Is this it?" Jack asked as the two men moved to quit the lean-to. "I am to be locked within like an animal?"

Dougal looked uncertainly at the man called Newton who glanced dispassionately at Jack. "Aye. At least until we've made proper accommodations, milord."

Proper accommodations sounded like a polite way of saying *a grave*. "Wait, wait," Jack said hastily. "Sir . . . Newton, is it? You seem a reasonable man. I appeal to your good senses as a Highlander and a Scot. I did no' ask to be put in this situation." He looked at Dougal. "Tell him, Dougal. Tell him I was forced into it every bit as much as Lizzie."

The two Highlanders exchanged a look.

"We'll fetch ye when it's time," Newton said, pulling the shed door closed.

"Time? Time for what?" Jack shouted. "Bloody bastard, you'll no' leave me here!" But the door slammed shut and he heard what sounded like something being pushed against the door. He kicked it with all his might, but the door did not budge.

"Damn you!" he shouted, and kicked the door again for good measure. He was as furious as he'd ever been in his entire life, and this—*this* was the final straw for him. Carson Beal could do whatever he liked, but he was not going to subject Jack to such conditions or treat him like an animal.

But as he fell onto the cot and threw an arm over his eyes, it was not his freedom he saw dancing about in his mind, but Lizzie Beal, straddling a horse.

Chapter Eleven

L izzie tried to scrub the last two days from her skin.
Failing that, she ended her bath and examined her
wardrobe.

For the first time since Papa had died, Lizzie was
displeased with her gowns. It seemed as if she'd been in
mourning for years, not months, and it had been an eternity since she had visited an actual seamstress, or, God in
heaven, a modiste.

Her life had changed dramatically in only a few short
years. Not so long ago her greatest concern had been
a proper coming-out. She had dreamed of a season in
Edinburgh. Her mother had debuted there and used to
regale Lizzie and Charlotte with tales of it. Lizzie had
never been to Edinburgh, but Papa had promised to take
her and Charlotte there.

Lizzie also once believed that she and Charlotte would
marry well and live near Papa, raising their children together, dabbling in Highland society and doing all those
things Lizzie supposed young wives and mothers did.
She never imagined they'd be making their home as a
pair of spinsters, or trying to keep an estate afloat. To
think of the money Papa had spent on pianoforte lessons
for the two of them! A bit of training in husbandry would
have been more useful, she thought with a wry smile.

It was Charlotte's accident that had brought Lizzie's dreams to an abrupt halt. The doctor from Crieff had known the moment he saw her that she'd never walk again. Whether or not Charlotte could bear children was unknown, but Lizzie silently agreed with Charlotte that it hardly mattered, for no Highlander would have her now. An invalid was too daunting.

The accident had changed their lives; Charlotte had slipped into despair and anger, and Lizzie . . . Lizzie felt entirely responsible. It was she who had begged Charlotte to ride with her that day, for Lizzie loved to ride. She loved the reckless release, the thrill of rushing headlong across the verdant land with a big sky overhead. That day, she'd convinced Charlotte to come along on the new Highland pony Papa had managed to obtain.

Papa sold the pony two days after the accident.

Charlotte had only just received her special chair when Papa died, and Lizzie's life—or her last remaining dreams for it—had been washed away in her tears of sorrow.

When Charlotte had wanted to extend their mourning of Papa into half mourning, Lizzie had scarcely given it a thought. Their situation left little room to be concerned about the sort or color of gown she wore, and Charlotte, dear Charlotte, was compelled to exert control in those little ways that she could. Lizzie understood it was Charlotte's way of trying to remain viable in a world that had no use for cripples. But, for the first time since her accident, Lizzie didn't want to do as Charlotte wished.

She glanced longingly at her best gown, a teal-colored silk that reminded Lizzie of the peacocks that once strutted about the grounds at Thorntree. It was gathered in the back and fell in soft folds, and the squared bodice was embroidered with a darker blue around the edges.

She'd had the beautiful gown made for the annual harvest celebration, but she'd never had the opportunity to wear it. Papa had collapsed while tending the garden one afternoon. There was no sign of illness in him, yet in the blink of an eye he was gone.

Lizzie toyed with the idea of wearing the gown. Having spent the last two days in various types of clothing that did not suit her, she wouldn't mind in the least if Jack saw her in something pretty.

"*Ach*, you're mad!" she muttered to herself. Why should she care what he thought of her? She would end this absurd *handfasting* just as soon as she and Charlotte determined how.

So Lizzie wore her gray gown, which was suitable for half mourning and spinsters (all that was missing was a fussy lace cap) and rejoined her sister in the drawing room, where two of the four dogs of Thorntree were sitting with her. Fingal and Tavish were a pair of sheepdogs, seldom used now that they had so few sheep. Red was a hunting dog that still went out with Mr. Kincade twice weekly. And Bean was a small Dinmont terrier with nothing more to recommend him than a cheeky personality.

The day was growing cold; Lizzie wore a wool plaid around her shoulders and was glad to see that Mrs. Kincade had put a lap rug over Charlotte's legs and rolled her chair closer to the fire.

The last thing Papa had invested in before his death was the big wheeled chair in which Charlotte spent so many hours. It had come all the way from Glasgow and Papa had been inordinately proud of it, but Charlotte had been horrified. She argued she would do just as well in the chair in her room, where Lizzie suspected she wished to remain and never be seen, but Papa had insisted. Thank God that he had, thought Lizzie as she shooed

Bean off the chair. She sat directly across from Charlotte and helped herself to tea.

"I've been thinking," Charlotte said as Lizzie stirred a bit of honey in her tea. They hadn't had sugar at Thorntree in six months now. "The damage Uncle Carson thinks he might have inflicted may no' be so great after all, aye?"

Lizzie snorted. "It is irreparable."

"But think of it, Lizzie. Mr. Gordon is in Crieff just now. Even if news has reached him, he canna know what has truly happened, can he? If you write him, you may deliver the first true word, aye?"

There was some validity to that—surely Mr. Gordon would treat whatever he might hear with a healthy dose of skepticism. After all, he'd spent quite a lot of time in Lizzie's company since meeting her last year at the spring planting festival in Aberfeldy. She thought he was an industrious, hardworking, and handsome Highlander. She admired his plans to bring more sheep to his Highland farm; he believed sheep and the export of wool was the way to make his family prosper.

Lizzie thought she and Mr. Gordon were compatible, and he'd said that he esteemed her. She esteemed him, too. He was a good man, a solid man—she would be quite fortunate to make a match with him.

"But if you summon Mr. Gordon here, that man canna possibly remain, for then Mr. Gordon will have no choice but to cry off," Charlotte pointed out. "That man must go home with Newton."

"Newton!" Lizzie exclaimed. "And where, precisely, does Newton live?"

"I hardly care," Charlotte said with an indifferent shrug. "But I am quite determined *both* men will leave Thorntree today." She smiled, resolute in her decision, and her face was transformed from the usual frown she wore.

Lizzie couldn't help but admire her. Even when she was in something of a snit as she was now, Charlotte looked beautiful, with her long locks of cornsilk hair gathered artfully at her nape, and pale blue eyes. To Lizzie's way of thinking, her beauty only made the tragedy of her broken back that much worse, for she would have had many more offers than Lizzie might ever hope to have, and all of them were lost.

"What is it? Why do you look at me in that way?" Charlotte asked when Lizzie did not respond.

"I would very much like for them to leave, Charlotte, but I hardly think they shall."

"Why no'? This is *our* home."

"Aye," Lizzie said carefully. "But Newton will no' depart until Carson gives him leave. Carson would no' send a man who gave him less than complete fealty. As for the other one . . ." She sighed. "He'll no' go until he can be certain he'll no' hang."

"Would he really *hang*?"

Lizzie shrugged. "He must believe it is a possibility. Why else would have have agreed to this handfasting?"

"Then what are we to do?" Charlotte demanded. "What will Mr. Gordon think if that man remains here with you?"

Lizzie tried to smile to put Charlotte at ease, but it felt odd. "I fear it is too late to fret overmuch, Charlotte," she said briskly. "What's done is done."

Charlotte eyed her skeptically. "Pray tell, what *is* done?"

"Pardon?"

"What is done, Lizzie?" Charlotte said, leaning forward. "You were handfasted, so that surely means—"

"No!" Lizzie cried as heat rushed into her cheeks. "Honestly, Charlotte!"

"Then what?" her sister persisted.

"I— We did no' sleep in the same bed, if that is what you mean."

"Did he kiss you, then?"

"No!" Lizzie cried, but had the absurd notion that she wished he had.

"Then what happened?" Charlotte whispered excitedly.

"*Nothing*," Lizzie said firmly. Charlotte frowned dubiously, and Lizzie sighed. "He . . . he was a gentleman. In a manner of speaking. Given the . . . the circumstances," she added uncertainly.

"Aye, and?"

"And he is no' as modest as he ought to be," Lizzie said flatly.

Charlotte smiled. "He is very handsome, is he no'?"

"Aye, but he is English for all intents and purposes."

"But he is an earl as well, and he is rather dashing, and—"

"Are you forgetting Mr. Gordon?" Lizzie demanded.

"No' at all," Charlotte said with a wicked grin. "I was merely wondering if *you* had . . . if even for a moment."

A moment? *Many* moments. So many, in fact, that Lizzie had wished once or twice for the fairy potion their grandmother used to pretend to give them when they were wee lassies to keep their thoughts chaste and pure. "Of course no'," she said briskly. "I've thought only of what we are to do now that this calamity has been put upon us."

"Now, you must write Mr. Gordon," Charlotte said firmly.

Lizzie frowned.

"You must! He has only your word that he may trust, and only you can explain what truly happened behind closed doors. Honestly, Lizzie! Mr. Gordon esteems you greatly! I think this the one time you could put propriety aside."

Charlotte was right, of course. Carson had forced her to put propriety aside.

"You must write him, and Mr. Gordon will come," Charlotte said firmly. "But what are we to do with *him* until Mr. Gordon arrives?"

Another excellent question, and one Lizzie could not answer.

Charlotte sighed impatiently at Lizzie. "He is handsome, Lizzie, but he's also cocksure, and there will be trouble as long as he is under the same roof as you, mark me."

"*Pardon?*" Lizzie exclaimed, almost spilling her tea. "What do you mean to imply?"

"Just that he *is* handsome, Lizzie, and you . . . *you* are very adventuresome, and you've been put away here like a spinster with very few prospects when you ought to have been out in society, and he is the sort of man who would tempt any woman and I can see in your eyes that you were tempted, no matter how vigorously you may protest."

"I was no' in the least!"

"Oh no? Then why are you wearing pearls? I canna recall the last time I saw you wearing pearls, and your hair all bound up with the bandeau so prettily. It surely is no' for my benefit."

Lizzie could feel herself color slightly. "Does it occur to you that perhaps I wanted to dress a bit having spent the last two days in dusty old gowns and trousers?"

"I only know that were *I* locked in a tower with him

for two full days, I might very well be tempted and more."

Lizzie put down her teacup with a clatter. "Charlotte, there are times I think you've taken complete leave of your senses! I am no' so easily *tempted* by a handsome face! There is far more at stake here, and honestly, what does he offer other than his good looks? He's a wanted man, for heaven's sake!"

Apparently unconvinced, Charlotte pursed her lips together. Lizzie rolled her eyes and picked up her tea. "You need no' worry after me, sister. You'd best exert your imagination in coming up with another plan, for Lambourne will no' toddle off to Newton's or the barn, you may trust me."

"Who is he to have a say?"

"He's no' the sort of man who is accustomed to doing a woman's bidding."

"He'll do *my* bidding, I assure you."

"As you pointed out, Charlotte, he is an *earl*."

"He is no' an earl here," she said, and picked up her teacup. "He is no' even a guest. We'll no' show him the slightest bit of hospitality. No Scotsman worth his tartan will abide accommodations where he must fend for himself."

"No Scotsman worth his tartan would fail to extend hospitality," Lizzie reproachfully reminded her.

"This is no' an ordinary situation, Lizzie. It is the only recourse open to us. The more uncomfortable the earl is, the sooner he will depart. Mark me—he will do as we wish after a day or two of foraging for food."

"Charlotte!" Lizzie cried laughingly. "He'll no' bend to your will!"

"So you say," Charlotte responded pertly.

"Madam."

Both women jerked their heads toward the door, where Mr. Kincade had entered without them realizing it. Bean jumped off his spot at the window seat and bounded forward to leap upon Mr. Kincade's trousers.

Mr. and Mrs. Kincade had been employed at Thorntree longer than Lizzie's three and twenty years on this earth. When Papa had died, and Lizzie had discovered the debts he'd left, she'd had to let the other servants go. But they could not let Mr. and Mrs. Kincade go—they were like grandparents.

Mr. Kincade was bent a little sideways, and he had a face that completely lacked animation. When Charlotte and Lizzie were girls, they delighted in trying to make him smile or frown, but his expression never changed.

Mr. Kincade possessed two brown coats. One he wore for his outdoor work, the other he wore for his indoor work. They were practically indistinguishable, but Lizzie assumed he wore his indoor coat now, because he was acting as a butler.

"Aye, Mr. Kincade?" Charlotte said.

"Mr. Newton and his men should like a word, mu'um," Mr. Kincade said. "One of them complains about his accommodations."

"That's some nerve!" Charlotte whispered heatedly to Lizzie. "He imposes on us and then has the gall to complain?"

"We've no' been particularly civil," Lizzie pointed out.

"I hardly see your point," Charlotte said crisply. "Very well, Mr. Kincade. Do please show them in."

Chapter Twelve

After what seemed like several hours, but Dougal insisted had only been two, Jack was escorted into the house once more. The day had turned gray, and in the dim light, the telltale signs of the Beal sisters' financial woes looked even worse. Although the furnishings seemed of the first cut and the place was pristinely clean, candles were scarce and the dimly lit corridors positively gloomy. The wallpaper in the entry was peeling and there was a pot in the corner of the foyer that Jack suspected had been used to catch rainwater, if the stains on the ceiling above were any indication.

He hardly had time to look as he was hauled to the doors of the same drawing room from which he'd been ceremoniously tossed only hours earlier. He was met at the door by two dogs, the smallest of them possessing the fiercest growl and baring his teeth at Jack. The other, a big red hunting dog, was more curious about the scent around Jack than his entry.

The two women were within, but Lizzie had undergone something of a miraculous transformation. She had bathed and changed into a drab gray gown that happened to fit her exceedingly well. *Exceedingly.* He could not help but admire her figure in it. Her dark hair was bound up in the ribbon she seemed to prefer and she wore a simple strand of pearls that rested against the hollow of throat. When she swallowed, the little strand moved like a tiny river.

Moreover, Lizzie looked considerably calmer and watched him evenly, as if they were engaged in a game of chess and she was awaiting his move.

Her sister, on the other hand, glared daggers at Jack, as if *he* had done something wrong. He supposed she believed he was there to wreak havoc. He couldn't possibly, even if he were of a mind, for Newton and Dougal remained at his back.

"Good afternoon, milord," Lizzie said, inclining her head. "Allow me to properly introduce my sister, Miss Charlotte Beal."

"So formal, Lizzie," he chided her. "And after all that we've endured together." He turned to her sister. "Miss Beal," he said, bowing low.

"Milord," Miss Beal said with a bit of a smirk, "we find ourselves in an unusual predicament." She primly folded her hands over the lap rug that covered her crippled legs. She looked very regal, Jack thought. Beautiful, regal, and a bit priggish.

"Unfortunately, our uncle's heinous actions have left us very few options as far as you are concerned. We donna like you to be at Thorntree, but we fear that if we refuse to house you, Uncle Carson may do something more wretched and drastic than he's already done. So it is with some . . . reluctance," she said, looking to Lizzie for agreement as to her word choice, to which Lizzie nodded enthusiastically, "that we will allow you to stay here. We shall make accommodations for you in the nursery."

Jack snorted.

"It is near the kitchens, where you may take your meals . . . if you can prepare one."

Now Jack gaped at her.

Charlotte lifted her hand. "I grant you, it is not an ideal situation, but Mr. Kincade assures me he can make it quite livable—"

"No," Jack said firmly.

"I beg your pardon?"

"*No*," he said again, folding his arms resolutely across his chest. "No, Miss Beal, I will not be relegated to the nursery. I am an earl, and I, too, have been through an ordeal, to say the least," he said, thinking of Lizzie. "You are right in that it is no' an ideal situation, and I assure you, I will take my leave as soon as it is possible for me to do so, but I will sleep in a bed and bathe in a hip bath and eat proper food prepared by a cook. I will no' sleep in a *nursery.*"

"I told you so," Lizzie muttered in a low aside to her sister.

"How dare you!" Miss Beal demanded of Jack. "You can no' sweep into our home and demand to be treated as a welcome guest!"

Her raised voice startled the little mutt of a dog, and he growled at Jack again, pouncing on his boot. "That is your first misconception, Miss Beal," Jack said as he shook the dog off his foot. "I did no' *sweep* into your home and demand anything. I have been threatened within an inch of my life." The dog pounced again. "If I defy your uncle today, it would seem there are some men about who would collect a very hefty bounty for my head. I donna intend to stay here a moment longer than I must, but until I can figure out, how, exactly, I might take my leave, I will no' be treated as some mangy cur!" he exclaimed, and shook the dog from his foot again.

"I *told* you," Lizzie muttered again with a sidelong look for her sister. "He's very obstinate."

"Miss Charlotte," Newton said evenly as Dougal tried to get the dog away from Jack's boot, "the laird was quite clear his lordship is to remain at Thorntree; and if he does no', the laird will begin a manhunt. In that event, I'm to bring Miss Lizzie to him."

"Why?" demanded Charlotte.

Newton's face darkened. "He will hold her responsible and punish her accordingly."

"*Punish?*" cried Charlotte. The sisters gasped with indignation and exchanged a look. But Charlotte was every bit as stubborn as her sister, obviously, for she shook her head and pressed her lips together, and Jack thought that it was remarkable that she could look so very handsome even when pouting.

The dog pounced again.

"That is unacceptable," Charlotte continued crisply, as if her miserable little mutt of a dog was not attempting to chew Jack's boot off his foot. "If he remains among us, free to come and go out of our company at will, it will compromise our reputations, and my uncle knows that very well! No, we donna want him here."

"*Diah,*" Jack groaned.

" 'Tis a fact that there are times we all must do what we donna want to do," Newton said.

"*No,*" Charlotte said adamantly.

In a moment of frustration, Jack bent down and scooped up the snarling little dog, holding him tightly beneath his arm. "I share your distaste for this charade, madam, but unfortunately, I am here, and I will take a proper guest room. Now, where shall I find it?"

"You are awfully bold, sir!" Charlotte exclaimed.

"I *told* you," Lizzie said in a very soft, singsong voice.

"He's to stay, lass," Newton said gruffly before Charlotte could object, and abruptly took the dog from Jack, stroking him behind his ears as he moved to put the wee monster on Charlotte's lap. "He will remain at Thorntree, and no' in the nursery." He walked back to where Jack stood. "Ye'll come with me now," he said, and put his hand on Jack's arm.

"Please remove your hand from me, sir," Jack said hotly, jerking his body clear of Newton's paw. "Have you no' a patch of land or a family that needs looking after more than me?"

"Very well, take him to the shed," Charlotte said.

Newton did not respond, for he had clamped his hand on Jack's arm, and this time held it painfully tight. "Ye will come with me, milord," he said, and forced Jack around. When Jack resisted, Dougal caught his other arm.

"Newton!" Lizzie cried. "There is no need to harm him!"

Jack would have said that he was beyond harming, but the two men had already dragged him out of the room.

They continued to drag him down the corridor with a red dog and two old sheepdogs who'd appeared from nowhere at their heels, strolling along behind as if they thought there might be a bone for them at the end of this walk. Much to Jack's surprise, they did not take him out of doors and to that wretched shed but up a flight of stairs and down a corridor that was bitterly cold. Apparently they kept only those rooms that they frequented heated. When they reached a pale green door, Newton flung it open and half tossed Jack across the threshold.

Jack caught himself before he tumbled to the ground and took a moment to look around.

He was in a bedroom. It was a wee bit dated in the décor but comfortable nonetheless. There was a four-poster bed, a pair of upholstered chairs near the hearth, and a writing table at the window. "This will do," Jack said, surprised by his luck. "There, Newton, do you see? I never asked but to be treated fairly, aye?"

Newton walked across the room and opened another door. Through it, Jack could see what looked like a small sitting room that had been turned into storage. There were bolts of cloth stacked in a corner, a table with a basin, and an old, cracked saddle, merely tossed onto the floor. There were crates, too, and a shelf that held children's boots.

Jack looked at Newton.

"This room," he said, gesturing to the bedroom, "belongs to Miss Lizzie. Ye'll reside with her as ye ought, being handfasted as ye are."

"That news likely will be met with shouts of joy," Jack drawled.

"It is Miss Lizzie's room, then, and she'll decide precisely where ye are to reside." He looked over his shoulder at the room behind him. "Given the lass's apparent feelings for ye, I reckon it might be here."

Jack looked at the room. "In *storage*? That's absurd."

"Mrs. Kincade will give ye a hand tidying up. And she'll bring what ye need to make a pallet for sleeping," he added rather nonchalantly.

"Pardon?" Jack exclaimed, gesturing toward the smaller room. "I'm to reside in there, in a closet, like some waif?"

Newton shrugged indifferently. "It's for Miss Lizzie to decide, then." He walked toward the door, but paused. "Oh, and by the bye, milord, Dougal will be right outside this door at all times. He'll persuade ye differently if ye decide to sleep elsewhere."

Jack laughed. "Do you think I will no' step over Dougal when he's snoring soundly in the middle of the night if I choose?"

"Ye might," Newton said, nodding. "But perhaps ye'll think what the laird might do to the lass should ye turn up missing."

Jack scowled at the giant of a man. "If you ever have occasion to call at Lambourne Castle, Mr. Newton, I should very much like to entertain you on *my* terms."

"That's no' likely to happen, then, is it?" Newton asked lightly. He looked at Dougal. "Keep him here, lad," he said, and, whistling for the dogs, walked out of the room, leaving Jack and Dougal.

Dougal looked curiously at Jack. "Dougal, lad, we're friends," Jack tried, but Dougal was already backing out of the room, closing the door behind him. He did not, Jack noticed, *lock* the door. After the events of the last few days, he considered that something of a personal victory.

Lizzie, like Charlotte, assumed Jack had been dragged off to the shed. She didn't like that at all, for it seemed like something Carson would do. Why could they not have put him in one of the servants' rooms? *Diah*, it wasn't as if they had any servants to fill those rooms any longer.

Lizzie made her way to her room after she and Charlotte talked and was surprised to see Dougal sitting in a chair outside her door. "Sir?" she said, pausing to look at him curiously. "What are you doing here?"

"Mr. Newton said to keep an eye on things," Dougal said.

"A guard? You are *guarding* me?" she asked incredulously.

"I suppose ye might call it that," Dougal said.

"Ha," Lizzie said pertly. "We shall see about that, sir!" And with that, she walked into her bedroom and shut the door behind her. She stood a moment with her back to the door, thinking of Jack in that shed. They'd put a cot in it years ago for Mr. Kincade's brother. He'd come round every now and again to pay a call but would fall so far into his cups on the strength of Mr. Kincade's whisky that they'd have to put him in the shed to sleep it off. The second Mr. Kincade had not been round in years, nor had Lizzie looked inside the shed in years.

She hoped it wasn't too terribly uncomfortable.

She pushed away from the door and moved to the center of her room, rubbing the nape of her neck. But as she stood there, she felt something odd . . . as if someone were watching her. Lizzie slowly lowered her hand and turned around—and cried out as she spotted Jack sitting in the shadows at her writing desk.

"*Diah,* what are you doing here?" she cried, her hand on her heart. "This is my room!"

"Aye, I am keenly aware of it," he said, and rose to his feet, moving languidly into the light.

"Get out," she said, pointing to the door.

"No," he said, shaking his head, his eyes narrowing on her. "We are handfasted, *leannan,* or have you forgotten it? No one else in this bloody provincial glen has."

"I want you to go straightaway!" she insisted, marching to the door.

"I can no' go—the large man with the larger knife has spoken. We are handfasted."

"*No,*" Lizzie said, shaking her head. "You will no' stay here in this room!"

"I *shall,*" he said, his eyes turning dark. As if to prove it, he fell into a chair and propped his boots on the table.

"No," Lizzie said. "No, no, *no*! Where is he, where is Newton, then? I shall put this all to rights!"

"I wish you luck," Jack said with a flick of his wrist. "I'd join you, but I have a keeper with strict instructions to leave me put."

Lizzie ignored him and stormed out of the room, almost tripping over Dougal in her haste.

She found Newton in the foyer. "He can no' reside in my room," she said, dispensing with any greeting.

"He must," Newton said impassively. "Ye have pledged yer troth to him, and now ye must abide by that troth."

"You know it was no' of my free will!" Lizzie cried.

"Aye," Newton said. "But ye agreed nonetheless. The laird would have the appearance of a handfasting at the very least."

Fury filled Lizzie. She was so angry she could scarcely speak. "So you will aid in the ruination of me, is that it?" she asked, her voice shaking.

"He will reside in yer rooms, lass. But *where* in yer suite of rooms is yer choice. No' mine. Mrs. Kincade is to put a pallet in the adjoining room."

"In the sitting room? Is that the best you can do, then?" Lizzie cried. "The entire glen will talk of this!"

He looked at her; Lizzie realized that was precisely what Carson wanted. "I've me orders, lass," he said, and walked on, effectively ending the discussion.

She watched him go, then picked up her skirts. "This is no' to be borne," she muttered angrily, "and I will *no'* bear it!" She marched off in the direction of her greenhouse, the only place she could find a moment's peace.

While Lizzie tried to find her way out of her quandary, Charlotte sat alone, brooding before the hearth.

She heard the creak of the door and assumed it was Mrs. Kincade with her afternoon tea, which the elderly woman served every afternoon at five o'clock. But the footfall was too heavy, and Charlotte twisted in her seat and groaned when she saw Newton moving across the carpet.

"You were no' given leave to enter!" she said crossly.

"Aye, so ye've said on more than one occasion," Newton said wryly, and proceeded to take the seat across from her. Charlotte cried out in protest, but he flippantly ignored her and settled his big hands on his knees, as if he and she were close acquaintances.

Truly affronted, Charlotte exclaimed, "Why do you question my orders?"

"Ye donna give me orders. The laird does. And I am to stay with ye."

"I donna want you here!" Charlotte cried.

Newton sighed. "Do useless legs give ye the right to be so ill-mannered?"

Charlotte could feel her face mottling with impotent rage. "How dare you say such a thing to me!"

"I think it high time someone spoke to you in such a manner," he said quietly, and stood up. "And I think it high time ye came out of this room."

Charlotte could hardly catch her breath she was so angry, but when he stepped behind her chair and began to move her, she cried out with fear.

"I donna intend to harm ye."

Charlotte cried out for Lizzie, but no one came. Newton pushed her to the door. He paused there and picked up a thick tartan blanket, which he wrapped around her shoulders.

"Stop this!" Charlotte screamed. "Stop this at once! *Mr. Kincade!* Help me! Someone help me!"

"Mr. Kincade is in the barn," Newton said, and proceeded to push her chair out the door.

It was no use. Only the dogs had come at the sound of her cries and they seemed more interested in her destination than in her abduction.

Newton maneuvered her down the corridor as Charlotte railed at him and tried to catch on to anything with her hands. The best she managed was to knock a vase to the floor. She was on the verge of tears—no one came to her aid and she was left to her own devices, as helpless as a fish out of water.

Newton wheeled her to the French doors that led to the terrace and paused to open them.

"Oh, dear God," Charlotte said breathlessly. *"Mi Diah!"* She had visions of herself lying helplessly on the cold ground, soaked to the bone by the mists and left to die, a useless cripple who could not even pull herself into the house. When he stepped behind her and pushed her onto the terrace, she screamed with terror.

"By all that is holy!" he exclaimed. *"Charlotte . . ."* He put his hand on her shoulder, squeezing gently as the dogs loped down the steps and onto the grass of the lawn. "Surely ye know by now I will no' harm ye." And with that, he slipped his hands beneath her arms and lifted her up, off that godawful prison of a chair. He caught her by the waist with one arm and held her against him, her back to him, as if she were standing before him.

He just stood there.

"What are you doing?" she asked anxiously. "What do you mean to do?"

"To give you a breath of fresh air. How long has it been, then? Take a breath, Charlotte," he urged her. "Take it, lass."

Her heart pounding, Charlotte drew a breath. It felt cool and fresh in her lungs. In spite of herself, she lifted her face to the cold gray sky. Newton stood silently as she breathed in the scent of the pines, of wet leaves and smoke.

She took another breath.

With Newton solid behind her, Charlotte relaxed and closed her eyes, and for a few moments, she soared high above the hills and the Scots pines.

Chapter Thirteen

Sometime after Jack had eaten the watery soup Dougal had fetched him, Lizzie returned to the room, slipping inside and standing against the wall. She was considerably calmer, but fatigue ringed her eyes.

"Lizzie," Jack said gruffly.

He was seated before the hearth; Lizzie looked at the book he held. So did Jack. "You are reading," she said, sounding quite incredulous.

"Aye," he said, and shut the book. "It is an occupation of last resort when there is no society to occupy me. And as there are no festive games, no one to ravish . . ." He shrugged.

"Well, then, perhaps you might do what others do when they find they've no occupation," Lizzie said. "Go to bed." She pointed to the door to the old sitting room. "In *there*."

Jack smiled. "You'll no' force me to sleep in an ice-cold sitting room, aye?"

If the narrowing of her lovely eyes was any indication, she would.

"*Diah*," he said crossly. "After all we've endured, you'd put me in the bloody sitting room?"

Her expression changed from frustration to supreme confidence. "And after all we've endured you'd see me ruined even further? You should be thankful for any accommodation," she said, folding her arms. "Charlotte wanted you in the shed."

"Aye, but what did *you* want?" he demanded irritably. He tossed his book aside and stood up. "I rescued you from Castle Beal!"

"*Rescued* me?" she cried. "You did no' rescue me! I rescued myself, I did!"

"And how is that, lass? By crawling out a window? I spotted you instantly, as did Dougal! You'd no' have gotten past the gate!"

"I certainly would have, and with no thanks to you!"

He snorted with disbelief. "You canna deny that I helped you out of a rather tight scrape, Lizzie! No one else! And in the course of it, I respected you as a gentleman ought to respect a lady, and *this* is the thanks I'm to have?" he exclaimed, gesturing angrily at the sitting-room door.

"This notion that I am somehow responsible for your comfort is absurd! I've my own worries, Jack. How do you think this will appear to Mr. Gordon?"

"If it does no' appear to him that I've been a veritable saint of patience, I may shoot him," Jack said testily. He meant to sit once more and resume his book, to simply ignore her, but she was too damned alluring in a provincial way, strangely seductive swaddled in wool and standing there in a high dudgeon with glittering blue eyes.

"I suppose you want to be congratulated for behaving like a gentleman, aye? That's a rogue for you! You behave yourself and think you deserve the master suite for it!"

"*No,*" he said angrily. "But at the very least I deserve . . ." He momentarily lost his train of thought as his gaze fell to her lips, dark and ripe against her pale skin. He was standing close enough that he could see the pearly hint of teeth, the tip of her pink tongue between them.

A strange thought occurred to Jack, and the thought was that he'd not been as aroused as this in a very long time. *Very* long.

"What?" she demanded, squinting up at him. "You deserve *what*?"

He felt himself on the verge of saying something profound, something to put this unruly lass in her proper place. But what came out of his mouth was a thick *"This,"* and in one swift and powerful movement, he caught Lizzie and hauled her into his chest. He gave her not even a fraction of a moment to react before he planted his mouth on hers. Firmly, possessively, hungrily.

He was not surprised when she shrieked into his mouth, but it hardly mattered. *This* was what he deserved, the taste of her succulent lips, the feel of them, soft and surprisingly warm beneath his. He deserved the kiss of this woman who had vexed him, perplexed him— even if there were mounds of wool between them.

Lizzie robbed Jack of all rational thought. Good sense, propriety, and decorum drained out of him. The cold seemed to crack around them, a large sheet of ice breaking under the heat and pressure of that kiss. Jack was aware of nothing but her and a desire in him that was growing more tempestuous by the moment.

He heard her little whimper of protest as he pushed her up against the bedpost, but he also felt her body drift into his. He dipped down, tightened his arm around her as he touched his tongue to the seam of her lips, and then her teeth.

The moment his tongue slipped in between her lips, Lizzie hit his chest with both fists. Jack did not let go; he was scarcely even conscious of the blow. Lizzie hit him again, harder, and solidly.

The gentleman in him forced the man to let her go.

Lizzie shoved him away. She stared at him wide-eyed, full of shock as she wiped the back of her hand across her mouth.

And then she slapped him across the cheek.

The slap stunned Jack, but only for a moment. He chuckled low. "Donna tempt me, lass, for you will surely part with your blessed virtue."

"Will that happen after I beg you for your affection?" she asked breathlessly.

That was the moment his restraint snapped. Jack grabbed the ends of her wool shawl and yanked her to him. For a brief but highly charged moment they glared at each other. Her eyes narrowed dangerously, but he could still see the blue glittering like tiny little crystals, openly daring him to touch her again.

Oh, he touched her. He touched her with his hands and his mouth and his body. He crushed her to him in his arms and kissed her soft, warm mouth as his hands ran over her body, over the curve of her hips and the swell of her breasts.

Lizzie made a sound deep in her throat, a sound of stark, unabashed desire. He plunged his tongue into her mouth, caught the back of her head in his palm, holding her there as he kissed her, as he caressed the velvet curve of her ear with his fingers, the slope of her neck, the line of her jaw. Lizzie grabbed his face, cradling it in her hands, returning his kiss with the same raw desire that was beginning to consume him.

Jack twirled about with her and pushed her up against the mattress. He slid his hands down to her bottom, cupping it, and up again, to the sides of her breast. Lizzie's fingers splayed across his ears, sinking into his hair. She was the only warmth in this room, a fire so hot and spirited that it sparked a deep, bone-melting heat in him. *Diah*, the need to feel her beneath him was almost primitive. Jack was on the verge of bursting with all that want, only moments away from putting her on her back on that bed when Lizzie suddenly wrenched herself free of his grasp.

She was panting and laid her hand across her heart, as if she sought to contain it.

Jack knew the feeling. His own heart felt as if it might burst through his chest at any moment.

She was staring at him with stark desire, for Lizzie was not one to mask her feelings. But then her gaze went hard. "Get out! *Out!*" she cried, pointing to the sitting room.

"Lizzie—"

"Go now, or I shall call the men to my aid!"

Jack's breathing was still ragged, the sensation of that kiss still raw. Something had just happened to him, something fundamental that rattled him and even alarmed him.

Lizzie pointed to the adjoining room again. Jack angrily swiped at the bed hangings and stalked across the room, slamming the door between them.

He sat on the bloody pallet, his back against the wall, his legs stretched before him, brooding about what had just happened between them.

A half hour later, maybe longer, Jack heard the door open. He knew one very hopeful moment, until a pillow was tossed in his direction. He snatched it angrily. A blanket followed and, with a sigh, he took that, too. A moment later, his book was slid across the floor and a candle placed carefully just inside the door, along with a flask of what he soon discovered was whisky—hardly a substitute for what he really wanted, but at least it numbed him past the point of caring for a short time.

Chapter Fourteen

A cold rain began to fall shortly after midnight and turned to sleet shortly before dawn. The sound of it against the glass panes woke Lizzie. She rose and washed quietly in the ice cold water, taking care not to make the slightest noise. When she'd dressed, she allowed herself only a glance at the door to the sitting room, which she'd left ajar to provide a little heat. She rather imagined it was freezing in there, and put another block of peat on the hearth and lit it.

She left the room very quietly, drawing the door closed with much care, only to forget about Dougal and trip over him in the dark. *"Dougal,"* she whispered, and squatted down beside him, put her hand to his shoulder. "Go inside, then, lie by the fire."

"Thank ye, lass," he said sleepily, and lumbered to his feet.

Lizzie made her way to the kitchen to help Mrs. Kincade.

"Now, Miss Lizzie, you ought to have Mr. Kincade do that," Mrs. Kincade said as Lizzie tried to force her frozen fingers to strike a match. She wore wool gloves with the tips of the fingers snipped out of them so she might at least feel the things she touched. She tried again.

Mrs. Kincade moved stiffly about the kitchen. The elderly woman wore her hair in the same severe bun she'd worn as long as Lizzie could remember, only it was completely gray now, not burnished brown. Mrs. Kincade was a wee bit heavier than average, and in the last few years she'd begun to complain about her back. She could scarcely stoop to pick things up any longer, and helping Charlotte in and out of chairs or beds or baths was very difficult for her. Lizzie did most of that now, and worried how much longer Mrs. Kincade could continue to work in the kitchen.

It was one of many things that worried her.

"Mr. Kincade has enough to do with the horses," Lizzie said, managing to light the match, which she quickly put to the kindling beneath the block of peat. She fanned the tiny flame that sparked until the block caught fire, and when she was satisfied it would not die, she stood and stretched her fingers to the flame.

"I feel snow in me bones." Mrs. Kincade sighed. "Me body aches all the way to me toes."

Mrs. Kincade's bones could be trusted to predict the weather, which meant there'd be no hunting or fishing for a day or two. And with a house suddenly full of people to feed! "We must have a pair of birds, aye?" Lizzie asked. They had a rooster and six chickens, only two of them laying hens. Lizzie had hoped to make it through the winter with all the birds.

"Aye, two if you can spare them, Miss Lizzie," Mrs. Kincade said apologetically. "We've got plenty of leeks yet. I'll make a stock."

"I'll fetch them as soon as it is light," Lizzie said. But first, there was something much more pressing she had to do. With the peat now blazing and warming the kitchen, she picked up a paraffin candle and walked down the dark corridor, Fingal and Tavish following behind. She picked up the estate's account ledger from the library, then made her way to her father's study. Normally, Lizzie could not bear to use her father's study—it remained just as it was the day he'd died.

But it was the only place in the entire house that Lizzie could go to be left completely alone without threat of interruption. She had her little greenhouse, which she dearly loved. She grew medicinal herbs and flowers and the time she spent there was a little bit of heaven. But everyone knew they could find her there, and she was rarely left alone for very long.

In her father's study, papers were still stacked high on his desk and his books scattered about the room and table surfaces, as were the curious little things Papa had found in walking about the Thorntree estate. There was a tree root that had curved into the shape of a heart, a rock with an impression that Papa swore resembled the profile of the king.

And there were the milestones of their lives. Crude pictures made with hand paints when they were wee girls, still tacked to the dark paneling of the wall behind the desk. A pair of portraits Papa had commissioned when Charlotte was twelve and Lizzie ten years old. A panel of gold drapes, still bearing the stains of an unfortunate accident with an inkwell.

Lizzie saw none of that this morning, however. She paced, walking around Papa's cluttered desk, trying to stay warm, alternately pressing her hands to her cheeks and then clutching her hands into fists as she tried to make sense of what had happened last night in her room with Jack Haines.

That kiss . . . that *kiss!* . . . had amazed her. Even this morning she could still feel it tingling through her limbs and in her chest. Lizzie had been kissed before, but they'd been chaste little pecks in comparison to what she'd experienced in Jack's arms. His kiss had not been of this world. It had been ardent and fierce and oh, so arousing. She'd felt as if she were the most desirable female between two shores.

She *liked* it. She liked the heady kiss of a rake, a felon, a man who, undoubtedly, made a sport of kissing as he'd kissed her!

"Bloody rogue!" she whispered hotly, and paused a moment, hands pressed flat against her belly to still the butterflies that still swarmed there, staring blindly at the dusty drapery as his enticing visage danced before her mind's eye. Even though the hearth in this room had not been lit in an age, and it was ice cold, Lizzie was strangely warm, almost hot. It made her cross, and she impulsively began to strip layers of a wool shawl and arisaidh from her shoulders until she was standing next to the greatcoat and a pile of wool shawls, wearing only an old wool jumper over an older shirt.

Almost unthinkingly, she rolled her sleeves up past her elbows and folded them across her body. "Donna be fooled, Lizzie," she cautioned herself. That may have been an arousing kiss, but she had no doubt he passed them around like sweetmeats. That kiss may not have been of this world, but *she* certainly was. To entertain a fanciful notion of something more was insupportable. It was madness!

Mr. Gordon was her only hope now. She had to write him quickly, for the sooner Gavin came the sooner that . . . that man would be dealt with properly. And his kiss—his insupportable, outrageously presumptuous, knee-bending kiss, would be forgotten. *Entirely* forgotten. "Insufferable man," Lizzie muttered. "Forgotten!" She would continue on as if it had never happened.

She picked up her arisaidh, threw it around her shoulders, and sat on the wobbly old chair before the desk. She blew on her fingertips and opened the ledger on the desk.

Nothing had changed. The figures had not miraculously transformed in her absence. The state of their household was pronounced in black and white on those ledger pages: they had four hundred and seventy-three pounds to their name. Four hundred and seventy-three pounds to provide for four adults, a menagerie of farm animals, and an entire estate for the foreseeable future, with not a bit of income. They'd sold the last of the ewes just two weeks ago.

Without any income from the estate, their situation was dire.

Lizzie bit her lower lip, put aside the ledger, brushed the errant curl from her eye, and opened the drawer of the desk. She withdrew a piece of foolscap and blew on her fingers once more. She had no choice but to summon Mr. Gordon.

She withdrew the pen from the inkwell. It felt strange in her hand. She was not the sort of person to ask for help. Mr. Gordon would certainly help her if he could, for he was a proud man. He was quite intelligent, too, Lizzie thought. He would be laird of the Gordons one day, she believed. He'd made great strides in building the clan's resources after economic hardships at the turn of the century, and in fact, he was in Crieff this month learning about the wool trade.

She could imagine Mr. Gordon in the wool markets. He was handsome, she mused. He was strong, too, and had won the caber toss during a Gordon clan gathering last fall. He was truly a perfect match for her; Charlotte was right about that. Lizzie had thought so, too, until . . .

Until she lost her mind recently.

Lizzie stuffed down the madness and put the pen to paper. She was not in the habit of writing letters to gentlemen, and was uncertain how to proceed.

"*Appeal to his vanity,*" Charlotte had counseled. "*Men are most susceptible to praise, whether it has been earned or not.*"

Lizzie rather assumed Charlotte would know, as there had been a time before the accident when she'd been quite sought after by the gentlemen in the glen.

Dear Mr. Gordon, she wrote, and stared at that a moment. "Dear Gavin," she muttered. "Mr. Gordon, sir. Dear sir."

She stuck with Mr. Gordon.

> *I hope this letter finds you well. Charlotte and I are quite well, but the weather is most disagreeable. It seems inordinately cold, even for January. I pray you have found your accommodations in Crieff to your liking.*

"*Diah*, how very tiresome!" she muttered. He'd not give a fig about the weather, given what he may or may not have heard about her. Papa always said it was best to be straightforward in matters of business. This was a matter of business, at least in part. Lizzie scratched over what she'd written—even foolscap was too expensive to waste—and began again.

> *My dear sir, I fear you have heard rumblings of a most egregious event in Glenalmond in your absence. I pray that you trust my good character and know that whatever you might have heard, I have held my head high and maintained my virtue and my good name. Indeed, it is true that my uncle has shown himself to be a vile man who will stop at nothing to see the happiness of his niece*

derailed. But I can assure you without equivocation that I did not participate in his wretched scheme.

Nevertheless, I implore you, Mr. Gordon, to please come to Thorntree at your earliest convenience, as I have desperate need of your wise counsel.

She paused to consider her wording. Was it praise enough? Did it appeal to his vanity?

I am convinced no one but you can possibly help me. Please do come straightaway if you are at all able.

Honestly, she didn't believe for a moment that Mr. Gordon could help her now. No one could help her. She and Charlotte were beyond hope.

My sister and I look forward to receiving you at Thorntree.

She studied the letter again, determined there was really nothing she could say that would soften it or improve the truth in any manner. She signed it and sealed it. And then she stuffed it into the pocket of her gown and went in search of Mr. Kincade so that he might find someone to deliver her letter posthaste.

Chapter Fifteen

The sitting room felt as if it were encased in ice. The bit of heat that had filtered through the small crack Lizzie had allowed him had dissipated in the middle of the night. Cold, damp air had seeped in through the floorboards and now it was so cold one could store meat.

As a result, Jack slept poorly and rose early in ill temper.

He did not in the least appreciate being stuffed into some storage room like a bad relation. If the situation had been reversed, he would have given Lizzie an entire floor of his bloody castle.

He stalked into the bedroom and stumbled over Dougal, who was curled in front of the hearth. "What in the bloody hell are you doing there?" he demanded.

"Sleeping, milord!" Dougal cried.

"No' any longer, lad," Jack said, and nudged him with his foot. "You will draw me a bath. Off with you now."

Unfortunately, the bath that Dougal reluctantly drew—which was as cold as the sleet that fell outside—did not lighten Jack's mood. Nor did the cold scone Dougal brought him. And that he donned the last articles of clean clothing only increased his ire, as he supposed he'd be made to launder his own clothing at this way station to hell. *That* he found insupportable. He'd never laundered as much as a handkerchief, and he would not forgive Miss Lizzie Beal—that blood-stirring kiss notwithstanding.

His first order of business was food. That damn kiss had left him hungry, and if he couldn't feast on Lizzie, he'd find something to fill him.

With a grunt of displeasure, Jack swept up his great-coat, marched across the room, and threw open the door of his ice cave.

The letter handed off to Mr. Kincade for posting, Lizzie strode to the kitchen. As she neared it she heard voices and slowed her step, coming to a halt just outside the door. That sounded like *him.* She laid her palms against the door and leaned in. The voices were muffled, but she could just make out Mrs. Kincade asking, "Is the belly *completely* bare?" To which *he* responded, "Aye, completely bare."

Lizzie pushed open the door and sailed through. Her entrance startled Mrs. Kincade, whose cap, Lizzie couldn't help but notice, was askew. But Jack looked up at her with sultry gray eyes and a hint of an unapologetic smile, as if he were expecting her, and with his gaze steady on her, he casually took a bite of a large piece of ham from a plate before him.

"Miss Lizzie, you gave me a fright, you did!" Mrs. Kincade said.

Lizzie glanced at Mrs. Kincade and noticed the feathers that lay on the table and the floor all around the elderly woman. She had a chicken. But Lizzie hadn't fetched the chicken yet.

Mrs. Kincade nodded at Jack in answer to Lizzie's

unspoken question. "He brung it in, along with the eggs."

Lizzie looked dubiously to Jack, who smiled imperiously as he ate another bite of ham. "*He* brought it in?"

"Donna let my refined manner confuse you, lass. I am quite capable of gathering eggs and catching old hens," he said dryly.

"Are you also capable of cooking food?" she asked, gesturing to his plate.

"Oh, 'tis my fault, Miss Lizzie," Mrs. Kincade said as she scraped feathers off the table and into a basket. "I got a wee bit caught up in his stories, I did," she said with a funny shake of her head.

Lizzie leveled a suspicious glare on him.

"I was regaling Mrs. Kincade with tales of London and the wonders of Oriental dancing," Jack said. He winked and popped another nice cut of ham into his mouth.

"It's scandalous, that dancing! Miss Lizzie, he knows the Prince and Princess of Wales!" Mrs. Kincade said, sounding awestruck.

"Mrs. Kincade has no' been to London," Jack added, and glanced up from his plate. "Have you had the pleasure, Miss Beal?"

Lizzie had never been even as far as Edinburgh. "If you donna mind, sir, Mrs. Kincade has quite a lot of work to do—"

"Oh no, miss, I'm quite all right. His lordship helped me. He made a new fire and brought more oats in from the pantry."

Jack smiled, obviously and inordinately pleased with himself. "Imagine that—eggs, chickens, *and* oats."

This was absurd! He was far too comfortable and inserting himself into her household. Just thinking of him being about gave Lizzie a tick of panic; he could ruin everything. "How very helpful of you," Lizzie said sweetly. "Mrs. Kincade, will you please go to Charlotte and help her from bed? I'll finish in the kitchen."

Jack lifted his brows and smiled as if that pleased him.

"Aye, of course," Mrs. Kincade said. She put down the bucket of feathers, paused to clean her hands, and then removed her apron.

Amusement dancing in his eyes, Jack blithely continued to eat what seemed to be an entire ham as Mrs. Kincade puttered about. When she finally quit the kitchen, Lizzie braced her hands on the table and leaned across to him. "You *helped* her, did you? You carried a bag of oats and a pair of eggs and thereby helped yourself to our ham?"

"Why do you seem so surprised? Have I no' shown myself to be *most* willing?" he asked, his gaze wandering the length of her body.

"You have shown yourself *quite* willing to charm meat from an old woman and . . . and . . ." She couldn't think when he was looking at her like that, as if he could devour her alongside his ham, head to foot.

"And?" Jack prompted. When Lizzie did not respond, he put aside his fork and wiped his mouth with a napkin. He stood from the stool where he sat, braced his hands on the table, and leaned forward, piercing Lizzie's gaze with his. "And charm the maidenhead from a young woman such as yourself? I'll have you know, *leannan*, that Mrs. Kincade heard my belly growl with hunger, understood the conditions to which I have been subjected here, and kindly offered me some bread and ham. I did no' *charm* her . . . any more than I charmed you."

The fire behind him suddenly crackled and flared, and Lizzie felt it reverberate in her. They were so close, only inches apart. How could she not think of the fiery kiss that still simmered in her veins?

She slowly leaned back, away from him and his gray eyes. She was not a debutante. She was not a shy, socially inexperienced woman who was easily intimidated by the unearthly magnetism of this man. Seduced by it, perhaps, but not intimidated. "You must think me awfully dull if you believe that I donna know what you are about, Jack."

"Oh?" he said, his gaze sweeping over her. "And just what am I *about*?"

"You think us fools here. You think yourself superior in every way and take advantages that no gentleman would dare take. You've been forced upon us like . . . like an ague we canna overcome. But donna mistake us—you're no' welcome here. So please keep your distance from us."

"From us? Or from *you*? What is it, Lizzie? Are you afraid you'll want me again?"

"I donna want you—"

"Ah," he said, putting up a hand to stop her. "I know want, *leannan*, and last night, you wanted me." His voice was a dangerously low caress. "As for Mrs. Kincade, I was hungry. Your cook fed me."

Lizzie swallowed.

Jack casually touched her cheek. "There is one more thing I would say. You may think me a rakehell, but for some inexplicable reason, I kissed you because I was attracted to you in a way I've no' been attracted to a woman before, aye? I apologize if I offended your tender sensibilities. And while I know quite well I was no' the only one who enjoyed it," he said, his eyes darkening, "you may rest assured that it will no' happen again."

A current of unexpected desire quickly slithered

through her, and Lizzie took a step back. "Good!" she said, folding her arms tightly across her chest.

"Never you fear, little Lizzie Beal," he said silkily. "I will be gone from your sight the moment I can find my way out of this calamity."

A small sliver of disappointment nicked her. "Splendid. Perhaps you will go now and find a quiet place to plan your departure that does not include anyone in this house."

His face darkened. He walked around the table, intentionally brushing against her as he passed on his way to the door. But he paused there beside her, his eyes sweeping over her face. "Say what you like, Lizzie. You may convince yourself until your toes cock up, but you wanted that kiss as much as I did. You may fool yourself, but you canna fool me."

She bristled indignantly with the sting of truth in his words. "You are too bold by half! Mr. Gordon is coming, and he'll no' abide your insolence!" The moment the words were out of her mouth, Lizzie wanted to kick herself. Not only did she sound like a miffed schoolgirl, but now she'd put herself out on a limb, for what if Mr. Gordon didn't come?

But it was too late. Jack was grinning wickedly. "How very sweet—the knight comes to rescue the damsel after all. I look forward to meeting the man who will saddle himself to you for all eternity."

That did it. Lizzie swiped up the butcher knife.

He chuckled. "I am going, damsel," he said, and kicked open the kitchen door as he strode through.

Lizzie dropped the knife on the table, gripped the edge, closed her eyes, and tossed her head back. "I am such a bloody *fool*," she moaned.

∽∾∾

Jack did not think Lizzie a fool, but he did think she was possibly the most exasperating woman he'd ever met.

Quite honestly, Jack had, from time to time, failed to charm a member of the opposite sex. It happened rarely, as he normally kept the company of women who were looking for a match or a lover, and he was, he recognized, a rather desirable match and a desirable lover.

But to Lizzie Beal, he was only trouble. Never had he met a woman who was as immune to his charm as she was. And never would he have believed he would care quite as much as he did.

He could not stop brooding about it. Lizzie had enjoyed that kiss. Jack would stake his reputation as a rogue and a lover on it—Lizzie Beal had savored that exquisite kiss every bit as much as he had. Bloody stubborn she was, as stubborn as an old mule.

Jack was so annoyed that he didn't see Newton until he was almost upon him.

The lumbering giant was standing in the entry, a pair of dogs with him, removing dead flowers from a vase. He glanced at Jack. "There you are, milord." He walked to the front door, opened it, and tossed the dead flowers outside.

Jack grunted and strode past the dogs, who were rather pleased to see him, judging by the furious wagging of their tails.

"I've something to show ye," Newton said before he could get around the dogs.

"What?" Jack snapped.

"A drawing room," Newton said.

"I have *seen* the drawing room."

"No' that one," Newton said. "Your drawing room."

"*Mine?*" Jack demanded dubiously.

"Aye. It is away from the lassies. They donna want ye near."

"I bloody well donna care," Jack said, and moved to continue on his path.

But Newton caught him by the arm. "Bloody well care, then," he said, and shoved Jack into a small receiving room just off the entry. It was painted the color of Lizzie's eyes, the drapery blue French toile. At least the hearth was lit, for which, had the circumstances been different, Jack might have kissed Newton.

But the circumstances were not different. "Is this some sort of jest?" Jack demanded irritably. "You'll keep me locked away, is that it?"

"No," Newton said. "But I found a room where ye might pass the time."

"Then please tell me a card table and three willing players will be arriving shortly."

Newton didn't even blink.

Bloody hell, so this was Carson's idea of freedom. "Splendid."

Newton returned to the door, but he paused there. "Milord?"

Jack glanced impatiently at him.

"If I may?"

Jack sighed heavenward. "If there is something you'd say to me, Mr. Newton, I beg of you, *say* it."

"Only that I trust ye will respect their privacy."

"What in the name of Scotland have I done to incur the low opinion of everyone at Thorntree?" Jack demanded, exasperated.

"These lassies are no' accustomed to the ways of high society, if ye take my meaning," Newton said stoically. "Donna toy with their affections, or ye'll have me to answer to."

Jack didn't know if he should be insulted or amused that a man who, he presumed, farmed sheep on some godforsaken hill would lecture him.

"And donna mind Miss Charlotte," Newton continued. "Her speech is her way."

"Her way of what, precisely?"

Newton shrugged. "Of hiding," he said, as if that was obvious. "She's frightened."

"Of?" Jack asked, expecting to be told that the poor lass lived in fear that he would steal her virtue in the middle of the night or something equally absurd.

"Of everything," Newton said. "Of life." And that was apparently all he would say on that subject, for Mr. Kincade entered the room.

"Miss Charlotte asks for ye," he said simply, and Newton immediately quit the room, the dogs trotting behind him as if he were lord and master here.

Chapter Sixteen

I f Jack thought he'd be allowed to roam the house freely, he was mistaken. He found Dougal outside his little drawing room, sitting in a chair he'd tilted back against the wall on two legs, a gun draped across his lap.

Jack cocked a brow as he looked at the gun.

"I'm to keep an eye on ye, milord," Dougal explained unnecessarily.

"And a gun cocked to my head?"

Dougal glanced at the gun in his lap. "Mr. Newton said ye might think to run. Or bother the lassies."

"Mr. Newton seems to have formed a swift and unalterable opinion of me," Jack drawled. "Is that loaded? Never mind—pick up your gun, Dougal. I should like a walk about the grounds."

Dougal dutifully picked up the gun and stood. As Jack walked down the corridor, Dougal followed like one of the ever-present dogs that appeared from nowhere.

"I am reminded of time spent with George in Bath," Jack said. "He'd decided to pen a bit of poetry and had a poor chap follow him about in the event the muse struck."

"George?"

Jack glanced over his shoulder at the man. "George. The Prince of Wales. Your future king."

"Ye . . . ye are acquainted with the Prince of Wales?" Dougal asked, in disbelief.

"He is—well, *was*, really—my friend. Aye, Dougal, I know him quite well." They had reached the front door. Jack opened it, walking outside into the gray light. One of the sheepdogs trotted out ahead of him to sniff about the hitching post. The clouds were beginning to break, and weak sunlight darted around Jack, teasing him as he walked, before disappearing behind the clouds again.

"Did . . . did ye meet him in London, then?" Dougal asked, hurrying to keep up with Jack's determined stride.

"Who?" Jack asked coyly.

"The prince."

"Ah, the prince," Jack said with a smile. "At Windsor, actually, in the course of a fox hunt many years ago. He's no' a particularly good hunter."

"No' a hunter?" Dougal asked in a tone that suggested he thought it impossible.

The Highlander listened with rapt attention as Jack regaled him with tales of the prince. This morning such tales had at least earned him a bit of ham. Jack hoped Dougal might be persuaded to put away that blasted gun.

Lambourne looked quite cozy with Dougal when Carson rode up the drive to Thorntree with his two men. The earl was leaning against a split rail fence, enjoying a cheroot Dougal must have given him, looking like a vicar in the throes of a philosophical rambling.

Dougal stood with his legs braced wide apart, a gun held loosely at his side, his attention on Lambourne. Whatever the earl was telling him had him engrossed.

The earl struck Carson as a glib man, someone who had made his way in this life on the strength of his silver tongue and his ability to ingratiate himself into fine salons.

When Lambourne spotted him, he gave Carson a derisive smirk.

As Carson dismounted, Lambourne tossed the end of the cheroot to the ground and crushed it with the heel of his boot. "And the day grows happier and happier," he said, bowing low.

"Spare me false pleasantries, Lambourne," Carson said, but Lambourne's smile only widened. He enjoyed annoying him, Carson realized.

"Rather cold day for riding, is it no'?" Lambourne asked, glancing in the direction from which Carson and his men had come. "What's down that way?"

"By the bye, milord," Carson said, removing his gloves, "I hosted two of the prince's men at Castle Beal last evening. When they did no' find you in Crieff as they'd hoped, they backtracked. But they brought along an additional six men—Highlanders all—to help them find you." He glanced at the earl.

"Indeed?" Lambourne said, looking damnably casual as his gaze flicked over the men who flanked Carson, their guns clearly evident in their belts.

"I thought you might like to know that Sir Oliver Wilkes was hanged a fortnight ago for treason and conspiracy," Carson said. "I understand he was a friend of yours."

The earl's arrogant smile faltered a bit. "Wilkes?"

"Then he was a friend, aye?" Carson said.

Lambourne laughed. "I am friend to all, Laird. Even to you."

Aye, but the man was smooth. Carson stepped forward and said low, "I know your sort, Lambourne. There are those in London and beyond who believe you had something in common with your friend Wilkes. The bounty has been increased by one hundred pounds. That would feed a man's family for more than a year, aye? I would suggest you stay close to my niece, lest the same end come to you. Where is she?"

"Oh, I hardly know," Lambourne said pleasantly. "Feeding chickens or stomping about the house in her boots, I'd wager."

"You are careless, sir," Carson said with disdain, and walked on, to the house, his men on his heels.

"You might clean your boots before entering," Jack called after him. "You'd no' want to muddy the clean floors, aye?"

Carson glanced down at his boots. They were covered with mud. He muttered a curse under his breath and continued on.

Lizzie heard voices through the flue in the library. She kept the hearth cold in this room, as she rarely occupied it for more than an hour or two at a time, and it was not worth the expense of peat. Bundled in her father's greatcoat as well as her fingerless gloves, she worked and reworked the figures in her account books, trying in vain to find a way to stretch the little money they had and pay the smithy for the repairs to their worn carriage: two new wheels and an axle. She'd had to do it—that carriage was the only means Charlotte had of leaving Thorntree, should the need arise.

" 'The worth of a thing is known by the want of it,' as Papa always said," she muttered to herself. But then she paused and frowned. "Aye, but Grandmama said 'willful waste makes woeful want.' " She shook her head. There was a Highland saying for everything, and if she looked hard enough, she'd find one to justify what she was doing. She resumed her work, her feet tapping an old Highland tune on top of Red's body, who had stretched out on the floor beneath the table.

When Lizzie heard the voices, she assumed they were those of Charlotte and Newton. But when the voices rose, she recognized the faint but unmistakable tones of her uncle. She was instantly on her feet, striding out of the parlor, Red trotting alongside her.

In the drawing room, Charlotte was sitting near the fire with Bean in her lap. Carson was standing over her.

"Someone should drown that bloody dog," Carson growled, glaring at Bean.

"Why are you here, threatening a small dog, Uncle?" Lizzie asked angrily. "Is there someone else you wish to abduct? Another life you wish to ruin?"

"And a jolly good day to you as well, Lizzie," her uncle responded as he unfastened the clasp on his cloak. He tossed it carelessly on a chair and ran a hand through his thick silver hair. "I have come to tell you that I have paid your debt to the smithy."

"*What?*" Lizzie demanded.

"Why, Uncle," Charlotte said with false lightness, as she gathered Bean in her arms, "how *generous* of you."

"We are perfectly capable of paying our debts," Lizzie said angrily.

"Oh? Then why did you no' pay it? What did you think would stop him from taking your carriage as payment?"

A flush of anger heated Lizzie's neck. Several months ago, a merchant had taken some of the furniture their father had commissioned when that bill went unpaid. "I intended to speak to him," Lizzie said curtly as she shed the greatcoat, "but I was taken from my home and forced into a handfasting."

"Speaking is no' *money*, Lizzie. You are a young woman and naïve to the ways of tradesman and merchants. I had to take matters into hand."

Oh, but she despised his domineering manner! Their debt to Carson kept mounting, and it was precisely what he wanted: the more they owed him, the tighter his stranglehold on them and Thorntree. "You've put us deeper in debt to you."

Carson shrugged indifferently. "If you honor your vow to the handfasting and turn that bloody Gordon away, we might find a satisfactory arrangement for you to repay your debt to me."

"I'd rather live in debtor's prison than be beholden to you. I donna understand why you go to such lengths, Uncle! What is Mr. Gordon to you?"

"A *Gordon*! The name itself is vile! I'll no' have a Gordon on Beal land!"

"Aye, but this is *our* land—no' yours," Lizzie said evenly.

"*This is Beal land!*" he thundered. "I might ask the same question of you, Lizzie—why do you go to such lengths to turn away an earl? He is wealthy and may solve all your troubles. He is titled—"

"He is wanted to hang and he was coerced into this union."

"As most men are," Carson scoffed. "How fares your husband?"

"He is no' my husband."

"Are you treating him as you ought? Is he sleeping in your bed?"

"Uncle!" Lizzie cried. The heat of humiliation spread up her neck, to her face.

But Carson was ruthless. "Get his seed in you. Carry his child."

Lizzie gasped with shock. *"Diah!"* Charlotte exclaimed.

"He'll go off and leave you, aye, he will as soon as he is able, but if you bear his child, he'll provide for you and all your problems will be solved, no?"

"You . . . you are reprehensible," Lizzie said, her voice shaking. She turned away from him, strode to the door, and yanked it open. "Please go."

"No' so fast," Carson said. "I have come to tell you that you'll be hosting a supper party on Friday evening. The McLennans and the Sorley Beals will be your guests. It is near enough to Candlemas that you will use the occasion to end your mourning. Now then, I have chosen the McLennans and the Beals to attend your supper party for they are family, and they will no' let on to an outsider that the man the prince so desperately wants in his custody is here. But you'd best show your regard and your happiness at your handfasting, Lizzie."

"I will do no such thing!" she cried. "You can no' command us to entertain and to pretend all is well!"

"Donna be stupid," Carson said coldly. "If you donna do as I say, it will no' be long before someone in this glen believes that a royal bounty is theirs for the taking, and they will justify it by your wretched behavior and disregard for the man. But if they believe one of their own is happily married, they'll protect his identity and your happiness. That is the way of the Beals, aye? We look after one another."

"Do you hear the irony in your own words?" Lizzie asked incredulously.

But her uncle was not listening. "In other words," he said, "if you donna want to see the man hang, you'll do as I say. Every Beal in this glen must believe that your troth has been happily pledged. If you would get yourself with child, that would ensure our secret is safe."

Lizzie gaped at him.

"God in heaven, will you leave us?" Charlotte cried.

Lizzie opened the door. Carson's two men, standing just outside, came to attention. Carson's face mottled with anger and, with a glare for Charlotte, he picked up his coat and walked to the door. He paused there and looked back at them. "You two are awfully high and mighty, eh? Just remember that I am the only one who stands between you and complete ruin."

"You've done nothing but hasten our ruin!" Lizzie snapped. "And for what? For a tiny estate with nothing to recommend it! How deep your greed runs, Uncle Carson."

His face turned darker and he clenched his jaw. "There are things that you are incapable of understanding." He shifted closer. "I'll say it once more, Lizzie. If you donna do as I tell you, you will feel the full force of my wrath," he said menacingly. "If you donna mind yourself and this handfasting, I will personally see to it that you are as incapacitated as your sister."

His threat had the desired effect—Lizzie was speechless.

"I'll be back," he said sourly, and quit the room, leaving bits of mud on the carpet.

Lizzie shut the door behind him and gaped at Charlotte in disbelief.

"What are we to do?" Charlotte asked helplessly.

Lizzie angrily removed the fingerless gloves. "Donna allow him to intimidate us, for that is precisely what he aims to do."

"He is succeeding," Charlotte muttered.

Chapter Seventeen

I n the library again, Lizzie pored over the books.
   She was worried. They needed food and more candles and proper clothing now that their period of mourning was coming to an end, but as things stood . . .

She dropped her pencil and rubbed her forehead in a vain attempt to stave off the headache that was building.

"Might I help?"

Startled, Lizzie looked up. Jack stood in the frame of the door, one leg crossed casually over the other, one arm braced against the frame.

"*Diah*, but you are forever appearing from the ether like a demon," she said.

"I'll take that as a compliment," he said and, walking into the study uninvited, paused to look around.

She did not need this distraction now, and gestured impatiently to the door. "Perhaps you might amuse yourself elsewhere?"

He looked at her, then at the ledger. "It is fairly obvious you are troubled, Lizzie. At least allow me to help."

"No." She adamantly shook her head. "This ledger contains our private affairs."

"You canna believe your affairs are particularly private any longer, can you, lass?"

She couldn't argue, given the handfasting and the gossip that must be flying about the glen. And although Lizzie had longed for someone to look at the old ledger and advise her, she couldn't bear to show this man of means the perilous state of their finances. "It is . . . kind of you to offer," she said, shutting the ledger. "But you've no knowledge about the affairs of an estate like this."

"Does Lambourne Castle run itself?" he scoffed, and moved closer to the desk.

"I mean one so triflingly small compared to your . . . position," she said carefully.

"They are all the same. So much comes in, so much goes out for this estate and many other types. I travel to Lambourne Castle once a year precisely to acquaint myself with such affairs."

"Only once a year?" she said, curious now. "Why?"

"Because . . . because there is little else for me there," he said. "Come then, let me have a look. You'd be doing me a kindness in giving me an occupation."

Desperate for the help he offered, Lizzie toyed with the worn corner of the leather binding. "We've no' a lot of money," she said stiffly.

"Well, now," he said, taking a wooden chair and twirling it around so that it was next to Lizzie's chair. "It's rarely the amount but how you've got it all arranged." He flipped the tails of his coat and settled in.

Lizzie straightened in her chair, her palms pressed against the closed ledger, debating whether or not she should do this.

Jack looked expectantly at Lizzie.

She sighed and slowly slid it to him.

Jack opened the ledger and turned his attention to it.

Lizzie could not bear to watch him or see his shock at the shambles he might perceive, and popped up out of her seat to pace anxiously beside the desk.

To his credit, Jack did not look appalled, nor did he laugh. He looked . . . studious. Quite studious, actually, as if he were very much at home with books and figures. Of course he would be—he was an earl. Where were earls educated, she wondered? What sort of school had he attended? She and Charlotte had had the tutelage of a governess for two years, but their father considered it a luxury and eventually let her go.

Lizzie looked at Jack. "Where were you educated, if I may ask?"

"St. Andrews," he said without taking his eyes from the ledger. "And Cambridge," he added, almost as an afterthought.

Lizzie paused in her pacing. He'd been educated in the best schools of Scotland and England. "And when you were a lad?"

"A series of tutors. Why do you ask?"

"Curiosity," she said. She imagined a boy in short breeches and a cap all alone in a dank nursery at Lambourne Castle. "Have you siblings, then?"

"A sister, Fiona."

"Where is she?"

"I couldn't really say. She has been in London of late, but the last I saw her . . ." He shook his head. "I donna know."

"What of your parents?"

"They are deceased."

A lost sister, departed parents. She actually felt a wee bit sad for him. The Highlanders had a saying, naturally: A lonely man has nothing to die for. "What were they like?" she asked.

Jack looked up, assessing her. "My mother died when I was seventeen years and Fiona only thirteen years. My father . . ." His face went blank. "He died a year later." The mention seemed to pain him.

"Oh. I'm sorry," she said.

"Donna be," Jack said low as he turned back to the books. "He was no' a happy man, and he rather enjoyed making everyone around him unhappy."

Lizzie allowed a few moments of silence to pass. "What is your age?" she asked almost timidly.

That caused him to glance up and peer curiously at her. "I've enjoyed thirty years on this earth. And you?"

"Three and twenty," she muttered.

"Three and twenty," he repeated as his gaze flicked over her. "I would say, Miss Beal, that it is high time your knight offered for your hand." He winked, then turned back to the ledger.

She thought to tell him that was abominably rude, but that idea was interrupted by the way his hair curled over his collar. It was brushed back from his face, and he was sporting a strong shadow of a beard. He was a handsome man, that could not be denied. Truthfully, he looked a bit more rugged than the first night she'd met him standing on the dais at Castle Beal.

She tried to imagine him at the Candlemas celebrations that were held annually at Castle Beal. Candlemas marked the middle of winter and meant that soon thereafter the fields would be readied for sowing. As long as Lizzie could remember there had been a celebration at Castle Beal, marked by a procession of children carrying candles, then sweetmeats for them and whisky for the adults, and a country dance.

It was impossible to imagine Jack at such a celebration, and frankly, every time she looked at him, she was reminded of the torrid kiss they'd shared. She was amazed the ice had not melted from the tree limbs and caused something of a flood, it had been so heated. One could only wonder how that heat would deepen if . . . *if* . . .

Jack suddenly looked up and caught her staring at

him. He gave her a slightly crooked, slightly knowing smile, then pointed to the ledger. "Is all your livestock recorded here?"

She nodded as she tried to collect herself from her deviant thoughts.

"Ah. A pity, that."

"Why?" she asked anxiously. "What do you see?"

"What I see," he said with a sigh, "is no' a lot with which to work. Were I you, I'd consider selling a cow."

Lizzie gaped at him. "Sell a *cow*? You're mad to suggest it!"

"Are you so attached to your cows? Sell one, and you will bring in more than what you presently owe and perhaps even have a bit to spare."

"Aye, and what shall we do for milk and butter?"

"One cow's milk can provide for this household if you use the milk wisely. And one can live without butter. Lord knows I have of late," he said with a sigh. "I think you have no choice," he added, leaning back, his expression far too superior to suit her. "It's simple economics."

"*Is* it?" she said, folding her arms. As if she were so daft not to understand that, at least!

He misunderstood her acerbic tone. "You have more expenses than you have income," he said patiently, as if he were explaining it to a child.

"Aha. I had no' noticed."

"You must reduce what you need while you look for ways to increase your income."

"*Thank* you." She walked around to the front of the desk and abruptly shut the ledger—on his hand.

"Ouch," he said with a grimace.

"I am aware that our expenses exceed our income, Lord Professor. But we *canna* sell a cow."

"I think you can."

"You know nothing about Thorntree! You donna understand the way it functions!"

"It functions precisely as one might expect an estate without a means of income to function—in debt! Tell me something, Lizzie. Why would Carson come from the north?" Jack asked.

The question, posed out of the blue, confused her mightily. What had that to do with cows?

"He came from the north," Jack said again. "What is north of here?"

Puzzled, Lizzie said, "I donna know. There is hardly a thing worth mentioning north of us."

"Nothing?"

"Nothing," she said impatiently, her mind on cows. "I have ventured several miles north in search of berries and nuts, and I assure you, there is nothing but hills and rocks entirely unsuitable for habitation or fodder. What has that to do with selling a cow?"

"Eh, what?" he asked, momentarily distracted. "No' a thing," he said, and looked at the window, his gaze distant.

"What are you thinking?" she demanded. "Do you think you can escape north?"

"There is a reason Carson wants to ruin your chances for marriage and keep you living in poverty at Thorntree."

"Are you just now coming around to it?" Lizzie sighed impatiently.

"And I think the answer lies north," he added, looking at her.

"All because he came from the north?" she said with disbelief, and picked up the ledger, holding it tightly against her chest. "How sinister that is! Did you think that he might possibly have gone for a ride? Or perhaps he went hunting?"

"The weather is hardly conducive to riding today. And one does not hunt in the middle of the day, aye? Moreover, there was quite a lot of mud on his boots, as if he'd done some trekking."

Lizzie laughed. "Of course there was mud on his boots, Jack. The weather has been rather wet of late."

"Scoff if you will," Jack said with a frown, "but there is something about Thorntree that has your laird's attention. A dislike of a man's last name is hardly reason to go to such extraordinary lengths to keep you from this Gordon fellow. I have a hunch that the answer lies north."

"And what am I to do, journey north until I find it?"

Jack smiled. He stood from his chair and peered down at her, his gaze drifting to her lips. "I donna expect you to journey north," he said, and surprised her by tucking a loose curl behind her ear. "At least no' without me."

Something inside Lizzie tipped, and the world seemed to tip with it. She should move, step away, discourage him from looking at her as he was. But she didn't. "Is that all?" she asked a little breathlessly. "Sell a cow and ride north?"

His eyes dipped to her décolletage, and then up again. His hand slipped to her neck, his thumb on the soft hollow of her throat. She silently cursed herself; she could feel the heat rise up in her, could feel her heart begin to beat at a clip. "No' all," he said, caressing her skin. "But all for now."

Lizzie sucked in a breath.

Jack dropped his hand, letting it drift over her bodice. His gaze was soft and . . . and . . . and he smiled like a man who ate women like her with tea.

"I've . . . I've sent for Mr. Gordon," she said uncertainly.

His languid smile dimmed a bit, but he said, "Splendid." His hand fell away from her, and without another word he walked from the room.

When he'd gone, Lizzie sank onto her chair, still clutching the ledger. Still feeling as if something was tipped at a strange angle inside her.

No, no, *no*, she could not be having such feelings of . . . of desire, of raging *desire* for that man. *No!* "Buck *up*, Lizzie," she muttered angrily to herself. "Think of Mr. Gordon." *Mr. Gordon, Mr. Gordon, Mr. Gordon*, she chanted in her head.

Chapter Eighteen

I t took the tale of a rather bawdy soirée at Montagu, the house in the Blackheath district of London that Princess Caroline called home, to earn Jack his supper.

Dougal was on the edge of his seat as Jack recounted attending a gathering there and playing an inappropriate game of charades. Even the old man Kincade was listening and staring at him with rapt attention. It was Kincade who went to fetch a bowl of chicken stew for him.

But, Jack noted lamentably, when he'd finished his tale, he was once more treated like a pariah. There was no hint of the hospitality for which Scots prided themselves. Just that afternoon, Dougal had suggested a cup of tea, then instantly reversed himself, saying, "Aye, that's right . . . no tea, then."

Frankly, Jack could not imagine what slight he'd given these people, what thing he'd said or trait he'd presented that had earned him such disdain. And they did not seem to trust him in the least—Old Man Kincade went about shutting doors and locking them in advance of Jack.

It had been a very strange day, all in all, beginning last night with that passionate kiss he'd shared with Lizzie, a kiss that was still churning his blood, prompting his imagination to run amuck.

In the library, where he'd reviewed her pathetic ledger, he could scarcely think of anything but that kiss. He wanted to kiss her again, feel the soft surface of her skin. But then she'd ruined it by mentioning Gordon, and Jack quickly filled with angry passion. He suspected that Lizzie would be an exciting lover, and he envied her knight in that regard.

Jack himself would give a fortune to taste her flesh, to feel her legs encircle him . . .

He shook his head. That was an unhelpful fantasy, one that would never come to pass. Pure Miss Lizzie had made that quite clear. She had to be the only woman in his acquaintance who was so very clear about it.

But Jack had made it quite clear too that, in spite of his reputation, he was not in the habit of bedding proper young women for the sake of it. Only once or twice. Perhaps thrice. All right, so he had. But that had all been long ago, before he'd realized how untidy those situations could become. And Lizzie was different. He couldn't do that to her. She exasperated him no end, but she deserved better.

So Jack took comfort in the fact that at least he had a roof over his head. He'd allowed Dougal to escort him up to her empty room and fell into a deep sleep in the storage room.

Jack spent a few days in this way, passing Lizzie in the house much as a ship would pass another at sea. She retired quite late and woke very early. Jack kept to his little sitting room when she was about, and even coerced Dougal into finding him a bed. To pass the time he plotted his escape, banking on the assumption that the prince would lose interest in him as soon as the social season started in London and there were other, more diverting persons— namely women—to capture his attention.

Several days into Jack's stay, a man who bore an undeniable resemblance to Dougal arrived. It turned out to be Dougal's brother, delivering oatcakes the lad's mother had sent along. Dougal's brother, Donald, also had a bit of news: the prince had hired Highlanders to comb the glens north of Lambourne Castle. The posses boasted they'd have the earl by Easter, and were methodically working their way north.

Diah, but George was quite angry, then, and apparently as irresponsible with his funds as the morning newspapers had always alleged, Jack thought. What an extraordinary expense to soothe a wound! But the news also meant he'd best stay put a few days more.

Every morning began the same for Jack. He awoke ravenous—there was something about the Highland air that stimulated his appetite—and Mrs. Kincade would inform him that breakfast was served promptly at the hour of seven o'clock and put away at eight o'clock and, as it was a quarter to nine, the breakfast was over.

"Seems as if someone might have mentioned it or made accommodation," Jack would mutter crossly, and then tell Mrs. Kincade another tantalizing story of London, for which he'd earn the bannock cakes she always seemed to have set aside for him.

From that point forward, he found each days activity around the manor to be crashingly dull. He caught glimpses of Lizzie here and there, marching past with a broom or a bucket, her boots echoing down the hall, and with at least one dog, if not all four, trotting after her.

He also stumbled upon Charlotte, who had been placed before a big window. Jack pitied her. She was a very handsome woman who should be dancing and riding and raising children. But here she sat, put away in a ramble-down manor, a prisoner of a wheeled chair.

He could not imagine how tedious it must be for her.

Even with two legs, Jack found nothing to occupy him—not even Dougal, his constant shadow. So he wandered about, making note of the many things that needed repair. He rather doubted that the ancient Mr. Kincade was up to the task of many of the most obvious tasks, what with all his other chores. Perhaps, Jack mused, if he were to be about a few days, he might make a few of the repairs to bide his time. Perhaps if he were useful, they'd feed him.

One afternoon, on a gray day with a flurry of snow falling, Jack begged some cheese and bread from Mrs. Kincade and wandered outside, where he spotted the very stoic Kincade and Newton. Dougal wandered over to the pair as Jack ate his bread, and seemed to be working very hard to convince Newton of something, judging by the way his hands flew about. When Jack approached, all three men stopped speaking.

If he wasn't very assured of himself, Jack might have believed they were speaking of him.

Dougal looked at his feet. Mr. Kincade, his arms propped on a rake, looked directly at Jack, but if he was embarrassed or curious or perhaps even dead, Jack could not say. Newton, however, folded his arms across his chest and eyed Jack closely.

"What now?" Jack asked, holding his arms wide, holding a half-eaten chunk of cheese. "On my word, I've no' done anything but wander about with Dougal nipping at my ankles."

"Ye tell outrageous tales, sir," Newton said. "Ye put ideas into the heads of good Scotsmen about the prince."

"You say that in a manner that would suggest that I am *no'* a good Scotsman, Mr. Newton."

"Ye've no' seen any of us living among the English, have ye, then?" Newton shot back.

"Living among the English does no' make me any less a Scotsman!" Jack said defensively. "And I've no' told outrageous tales! I've merely relayed my experiences in the company of both the Prince and Princess of Wales."

"Aye, indeed, you have relayed yer *experiences*," Newton said. "And ye'd have these good men believe that our prince impregnated a lowly innkeeper's wife?"

"Among others," Jack replied evenly.

The poor giant looked sincerely shocked. "But . . . he's the prince, the king's heir," he said, as if trying to work out the moral decay in the royal family. Oh, but if he knew. . . .

"*Diah*," Newton muttered.

"Once, a young woman wearing a white muslin of the finest fit in all of England," Jack said, moving closer and tracing her curves in the air, "approached the prince. Gentlemen, you must believe me when I tell you that this young woman possessed a most *spectacular* bosom," he added conspiratorially, holding his hands up to his chest to demonstrate just how spectacular. "She said, 'Your Grace, there is something I would show you, if you give me leave.' "

The three men seemed to hover, moving so close as to not miss a word. Jack did not disappoint them. He went on to tell them about a very shapely leg, a breast as smooth and plump as a baby's bottom. He told them of a young woman's promise that was so promiscuous, so morally perverse, that no man could turn away from it.

Certainly George had not turned away. Jack did not add that the young woman need not have promised him anything, for a dog never turns away from a bone, but Newton seemed troubled by the prince's moral fabric as it was.

Jack had just begun to tell them about a private party

in the prince's apartments when Newton suddenly looked at something over Jack's shoulder and cleared his throat. No one had to tell Jack that Lizzie had walked into their little gathering. He could tell by the averted gazes and shuffling of feet. He steeled himself and turned around. "Lizzie!" he said, as though they'd been expecting her.

She was wearing a drab muslin gown and an arisaidh, but her eyes were shrewd and bright blue, peeking out from under the plaid hood. She had an empty basket on one arm. She narrowed those lovely eyes and, one by one, gave them each a withering look that only a woman could manage. When she'd eyed them into feeling sufficiently guilty, she looked pointedly at Jack again. "What are you about?" she asked, dispensing with any greeting.

"Lass!" he said jovially. "What makes you think I am about anything at all?" He tossed the last bit of bread into the grass and clapped Dougal collegially on the shoulder.

Lizzie frowned at him, then shifted that frown to Kincade. She didn't have to speak; the old man picked up the rake and walked on, almost as if he'd paused only to straighten his cuffs and hadn't heard a word of what Jack had said.

"He knows the Prince and Princess of Wales," Dougal interjected helpfully.

That did nothing to appease her. If anything, it seemed to agitate Lizzie even more. "Aye, so I have heard on *several* occasions now. I believe that His Lordship must leap from person to person claiming, 'I know the Prince and Princess of Wales,' " she said, gesturing in a leap-about sort of way. "I suppose that at the very least I should be happy that you are all thus engaged and no' a bother to me or to Charlotte, aye?"

Dougal and Newton sheepishly hung their heads, but Jack grinned.

"If you will excuse me," she said regally, "there is *real* work to be done." She sailed past them, the basket bouncing against her hip as she walked down the path and turned left, disappearing behind a brick wall.

The men looked at one another when she was gone.

Newton glared at Jack, then strode toward the house, muttering in Gaelic under his breath. Dougal looked eagerly at Jack, obviously wanting to hear more, but Jack shook his head, and Dougal winced with disappointment.

"Where's she gone, then?" Jack asked, nodding in the direction Lizzie had marched.

"Hothouse, I'd wager," Dougal said.

"Ah," Jack said. "Come along, my friend. I'd like to see this hothouse." He set off, not caring if Dougal followed. Jack couldn't help himself; she was like a siren, her impatience and indifference sparking a longing Jack had never felt quite so acutely. Not physical longing as such but that unfortunately desperate feeling one experiences when one desires to be at least *liked* by another human being. Part of him feared he might suffer from the same desperate longing his mother had felt for his father. That was hardly appealing, yet he could not seem to help himself.

The hothouse was the smallest hothouse he'd ever seen, barely larger than the laundering room that stood nearby. He could see Lizzie through a window, bent over a plant, plucking dead leaves. "Wait here," he said to Dougal.

"Milord! It's freezing!" Dougal complained.

"Then go and tell Newton where I've gone," Jack said impatiently, and opened the door to the hothouse. As he stepped inside, he saw that Lizzie had lifted a pair of pots, apparently with the intent of moving them, but one of them was slipping from her grasp. Without thinking, Jack strode in and grasped the pot.

Naturally, Lizzie surprised him with a cry of alarm and tried to wrest it away from him. "Stop that!"

"You are about to drop it. I'll hold it for you," he said, surprised by her strength.

"I donna need your help, Jack."

"Aye, so you keep insisting, but as usual you are too stubborn to admit what is obvious. Let *go*."

Lizzie shoved with all her might, thrusting the potted plant into his abdomen at the same moment she let go. Jack smiled triumphantly.

"A scoundrel of the first water, that's what you are," she said, and set the second pot down with a loud *thwap*.

"Mary, Queen of Scots, why does everyone in this blasted glen seem to believe that I am?" an exasperated Jack exclaimed heavenward.

She whirled around to face him, grasped the pot he held with both hands, and yanked hard, managing to pull it from his grasp. "Hmm, let me think on it," she said as she put that one on the table beside the other one. "Ah, here's a thought—perhaps it is your chaste tales of London, aye?"

"And how would you know if they are chaste or no'? I've no' told you a single tale, have I?"

"I *heard* you, Jack! I heard you relate that . . . that unspeakable gossip to Newton and Dougal, and, *Diah*, even Mr. Kincade!"

"If I'd known you were eavesdropping—"

"—I most certainly was *no'* eavesdropping—"

"—I would no' have finished the account. It was a story for *men*, Lizzie. And the men liked hearing it! That is what men do, they tell one another bawdy tales!"

"That's preposterous! Gentlemen do no such thing! You do yourself a disservice, Jack."

And now this provincial miss would chastise him? "Do I, indeed?" he snapped. "Perhaps I should have sung for my supper then. Is that what you wanted?"

She looked at him as if he were speaking Greek.

He made a sound of utter disbelief. "You will stand there and pretend that you've no' tried to starve me out of Thorntree? Ach, donna deny it, woman! Yet, in spite of your manipulations, I have managed to survive by my wits and stories of a life in London that these men will never know!"

"Go on, then," she said, gesturing wildly to the door. "Go and tell them all your awful tales!"

"Thank you, but no," he said curtly. "I've had quite enough of your disdain, and Dougal shadowing my every step, and Kincade locking every door ahead of me. And as I am allowed no suitable occupation"—he glanced at the table and the array of pots lined along the center of it—"I shall help *you*."

The words that fell out of his mouth appalled him, particularly when Lizzie laughed. She laughed!

"No, please, milord, I beg of you, donna help me!" She laughed again.

He scowled and picked up one of the pots.

Lizzie snatched it from his hands and put it down again. "All right, all right, if you want to help . . ." She paused and looked around. "Here, then. The thistle needs to be crushed." She shoved a bowl and pestle at him. "It needs to be made fine or the horses won't eat it."

"They eat thistle?" he said, grimacing at the long, prickly, purple flowers.

"Aye," she said and gestured to several of them. "They all need to be ground."

Grinding thistle seemed a rather tedious task to Jack. If Lizzie were his, she'd never have cause to indulge in such labor. She'd be at her leisure, doing all the things ladies did. Not laundering. Not feeding chickens or milking cows. Not grinding thistle.

Lizzie a lady . . . That absurdly forbidden thought startled Jack into picking up a small knife and cutting one of the thistles.

"May I ask you something?" Lizzie asked as he attempted to grind the bulbous flower in the bowl. "And do promise me that you will speak the truth, aye?"

He gave her a curious look. "All right."

"Why does the prince want to see you hanged? What did you do?"

"He does no' want to see me hanged," Jack said. "He wants to make a point."

"A point," she repeated dubiously. "And you are so fearful of this point being made that you fled to Scotland and agreed to a handfasting with a stranger?"

Diah, she had him there. Jack glanced at her again, debating. She was tying winter roses by the stems, hanging them upside down to dry. When he didn't answer her, Lizzie looked at him curiously with wide blue eyes that would disturb a lesser man's sleep.

Jack sighed. "All right. I shall tell you," he said, and put the pestle down. "But I'll no' have any of your maidenly vapors."

"My *maidenly vapors*?"

"Aye, aye, you know very well what I mean," he said. "You are easily offended."

"I am *no'* so easily offended—" Lizzie stopped herself with a groan and dropped her head back, closing her eyes for a moment. Then she straightened and picked up another bundle of flowers. "Never mind that. I would merely like to know why you would be hanged, and I think it is my right, as I have been handfasted to you."

He paused.

She waited expectantly, roses in hand.

This could not possibly go well, he thought. "There is some . . . speculation, for lack of a better word, and all of it untrue, I might add, that I . . . that I committed a treasonable offense with the Princess of Wales." There, then—if she had half a wit about her, she'd understand what that meant.

But her brows furrowed with confusion. "What do you mean?" she asked curiously. "You and the princess plotted to overthrow the prince?"

"Overthrow! No, no—"

"But you mean a conspiracy, or that sort of thing," she said, nodding her head.

"No' *conspiracy* in the manner in which you are thinking, but . . ." He didn't want to say it, but Lizzie obviously had not the slightest idea of the range of treasonable offenses. "*Adultery*," he blurted, perhaps a bit too hastily. "They say I took the princess to my bed."

Lizzie gasped. Maidenly vapors did indeed overwhelm her—Jack knew all the signs. Wide eyes, chest moving up and down with little gasps of breath. Hands clutching the roses' stems too tightly for want of something better to hold onto. Lizzie gasped again, whirled around, bracing herself against the table with both hands for a moment, then busying herself by madly tying string around the flower stems.

"It's no' true, of course," he added, far too late.

"Of course!" she agreed in an oddly lilting voice. "Undoubtedly you never even visited her . . . her *chambers*, or wherever it is a princess resides."

"Never!" he swore adamantly. "I will admit that I have

attended more than one gathering at her home, and, aye, I have a wee bit of a . . . a *reputation*, but I assure you, I never saw her private rooms, and any accusation to the contrary is egregious and entirely false!"

"But of course!" she cried in that lilting voice again. She put down the bunch of flowers and began to gather another bunch from a stack of them. "Why should anyone say something so very wretched? You are a perfect gentleman!"

"For the love of Scotland," Jack said irritably, and strode forward, putting his hand on Lizzie's to still it. "I did no' take Princess Caroline to my bed. I've naugh' been less tempted in my *life*. But the situation in London right now is rather tense, what with the Delicate Investigation—"

"The what?"

"The rather delicate investigation into the princess's behavior. With the Lords Commissioners examining the accusations against her, more accusations are flying about and most of them untrue. Someone is disgruntled with me for reasons I canna guess, and has chosen to make a false accusation."

"You canna guess," she said, her voice full of disbelief.

Why was he working so hard to convince this little fairy of the glen? "No," he said evenly, "I canna guess."

She snorted.

But Jack had had quite enough and suddenly caught her by the shoulders, forcing her around. "What do you know of me truly, Lizzie? How can you judge me so quickly and thoroughly?"

"Thirty years and unmarried?" she said derisively.

"Aye?"

"Does that no' sound like a rake to you, Jack?"

He bristled. "I was reared in a household that was made most unpleasant by *marriage*," he said harshly. "Couple that with the fact that I rarely meet an unmarried woman whose interest in me extends beyond my purse, and you will understand why. Why are *you* no' married at the age of three and twenty? Should I assume you are a loose skirt?"

"Why did you kiss me, Jack?" she demanded, tossing the loose bundle of flowers aside. "*Why* did you kiss me? Was it because you fancied you *loved* me?"

"God's blood, what are you—"

"Oh, I'm no' so foolish to believe it, if that is what you think. You kissed me because you are a *rake*, Jack, in every manner and deed! And if you did no' do what they accuse you of doing, I'd wager you came perilously close!" She pushed his hands from her shoulders. "Close enough to warrant hanging you." She turned back to the table.

Jack grabbed her by the shoulders again and forced her around. The movement caused a curl to fall over her eye, which she defiantly blew away. It fell right back, and Jack was suddenly filled to absolutely bursting with the desire to kiss her again. "I kissed you, Lizzie, because, just as I told you, I was, for reasons that suddenly seem *quite* mad at present, drawn to you! I kissed you because you are beautiful and alluring, and you are a woman and I am a man! But I did no' kiss you to satisfy some carnal beast." Although he wouldn't mind in the least satisfying the carnal beast. "If you turn that wee nose up at me once more, I will remind you that you esteem me, too."

"*Esteem* you?" She tilted her head back to look up at him. "You think well of yourself, sir! I have tolerated you! I have done only what I must to survive!"

Oh, this provincial little glen nymph was vexing! Jack was accustomed to women who were demure and skilled in the art of subtle flirting, not the sort who spoke frankly and unabashedly. He looked at her lips. Succulent, dark lips that called on every male sinew in him to refrain from kissing her again. "Would you truly have me believe," he said gruffly as he slid one hand to her neck, to the point where it curved into her shoulder, "that you merely tolerated my kiss? That you did no' find it the least bit stirring?"

Her eyes turned a dusky blue, but her gaze did not waver. She slowly lifted her hand to his wrist and closed her fingers around it. He expected her to yank his hand away, but Lizzie surprised him. She gripped his wrist tightly, almost as if she were afraid he would remove his hand. He could feel her skin warming beneath his palm. When she swallowed, he could feel it beneath his thumb. Their argument was suddenly forgotten; Jack's gaze drifted down to a bosom concealed behind a blouse and more thick wool, but the curve of it strained against the fabric. It was, by some strange and devastating measure, more enticing than a bosom bared to him.

The carnal beast stirred inside Jack, that beast that defined him every inch a man. It was a beast that could drive a man to do unfathomably stupid things, and he felt it with alarming and erotic intensity. It confused him. On the surface, Lizzie was not the sort of woman who typically attracted him, but, God in heaven, she had. She'd attracted him as the sun attracts all living things to turn toward it.

She was still holding his wrist, but he moved his hand down, to the swell of her breasts, his eyes never leaving hers. She drew a slow and tantalizing breath that lifted her chest.

"Would you truly have me believe you donna want me to kiss you again?" he asked low.

"I do no'," she said, but she shifted almost imperceptibly closer.

He smiled a little. "Your words belie your actions, lass."

"You think you know so very much," she said.

"I know," he said softly, bending his head, putting his lips so close to hers, "that you are wishing my mouth would touch yours," and he teased her by almost touching hers. Lizzie tried to touch hers to his, but he moved—enough to keep her from touching him. "I know that you would like my hand to touch your flesh," he said, running one hand down her rib. "And I know that just about now, you are feeling the dampness of your longing and your body is pulsing in lovely anticipation of it. And I know, Miss Lizzie Beal, that if I kissed you now, you would succumb, freely and eagerly."

Her lips parted at her soft intake of breath. Her gaze fell to his mouth.

"Ask me," he said softly.

"Ask you?" she whispered.

Jack moved again, so that his mouth was next to her ear. "*Ask me to touch you.*"

Lizzie did not ask, for that highly charged moment was interrupted by the sound of the door opening behind them, the clearing of a throat, and the unavoidable "Beg your pardon, miss."

Jack would kill him. He would kill old Kincade with a pestle.

Lizzie shunted away from Jack. "Aye, Mr. Kincade?"

"Mr. Maguire has come requesting an audience."

"I'll be there straightaway. Thank you."

"Shall I send the missus to help in here?" the old man asked.

"That's no' necessary, Mr. Kincade. Lambourne has offered to lend a hand."

Jack winced at that as Kincade's measured steps moved out of the hothouse.

The slightest hint of a smile curved Lizzie's luscious lips. Her eyes were shining with feminine triumph as she stepped away from Jack. At the door she paused to glance at him over her shoulder, but as Jack had yet to find his tongue, she put a hand to her hair, tucking the loose curl into the bandeau, and walked out.

He watched her walk away, watched the sensual sway of her hips, and felt their rhythm in his veins.

When he could see her no more, he looked at the pots of thistle that needed to be ground.

He had just crossed his own line.

Chapter Nineteen

M r. Maguire was a man with very little meat on his bones, which Lizzie had always found ironic, given that he was the proprietor of a rather large mercantile in Aberfeldy. Mr. Maguire was hoping he might collect the debt Lizzie owed him for flour and oats.

He apologized profusely for having to ask at all, as if he were somehow imposing on her, when in fact, she had imposed on him. She quickly and sheepishly wrote a bank draft for the ten pounds she owed him and asked him to stay for tea, but he assured her he had to return to Aberfeldy before nightfall.

With the bank note tucked securely in his coat pocket, Mr. Maguire stood up and offered his bony hand to Lizzie. "Thank ye kindly, Miss Beal. I'd no' ask—"

"No, no, please," she said, lacking the energy to go through the round of apologies again.

He gave her a gap-toothed grin and shook her hand. "Then allow me to offer my sincere felicitations on your handfasting. You'll no' worry about money when it's made permanent, aye? The wife and I, we look forward to making his acquaintance at Candlemas. Ah, but that reminds this old head—your uncle asked that I give you venison. It's in my cart, it is."

"My uncle?" Lizzie asked, confused. "How very kind

of him." She forced a smile. "And how fares Mrs. Maguire?" Lizzie asked brightly, changing the subject before he could say more.

By the time Mr. Maguire had catalogued all of his wife's health complaints, she'd shown him out. Mr. Kincade had the venison and the propreiror hauled himself up on his horse and trotted away from Thorntree, scattering the chickens and rooster as he went.

Lizzie watched him round the bend. She hardly felt herself just now—her usual worries filled her brain as they always did, but crowding in around those worries and pushing them aside were thoughts of Jack. Tomorrow she would be forced to sit at his side, and these unwanted, shamelessly bold thoughts of him would fill her brain.

Ask me to touch you.

She walked back into the house, but as she turned to close the door, a few errant snowflakes made their way in through the opening. Lizzie gasped softly as they scudded across the floor. There was an old Highland saying that snowflakes in the house meant that someone would be departing before Candlemas.

There was only one possibility of that.

Lizzie made her way to her small suite of rooms, and there she threw herself facedown onto the bed, her eyes squeezed shut.

After a moment she rolled over onto her back and pressed a hand to her collarbone, precisely where his hand—warm and large and powerful—had rested against her. The feeling that had exploded inside her when he'd touched her so delicately had taken her breath away.

She hadn't caught her breath yet, and she might have languished all day trying, but there was still much work to be done.

Lizzie wearily pushed herself up and made herself continue on, with that strange, tingly sense of anticipation inside her, just as he'd described.

Jack did not actually grind the thistle, although he did, in uncharacteristic fashion, consider it. But he dismissed the notion quickly—he could not bear the thought of being brought so low. So he called Dougal in, who he guessed might be more familiar with such a mundane task.

He left Dougal with the excuse that he was hungry. In the house once more, he happened to pass by the open door of the drawing room and noticed Newton inside with Charlotte. Something about the two of them engaged in a tête-à-tête made Jack slow his step. Newton apparently had the ears of a bird dog, for he suddenly turned his head and leveled his gaze on Jack.

Miss Beal looked at Jack, too, releasing what could only be called a put-upon sigh, and turned her head to the fire.

"I beg your pardon," Jack said. "I heard voices. . . ."

Newton came to his feet as if he expected Jack to bolt. Miss Beal sighed and looked at Jack. "Please come in," she said curtly.

Jack did not want to go in. He glanced uneasily up the corridor, wishing for Dougal or Kincade, anyone who might divert him.

"Please, milord," she added.

Bloody hell, then. He stepped warily across the threshold as Charlotte eyed him skeptically, her mouth turning down at the corners in a frown. "Do come in, sir," she said. "Please donna make me shout."

He wasn't trying to make her *shout*. "I beg your pardon, I was just passing by," he said, gesturing to the corridor.

"There is hardly anyplace to pass by *to*. Come in, will you?" she asked, clearly perturbed at having to ask again.

This was immensely uncomfortable; Jack was clearly intruding. "My apologies for disturbing you."

Charlotte ignored him and said stiffly, "I should like to invite you to dine with us tomorrow evening. We will have four at our table who would like to acquaint themselves with Lizzie's . . . ah, mate."

He was shocked. The invitation was so warmly given that Jack could hardly think of a thing he'd rather do—except, perhaps, gouge his eyes with knitting needles or throw himself beneath the hooves of stampeding bulls.

Charlotte frowned at his hesitation. "That is . . . we will have wine before supper and dine at eight."

"Thank you, but I . . . I would be . . ." *Tortured. Plagued.*

" 'Tis no' an invitation," Newton rumbled. "There are bounty hunters as near as Aberfeldy looking for you now. The laird believes you will appreciate the need to keep your neighbors and family close."

"No' entirely, but I shall be delighted," Jack said, inclining his head.

"Lambourne, may I inquire—is it true?" Miss Beal asked. "Are you acquainted with the Prince and Princess of Wales?"

Jack was beginning to wonder whether he might have been spared a problematic handfasting if he'd told the men who'd captured him in the forest he was personally acquainted with the Prince and Princess of Wales. "I am."

"I have read that Carlton House is quite magnificent. Have you seen it?"

"I have."

"Is it very big?"

"Astoundingly so."

She twisted in her seat as much as she could and looked at him curiously. "I have read that it cost more than one hundred thousand pounds to refurbish."

Newton suddenly coughed harshly and turned his head toward the hearth.

"I was no' privy to the cost of it," Jack said, "but I should no' be surprised if that were true. It is very grand. Are you familiar with the French neoclassical style of architecture?"

Miss Beal shook her head.

He took a tentative step into the room. "It is based in the Greek style but, as with everything French before the revolution, the interpretation is very grand. One enters through a portico held up by massive columns. The entrance hall is two stories high, made of marble, and shaped on the octagonal."

"Marble?" Charlotte repeated, her eyes growing wide.

"Indeed," Jack said, as Newton quietly crossed to the window and returned with a chair. "There is a dual staircase that curves upward," he said, sketching it with his hands, "and sculptures made in the style of the Greeks line the octagon." Without missing a word, Jack moved forward. He continued to describe the opulence of Carlton House as he flipped the tails of his coat and took a seat close to Charlotte.

Whether she noted it or not was hard to say—her pale blue eyes were riveted on him, and her eagerness to hear what he was saying was obvious. She hung on every word, and at one point her eyes seemed to fog, as if she were seeing Carlton House, perhaps even walking through it as he described it.

Suddenly Jack wanted to give her every single detail, to let her truly see it through his eyes. He described the private apartments of the Prince of Wales, of the Crimson and Satin drawing rooms. He described the Throne Room, the Blue Velvet Room, the music room that opened onto a lush garden, and the massive dining room. When he'd exhausted his description of the house itself, he began to describe life within Carlton House, and the *beau monde.* He promised to give her a book he'd carried with him. It was *Cecilia,* by his acquaintance Frances Burney— a fictionalized account of the world of privilege.

Somewhere in the course of it, he felt Charlotte begin to thaw.

The discovery that Dougal had been left to grind the thistle needed for the animal's fodder caused an uproar with Mrs. Kincade. It seemed he'd made quite a mess of things, and Mr. Kincade had fetched his wife to help. "Miss Lizzie will be undoing for a week what he's done," Mrs. Kincade said bitterly.

Lizzie doubted it would take that long, but she offered to prepare Charlotte's tea while Mrs. Kincade swept up the mess. She sent Dougal to find his captive.

Lizzie was carrying the tea down the corridor when she heard voices coming from the drawing room. Accustomed to silence in the afternoon while Charlotte sat and brooded, Lizzie drew up, listening.

That was Jack's voice. Charlotte must be beside herself, Lizzie thought, and hastened her step.

She crossed the threshold of the drawing room and stopped mid-stride. The three of them—Newton, Jack, and Charlotte—looked at her expectantly, as if she'd interrupted them.

Then Charlotte suddenly smiled. "Lizzie! Come,

come! I knew you'd be along. You will no' believe what his lordship has been relating!"

His lordship? Smelling a scoundrel, Lizzie marched across the room and deposited the tea service on the table.

"He's been to Carlton House," Charlotte continued far too eagerly. "Where the Prince of Wales resides! And he's given me a book. It is about the *haut ton*. Do you know what that is? It is London's highest society. Come and sit, Lizzie—you should hear what he tells!"

Oh aye, if only there was ever a moment in her day to *come and sit*. "No. Thank you," she said, her gaze going to Jack. "There is too much work to be done."

One corner of Jack's mouth tipped up ever so slightly. "I could wait until Miss Lizzie is available," he said. "Perhaps over supper tomorrow, aye?"

"Oh yes! That would be exciting!" Charlotte said.

Shocked, Lizzie looked at her sister, noting that Newton smiled kindly at Charlotte—*smiled*—as if to encourage her!

Something disastrous had happened at Thorntree in the last several days. Lizzie's world, as she knew it, had turned completely upside down and was skipping off toward the sun, destined for a grand collision.

"Lizzie, Mr. Kincade tells me there is a bit of Papa's wine in the cellar," Charlotte suggested. "What do you think?"

This couldn't be happening. This man would not sit at her table, smiling at her in that way he had of making her feel weak, regaling them all, ingratiating his way into their lives, only to escape at first opportunity and leave her to relive the small moments when her flesh had heated, her heart had pounded, her palms had dampened. Those moments in which she'd felt absolutely alive, could believe herself alluring, could believe in excitement again.

"Lizzie?" Charlotte said uncertainly.

"Splendid!" she blurted with false cheer. "We shall make a soirée of it, shall we, Charlotte?"

Jack looked entirely too pleased with himself.

It was more than she could bear, and Lizzie strode from the room. *When would Mr. Gordon come? When would he come and save her from this madness?*

Chapter Twenty

When one cannot possibly win, one must concede, and Lizzie conceded. Charlotte looked horrified when she appeared in her room before supper the following evening, dressed in the teal blue silk that had hung in her wardrobe for so long.

"Lizzie . . . you look beautiful," Charlotte said.

Lizzie blushed self-consciously. "You think so because I've worn only common mourning clothes these long months." She walked to Charlotte's wardrobe, throwing it open.

"What are you about?" Charlotte asked. "I'll no' throw off the mourning before decorum and propriety allow, merely because Carson decrees it."

"Decorum and propriety finished mourning Papa two months ago," Lizzie said irreverently, ignoring Charlotte's gasp. "If you want to be angry, be angry that Carson has forced this interminable supper on us, as if we are a pair of debutantes! We've no' had anyone to dine at Thorntree in over a year!"

"It canna be avoided, Lizzie," Charlotte said morosely.

"Apparently, it can no'," Lizzie agreed, and withdrew a gold brocade gown from the wardrobe. Charlotte had worn it the night of the MacBriar party celebrating fifty years of connubial bliss. She'd adored this gown and had twirled round and round before the looking glass, admiring herself in it.

Not a fortnight later, she'd been thrown from the horse and broken her back.

When Lizzie turned around and held it up, Charlotte blanched. "You're being cruel. No, I donna intend to end my mourning."

Lizzie tossed the gown onto the bed. "You've worn black or gray for more than a year now. It is time that life carried on, Charlotte. You will wear it tonight and preside over a supper party as a good hostess ought."

Charlotte refused to look at it. "It's too fine to be sat upon in a chair. *You* should wear it."

"I happen to fancy my gown!" Lizzie cried. "And *this* gown," she said, indicating the gold, "is fine whether one is sitting or standing or climbing a tree."

"Lizzie, please! It's humiliating!" Charlotte protested as Lizzie turned her chair around to the vanity Papa had put up on legs so that Charlotte's chair could roll up to it. "I'll look a fool in such a lovely gown."

"Why? Because you canna' stand?"

Charlotte's face melted into anger, and then suddenly into despair. "Because I am hardly a woman at all."

"Charlotte! That's absurd!" Lizzie exclaimed.

"Absurd? I am a burden to everyone! I canna take care of myself, I can no' even preside over a dining table. Newton says that I am unkind, but he scarcely understands me at all."

"He's free with his opinions, is he no'?" Lizzie asked angrily.

"*Quite*. He told me I should smile, that I have a lovely smile, but when I said there is precious little over which to smile, he said, '*you're alive, are you no', lass?*' " she said, mimicking his gruff voice. "Aye, Lizzie, I am alive, but I am bound to a *chair*, and Newton said that I'm bound to it because I *want* to be bound to it, that I feel safer in this chair, and were I only to ask for help, the world would open to me," she said tearfully.

Shocked, Lizzie blinked. "*That* man said all that?"

"Oh aye, he talks and talks and *talks*," Charlotte said and, covering her face in her hands, began to cry.

"Charlotte, darling! What's wrong?" Lizzie asked, sinking down next to her.

"It's *him*, Lizzie!" she said tearfully. "He's so stubborn and unyielding, but somehow, he makes me less angry. Can you imagine it? I am always so angry," she said, balling one fist, "but when I am with him, I donna feel the anger. I feel as if there truly is a world out there that could open for me."

"But Charlotte! That's wonderful!" Lizzie said, taking her hand and forcing her to uncurl her fingers. "Why should that make you so unhappy?"

"No, no, Lizzie, it's awful. He's a crofter, aye? He lives in a cottage south of Castle Beal and he has a bit of land he farms and a few cattle. He could no' be less compatible with me! And even if we were completely suited, how could he possibly bear *this*?" she asked, gesturing to her legs.

"That's ridiculous! A man once told me that love comes from the most unexpected places."

"*Diah*, Lizzie!" Charlotte said, wiping the tears from beneath her eyes. "I donna *love* him. Come, come, we are expected in the drawing room," she said, and began to fidget with the jewelry in a velvet box on her vanity.

Lizzie stood up. "Aye. But I think you should wear the gold," she said, watching her sister in the mirror.

Charlotte did not object, but continued to fidget with

the things in her jewelry box. "What will we feed our guests?" she asked, slyly changing the subject.

"Carson sent round some venison," Lizzie said, and told her all that she and the Kincades had done to prepare for the evening as she helped Charlotte into the gold gown. The gown transformed Charlotte. She was beautiful. "Look at us," Lizzie said as she began to dress Charlotte's hair. "On my word, the earl has succeeded in turning our house topsy-turvy, has he no'? Were it no' for his arrival in Glenalmond, we'd no' be forced to endure this evening." She rolled her eyes.

"Oh dear," Charlotte said, watching Lizzie's reflection in the mirror. "There you are speaking to *me* of love, and all the while, you've come to esteem him, Liz."

"Donna be ridiculous," Lizzie said. "I donna esteem him. It was no' my invitation that put him at our table, was it?"

"Look at you, you're as angry as a bee. And I've no' seen you look so lovely as this in an age! Little wonder you were so eager to throw off your mourning clothes, aye?"

"I dressed as I should for supper guests," Lizzie said briskly.

"Mmm . . . of course you did," Charlotte said, her eyes narrowing on her sister. "Yet you must admit he's rather interesting," she prodded.

"Aye, rogues are always captivating in their own way."

Charlotte giggled.

"Laugh if you will, but he is a rogue and more," Lizzie said sternly. "He has a bottomless well of fantastic stories that he uses to gain favor wherever he might need it. He is charming to the point of melting the boots off the women he meets—including *you*, Charlotte. Oh, and he is wanted for treason. Fancy that! Wanted for treason! He is a *rogue*, Charlotte, a rogue with criminal leanings."

Charlotte laughed outright. "Very well, he is a rogue! But he is a handsome rogue—*ouch!*" she cried, putting a hand to her hair where Lizzie pulled too tightly. "There, you see? You do esteem him!"

"The only gentleman I esteem is Mr. Gordon, and the sooner he arrives at Thorntree the better it shall be for all of us!" Lizzie insisted as she threaded a ribbon through Charlotte's thick blond tresses.

But Charlotte continued to watch Lizzie closely, her expression dubious. "Admit it, Lizzie. There is something about him that is rather appealing. He is quite handsome, and the most charming man to have ever been in Glenalmond. And he is *rich*."

"Really, Charlotte, Mr. Gordon is all of those things. He's no' rich, I'll grant you, but he will be."

"Has Lambourne touched you?"

"Charlotte!" Lizzie cried.

"Honestly, how can one spend as much time in your suite of rooms alone with that man and no' have a wee bit of passion, then?"

"You are incorrigible! I'll have you know that our paths rarely cross, and really, you must stop saying such things, Charlotte! Mr. Gordon must believe that nothing has gone on between us."

Charlotte snorted. "Then you'd best hope he comes as soon as possible."

Lizzie ignored her and focused on the task at hand. She didn't really care to be examined by her sister. . . .

All right, perhaps she did esteem Jack in some small way. Charlotte was right, he was interesting. Frankly, he was the most interesting thing to have happened at Thorntree in years. But what in blazes did it matter? He'd be gone just as soon as he was able, and even if he *had* told her the truth about his feelings, she would never be anything more than a dalliance to him. It wasn't as if he was going to sweep her and Charlotte from Thorntree to live in London or Lambourne Castle. And to think of him at Thorntree was laughable.

Whether or not she esteemed him at all seemed beside any rational point. Best put out of her head. Best ignored. And when Lizzie paused to review her appearance and tucked a curl behind her ear that had fallen from the pearls she'd wrapped through her hair, she reminded herself she'd donned her favorite gown only because she wanted to be a presentable hostess.

Nothing more.

Newton poured Jack a tot of whisky as if he were lord of the manor. "*Uisge-beatha,*" Newton said proudly, reciting the Gaelic word for whisky. "I distilled it." He clinked his glass against Jack's.

Jack tossed it back, managed to keep from choking at the bitter burn of it, and smiled through a watery-eyed gaze at Newton. "There you are, a very fine whisky," he lied.

Newton beamed with pleasure and lifted the flask, offering it to Jack.

Jack quickly threw up a hand. "Ah, no, but thank you kindly," he said, and gingerly put the tot down. He'd already donned the kilt Newton had told him he must wear. The whisky was a wee bit more than he wanted from the man.

Newton shrugged, poured himself another tot of the liquid fire.

"Well, then, Newton," Jack said. "You're still here, are you? I would think Carson would be satisfied that the damage is done, and would allow you to return to your flock. You do have a flock, aye?" Jack asked. "Lots of sheep on a craggy hill somewhere? Perhaps a dog to keep you company on long winter nights?"

"Ye know very well I canna leave Thorntree. Who would keep ye, then?"

"Very noble of you," Jack said. "Yet surely if this is a true handfasting as your laird would have us all believe, then why should I need anyone to tend me at all? What am I keeping you from?"

Newton's gaze flicked over him. "I have a small croft," he said, a bit hesitantly. "My flock, as ye call it, is well cared for in my absence by my cousin."

"Have you a wife?" Jack pressed.

"Widowed," Newton said, refusing to offer more.

"Then do you live all alone, Mr. Newton?"

He shrugged. "My cousin's land abuts mine. My sister comes round on Sundays."

He seemed quite at ease with that life. Frankly, he looked like a man who lived alone, Jack thought.

He wondered idly if he himself looked like a man who lived alone.

The thought bothered him, however, and he looked away from Newton and strolled to the hearth. "Were I in *your* shoes, I would no' abandon my livelihood to serve a dubious master."

Newton gave him a rare and wry smile. "But ye'd abandon it for London, aye?"

"If I had the freedom, I'd be in London now," Jack said.

"Ye might be in London in a fortnight, if the prince's men find ye, aye?"

Touché. "Tell me," Jack said, "what is to keep anyone—supper guests and all—from pointing a finger in my direction? Does Beal honestly command such fealty?"

"Among the clan, aye. We'd no' hand one of our own over to anyone, much less the English. And if one was tempted by the bounty, the laird would match it."

"That seems rather extreme, does it no'?" Jack said.

"He has his reasons."

Jack wanted to ask what those reasons were, but his thoughts were interrupted by the arrival of Lizzie and Charlotte.

Jack—and Newton, as well, for that matter—was not the least prepared for their appearance. Jack had grown accustomed to Lizzie's drab gray gowns and the miles of wool she wore. The gown she wore this evening was the farthest thing from drab or gray. It was the color of a Scottish sky in summer, the underskirt the ruby shade of dusk. The fit of the gown was so remarkable that Jack had to force himself to look away lest he be accused of ogling.

Yet that was precisely what he was doing, and he could scarcely keep from it. She moved like a cloud in that gown, gliding into the room even when pushing Charlotte in her chair. She wore the annular brooch—a wreath of thistles—and her auburn curls had been corralled prettily by a string of pearls.

Jack had seen some beauties in his time, women dressed in rich fabrics and dazzling jewels who moved gracefully, spoke eloquently, and made love elegantly. Lizzie made them all look common to him now. There was something about her that struck at the very core of him. She was a Scottish princess, a woman who exuded health as well as beauty, who had a sparkle in her eye that reflected a lust for life. Jack was utterly enchanted. So enchanted that Lizzie had to say once more, "Good *evening*."

"I beg your pardon," he said, instantly extending his hand to hers, "I was so taken I quite forgot myself."

"Save your flattery, milord; I am immune," she said playfully, and delicately put her hand in his palm, allowing him to lift it up to his mouth. He watched her as he kissed her knuckles; she smiled a little, but her eyes were full of challenge.

"Miss Charlotte, how lovely you are this evening," Newton rumbled from somewhere nearby.

"Hmm . . . thank you, Mr. Newton," Charlotte said coolly, looking at him and Jack. "The gentlemen are looking rather regal, are they no', Lizzie? Lambourne, I am surprised to see you in a kilt."

"It was Mr. Newton's suggestion," Jack said. Charlotte said something to that, but Jack failed to hear her—he was watching Lizzie as she crossed to the sideboard, letting his gaze drift down her curves . . . delightful, delectable curves.

But Mr. Kincade, who entered the drawing room and announced that the guests had arrived, interrupted his leisurely perusal.

Chapter Twenty-one

"May I introduce my uncle Beal, once removed," Lizzie said when the four adults had been shown into the drawing room and Jack was introduced to them. "Mr. Sorley Beal is my father's cousin."

"Nephew," Mr. Beal corrected her, and bowed smartly before Jack.

"And Mrs. Beal," Lizzie said.

Mrs. Beal, who was almost as wide as the door frame, beamed at Jack and offered him her round hand. "I've so longed to make your acquaintance, milord!" she said, and startled Jack by bouncing up from her surprisingly deep curtsy to kiss his cheek.

"Mr. and Mrs. McLennan," Lizzie said, ushering the other couple to him. "They are related on my mother's side, but I could hardly tell you how."

"It's all so very complicated," Mrs. McLennan said as she dipped a curtsy. "I'd wager it's just as complicated at Lambourne, aye?"

"It is indeed," Jack assured her.

Mr. McLennan quickly shook Jack's hand as he passed him on the way to the sideboard, where Mr. Kincade had put out whisky and wine.

"We're so sorry to be tardy!" Mrs. McLennan said. "We were briefly detained by bounty hunters."

Lizzie, Charlotte, Jack, and Newton all turned to the woman.

"Where did you see them, then?" Newton asked.

"Where did we see them, Mr. McLennan?" Mrs. McLennan asked. At her husband's grunt, she said, "I could hardly say—I am wretched at directions, am I no', Mr. McLennan? But the bounty hunters are everywhere of late, it seems."

Jack and Lizzie exchanged a look.

"You must be quite delighted with our Lizzie, milord!" Mrs. Beal exclaimed.

"Supremely," Jack said, suddenly appreciating Carson's advice to keep friends and neighbors close, and put his arm around Lizzie's shoulders. He could feel her resist, but he held her tightly, patting her arm. "She's made me indescribably happy. She is a delight, the sun in my dreary world."

"Oh," Mrs. Beal said with a sigh. "How *lovely*. She and Charlotte have long been favorites of ours."

Lizzie laughed, folded her arms, and pinched Jack's side.

"What of Mr. Gordon, Lizzie?" Mr. Beal asked. "I rather thought you had an understanding with him, aye?"

"It was a very tentative understanding," Charlotte said. "*Very* tentative."

"I reckon they've a different understanding now, aye?" Mr. Beal said, and the four guests laughed heartily.

"A handfasting, too!" Mrs. McLennan said. "Is it no' so very quaint? I've no' heard of one in my lifetime."

"Mr. Beattie, dear. Mr. Beattie and his wife were handfasted," Mrs. Beal reminded her.

"Aye, that they were. How could I forget it? And as Mr. McLennan so rightly pointed out, given your age,

Lizzie, it was probably one of the more expedient ways to do things, aye?"

Lizzie coughed; Jack squeezed her shoulders. She stepped away, but he caught her hand and held it firmly.

"Oh, look at the two of them, will you, Jane," Mrs. McLennan said. "Just like a pair of doves, are they no'?"

"I am so happy for you, Lizzie," Mrs. Beal said, and grasped Lizzie's shoulders, gave her a warm shake. "Do you remember when you were but a wee lass, how you would dress in your mother's gowns and have your pretend weddings? On my word, they'd go on for days!"

"She made Robert Duncan stand in," Charlotte said with a snicker, and everyone laughed.

Lizzie stole a glimpse at Jack. "I was eight years old," she muttered.

"You were such a dreamer, Lizzie! Always dreaming about this romantic adventure and that. I had despaired that your dreams would ever come true, but now look at you, all beautiful and handfasted. And to an *earl*, no less!"

"I am a very fortunate man." Jack smiled at Lizzie. "I've always fancied a dreamer," he said.

She smiled, too, but there were sparks in her eyes.

"Aye, she was a dreamer, and she was a wee bit of a hellion," Mr. Beal said. "She's quite good in archery. Were you aware of it, milord?"

"They've hardly talked about archery, Uncle," Charlotte said.

"My wee darling is an archer?" Jack asked, and grinned with delight at Lizzie. "Bows and arrows in her graceful hands?"

"Bested the whole lot of us one summer during a wedding celebration. Do you recall that, Lizzie?" Mr. Beal asked.

"I do," Charlotte said. "Mamma was nearly apoplectic, thinking she'd ruin any chance of ever making a match if she continued to best all the young men."

"*Diah*," Lizzie said. "I was hardly in danger of gaining an offer, much less chasing them away."

"You're too harsh!" Mrs. Beal cried jovially. "Granted, you are no' as comely as Charlotte, aye, but you are a handsome lass all the same. Is she no' handsome, milord?"

Handsome? That hardly began to describe Lizzie. She was so much more than handsome, so beautiful in her own way. "A fairer lass has no' graced mine eyes," Jack said.

That was met with a round of *bravo*s and laughter. But Lizzie . . . Lizzie looked up at him with those crystal blue eyes and for once, Jack wondered if there were words that could adequately describe what he saw in her.

Fortunately, he was not pressed to do so, for Mr. Kincade appeared to announce that supper was served.

Given that they had few vegetables to add to the stock, the soup was actually very good. In addition to the soup and venison, there was freshly made bannock bread with raisins, and an extravagant, very delectable plum pudding. There was not a crumb left when they'd finished dining.

The conversation at the supper table was lively and included lots of advice about marriage. "Share your bed stones," Mr. McLennan advised.

"Share them!" Mrs. McLennan cried. "You've no' shared one warm stone with me in all the years we've been married!"

"I am happy to announce," Jack said, with a wink at Lizzie, "that Lizzie has been remarkably charitable with

her bed stones. She frets whether I am warm enough."
He smiled.

Lizzie blushed furiously. He was *enjoying* this!

"Ach, lass . . . there are better ways to keep warm," Mr.
Beal said with a laugh.

"Aye. She's shown me that, as well," Jack said, to the
delight of everyone at the table. Even Charlotte, seated
at the head of the table, seemed to be enjoying Lizzie's
discomfiture.

"Did you know," Lizzie said, returning Jack's smile,
"that the earl is a close acquaintance of the Prince of
Wales?"

"I rather gathered as much, given that they are looking high and low for him," Mrs. Beal said, to which the
guests laughed roundly.

"Have you visited the museums in London, milord?"
Charlotte asked.

"I have," Jack said, and answered her questions with
elegant ease. He said he particularly liked the work of the
Masters and believed they compared favorably with the
works he'd had opportunity to view in Paris and Rome.
Aye, he was a patron of the opera and had a box near the
Prince of Wales, who likewise was an avid fan of opera.
Jack believed the operas written by Mozart to be most to
his liking. No, he'd not dined at Windsor with the king,
but he had hunted with him for a fortnight in Balmoral
and had dined with him there.

"Balmoral!" Charlotte said dreamily. "Lizzie, remember the picture book?"

How could she forget it? Lizzie's eyes misted a little
as she watched her sister. They had a picture book of
grand estates, Balmoral among them, and when they
were young girls, Charlotte and Lizzie would pore over
the pictures together. Lizzie could still remember Char-

lotte, dressed in the gowns of their late mother, dipping and holding her hand aloft as she supposed all ladies of grand estates did. She was determined to visit each and every one of the estates when she was of age.

Lizzie lowered her gaze and stared at her plate. She'd been long accustomed to Charlotte's tragedy, but there were times when she was caught completely unawares and forced to rethink it all over again.

"Balmoral is a lovely old castle," Jack said. "Cozier than Lambourne but quite a lot more comfortable. Lambourne is hard angles and harsh stone, whereas Balmoral is gentle and refined. And the hunting there is superb."

"Tell us more," Charlotte urged him, and once again, Lizzie was touched by the way Jack indulged her sister, refusing to omit even the smallest detail. And Charlotte glowed with the sort of pleasure Lizzie had not seen for years.

Newton, on the other hand, seemed to be fighting the urge to sleep.

When supper was finished, and Mr. Kincade had methodically removed the dishes, the party retired to the drawing room. In a rare act of beneficence, Charlotte happily invited the Kincades and even "the other man" to join them.

The Kincades were so delighted by the invitation that they brought along Mr. Kincade's bagpipes and Mrs. Kincade's specially made whisky. Lizzie was mortified that the elderly couple should appear with a jug, but her guests seemed to think nothing of it—even less so when tots were passed all around and they were warmed by what did seem to be an excellent blend.

So excellent, in fact, that when Mr. Kincade took up his pipes and began to play "Highland Laddie," a song known to all Highlanders, Dougal did not need to ask twice for Lizzie to dance, particularly when she was soundly encouraged by her guests. She held up her skirts and kicked up her heels as if she were dancing at her own wedding, laughing when Newton encouraged her to dance faster by shouting, "*Suithad, suithad!*"

Lizzie could not recall the last time she'd danced. But the whisky, the music, the evening all made her feel light and free for a few short hours.

Dougal was a passable dancer, but too enthusiastic given the small confines of the room. He put his hand on Lizzie's waist and twirled her around and around as they mirrored each other's steps. When Dougal accidentally danced himself into a chair, he stumbled and let go of Lizzie. She was more sure footed than he, and with a laugh, she twirled around—right into Jack's chest.

He caught her with an arm around her waist. His eyes locked on hers, and for a fleeting moment she saw something there that sent an alarmingly sensual shiver through her as the ladies gleefully applauded. "Well done, milord!" Mrs. Beal cried.

He smoothly let her go. "Mind your step," he said. "And my foot," he added with a hint of a smile.

With a laugh, Lizzie ceased her dance and tried to catch her breath.

Mr. Kincade stopped blowing his pipes.

"The room is too small, really, for such lively dancing, aye?" Lizzie said breathlessly, her eyes still on Jack.

"Aye!" Dougal agreed as he collapsed into a chair to catch his breath.

Jack said idly, " 'Tis a pity there is no' a ball we might attend. It would be an honor to lead the ladies round the dance floor so that they might be admired by many."

Dougal laughed, as if Jack had intended that as a jest.

"You do enjoy a ball now and again, aye?" Jack asked, looking around at the lot of them.

"A *ball*," Charlotte said, as if that amused her.

"We have our country dances once or twice a year," Mrs. McLennan said, to which they all nodded enthusiastically.

"No' a ball?" Jack said, and looked at Lizzie. "Then I suppose you have no' had the pleasure of dancing a waltz."

All eyes turned eagerly toward Jack. "A waltz!" Charlotte cried. "Tell us, milord!"

"It is more sedate than a highland dance, but perhaps better suited for this room," Jack said. "It is relatively new. It has no' been danced publicly to my knowledge, but it has become quite the thing in private salons."

"Oh, you must show us, milord!" Charlotte cried.

"Are you certain?" Jack asked, looking at Lizzie. "Some consider it to be a dance of subtle seduction."

Everyone seemed to draw the same startled breath. Lizzie's heart leapt in her chest, and she looked anxiously about the room.

"It is a dance done face-to-face," Jack calmly continued.

"You must demonstrate!" Charlotte cried.

"You *must*!" Mrs. Beal exclaimed.

Lizzie saw the glimmer in Jack's eyes, the hint of lust, the challenge of seduction.

"I should happily demonstrate if Miss Lizzie is a willing partner," he said, openly challenging her now.

"I—"

Jack's gaze was so penetrating, so daring, so inviting, that Lizzie was powerless to stop herself. In a moment of true abandon, she stepped forward and curtsied. Jack quickly put out his hand for hers, as if he feared she might change her mind, and helped her up. He turned his hand slightly under hers so that their palms touched, and closed his fingers over hers. "Put your hand on my shoulder," he instructed her.

Lizzie looked at his shoulder, broad as the length of her hand, covered in black superfine wool. A ghost of a smile graced his lips; he put his hand on her rib cage, eliciting a soft gasp of surprise from her, then moved it around to her back and pressed against her, pulling her in closer. "Your hand," he reminded her.

Lizzie took a tiny step closer, but dared not go further than that, and put her hand on his shoulder.

"It is very simple, really," he said, and moved smoothly to his left, guiding Lizzie along with him, counting the steps. "*One* two three, *one* two three," he repeated as he slowly moved her back and forth, until she had learned the step.

Lizzie glanced anxiously around at the others, who were watching her intently. "Is that all there is to it, then?" she scoffed. "It's hardly a dance at all!"

The ghost of his smile spread into a confident one. Without taking his gaze from hers, Jack said, "Any song played in three-quarter time will suffice, Mr. Kincade."

The old man picked up his pipes, played around with them a moment, then began to play a song Lizzie had never heard before. The tune startled her—she'd heard Mr. Kincade play many times in her life, but this was a hauntingly lyrical song that reminded her of the winds that often swept through Glenalmond.

Jack began to move, his steps fluid. With his hand on her back, he pressed Lizzie forward, and, whether by desire or the force of the music, she could not resist him. She was suddenly only inches from him as he guided her with pressure on her back to the left, then to the right.

They were so close that she could feel the power in his body, the grace of his lead. He held her hand out from their bodies, kept his other hand high on her back, and moved her effortlessly about the room.

Lizzie could hear Charlotte's tittering, the ladies' *ahs* of approval, yet she could not take her eyes from Jack's. They looked almost silver in the low light of the room, almost liquid. She could feel every inch of his hand on her back, every finger surrounding hers.

Mr. Kincade seemed to pick up the tempo of that mournful Scottish song, and Jack twirled her about, putting his leg against her skirts, pressing against her legs, spinning her around so quickly that she felt almost as if she were flying. Lizzie understood fully why this was considered a dance of subtle seduction, for as they twirled about that small drawing room in a manor high in the Highlands, she could believe she was in a grand ballroom, could believe she was the object of a man's desire, because Jack's expression said all of that and more.

His gaze bore into hers, burning with the same heat she felt, the burn of it radiating through her, taking her breath away. For a few moments the walls fell away, the people disappeared, and stars spun over her head. There were no words, nothing but his warm body, his dark silver gaze, and a haunting melody that held them together and allowed them to move as one, swirling and gliding with the crescendos and downbeats of the music.

And just like that, it was over. Mr. Kincade came to the end of his hastily retimed song and lowered his pipes. Jack's hand drifted from Lizzie's back and he released her hand. But his eyes were still on hers, still boring into her, still holding her close as he stepped back and bowed low.

Lizzie faltered, sinking awkwardly into a curtsy.

"Oh my." Mrs. Beal sighed longingly. "How *lovely* that is."

Lovely was too paltry a word to describe what had just happened, Lizzie thought, and the look on Jack's face suggested he knew it as well. He absently traced a finger along his lower lip before turning away from her to the group. "There you have it," he said. "The illicit waltz."

"You must perform this dance at Candlemas!" Mrs. McLennan cried.

"Oh, I donna think—"

"What more have you for us, milord?" Charlotte asked, her face beaming with delight, cutting off Lizzie's protest.

"I'm really no' much for dancing, but the Princess of Wales enjoys it very much. When a guest in her house, one is practically required to dance. I distinctly remember a time when there were but eight of us dining at Montagu House. The princess had brought in her favorite pair of musicians and we proceeded to dance a quadrille, but one quadrille quite different from what you might expect. When called upon to repeat a pattern of steps, one was required to remove an article of clothing."

Mrs. McLennan gasped with horror, but Charlotte and Mrs. Beal were clearly enthralled with the untoward royal gossip—almost as enthralled as Dougal. Only Newton scowled disapprovingly.

Lizzie stepped into the shadows of the room where she might find her breath while he titillated them with his tale. There was, she realized, a breath of fresh air blowing through Thorntree, a diversion that could rival no other. Jack was the faery Lizzie had always wished would sweep in and change her and Charlotte's lives.

She'd just never imagined it in precisely this way.

But it was still a fantasy, for it would end soon. *Too* soon, considering how her heart still pounded in her chest and her breath still came in little snatches.

Later that night, when she finally reached her bed, Lizzie tried to think of Mr. Gordon. But every conscious thought was obliterated by the memory of Jack's hands on her body, the smoldering look in his eye. She could not stop imagining those hands on her bare skin, those eyes raking over her naked body. . . .

The room was stifling. Lizzie threw back the heavy covers and climbed out of bed. She looked at the dressing room door. Through that door, Jack lay sleeping. Lizzie padded across the rug to it and pressed her palm against it, just as he had pressed his palm against her back. She leaned forward, rested her cheek against it.

Lizzie didn't know what she expected, but she didn't hear anything. Yet she stood there nonetheless, her eyes closed, her cheek against the door, reliving the waltz step by step. She toyed with the idea of stepping through, to him. But she lacked the courage and the desire to ruin herself completely.

She returned to her bed restive and out of sorts. She sought sleep by whispering Mr. Gordon's name over and over. He was her only hope, the only salve to the laceration Jack had lashed across her life. Before Jack had come into her life, she'd been happy—at least as happy as one could be, facing the poorhouse and the constant worry of how to care for Charlotte—she'd been free, and she'd been happy. But she'd felt an oddly enticing unrest since she'd been put upon that dais beside Jack.

Mr. Gordon. Mr. Gordon needed to come soon, before Lizzie fell from grace and did something so wildly reckless that she would live to regret it all her days.

∽

In the dressing room, with Dougal just outside and Lizzie only God knew where, Jack lay with his arms folded, his hands behind his head, staring up into thick darkness.

He was thinking of Lizzie, but not consciously. Of late Lizzie seemed intrinsically part of his being, whether he was fully aware of it or not. She was just . . . *there,* existing inside him somehow, her presence never far from his mind.

Or his desires. *Diah,* he'd been spectacularly aroused by that waltz. Not so much in the flesh—not that he hadn't felt the familiar stirrings of lust—but he'd discovered in that waltz a heightened sense of her. *All* of her. He was acutely aware of how she felt in his arms, her delicate frame, the small bones of her hand. And the rosy scent of her unruly hair and the soft glow of fine, smooth skin. And her *eyes.* Lord help him, her eyes seemed to reflect the lowest light, sparkling back at him, and making him believe he could feel that sparkle in his blood.

It had been a waltz for the ages, the one dance he would never forget.

But while he had Lizzie floating about his brain, it was Carson Beal who had Jack's foremost attention. Whatever it was the man was hiding, whatever compelled him to keep Lizzie and Charlotte captives in their own home, Jack was increasingly determined to discover what it was.

While the rest of the house lay in their beds, Newton stood at the windows in the old nursery that overlooked the sought lawn. He wore a thick wool cloak lined with shearling. There was no peat for this hearth. There was precious little peat for the entire house. Newton knew, for he'd gone to see for himself this afternoon.

Despite the late hour, he felt oddly cross and very much awake. He stared down at the unkempt lawn, illuminated by a full Scottish moon, and pictured a gazebo there, into which Charlotte could be wheeled without trouble. One that overlooked the river and the hills, one to which ducks might wander up to be fed a bit of bread if Charlotte wished. He could picture her now, leaning over the arm of her wheeled chair, letting ducks—or dogs, or even children, perhaps—take food from the palm of her hand.

Newton scratched his chin, thinking of the expense. The Beal lassies had no money, everyone knew that was so. But he'd put a little aside for emergencies. He mulled it over, standing at the window until he'd lost track of time, thinking of a beautiful woman cruelly bound to a chair.

Chapter Twenty-two

M rs. Kincade actually smiled—and warmly, at that—when Jack and the dogs Tavish and Red appeared in the kitchen in search of breakfast.

He returned her smile, surprised and pleased, and asked if he might have a bit of food to break his fast. She was more than happy to prepare some porridge and eggs for him, and even shooed the dogs outside.

Seated at the long wooden table with a steaming cup of coffee and eating some freshly baked bread, Jack asked if Lizzie was up and about. He imagined her chopping down a tree for firewood or herding a flock of sheep to the shearer or some such thing.

"Oh, aye," Mrs. Kincade said in a tone that suggested it was a ridiculous question. "She's gone on to Aberfeldy this morning. She and Mr. Kincade took the old milk cow to market."

"Without me?" he asked, a little miffed that she'd taken his advice but not him.

"They left well before dawn. We donna wait for the sun to rise up here, milord."

Jack disregarded her remark and continued with his porridge.

"Milord, if you donna mind me saying . . ."

The woman's voice trailed off, and Jack glanced up

from his bowl. Dear Lord, was he seeing things, or was she blushing?

"Your dance," she said, her blush deepening.

"Aye?"

"Mr. Kincade and I tried it ourselves and found it . . . well, we found it very much to our liking, then."

Jack put down his spoon. He grinned. "Why, Mrs. Kincade, you do scandalize me!"

She laughed nervously and put a hand to her nape. "A bit of snow on the roof does no' mean a lack of fire within."

"How happy I am to hear it," he said, and laughed heartily.

Mrs. Kincade laughed, too, the sound of it girlish.

When Jack finished his breakfast, he left a smiling Mrs. Kincade to her chores. But with Newton undoubtedly moving Charlotte about, Jack faced another day with nothing to occupy him. He walked about the manor, noting again the repairs that needed to be made. The roof seemed to be in the most desperate need, judging by the number of stains on various ceilings.

Jack donned his greatcoat and strode outside. It was a crisp day with a cobalt blue sky, and after walking around the perimeter of the house, he decided to climb up on the roof and have a look. He really had no notion of how to go about repairing a roof, but as a lad he'd followed behind Mr. Maxwell, the groundskeeper at Lambourne Castle, and had learned a thing or two, he reckoned.

He also fancied himself a clever man, and as he and Fingal headed for the outbuildings in search of a ladder, Dougal trailing lazily behind, Jack imagined that repairing a roof could not be so difficult.

He'd imagined incorrectly.

While Fingal, and eventually Tavish and Red, napped at the foot of the ladder, Jack discovered several places that needed patching, and two through which he could put his gloved fist. The roof was made of slate, and many of the tiles were broken or missing. He needed ash and tar to patch the worst holes and slate tiles to replace those that were broken.

When he had inched his way across the top of the roof back to the ladder, he found Newton standing at the base, one large foot on the bottom rung, his look condemning.

"You have that look about you of wanting to accuse me of nefarious deeds, sir," Jack said amicably. "But you'd be in the wrong. I'm only having a look at the roof. It leaks."

"Aye, it leaks. What can ye do about it, then?" Newton asked in a tone that suggested he believed Jack entirely incapable of patching a roof.

"I can *repair* it," Jack shot back. "If I had the proper materials, that is. Where might I find slate and tar?"

"You're no' serious, aye?"

"Aye, I am! " Jack said impatiently. "Now look here, Newton, I should think Kincade would have some tar about, so where might I find slate?"

Newton shook his head. "It's no' mined round here, milord, but ye might inquire of Old McIntosh up glen. He often has such things as slate tile lying about that he'd be happy to give over for a few coins."

"What do you mean, it's no' mined here? This roof is slate."

"Aye," Newton said patiently, as if speaking to an imbecile. "There was a bit of mining many years ago, but that mine was depleted."

"McIntosh, is it?" Jack asked curtly and swung one leg onto the ladder. He came down quickly, landing before

Newton. He calmly dusted his hands together as if he lived on ladders and scampered up and down them at will, and said, "Thank you. You've been quite helpful. I should like my horse brought round, and one for Dougal, I suppose."

If Jack wasn't mistaken, the growl in Newton's chest was a laugh. "No need to send Dougal with ye, milord. Ye'll return to us soon enough, ye will."

"You're bloody certain of it, are you?" Jack asked testily.

"Aye. 'Tis wild country north of here, naugh' but wild country for miles. If you think to escape, ye'll no' last a day without provisions, especially during the height of winter. One snow, and the trail is lost. And if ye head south, ye'll no' escape the bounty hunters, aye?"

"Donna tempt me, lad," Jack said.

Newton laughed again. He picked up the ladder with one hand and balanced it against his shoulder. "I'll handle the ladder for you, if you'd like."

"Thank you," Jack said, and strode away, the dogs trotting behind him once again as he headed for the barn.

The dogs were not of a mind to go any further than the manor grounds, however, as they stopped at the edge of the drive and sat, their heads cocked as they curiously watched Jack and the mare trot down the only road that led deep in the glen.

Newton hadn't been entirely certain where Jack might find McIntosh, but he was right about the terrain. There was scarcely a trail at all, and what was there was rough and overgrown. Aye, but someone had been along this trail recently. Jack knew Carson had been; he sincerely hoped Carson and his men were the only ones to come along this path, as he did not relish the thought of encountering the bounty men.

The ride seemed long, but if Jack had a talent, it was hunting and tracking. If there was a McIntosh to be found in this glen, Jack would find him.

He rode for a half hour and came upon a fork in the path. A smaller, rougher path led into the forest, while the main fork carried on north. As his mare sauntered past, Jack noticed a mark in the mud on the smaller trail. It looked fresh, and that interested him. He wondered what sort of game might be wandering this glen and reined his mount up, swung off, and walked onto the path, crouching down on one knee to look at the marks.

It wasn't game at all but the marks of horses. Four, Jack counted, all of them shod. He stood up, peering up the path. From where he stood, the path seemed to get narrower and the terrain wilder. He seated himself on the mare once more and turned her onto that rough path to follow the trail.

He lost the tracks at a stream. He dismounted and crossed the stream, looking carefully at the ground. The tracks led right, but they were lost in the thick heather. Jack looked around him. The stream ran down a particularly steep hill. There was no place for horses to go, really, but up, and that seemed unlikely. Even Highland ponies weren't that sure-footed, particularly in heather as thick as this and climbs so steep.

Perplexed by the tracks of four horses that seemed to disappear, Jack returned the way he came. It was exceedingly strange; he decided he'd have another look once he found this McIntosh fellow and divested him of his slate.

As it happened, McIntosh found Jack when Jack stopped to water the mare. The old man appeared out of the woods, a grimy rucksack over his shoulder, a gun carried loosely in his hand, eyeing Jack suspiciously.

"How is the hunting, then?" Jack asked casually.

"Two hares," the man said, his accent so rustic that Jack could hardly make out the words. He squatted down next to the creek to wash his hands.

"You're McIntosh, are you?"

The man glanced up. "Who's asking, then? Are you an authority?"

"Hardly," Jack drawled.

McIntosh did indeed have a sheet of slate for sale, a broken piece left behind by carpenters in some hamlet, he said. The old man had seen the value in it and carried it back to his home—which, Jack discovered, was a hovel deep in the forest.

McIntosh took two shillings for the piece. Jack thought the price outrageous, but he couldn't help but notice the disrepair of the man's hovel. He handed over the two shillings, strapped the slate onto the mare's rump with a bit of rope, and started back for Thorntree.

The day had warmed considerably, the sun shining brightly and a crisp breeze rustling the tops of the pines. As Jack neared the spot where the path diverged, the mysterious fork going up into the hills, he heard the sound of an approaching rider.

His heart skipped. He didn't want to meet the rider head-on—the last time he'd met riders in the woods, they'd deprived him of his liberty and his gun. Jack quickly dismounted and led the mare into a copse of pines.

The rider was pushing hard and rode by so fast that Jack could scarcely make out the identity, but the bouncing bonnet and flying auburn curls gave Lizzie away. "Lizzie!" Jack shouted, and threw himself up onto his horse, spurring her out of the trees and after Lizzie.

She was too far ahead to hear him, at least two lengths,

but as the trail grew uneven, her mount slowed, and Jack was able to close the distance. "*Lizzie!*" he shouted again. She bent over the neck of the horse and glanced back, but when she saw it was Jack, she reined the horse hard, forcing it to wheel about.

Jack reined hard, too, to avoid a collision with her. "What the devil!" he exclaimed as the mare danced around in a tight circle to face her again.

"Are you following me?" she demanded.

"No!" he exclaimed, affronted, and looked back to assure himself the slate had remained on the mare's rump. It had not. "Bloody hell," he muttered, and looked crossly at Lizzie. "Is Thorntree burning? Has the sun fallen from the sky? Do the English invade?"

"Pardon?"

"You're riding recklessly, lass! Too recklessly—you might have been thrown and seriously harmed!"

"I was no'!" she protested, and pulled up her bonnet—which was quite possibly the strangest bonnet Jack had ever seen. While the bonnets in London were demurely festooned with ribbons and sprigs of violets, this one boasted all manner of clusters of silk fruits and showy flowers.

"What are you doing out here? Where is Dougal? Are you escaping?" she demanded.

When Jack did not answer straightaway, she put a hand to her bonnet. "What?" she asked accusingly.

"I . . ." He dragged his gaze from her bonnet to her face. "Of course I am no' plotting an escape," he said, perturbed by the implication, when that was precisely what he might have done only two days ago. "I would no' go *north* were I to escape."

"Aye, for everyone knows all the good escape routes lie south," she said smartly.

"And so do bounty hunters," he said, his eyes narrowing. "What of you? I was told that you'd followed my excellent advice and had toddled off to sell a cow."

She colored. "What of it?"

"You are welcome," he said, enjoying the high color in her cheeks. "I'd wager you got a very good price for it. So good, in fact, that you treated yourself to a new bonnet."

She gasped. Her cheeks turned even rosier. He was right, he could see that he was right—but of all the bonnets in Scotland, why on earth would the lass choose *that* one?

She suddenly lifted her chin and straightened the brim of her godawful bonnet. "If you have had your fill of interrogating me—"

"I have no'. Why are you riding so hard?"

"You are presumptuous, questioning me!" she exclaimed in disbelief.

"I am *handfasted* to you, lest you've forgotten it, although I can hardly see how you might, given our performance as the happy couple last night. But in the event that you have taken complete leave of your senses, allow me to remind you that were I your husband, I would do no less."

"You would never *be* my husband."

"What, then, you would refuse the offer of an earl?" he scoffed.

"Are you offering?" she asked mockingly.

"If I were mad enough to do so," he said, gliding over her challenge, "would you have me believe you would *refuse* it?"

"In the space of a heartbeat," she said pertly. "I am no' one of your London mistresses, Jack."

Truer words were never spoken—she was nothing like those women, nothing at all. "Aye, you are different,

I will gladly grant you that, but show me a woman who does no' seek to improve her situation by marriage and I will show you an old widow with more than she can spend."

Lizzie laughed. "That's outrageous!"

"No' as outrageous as you might think. But if you donna seek to improve your situation, then what exactly do you seek, Lizzie?"

She was just beginning to rant, if the square of her shoulders and the puff of her chest were any indication, but his question jolted her somewhat.

"What do you seek in exchange for your heart?" he demanded, spurring his mount a step or two closer. He was surprised by his own words, but he suddenly needed to know.

She looked unnerved by the question. "*Why?*" she demanded.

Why? He had no idea, but it seemed of the utmost importance. "Answer, if you dare."

"You must believe I am afraid to admit it. But I'm no', Lambourne. I want *love*, if you must know. I want the promise of forever," she added, looking wildly about. "To know that there is one person who loves and respects me above all others, one person who will come into my heart and fill all the holes and patch all the cracks and make it sing as it ought! No' a bloody castle or a husband who will honor his vows only with his purse!"

"Poetic," Jack said, nodding appreciatively.

Lizzie's expression darkened. "And what do you seek in exchange for *your* heart?" she asked crossly. "A gambling debt reduced? A felony whisked away? A doxy to share your bed?"

The moment the words *doxy* and *bed* tumbled out of her mouth, her eyes widened. But Jack was not fazed by it. He grinned at her and her hat. "There are far worse things than sharing a bed, lass. Someday, when you climb off your celestial perch, you might understand it."

"And I suppose in that I have my answer," she said, and reined her horse up, preparing to turn him around.

"Wait, wait—for the love of Scotland, Lizzie, where are you off to?"

"Mi Diah!" she cried heavenward. "Will you begin the interrogation again? I am merely *riding.* I enjoy it and I rarely have the opportunity, and I prefer to do it *alone.*"

"Rarely the opportunity because you work all your horses into a painful lather?"

"No," she said pertly. "Because Charlotte does no' care for it." At Jack's puzzled look, she gestured impatiently to her legs.

"Ah," Jack said, leveling a gaze on her. "Your sister has a valid point, for you ride like the *diabhal.* Give the poor animal a bit of a respite and come with me. There is something I would show you."

"Something *you* would show me!" She laughed a bit frantically as she adjusted her ridiculous bonnet. "I think you've shown me quite enough, have you no'?"

So she was thinking of the waltz, too. "Oh lass," Jack said with a wolfish wink, "I've only begun to show you."

Lizzie understood him completely, he knew, because it was her infuriating habit to challenge him boldly, then retreat when he overstepped the bounds of her innocence. She retreated now, averting her gaze by looking down at her saddle. Two silk apples pointed at him like a pair of eyes.

"What I would show you now are tracks."

She glanced up. "Tracks?"

"Aye. Tracks that lead nowhere."

"What sort of tracks?" she asked, obviously intrigued, and looked up the road. "Up here? No one comes from up here."

"Come," Jack said, and led her up to where the paths diverged. When he pointed out the tracks, Lizzie leapt off her horse before Jack could dismount and assist her, and knelt down next to the tracks to have a look. "Horses," she said. "I count three."

Surprised by her tracking skills, Jack went down on his haunches beside her. "Four," he said, pointing to the distinct hoof marks.

Lizzie nodded and peered curiously up the path.

"Where does this path lead?" he asked.

"Nowhere," she said, sounding puzzled. She stood up and peered into the forest much as Jack had done a few hours earlier. "There is nothing but the rough side of a hill and a few deer trails beyond this point."

"But there is something," Jack said, and glanced at Lizzie. "Shall we have a look?"

"Aye," she said, nodding, thereby causing a large, showy flower that looked wildly out of place at the tail end of January to bounce erratically.

Lizzie knew of a clearing where they could tether the horses. Together they walked up the path, following the tracks. When they reached the stream, Lizzie deftly navigated it by hopping across exposed rocks until she reached the other side.

Jack walked across.

She leaned over, examining the ground.

"The tracks disappear into the heather," Jack said, leaning over her. "It is difficult to track through heather, and particularly without proper light," he added, glancing up. Between the towering pines and the height of the hill, it was darkly shaded.

"Do you always concede so quickly?" Lizzie asked with a playful smile. She stepped into the heather, her head down.

Jack followed her. A few steps ahead of him, Lizzie made her way slowly, and skirted around an outcropping of rock. She abruptly whirled around, her smile beaming, and pointed at something.

There was a small clearing where the heather broke on the other side, and horses had trampled the ground there. Jack turned fully around, looking at his surroundings, and looked at Lizzie. "Why?" he asked her. "Why come here?"

She shrugged. "An outing, I suppose. A walkabout."

"When the weather can change without a moment's notice?"

She shrugged again. "There you have it. We found where the tracks lead. Now that I've shown you the proper way to track through the heather, I should return to Thorntree."

But Jack was far too curious to turn back now. He walked in the opposite direction, where the hill began a steep ascent again.

"Wait!" Lizzie called. "Where are you going?"

The trail was faint but obvious. He felt Lizzie at his back and turned slightly, gesturing to the trail. "I'm going to have a look. Wait here."

"Wait! I'll do no such thing! If you are going up, so am I."

"No, Lizzie, it's quite steep."

"And you're better suited to it than me because you're a goat?" she asked. "I can climb a hill, Lambourne." And, to prove it, she pushed past him and started up.

But Jack caught her hand and stopped her. "*I'll* go first, if you please." When she looked as if she might argue, he tugged her back a step. "Unless you are quite at ease meeting anyone who might happen along this path head on, you'll allow me to go first."

That seemed to give her pause. She stepped back, gestured for him to carry on.

They climbed for a few minutes, Jack pausing every few steps to assure himself Lizzie was behind him. Lizzie remarked that he seemed rather at home on the side of a hill.

Jack looked at her. "You seem surprised."

"I am indeed," she said gaily. "I would think you better suited for tea and crumpets than walkabouts."

"Very amusing."

Her eyes danced as she mimicked sipping from a teacup, her little finger extended in a most affected manner.

Jack resumed the climb up. "As you very well know, one is no' reared in the Highlands without climbing a few hills."

"Ah, but that's been a very long time ago, I gather. You canna claim to be a Highlander now," she cheerfully reminded him.

Oddly enough, that remark chafed. He *was* a Highlander, just as much as she was. Aye, he'd been away what seemed a lifetime, eleven years now, but he was nevertheless a Highlander!

Wasn't he?

"These hills are no' the only ones I've climbed."

"Oh?" she said, seeming genuinely interested. "What hills, then?"

"Switzerland," he said. "France, naturally." He offered his hand to help her up over a rock.

She slipped her hand into his and allowed him to pull her up. The path was narrow; she landed practically on his feet. It amazed Jack that he could feel the heat be-

tween their bodies even when they were both encased in
wool like a pair of sheep. Lizzie had a unique power to
make his blood race.

"You've climbed hills in Switzerland and France?" she
asked breathlessly.

He looked into her sky blue eyes. "Aye."

"Why? Were you to be hanged there, too?"

He laughed and squeezed her hand. "*No*," he said with
the patience one might use when speaking to a child.

Lizzie laughed, too, the sound of it as sweet as bird-
song to him. "Please tell me," she said. "When we were
girls Charlotte and I were very fond of looking at the
atlas and imagining such places," she said, and slipped
her hand from his.

He wanted to keep holding it. He wanted to stay right
here, on the side of this steep hill, and look into her blue
eyes. But he moved on, leading the way again. "It was
my grand tour of the Continent," he said, and proceeded
to tell her about it. It had lasted longer than he'd anticipated because his friends—Nathan Grey, the Earl of
Lindsey; and Declan O'Conner, Lord Donnelly; Grayson
Christopher, Duke of Darlington; and Sir Oliver Wilkes
had accompanied him and had enticed him into more
trouble than a proper young lass ought to know about.

She seemed very interested in his travels, asking questions about what sort of places they were, what the people ate, what they wore, the languages they spoke. She
seemed surprised and impressed that he spoke French
fluently. He was privately surprised that she didn't know
at least a little of it.

They reached a flat point on the hill, where Jack
paused so that Lizzie might rest. The day was turning
into one of those rare and gloriously warm winter days,
and Lizzie paused, removed her awful bonnet, and swept

a curl from her forehead with the back of her hand. She was about to put the bonnet on again when they both heard voices.

She gaped at him; Jack indicated she should be silent.

There were the voices again, coming up the trail behind them. Bloody awful timing, Jack thought and, even worse, he had no gun. In the Highlands, one could never be too careful.

Jack looked around, saw the flat of the hill extended around a rock outcropping, but the trail continued up. He grabbed Lizzie's hand and pulled her along the flat stretch. But when he reached the outcropping, the flat gave way to a narrow ledge high above a rocky ravine.

This was not the least bit encouraging: they were trapped between the hill and whoever was approaching—and to date, Jack's experience had been bloody well awful when he found himself trapped in Scotland.

Chapter Twenty-three

❧

The voices were drawing closer, and belonged to men, Lizzie quickly determined, speaking Gaelic. At least that suggested it was not the prince's men come to carry Jack off to hang.

Lizzie glanced over her shoulder in an effort to see them; at the very same moment Jack yanked her around the outcropping and onto a ledge. Lizzie gasped as she looked down; they were standing twenty to thirty feet above a rocky ravine. One clumsy move and they would fall to their deaths. *"Are you mad?"* she whispered hotly.

He put a finger to her lips and narrowed his gaze with implicit warning.

The sound of the voices so very near to them startled Lizzie right into Jack's chest. She tried to gain her footing, but her right foot met with nothing but air. She grabbed the lapels of his coat, but in the process of trying to maintain her balance, she dropped her bonnet. It landed on the very edge.

Jack gave her another look full of warning, then tried to glance over her. Her hair must have been a fright, for he put his palm squarely on the top of her head and pushed down.

Lizzie looked at the bonnet she'd purchased from Mrs. Bain, the proprietress of the lady's shop in Aberfeldy, for two shillings instead of the three she'd wanted for it last summer. Lizzie began to squat down to retrieve it, but her left foot hit a loose rock that went tumbling off the ledge, pinging off several rocks on its way down. She made a sound of distress; Jack caught her around the waist with one arm, grabbed onto an exposed root with his other hand, and jerked her back hard, into his chest. She gasped; he let go the root and clamped his hand over her mouth and hissed, "*Sssh*," into her ear.

Neither of them moved. The tips of Lizzie's boots were hanging over the ledge. She held her breath but heard nothing—no voices, not so much as a bird chirping. Whoever had been coming up the path had paused, the sound of the fallen rock obviously having gained their attention.

Another moment passed. A slight breeze picked up, rustling the tops of the trees. She was aware of Jack at her back, long and solid against her. She was aware of how tightly he held her, of the strength in him. She slowly leaned her head back and rested it against his shoulder, looking up at the clear blue sky.

"*Ainmhidh*," a voice rumbled, and the men continued on the path.

Animal. They thought they'd heard an animal. Lizzie sagged with relief; Jack tightened his grip on her.

It seemed to take an interminable time for them to pass. Lizzie was certain she could feel Jack's heartbeat. His was not skipping about in his chest as hers was; it beat a strong and steady rhythm, and she found that comforting.

The men reached the flat part of the trail and passed just inches from them. By that point, Lizzie's heart was pounding so loudly in her ears that she couldn't really concentrate on what they were saying, but she managed to pick up *seachd miltean*—seven miles—and a few words here and there, *crois a' rothaid* and *cairt*. Crossroads and cart?

When the men passed them, and they could hear no more, Jack slowly maneuvered them off the ledge and onto the flat part of the trail.

"My bonnet—"

"I'll buy you a new one," he said dismissively, glancing up the trail.

"It cost two shillings!"

He looked at her with surprise. "Are you mad? You paid two shillings for it?" He shook his head. "Never mind that now. There are more than enough bonnets to be had. Lizzie, I need you to stay here. Please donna argue with me," he said when she opened her mouth. "I must see where they've gone. Donna go down without me, donna try and follow me. Stay *here*."

"But—"

He'd already started up after the men. In two great strides he'd leapt up the trail, moving swiftly and disappearing into the trees.

He was back minutes later, shaking his head as he jogged down the trail. "I lost them. I donna know how— on the other side of this hill there are only more trees, yet they've disappeared."

"How? Where could they have gone?"

"One can only guess," he said, and put his hand on her elbow, turning her about. "Presently, I am more concerned about taking you away from here." He began to usher her down the trail.

"What of my bonnet?" she exclaimed as he hurried her along.

"Lass, on my word, I shall buy you the finest bonnet in all of Britain, but that one is best left at the bottom of the ravine."

Lizzie was greatly offended by that—she'd thought it a lovely bonnet with lively trim—but Jack was moving quickly.

"Did you know the men?" he asked as they made their way down.

"No, but I think one of them might have been Carson's man."

"I'm shocked," Jack said flippantly. "What did they say?"

"I couldna understand them clearly. I was able to hear the words *crossroads*, *cart*, and *seven miles*—no' in that particular order." She paused, trying to remember. "Or in the same sentence. What can it mean, seven miles, and crossroads, and cart?"

"Maybe nothing at all," Jack said. "Then again, maybe quite a lot. Perhaps we will have a look at your atlas and see if anything leaps out at us."

"Aye, but please donna tell Charlotte of this. I donna want to alarm her."

They had reached the clearing where three horses were grazing.

"Recognize them?" Jack asked.

"No," Lizzie said. "But Mr. Calder keeps quite a lot in this glen. Men are constantly trading horseflesh."

The three horses barely lifted their heads from the grazing as Jack and Lizzie passed.

"Two trips in as many days," Jack said as they walked through the heather. "That would suggest more than an outing, aye?"

"Aye," Lizzie agreed. She was suddenly very glad she'd left their mounts in another clearing. She couldn't begin to guess what was happening here, but she had an uneasy feeling that it was for the best that no one knew she and Jack had stumbled upon it.

∽∾∾

They agreed to meet in the library after supper.

After a private meal with her sister, Lizzie wheeled Charlotte into the drawing room, where Newton waited. Lizzie suggested they have a game of cards, but Charlotte declined and picked up her knitting needles. "I should like to hear Mr. Newton read. Lizzie, you donna mind, aye?" she asked.

"I'm really rather tired. I think I shall retire early tonight."

"Oh." Charlotte said as she began to knit. "Good night, then. Sleep well."

While Lizzie was settling Charlotte, Jack convinced Dougal to go and inquire about tar of Mr. Kincade.

Dougal frowned in confusion. "You mean to patch the roof now, milord? It's black as ink outside."

"I mean to do it on the morrow, weather permitting, but if there is no tar to be had, I'll need to send someone to Aberfeldy at first light."

That seemed to satisfy Dougal.

Jack found Lizzie in the frigid library. She was wearing her peculiar fingerless gloves. "It's as cold as a witch's scorn in here!" Jack complained as he blew on his cupped hands to warm his fingers. He was beginning to appreciate the utility of fingerless gloves. "There's no wood or peat in the bin."

"We donna have enough peat to warm every room," Lizzie said crisply as she sailed across the room to a bookshelf, set aside her single candle, and pulled down a very large leather-bound atlas.

Jack caught it before she dropped it and carried it to the table. They laid it open to Scotland, and together leaned over the dusty pages, poring over the map, looking for something significant within seven miles of Thorntree.

There was nothing. There was no major crossroad, which Jack had hoped to find. There was no minor crossroad, for that matter, as roads in the glens tended to be long and narrow and fairly straight. Within a seven-mile radius of Thorntree there was little more than hills and glens and rivers, a farming settlement or two that amounted to nothing more than a pair of crofters' cottages and some enclosures, and Ardtalnaig, a settlement on Loch Tay.

"Nothing," Lizzie said, frowning with disappointment. "Only a loch and flocks of sheep."

"I suppose it was a bit of a guess to begin with," Jack said. He leaned over the map again, so close that she could feel the energy of her body radiating off his. "A pity." He sighed, braced his hand against the map as he squinted at the name *Ardtalnaig*, then turned to look at Lizzie.

She was leaning forward too, her face only inches from his. He could kiss her now if he liked. But Lizzie was frowning studiously at the atlas, apparently heedless of the current Jack felt running between them.

"You heard nothing more, you're certain, then?" he asked softly as he touched the tips of his fingers to hers.

"Nothing."

He casually entwined his fingers with hers.

Her cheeks flushed a little. "Perhaps it was nothing more than a walkabout," she suggested, and shifted away, disentangling her fingers from his and trailing them across the open page of the atlas. She rounded the corner of the table, her gaze on the map. "A diversion."

"No," Jack said firmly, watching her. "Grown men

who possess normal responsibilities do no' go traipsing about the Highlands for the sake of diversion. It has to do with this estate, Lizzie. Your uncle is determined to have it. But why should he no' make a claim for it as the closest surviving male heir? One would think he'd have better luck with a claim before a magistrate than with his handfasting."

"Oh, that's simple, really," she said casually. "The magistrate spends his winter in Inverness. He'll no' come round to the glens until spring. And besides, a Beal man can no' inherit land."

She said it as if it were a well-known fact. "Pardon?" Jack asked, certain he'd misunderstood her.

"Beal men canna inherit land," Lizzie said again.

"What precisely do you mean, a Beal man canna inherit land?" Jack demanded.

"It's an old story," Lizzie said dismissively. "There was a royal decree of some sort issued after the Jacobite rebellion of forty-five."

"Go on," Jack urged her.

"The Beals of Glenalmond fought on the wrong side of the Crown, and when the rebellion was over, King George retaliated by forfeiting their lands to the Crown. There are many Beals who still hold a firm grudge against the king today, and I can assure you a Beal will no' hand you to a royal bounty hunter," she said proudly.

But Jack hardly cared at the moment. "Am I to understand that all Beal lands were forfeited?"

"No' all of them. Those lands that were in possession of William Beal—my father's grand-uncle, or something near to that—were saved, for William Beal was married to the king's cousin, Anna Beal. The king allowed that Anna might possess land, but no' her traitorous husband and his kin. So he gave the lands to her, prohibited Beal men from inheriting property, and decreed that only Beal women may inherit."

Jack was stunned. "That means you've inherited Thorntree free and clear? Carson canna claim a sister, a mother?"

Lizzie shook her head. "He had only a brother, my father. Really, there are precious few girls born to the Beals. Charlotte and I are the only ones in our immediate family."

"*Diah*, Lizzie, do you see?" Jack said eagerly. "This might explain why Carson does no' want to see you married so much as ruined for a Gordon, aye?"

"Why?" she asked.

"If your Gordon cries off because of the handfasting—which any man of sound mind would do—and you donna marry, the lands will remain in possession of a Beal. Carson might force you to marry one of his men—a Beal man, that is—so that he might have control of Thorntree."

Lizzie snorted at that. "Who? Dougal?" She laughed but quickly sobered. "*Mi Diah*, perhaps he is planning something *precisely* like that. Yet . . . yet there is naugh' to control. You've seen it yourself, Jack: Thorntree requires more income to operate than what we manage to bring into the coffers."

"Aye, but that is precisely the question, Lizzie. What exactly is it you've inherited?" Jack asked, trying to sort it out. "Thorntree could only be a drain on his accounts. I should think Carson would be happy to put the burden of it on a Gordon."

"Perhaps he does no' want a Gordon to reside so close to him," she suggested.

Jack shook his head. "Carson Beal does no' strike me as the sort of man who would value principle over coin."

He thought a moment, then looked at Lizzie. "You said it was a royal decree, aye?"

"Aye."

"Can you locate it? Perhaps there is something there that might clarify matters for us."

"My father showed it to me once," she said. "He was worried someone might take advantage of us after he was gone, and Charlotte in particular." She smiled wryly. "Perhaps he knew Carson better than I realized, aye?"

"Do you think you might find it, then?"

"It would be in my father's study." She hesitated, folding her arms tightly across her body. "That was the room he preferred, his private space. We've left it as it was the day he died."

"I understand," Jack said, and he did. It was many months before he'd been able to disturb his father's sanctuary after his death. Clearly not for the same reasons as Lizzie's—Jack had needed time to convince himself the old man was truly gone. His father had told Jack from his deathbed that he'd never amount to much. Jack had been a young man then, and there was a part of him that feared his father would rise up from his grave. But he'd been forced to face it sooner rather than later—he'd become an earl at the age of eighteen, and there were matters that needed his attention.

To Lizzie he said, "I rather think your father would want you to discover what Carson is about, to keep you and Charlotte safe."

Lizzie bit her bottom lip and nodded. "Aye, he would. I think I can find it."

Chapter Twenty-four

Her father's study was filled with stacks of papers and books and estate ledgers even older than Charlotte, and perhaps older than the Kincades, by the look of them. Lizzie had to think hard about where the document might be. She strained to see by the light of a single candle.

Jack followed her about, leaning over her shoulder, his hand brushing hers, his shoulder pressed against hers, making it difficult to concentrate on the task at hand. As Lizzie searched through stacks of papers, he began to complain of the cold. "It is ridiculous to be looking for something when one cannot feel the tips of one's fingers," he groused. "And by the light of a single candle! You will ruin your eyes, lass. We need light and warmth."

Handfasting notwithstanding, Jack had a tendency to be imperious. "I've told you, we canna afford either," she reminded him. "There's no' enough peat to warm the entire house, and candles are a precious commodity in the winter while the bees are dormant."

"You can spare one block of peat," he insisted.

"We can *no'*."

"Where is it, where is the peat? I'll no' have you freezing unto death."

"Have you heard a word I've said?" Lizzie exclaimed impatiently. "We canna spare the peat!"

"Mi Diah," Jack muttered under his breath, and then something else about stubborn women she didn't quite catch. He put down the candle with a *thwap* and strode from the study, leaving the door wide open. Lizzie blinked after him, wondering if she'd just witnessed a vainglorious man in a snit.

A quarter of an hour later, Jack returned with a block of peat on his shoulder.

Lizzie clenched the papers she was holding and pointed them at the block of peat. "You donna mean to light it!"

"I do indeed." He kicked over a footstool that stood before the cold hearth, pushed aside the fire screen with one hand, and tossed the peat inside. From his pocket he withdrew a match and a flint, and Lizzie watched in angry astonishment as he lit the block of peat. It flared, filling the small study with light, and began to burn. He stood up and turned around to face her victoriously.

"You have no . . . no *authority* to use that peat!" she cried.

"Aye, I think I do," he said confidently. "I am hand-fasted to you, lass. That makes me king of a sort in this little castle, and I will no' tolerate your freezing for no other reason than that you are stubborn and fearful of squandering a block of peat when it grows in abundance all over this glen!"

"You are entirely too arrogant! It hardly matters what you will tolerate, for this is *my* home, and that . . . that bloody handfasting is a farce. It gives you no rights here!"

"Does it no', indeed?"

"It does no'!"

Jack smiled wickedly and withdrew two tapers from the pocket of his greatcoat. He held them up just out of her reach, wiggling them playfully. "Then you best tell Mrs. Kincade so, for she gave them over the moment I asked."

Two beeswax tapers! Lizzie used them sparingly, and only when Charlotte complained of the smell the cruder tallow candles emitted. She lunged for the candles, but Jack held them high above his head, just out of her reach. She gasped with outrage and tried to slap his arm down and Jack . . .

Jack . . .

The color of his eyes changed before her very sight, turning a dark, smoky gray that snaked through her body like a trail of smoke. "Ask me," he said huskily.

He confused her—Lizzie wasn't certain what he meant.

"Ask me," he said again. "Beg me. If you want it, Lizzie, you must say it."

Say it. Say it. "I want it," she said softly.

"Want what?" he pressed her.

Lizzie looked at his mouth, words failing her. The moment was powerfully magnetic; Jack let the candles drop carelessly from his fingers and grabbed her up in both arms at the same moment his lips found hers. He did not ask her permission, just kissed her passionately as he tightened his embrace, crushing her to him as if he were afraid she would fly away if he let go.

Lizzie didn't recognize herself—the thing between them that had been building since their first night in the turret, the thing that had vexed her, disturbed her, but had also given her a sense of security on a narrow ledge today, erupted. The tormenting touch of his lips on hers jolted her to the core and rattled every bone, lit every patch of her skin that he touched. Her body seemed to blend into his before her mind could register what was happening. She clung to the warmth of his lips, to the breadth of his shoulders, the strength of his arms.

A moan rumbled deep in Jack's chest; he crushed her to him, nipping at her lips, sucking them, licking them, his tongue swirling around hers. Lizzie forgot the cold, the candles, she forgot everything but Jack. She was emboldened by the clash of his hunger, her emotions and her desire.

Lizzie's heart was pumping furiously, her breath snatched from her lungs. She eagerly explored his mouth with hers, his body with her hands, dragging through his hair, stroking his face, cupping his chin.

He groaned again and suddenly lifted her off her feet, setting her on her father's desk and dipping down to the hollow of her throat, the only bit of skin he could see outside all the wool she wore. "I can feel your heart beating here," he said roughly.

"It's beating too fast," she whispered fearfully, for it felt as if it would fly out of her chest.

"No, no," he said, and took her hand, pressed it against his chest so that she could feel his heartbeat. "Your heart leads all else," he said. "It is life, it is instinct, and it is the essence of a woman, aye? What you are feeling is quite normal. But when your heart moves, it causes mine to move. When it beats so quickly, it warms your skin, and I . . ." He drew a breath, brushed his knuckles across her cheek. "I must touch it. You lick your lips, and I canna resist kissing them."

Lizzie's lips parted; Jack kissed her tenderly.

"You close your eyes," he said softly, "and I must wake the woman in you. You feel the desire for it between your legs, and I must satify it. I am a man, and that is what a man must do for a woman."

Let a man be a man. . . . Mungo Beattie's words came

floating back to her, and as a bit of peat flared bright and hard, Lizzie dropped her head back.

Jack ravished her neck, his mouth exploring, his hands caressing. His lips seared her skin; his tongue scorched her earlobe, and his warm breath on her neck sent a white-hot shiver of anticipation shimmering down her spine. His hand swept the swell of her hips, pushed her body into his. The hard ridge of his erection excited her and she inhaled a ragged, ravenous breath.

"*Mi Diah*, Lizzie," Jack said, cupping her face with his hands, pressing his forehead to hers. "*Mi Diah*. Do you know the power you possess? Do you know that with a look, a sigh, you can reduce a man to such need?"

He kissed her again, slid his hands to her shoulders, then her rib cage, sliding them down to her hips. One hand slid down her leg, to her ankle, his hand beneath the hem of her gown and her cloak.

His hand on her leg. Her skin shivered where he caressed her. *She should stop him, stop him before it was too late, before she did the very thing she would surely regret all her days, the thing that would lead her to complete ruin.*

"I shouldn't," she whispered.

"But you can no' stop yourself, aye? The power you hold over me excites you and makes you mad with desire. You can no' stop because you take pity on my need to bring your release; and by your kiss, you show me mercy."

Oh, he was a rogue, a rogue with the poetry to seduce her! But he was correct that her response to him was instinctive, flowering inside her, freed by Jack's masterful lips, by his words and the way he said her name, the way his hands glided over her body as if she were fragile.

She encircled his neck with her arms, pressed her lips to his cheek, to his ear, his jaw, teasing him with the tip of her tongue. She kissed him as if she'd kissed a million times before, when in fact he was the first man she'd ever truly kissed.

As his hand moved up her leg to the soft flesh of her inner thigh, she felt almost frenzied. She wanted to breathe, to laugh, to cry out and demand he stop all at once. He stroked her thigh, kissed her face and neck, but when his fingers brushed the apex of her legs, Lizzie gasped at the sensation.

"You must allow me this," he said breathlessly and stroked her again, the sensation of it running through her like a river. "*Leannan*, have mercy. Allow me this," he whispered, and sank his fingers into her folds and began to stroke her.

It was astounding and searing. She fought for breath, clinging to his shoulders. Jack was transporting her away from Thorntree, away from the hardship of her life, from Carson, from debt, from everything but him. She could feel the pleasure building in her, the damp warmth. He anchored her with one arm around her waist as his strokes grew fevered. His dark eyes were intent on hers as he watched her succumb to his touch.

"*Jack*," she said, her voice rough and hoarse and strange to her own ears.

He whispered something, words she couldn't grasp as he moved his hand boldly and intimately between her legs until her body shattered with physical pleasure. Over and over again she felt the waves of it spilling over her, and as she tried to find her bearings, she was certain she heard him say, "*For you . . .*"

When at last she could breathe, Jack slowly removed his hand from beneath her skirt. He was as breathless as she. He pulled her hands from his neck and kissed them both.

Blood was pumping through her veins again, and Lizzie's senses slowly swam to the surface. She was captivated, entranced by what had just happened to her, but she was also mortified by her behavior. How could she have allowed it to happen? "Jack—"

"No," he said, and pressed his palm against her cheek. "Donna say a word, lass. Donna deny what you are feeling."

She did not deny that she was feeling elation. Adoration. And shock at her headlong fall from virtue without so much as a whimper of protest. Lizzie did not speak, for if she did, she feared she would ask for more, far more than Jack could or should give her.

She looked away and pressed the rumpled decree that she still held in her hand against Jack's chest.

He covered her hand with his. Lizzie slid her hand out from beneath it, leaving the decree pinned against his chest, and looked at him from the corner of her eye.

Jack offered his free hand to her and helped her off her father's desk.

"I'll have a look," he said, indicating the decree, watching her closely. But that was all he said. *I'll have a look.* There were no declarations of esteem, no smiles. "I'll work here, if you donna mind."

She was more than happy to let him do so—she had the urge to flee, to think. But as she walked out of her father's study, there was one thing Lizzie was entirely certain of—Jack might regret what had just happened, but he had seen the heavens shimmer a little too.

She walked away without looking back, her arms folded tightly across her, her curls, having come out of the ribbon, bouncing around her shoulders. An exquisite warmth still tingled through her and the feel of his hands on her body still lingered.

So did the very real fear that she was in serious trouble because of it, that she'd made a horrible, irrevocable mistake.

If she'd looked back, she might have seen Jack sink heavily onto a chair, grasp his head in his hands, and stare dumbly at the decree, for his heart was still divining, still seeking her, and that had sent him into a vortex of discomfiture.

Chapter Twenty-five

In the sitting room, Jack fought the urge to slip back through the door into Lizzie's bedroom and finish what he'd started. Heaven knew his body was desperate for him to do so. But as he stood at the door, one hand on the knob, he knew he could not take her virtue, the only thing she had left to her.

He couldn't do that to himself for that matter. He'd have a difficult time leaving her if he did, and he would eventually leave. He could not remain here. Lizzie could not come with him, not with a sister who needed her, and London was impossible for Charlotte. It would never work.

Jack removed his hand from the doorknob and moved away.

He crept out the next morning, stepping over a sleeping Dougal. He had his horse saddled before dawn and spent the better part of an hour waiting for the day's light to show itself.

He was feeling uncommonly restive, his emotions and actions increasingly unmanageable. He'd told himself after the first kiss in her bedroom that he was a bloody fool. But after last night . . .

After last night he felt his head and his heart engaged in some internal war. He couldn't sleep for it, and had decided, somewhere in those predawn hours, that he should find something to occupy his hands and his thoughts other than Lizzie.

He'd toyed with the idea of riding on, leaving the handfasting behind. But he obviously didn't like the idea of encountering bounty hunters, who, if Dougal's brother Donald could be believed, were nearing Glenalmond. But, more important, Jack didn't like the idea of leaving Lizzie with Carson's scheme. He didn't trust that man, and believed Carson had an evil streak. He was afraid what might happen to Lizzie if he didn't discover Carson's scheme first.

Jack knew the answer was in the hills north of Thorntree. He just had to find it. When the sun at last began to pinken the day, Jack set off to find the piece of slate for which he'd paid handsomely, and he intended to spend the better part of the day on the roof. Let Lizzie walk about the house with her hair down around her shoulders and her blue eyes glittering with the happy occupation of housework.

Jack found the slate easily enough; it was still beside the road where it had fallen. He also found the forest path, and leaving his horse behind, he walked up again.

Three quarters of an hour later, Jack returned to where he'd tethered the mare, lashed the slate on the horse's rump, and set off in the direction of Thorntree. He'd found nothing when he'd gone farther up the hill. Where the men had disappeared to yesterday was an even bigger mystery today.

Fortunately, his ploy of sending Dougal along to ask about tar last evening had worked very well—Dougal and Kincade met him in the barn with a block of peat and a kettle. The ash from the peat would make the tar.

Dougal was quite agitated. "Ye're no' to go off without me, milord," he said sternly.

"Aye. I apologize, Dougal," Jack said, clapping him on the shoulder.

Dougal frowned. He clearly expected an argument, and when he didn't have one from Jack, he gestured to the contents of the kettle and said cheerfully, "Far sight from yer normal occupation, aye, milord?"

"Mmm," Jack said.

Dougal scratched his belly. "I fancy ye donna see the inside of a barn often, aye?"

"Rarely."

"But have ye seen inside the king's barns?" Mr. Kincade asked, peering up at him. "What's it got, bits of ermine and mink for the horses to lay on?"

Dougal laughed, but Kincade's expression never changed.

"No ermine or mink," Jack said. "I've seen only one royal stable, mind you, and it didn't seem very different from most, other than it was rather large."

"Oh?" Dougal said, his eyes lighting with the hope of another tale. "The king rides, does he?"

Jack told them a little tale about hunting with the king. There was nothing remarkable about the story; it was really rather lackluster. But Dougal and Kincade were so enthralled with the image of the king hunting, particularly having heard from Jack that the prince was not an avid hunter, that Jack embellished the tale a wee bit for their benefit. In his version, the king brought down a stag instead of riding back to Balmoral empty-handed.

When the tar was of the thickness and texture Kincade deemed appropriate, Jack climbed up the ladder. It was quite strenuous, he discovered quickly. His shoulders and back burned with the repetition of the work, but Jack ignored it. This was something he could do, and would keep him away from Lizzie. With Dougal's assistance, he moved methodically across the roof, patching holes.

After working a solid two hours, Jack sent Dougal in search of Kincade and more tar. He sat on the roof for a bit, admiring the view of the glen from his perch.

He'd forgotten how beautiful Scotland was. There was really no place quite like it. He felt drawn to the hills and the people in a way he'd never been drawn to London. Even his distaste for Lambourne Castle was a result of the memories there, not for the land itself. He closed his eyes and turned his face to the sun until a voice lifted him from his rumination.

His breath caught at the sight of Lizzie walking up from the hothouse, her hair around her shoulders. She was singing softly to herself, an old Highland tune he recognized from his youth. She wore a plain blue muslin gown, the arisaidh wrapped loosely around her arms, apparently unaware that the tails of it were dragging the ground behind her. On her arm she carried a basket filled with what looked like foxglove.

She suddenly paused and looked up, directly at him.

Jack raised his hand in greeting.

Lizzie shielded her eyes from the sun and took several steps forward. "*Jack?*"

"Good morning!" he called.

She hurried toward the house, disappearing from his view.

A moment later her curly auburn head popped up at the top of the ladder. "What are you doing up here?" she exclaimed.

"Patching your roof, which it desperately needs. You should no' be on the ladder, lass. You could very well fall and break your neck. Go down, now," he said, gesturing for her to go down.

But Lizzie wasn't listening to him. She glanced around, noticed the freshly patched spots on the roof. "Did Dougal do this?" she asked, her voice full of confusion.

"*Dougal?*" he responded indignantly.

"Newton, then?"

"I beg your pardon, but I am perfectly capable of patching a roof!"

"Are you?" she asked, peering at him curiously. "I would no' have thought it."

Jack sighed, exasperated. "Tea and crumpets again?"

"Well . . . now that you mention it," she said with a winsome smile. "But you need no' patch our roof, Jack."

"*Leannan*, you are in dire need a new roof altogether. Frankly, all of Thorntree is in need of repair."

"Aye, I am aware," she said with a sigh. She glanced around the roof, then turned to him with a smile so sunny that he felt a little weak for it. "How shall I ever thank you?"

He could think of a way or two, but said, "*Ach*," and flicked his wrist.

"It is *quite* something, all this work, for a man who is unaccustomed to . . . well, to working," she said gingerly.

"Might you say it in a way that does no' make me seem such a wastrel?"

"Thank you," she said, still beaming. "And before the spring rains! Charlotte will be so pleased no' to worry over leaks."

"Ho, there, milord!" Dougal called from below. "More tar!"

"I'll be down straightaway, Mr. Dougal!" Lizzie called down, then looked at Jack. "I am learning," she said with a smile as she started down, "that you are no' as underfoot as I'd feared."

He wished she wouldn't smile. At least not *that* particular smile, the one punctuated by pretty dimples on her face, for it warmed him like a good wine. In all honesty, he was mortally afraid of what he might do for the favor of that smile. "Your flattery is obvious and will earn you naugh'," he said with a smile. "Mind that you have a care going down."

She waved her fingers at him, and just before her head dipped below the eaves, Jack waved his fingers at her, already wishing she'd come back.

He didn't see Lizzie again that afternoon, not until he'd finished the last hole and stood up, straddling the roof's ridge, to stretch his aching back. The sound of an approaching horseman reached him and Jack looked up the road toward Castle Beal. The rider was moving far too fast on the pitted road. He assumed it was Carson or one of his henchmen, come to ensure his stranglehold on Thorntree and renew his threats to Jack of hanging and ruin. But as the rider neared, Jack could see it was not Carson.

Bounty hunter, he thought.

A feminine cry of delight just below startled him. Lizzie ran out onto the drive and up to the iron gate, clinging to the bars, craning to see around the posts.

The rider came to a hard stop outside the gates, and the man threw himself off the horse and strode toward her. He was a tall, well-built man. He had golden brown hair, and clothes that suggested he had some means.

As he neared the gate, Lizzie flung it open, and while Jack stood on the roof feeling like an arse, Lizzie ran to that man, threw her arms around him, and hugged him tightly. They exchanged words that Jack could not make out, the man kissed Lizzie's forehead, and then, with their arms wrapped around each other's waists, they hurried to the house, disappearing from his view again.

A strange weight suddenly descended on him and Jack sat heavily on the roof, drew his knees up, and planted his arms on them, staring out into blue sky. It was ridiculous that he should feel so cross of a sudden, but he did, monstrously so.

Lizzie's knight had arrived.

Chapter Twenty-six

Of course Gavin had come as soon as he'd received Lizzie's letter. How could he not? He was a gentleman, and a gentleman did not ignore a lady's cry for help. He was also a Highlander, and a Highlander had his honor—and the honor of his woman—to defend.

He was fond of Lizzie and always had been; she was a pretty Scotswoman with a lot of spunk. Granted, Gavin was three years her junior, but nevertheless, when he thought of conjugal felicity, and he thought of that quite a lot, Lizzie seemed perfectly suited to him.

Gavin was enraged by the bloody handfasting. He knew Carson Beal was a bastard, but this went beyond the pale. He could not imagine what Carson hoped to achieve by it. He agreed it was a ridiculous ploy to make him cry off, and he steadfastly believed Lizzie's letter in which she'd written that nothing had happened between her and the earl.

If Carson Beal thought a handfasting would run Gavin off, he was mistaken. If anything, it had only heightened a stubborn determination to marry Lizzie.

Oddly enough, Gavin's father wasn't as bothered by the handfasting. He treated Gavin's concerns about the recklessness, the impropriety, and the potential reflection on the Gordons lightly. But his father had agreed with

Gavin that he must go to Lizzie and confirm his commitment to her and attempt to have the forced handfasting set aside.

In Thorntree's small library, Gavin admired Lizzie as she paced in her blue gown and with her hair tied loosely at her nape, her eyes wide and shining. His mind wandered briefly to the children they would have, with their mother's auburn hair and blue eyes, and with his strength and stature and last name. He thought about the long, cold Highland nights and imagined Lizzie lying naked beside him, her eyes glittering with the satisfaction of lovemaking.

Those thoughts made him even angrier about the handfasting.

"Lizzie," Gavin said, attempting to interrupt a very long discourse on the depraved animal her uncle Carson Beal had turned out to be.

"A *jackal*," she said firmly. "That is the kindest thing that can be said for him."

"*Lizzie.*"

She paused in her pacing, blinking at him. "Aye?"

"Where is this"—he waved his hand a bit—"earl?" he asked tightly.

"Oh. Him. Patching the roof. Or at least he was the last I saw him." At Gavin's startled look, she shrugged a bit. "I . . . I think he desired an occupation."

Gavin would give the earl an occupation—shining his boots. He stood up and took Lizzie's hand, leading her to a chair. "Sit, lass," he said firmly.

Lizzie paled as she looked at the seat he indicated. She pressed her palms against her gown and carefully took the seat, sitting on the very edge of it, her hands folded in her lap, looking up at him with luminous blue eyes.

Gavin flipped the tails of his coat and sat across from

her. He reached out, put his hand on hers. "You need no' look so fearful, Lizzie," he said, trying to remain calm in spite of his anger. He did not want to frighten her. "I believe what you've told me. I believe Carson has done this to ruin any understanding between us. But I am no' a coward, lass. I will no' back down so easily."

"Thank you," she said, looking quite relieved.

"What is the arrangement here?" he asked.

Lizzie blinked.

"Where does he sleep?"

"Ah. *Ahem.* Ah . . . Mr. Newton p-put him in my rooms. But I have made him sleep in the sitting room," she added quickly.

"Pardon?" Gavin asked.

Lizzie pressed her lips together.

"A sitting room that we use for storage. *Ahem* . . . adjacent to my bedroom."

"Is this known to everyone?" he demanded, removing his hand.

"To Charlotte and the Kincades," she said.

"Anyone else?"

She seemed to shrink. "The Sorley Beals and the McLennans."

"*Mi Diah.*"

"I must—"

"Donna say it," he said, throwing up a hand. "Lizzie, he must cry off. I donna care that he is a wanted man, he must cry off."

"Aye," she said, nodding adamantly that he should. "We signed only one paper."

"A paper."

"We put our names to the vow," she said weakly.

Gavin stood and walked to the window, looking out at the sunny day.

"What if . . . what if he will no' cry off?" she asked.

"We'll find another way to dissolve the handfasting," he said gruffly. He had no idea how he might accomplish it, but he would find a way. He glanced over his shoulder at Lizzie. She seemed to have wilted in her chair.

"I'll have a word with the earl," Gavin said authoritatively. "You've been through quite enough as it is, and really, this is a man's business."

Lizzie drew a breath as if she intended to speak.

He looked curiously at her. "Aye?"

"I . . . I'd no' consider it . . . *completely*, that is . . . only a . . . a *man's* business."

"Pardon?"

"Well," she said, squirming a bit, "it would seem that it is *all* of our business . . . would it no'?"

That was one thing he admired about Lizzie. She was intelligent and appreciated her independence. He returned to her side, took her hand, and squeezed it. "This is between me and the earl, lass. And once I've dispatched him, we may turn our attention to our future."

She blinked again. Her plump lips formed a perfect *O*, and her gaze darted to the window, then to him. "Ah," she said. And smiled. "Thank you."

Such a lovely smile. He ran his hand up her arm, to her cheek. "I've missed you, Lizzie," he said softly. "It seems that sometimes we are separated by an ocean instead of a few hills, aye? I should like a way to see you more frequently until we can begin our life together."

"I would welcome that," she said.

He wanted to say more, but the earl was looming in his mind. He could not think of the future with the man about. "Where are Carson's men?"

"Mr. Newton and Mr. Dougal donna know you've come. Once word reaches Carson . . ."

"Donna fret—I'll have this all tidied up for you in no time."

She nodded and smiled, but the smile did not radiate through her eyes. Ah, well, she fretted yet. As far as Gavin was concerned, this charade was coming to an end. "Where is the earl?" he asked.

Lizzie stood up and looked at him with clear blue eyes. "On the roof," she reminded him quietly. "Thank you, Mr. Gordon. You are too kind to have come so quickly to my rescue. I shall never be able to thank you properly."

Gavin smiled warmly, imagining all the ways that she might thank him properly.

Once the business of this handfasting was done, naturally.

The roof patched, and the instruments of his labor returned to the barn, Jack glanced down at his hands and clothing. He was covered with the soot of ashes and streaks of tar.

"You've a bit of tar on your face, milord," Kincade noted.

"Mmm," Jack said.

" 'Tis a heavenly foresight ye must have, then, to patch that old roof, milord, for the missus feels snow in her bones again."

"Oh?" Jack asked casually as he tried to wipe his hands with a cloth. "And do her bones portend when?"

"A day or two, milord." He handed Jack a cake of lye soap. "Ye canna wipe the tar."

Jack took the cake of soap and the cloth. "Tell me, Mr. Kincade, what magic must a man possess to have a hot bath drawn here?"

"I'll ask me wife, milord, but she'll be about the business of the evening meal and need the kettle for that."

In other words, she'd not be very happy to turn the kettle over to the task of heating water. Jack sighed. He took the cake of soap and the cloth and headed to the icy waters of the river.

He cleaned himself as best he could—he would insist on a hot bath this evening if he had to draw it himself—and started back to the house. As he trudged up the path to the unkempt back lawn, he thought he heard the sound of laughter and paused.

His first thought was Lizzie with her bloody knight. How quickly she'd found the time and place to entice him! He moved immediately toward the laughter, abandoning the path and following the sound, picking his way around the detritus of the forest floor until he could see a stretch of grassy bank of the river. But instead of finding Lizzie laughing and carrying on with her knight as he fully expected, what he saw took his breath away.

Charlotte was seated in a chair at the river's edge, holding a fishing pole of all things. Behind her the prodigious Newton was leaning over her shoulder, instructing her how to hold the pole, how to bring the line in.

In the course of his instruction, something caught Charlotte's line. She gave a squeal of delight at the tug as Newton scrambled around her chair and steadied her pole. Charlotte laughed at him, and the sound of it was so sweet, so full of unexpected joy, that Jack was moved by it.

He slowly backed up and quietly returned to the path that led up to the lawn. He walked with his head down, his thoughts on Charlotte. The most remarkable thing about Charlotte on the banks of the river was not her gay laugh, but the fact that she was smiling. Genuinely *smiling*.

As he was thinking of that glorious smile, Jack did

not sense that anyone shared the path with him until he heard someone clear his throat. His head snapped up and his gaze landed on the young man who had ridden so recklessly to the gate.

The man's gaze narrowed menacingly, and Jack suppressed a tedious sigh.

"Lambourne?" he asked coldly, bracing his legs apart, his fists at his sides, as if he were prepared to grapple with Jack should the need arise.

"You must be Lizzie's knight, then," Jack said.

The knight's gaze raked over Jack's soiled clothing, the wet ends of his neckcloth, and the soap and cloth he carried. "I'll ask only once. Who are you?"

"I am Jankin Haines, Earl of Lambourne, at your service," Jack said, and clicked his heels, bowing low with an exaggerated flourish.

"I thought as much," the young man said, his voice dripping with derision.

"And you, sir knight? Have you a proper name, other than Lizzie's savior?"

"I am no' a *knight*," the young man said. "I am Gavin Gordon of Glencochill."

"How do you do, Mr. Gordon," Jack said. "And now that we've made the inevitable and unavoidable introductions, will you please excuse me? I've had a rather long day and I should like a bath." Jack moved to step around Gordon.

But Mr. Gordon was indeed Lizzie's knight, for he threw up his hand, his palm facing Jack. "You are too hasty, milord. I would have a word. The situation in which Miss Beal finds herself with you is insupportable and must be dealt with straightaway."

"I could no' possibly agree more," Jack said, and attempted to step around him again.

"You must cry off," Gordon said sternly. "You must cry off and leave Thorntree at once. After the damage you've wrought, it is the only gentlemanly thing you might do."

All right, then, Jack was prepared to let this young buck feel his oats, but he would not stand for *that*. "The damage *I* have wrought? The only gentlemanly thing I might *do*? Do you think, Mr. Gordon, that I somehow concocted this ridiculous scheme to steal your precious Lizzie from you?"

"Donna speak about Miss Beal as if you are a close acquaintance, sir," Gordon snapped. "You may no' have concocted this scheme, but you are a man and you should no' have agreed to the handfasting if Miss Beal did no' desire it. Your actions could very well have ruined her."

Jack turned to face him fully, looking him over head to foot, assessing him. He was at least ten years younger and not without good looks. He had a strong build, but he was not as muscular as Jack, or as tall. His clothing was not of the first cut, but it was suitable. At the very least, Jack reckoned the knight would keep food on a table and a roof over Lizzie's head. And he did possess a bit of mettle. He'd need that in order to go toe-to-toe with her.

Aye, Jack supposed Gordon would do for Lizzie in the absence of any suitable man in Glenalmond. "Lad," he said, "you need no' fear my intentions. There is naugh' at Thorntree that could possibly entice me to stay. As soon as I might slip away without causing a bit of trouble up the hill, I'll be gone." He gave him a smile and stepped around him.

Gordon caught his arm. "You'll cry off and you'll go," he said flatly.

His grip was strong, and that infuriated Jack. With a violent jerk, he freed his arm. "Do no' presume to tell me what to do."

"You will remove your presence from her private rooms, put yourself on a horse, and go."

"I may as well hand myself over to bounty hunters," Jack said.

"Hand yourself over to the *diabhal* for all that I care," Gordon said icily. "Just leave."

"Bloody simpleton, suppose I did precisely that?" Jack said angrily. "You'll still be left with the issue of Carson's desire to have Thorntree. Are you prepared to marry her without that as a dowry, Gordon?"

Gordon blinked.

"As I thought," Jack said acidly. Gordon was playing the part of the noble gentleman quite well, out to protect the virtue of the woman who would, by all indications, become his wife . . . unless the dowry should slip away. Jack ignored the sharp prick that thought gave him and decided that the best way to soothe the young man's ruffled feathers was to allow him to think he'd won the battle and perhaps even the war.

"I happen to agree that Miss Lizzie deserves better than the likes of me." He smiled down the small irritation to his conscience that remark caused him. "I'd be gone from Thorntree now if I could but determine what it is that Carson Beal wants from it."

Gordon's face mottled with his confusion.

"Aye, there is something at Thorntree that he wants," Jack continued. "Something he'd have for himself, something that he is loath to leave to Miss Lizzie . . . or her future husband."

"What do you mean?" Gordon demanded.

"I donna rightly know. But once I've determined what it is he wants, I might negotiate with him, aye? Perhaps I might save my neck and Lizzie's reputation."

"That's ridiculous," Gordon said sternly. "There can

be nothing at Thorntree that he'd want. Look around you, milord. It is a small estate with no income."

"Aye, a small estate with no income, but mark me—there is something here that does no' meet the eye."

"You can study it from some place other than Thorntree," Gordon said stubbornly, clearly not as concerned about bounty hunters as Jack was. "I donna want you near her, aye?" He stepped forward, so that his face was quite close to Jack's. "I donna want you to speak with her, to look at her, to touch her. You do any of those things, and I will kill you."

"If I were you, I'd cease threatening me," Jack said evenly.

"Or *what*, pray tell?" Gordon sneered.

"Or I will kill you first," Jack said, and swung so fast that Gordon didn't have time to react before he connected with his jaw. But Gordon was quick on his feet and swung right back.

Jack had no idea how many blows were landed before someone pulled them apart—pulled Jack off Gordon, he smugly noted, and held him back. It was Dougal; Newton had Gordon in hand.

"Ye're no' to be here, Gordon," Newton said angrily, and began to drag him away. When they had cleared the path, Dougal let go of Jack and handed him a handkerchief. Jack touched it to his lip. It was bleeding. He could not remember the last time he'd fought another man with his bare hands, but he'd found this scrap oddly invigorating.

Gordon thought he would keep Jack from Lizzie? Preposterous! The place was so small he couldn't avoid her if he tried. As if he could inhabit the same bit of Highland air as she and not breathe it!

Preposterous. *Impossible.*

～～

Lizzie heard about the commotion from Mrs. Kincade, who sought her out in the hothouse, where she'd taken refuge. "It's an awful to-do, Miss Lizzie," she said with a shake of her head. "They've bound your Mr. Gordon to a chair!"

Lizzie cried out with alarm, dropped the spade she held, and flew to the house, still wearing her apron.

She found them in the small front parlor. Newton and Dougal flanked Mr. Gordon, who was indeed trussed to a chair. Jack was sitting on the settee, nursing a cut on his lip. It was obvious both men had been involved in a fight. *"Mi Diah!"* Lizzie cried. "Untie him! Untie him at once!"

"I canna do that, Miss Lizzie," Newton said stoically. "Gordon is no' allowed here on my laird's orders, and if I let him go, he'll bring the prince's men down around our ears."

"By all that is holy, I'll see you all brought down!" Mr. Gordon roared, and tried to wrest free of his ties, managing only to move the chair a few inches before Dougal stopped him.

"You can no' leave him tied up like this!" Lizzie cried.

"You had no objections when they restrained me," Jack pointed out petulantly.

"And why should she? You're a bloody nuisance!" Mr. Gordon shouted.

Newton suddenly pointed a gun to the ceiling and cocked it, gaining everyone's attention instantly.

"Rather dramatic, is it no'?" Jack asked tetchily.

"Lads," Newton said with a scowl for Jack, "we'll come to a reasonable solution, aye?" He looked at Mr. Gordon. "As I see it, sir, ye donna want to leave Miss Lizzie alone here with the earl, and no one here blames ye in the least."

"I beg your pardon!" Jack protested.

"And *ye* donna want anyone handing ye over to the prince's men," Newton said to Jack. "No one here will fault ye for no' wanting to hang just yet, aye? Ye both need a bit of time to put everything to rights, so I think we might agree to a gentleman's understanding."

"What in *diabhal* do you mean?" Mr. Gordon demanded.

"I mean that we'll hide ye from the laird, as much as it pains me to do it," Newton said. "And we'll hide the earl from the bounty hunters. Ye'll both be safe here for a time."

"Toward what end?" Jack demanded.

Newton shrugged. "Until ye determine what is to be done."

"Ridiculous," Mr. Gordon said. "I'd rather remain tied to the chair."

But Newton looked at Lizzie. "Miss Lizzie?"

She looked at Jack, then at Mr. Gordon. "We've no other choice, aye?" she said reluctantly. "Mr. Gordon, we've no choice," she said again. "I canna let you bring the prince's men here. And if Carson discovers you are here, I shudder to think what he might do. We must have a plan, would you agree?"

He considered that a moment before giving her a terse nod.

She looked at Jack.

He glared at Lizzie, then at Mr. Gordon. "I shall do whatever allows me to quit Thorntree at the earliest convenience—short of being handed over to those wretched bounty hunters."

"Then you must move out of her suite," Mr. Gordon said. "I will no' settle for less!"

"I will keep to Charlotte's suite," Lizzie said quickly.

"And precisely where will *you* be?" Jack snapped at Mr. Gordon.

"The nursery," Newton said. "I shall keep an eye on him as Dougal has kept an eye on you."

"Splendid," Jack said, and gained his feet. "Then it seems we've solved today's dilemma. So if you will excuse me, gentlemen. Lizzie." He bowed and stalked out of the room.

Lizzie looked at Mr. Gordon. He was watching her closely. Too closely. "I should see to Charlotte," she said, and hurried away from the parlor.

Chapter Twenty-seven

L izzie quickly removed her apron, straightened her clothing and her hair as best she could, then went to Charlotte. The day was growing very gray, she noted; it would snow soon. So many angry men in the house made her nervous.

Fortunately, Charlotte seemed unaware of the fracas and quite at ease. She was in her room, reading. It was the same tableau Lizzie had seen countless time, but this time there was something slightly different. "Your hair looks as if you've been outside without a bonnet," Lizzie said curiously as she pulled the pins from it to brush it. "Did Mrs. Kincade no' come to you, then?"

"She came," Charlotte said idly. "But Mr. Newton took me out of doors."

"What?" Lizzie cried. "He took you *out*? How dare he!"

"It's all right, Lizzie," Charlotte said. "It was a lovely day, and I've no' been out in some time."

"But—"

"He was very kind to do it," Charlotte said calmly. "I thought there was no harm. After all, the only thing I do is sit and sit and sit, aye?" She turned the page of her book. "I had forgotten what it smells like."

"What?" Lizzie asked, confused.

"Winter," Charlotte said.

Lizzie took so many things for granted. She brushed Charlotte's hair a few moments. "Did Newton happen to say anything of Carson? Anything that might help us?"

"No' a word!" Charlotte said. "He'll chat *my* ear off, he will, but he's stubbornly loyal to Carson and will no' speak ill of him."

Amazingly, Charlotte did not scoff when she said it, nor did she make a face. Lizzie peered at her closely in the mirror but Charlotte averted her gaze. "What will Mrs. Kincade serve this evening? We've no' enough chickens to feed the masses, have we?"

"Rabbit hotpot," Lizzie said.

"Rabbit hotpot!" Charlotte exclaimed. "If that is no' an indication that we've got one foot in the poorhouse!" She began to complain about the strain so many people were having on their paltry stores, concluding that only Jesus and his ability to change water into wine would save them now.

Lizzie did not interrupt Charlotte's nattering on about the poor quality of their evening fare, and watched her shrewdly. She knew very well that her obstinate sister had somehow come to esteem Mr. Newton, whether she chose to admit it or not. Lizzie was pleased for her, then, for Charlotte was in desperate need of a friend, and really, beyond his unfathomable attachment to his laird, Newton had shown Charlotte a kindness that no one else had. Lizzie grudgingly realized that she was glad he was about.

"I have news," she said as she put the finishing touches on Charlotte's hair. "Mr. Gordon has come."

"Oh, Lizzie!" Charlotte said brightly. "At last! Wait . . . why do you look so unhappy? I thought you'd be over-joyed!"

Lizzie started. Did she look unhappy? "I am happy, of

course I am! But there has been a wee bit of . . . of friction between Mr. Gordon and the earl."

"Naturally!" Charlotte said laughingly. "What did you expect?"

"I hardly know what I expected," Lizzie said truthfully.

"Make haste," Charlotte said eagerly, sensing a bit of excitement. "Let us go and greet Mr. Gordon."

A quarter of an hour later, when Lizzie wheeled Charlotte into the drawing room, or rather, tried to maneuver past the four dogs who met them at the threshold, they found Mr. Gordon and Mr. Newton within, the tension between them as thick as Highland fog.

Jack, Lizzie noted with a twinge of disappointment, was nowhere to be seen.

"Miss Charlotte," Mr. Gordon said tightly, moving to take the chair from Lizzie. "How well you look this evening."

"I am so happy you have come, Mr. Gordon," Charlotte said. She looked at Newton and smiled. "Mr. Newton."

"Good evening, all," Lizzie said.

Newton nodded curtly and stood with his arms folded, watching Mr. Gordon closely as he wheeled Charlotte to the hearth. Bean jumped into her lap, settling there and eyeing Newton suspiciously. Fingal and Tavish, the largest dogs, meandered about the room having a good sniff of it, while Red plopped down near the door.

"Whisky, sirs?" Lizzie asked.

"No, thank you," Mr. Gordon said. Newton likewise shook his head. Lizzie moved to the sideboard nonetheless. She would not subject herself to such a strained evening without a wee bit of wine. And if a wee bit would soothe her, a generous amount would drain her of all anxiety, so she helped herself to a full glass of it, and set aside a glass for Jack, for when he appeared. She had no doubt he would appear. The only question was when and in what frame of mind.

"Are acquainted with Newton?" Charlotte asked Mr. Gordon.

"I was forced to make his acquaintance," Mr. Gordon answered curtly.

"Pardon?"

"Mr. Gordon wanted Lambourne to leave Thorntree, naturally," Lizzie explained, catching Charlotte's gaze, "but Newton thought perhaps Mr. Gordon should go instead."

"Why?" Charlotte asked, her brow furrowing.

"Because Newton is Carson's man, and Carson prefers the sham handfasting to a legitimate marriage," Mr. Gordon said irritably.

"Ah." Charlotte looked at Newton, who did not dispute it. "Well, then," she said brightly as Mr. Kincade entered the room. "How do you like rabbit hotpot?" she asked Mr. Gordon.

"The hotpot is served, Miss Charlotte," Mr. Kincade said, bowing crookedly.

"But . . . but we are no' all present, Mr. Kincade," Lizzie said with a smile, knowing that the elderly man was not accustomed to playing the part of butler. "The earl of Lambourne has no' yet joined us," she reminded him.

"The earl took his supper with me and the missus, Miss Lizzie," Mr. Kincade said. "He and Mr. Dougal are bedding down the animals. Missus says it will snow tonight, it will."

"Let us dine," Mr. Gordon said, and took Lizzie by the

elbow. He nodded at Charlotte and steered Lizzie out of the room as she absorbed the news that Jack was not coming to supper.

She didn't know why she should be surprised, she thought, as Mr. Gordon helped her into her seat at the dining table. Jack had done precisely what she had tried to make him do from the start. He'd stepped aside, left her to Mr. Gordon. It was the gentlemanly thing to do, wasn't it? Considering that he might have put himself in harm's way, some might even say it was a noble gesture from a man who was unaccustomed to making noble gestures.

So why, then, did she feel so wounded by it? Why, in the course of the meal, did she think of Jack and scarcely hear a word from the man she hoped to marry? Was Jack so charming that he could—

"Lizzie, is the food no' to your liking?" Mr. Gordon asked, peering closely at her.

She reared back and looked at her bowl. She'd hardly touched it. "No, no, it's fine. I have very little appetite this evening."

"You, with the normal appetite of a horse, have none?" Charlotte asked, her tone far too disbelieving to suit Lizzie.

"No' tonight, Charlotte," Lizzie said with a pointed look for her sister.

"I am tiring you," Mr. Gordon said.

"No' in the least!"

"You're certainly no' tiring me!" Charlotte said. "Please go on, Mr. Gordon. You were saying?"

"Just that sheep is the future of the Highlands. The more sheep we can put on these rocky hills, the more wool we will export, and there is a voracious demand developing for it."

Lizzie had no idea what Charlotte said to that—she was concentrating too hard on forcing the image of Jack from her mind.

When the dishes were cleared, Mr. Gordon suggested he escort Lizzie and Charlotte to a drawing room. Newton stood.

"No' you," Mr. Gordon said coldly.

"I will invite myself, then," Newton responded just as coldly.

"Shall we have Newton read aloud?" Charlotte asked quickly. "I find him far more tolerable with an occupation than when he sits and stares at me. He's been reading to me from the novel *Cecilia*, by Frances Burney," she said. "The earl gave it to me and it's really quite good. I should like to hear more of it—that is, if it suits Mr. Gordon and you, Lizzie."

Mr. Gordon clasped his hands behind his back. "Perhaps Mr. Newton might read to you, Charlotte. If you are agreeable, I should like a private word with Lizzie."

Newton cleared his throat.

"Stand down, sir," Mr. Gordon said irritably. "I donna intend to whisk her away. I want only a word."

"It's all right, Newton," Lizzie said softly.

Newton didn't look as if he thought it was all right, but at Charlotte's nod, he took her chair in hand and quit the small dining room, with Fingal and Red accompanying them.

In the drawing room, Newton rolled Charlotte to the hearth. "There's trouble brewing," he muttered.

"Trouble has been brewing for quite some time," Charlotte said. "Go on, then, Mr. Newton. The last we heard, Cecilia was in London," she said eagerly.

Newton sighed wearily but took his seat and opened the book to the marked page. "She had met with an object whose character answered all her wishes for him with whom she should entrust her fortune, and whose turn of mind, so similar to her own, promised her the highest domestic felicity; to this object her affections had involuntarily bent. . . ."

Charlotte perched her chin on her fist, watching Newton's fine lips as he read aloud.

Chapter Twenty-eight

They repaired to the library, where Gavin insisted that the hearth be lit. He went in search of Mr. Kincade and the two of them returned with a block of peat. As he lit the fire, Lizzie perused the shelves. She withdrew one book and was scanning the pages when Gavin walked up behind her and put his hand on her waist and pressed his face to her neck.

"Mr. Gordon! I did no' hear you behind me!"

The woman had a perfect mouth. "Come and sit," he said, "I want to speak with you."

"Of course." She allowed him to show her to a settee, and sat with her hands folded over the book in her lap.

Gavin flipped his tails and sat beside her. He studied her face a moment until Lizzie smiled self-consciously. "When the snow passes, Newton will send me from Thorntree," he said abruptly.

"He will no' do such a thing," Lizzie tried to assure him.

"He will. When he does, I intend to find a magistrate to help us."

"But a magistrate will no' come to Glenalmond before spring."

"Then I will go to him," Gavin said. "And while I am

gone, you must call someone to you, aye? Mrs. Sorley Beal, perhaps."

Lizzie's confusion was evident in her slight frown. "But why?"

"*Why?*" Gavin echoed incredulously. Must he explain it? "To protect your reputation, of course, Lizzie!"

She colored. "I fear it is too late for that."

Was she so blind to what was happening here? Or was he? "Perhaps I waited too long to offer for you properly," he said in a sudden rush of guilt. "If I have no' made myself entirely clear, Lizzie, I want to marry you. I blame myself for what has happened—I wanted everything to be perfect before I asked for your hand and set a firm date."

"No, Mr. Gordon, you are no' to blame."

"I am," he insisted. "But I will set everything to rights, Lizzie. You have my word that I will." He suddenly stood up and paced before the settee. She was lovely. Had he realized how lovely she was? He looked away a moment, then looked at her again. He abruptly sat beside her. "There is something I feel compelled to tell you."

"Aye?"

"I have long—*long*—admired you. You know that I have. But I've no' been as attentive as I ought to have been—"

"You've been working hard," she offered kindly.

"Aye, but look what has happened while I was working hard, will you? We can overcome it yet, I am certain of it. But Lizzie . . . I must know what your feelings are."

She blushed and smiled uncertainly. "What do you mean?"

"You seem almost solicitous of Lambourne."

She gasped; her color deepened. "That is no' so!"

"I must know, Lizzie. Do you still esteem me as you once did? Do you still wish to make this match?"

She gaped at him. Her hands gripped the book tightly. "I would no' have sent for you otherwise! And I should be asking *you* that question," she said in a low voice. "What if this . . . this catastrophe canna be undone?"

"It can," he said firmly. He had no doubt of it.

"Carson is determined," she warned him.

"It will take a bit of maneuvering, aye, but I donna believe for a moment that Carson Beal might force you into a handfasting against your will and succeed! He's no' God, is he?"

She did not look convinced. "But if it canna be undone, for whatever reason, would . . . would you wait a year?" she asked.

Gavin hesitated. "It will no' come to that," he said flatly.

At the same moment, Fingal began to scratch at the door to go out. "Excuse me, please," Lizzie said softly, and rose to let the dog out. When she returned to her seat, she said, "I think Jack is right, Mr. Gordon. There is something here that Carson wants."

"There could no' possibly be," he scoffed. He knew these Highlands better than most. If there was something here worth having, he'd know it.

"Aye, but it is worth looking, is it no'?" Lizzie pressed. "For us?"

Us. She said it in a way that put Gavin on firm ground again. "How it fills my heart to hear you say it," he said, and took her chin in his hand, lifting her face, kissed her. "*Diah*, Lizzie, I've no' realized until now how much I care for you. And how much I *need* you." He moved to kiss her again.

But Lizzie hesitated. Her eyes were shining, full of what he believed was hope—or perhaps convinced himself was hope—and he chalked up her hesitation to maidenly nerves. He would not allow himself to think of any other possibility, not when she was looking at him as she was. He slipped his hand to her nape and touched his mouth to hers, shaping his lips to hers. He caressed the curve of her ear, her neck, and the swell of her breasts above the bodice of her gown. It was a tender, respectful kiss that belied the desire rampaging through him with each touch of her skin. He wanted to have her, all of her, and he thought himself a fool for having waited so long.

His hand slid down her shoulder to her hand, and he laced his fingers through hers, lifting it to his heart, so that she might feel how much he desired her.

When he lifted his head, she stared at her hand, pressed against his beating heart.

Gavin touched his fingers to her cheek. "I give you my word," he said solemnly, "that I shall see us through this ordeal. I shall honor and defend you as I ought, and we shall be married, and then you will know the true strength of my ardor for you, aye? I shall give you all that you deserve, Lizzie. A comfortable home. Children . . . all that you need."

"Aye," she said softly. "You will never know how grateful I am for your help."

He smiled. "I look forward to the time you might show me."

She blushed, kept her gaze down.

The sound of voices reached them; Gavin looked at the open door. The hour was late and there was much to think about, to do. "Shall we retire for the evening?"

"Go ahead if you'd like. I'll wait a bit longer so that Charlotte might have her reading before I take her up."

He didn't like leaving her alone with Lambourne skulking about, but he took Newton at his word that Lambourne would be kept apart from her. "Very good."

He leaned over and possessively kissed her forehead. "Good night, Lizzie."

"Good night, Mr. Gordon."

Lizzie watched him walk out of the library. He paused at the open door and smiled at her before walking on. But when he'd gone, Lizzie tossed aside the book she'd clung to, dropped her head against the back of the settee, and stared up at the peeling ceiling.

Funny, she'd dreamed of this for so long now that she could hardly believe it was happening. Gavin Gordon would save her from ruin. He was a gentleman, a stalwart companion, and any woman would be very happy to make a match with him.

She was happy. Aye, she was!

"Please tell me you haven't swooned with rapture," a voice rumbled from inside the room. With a squeal of surprise, Lizzie came out of her seat and whirled toward the door.

Jack was leaning against the doorjamb, a lopsided smile on his face. "My, my, Miss Lizzie, you look a wee bit flushed. Gordon's kiss is that titillating, is it?"

"You were *spying* on me?" Lizzie exclaimed angrily.

"I was no' spying," he said, shoving away from the door and walking into the library. "I was merely passing by."

"The devil you were! You seem to be constantly passing by one private conversation or another!"

"You should no' leave your door open."

"I—" She paused and frowned at the door. "Was it open, then?"

"*Wide* open," Jack said. "So very open that all the talk of devotion wafted down the hall to my eager ears."

Lizzie colored.

Jack chuckled. He glanced at the hearth. "I see that Gordon is allowed a bit of peat."

Lizzie pressed her lips together.

"Will you marry him?" Jack asked bluntly.

As if she had any other prospects. As if someone like Jack might sweep into Glenalmond and suddenly determine the bucolic life was much more to his liking than the highest reaches of London society. "Aye," she responded just as bluntly.

"Splendid. Gordon seems a pleasant enough fellow . . . if you prefer the country type."

"Is there something wrong with that?"

Jack shrugged and nudged Red with his boot. "No. In truth, he seems a good solution for you, Lizzie. Apparently you want to live a sedate life in the country. A comfortable, safe life."

Lizzie's pulse leapt with umbrage. She felt uneasy and cross.

"One lacking in true passion," Jack added silkily.

She wanted to strike out, to slap those words from his mouth. "Thank you for your unsolicited opinion, Jack. Now that I have it, I may rest easy, aye? I'm going to bed," she said, and turned away from him.

"To your safe, comfortable bed, then."

It was more than Lizzie could bear. She didn't know what made her angrier—that he could be so ill-mannered, or that she feared he was right? She jerked around, her fists clenched at her sides. Honestly, Lizzie didn't trust herself to keep her hands from his neck. And when she moved—toward him or away from him, she would never really know—a slow, languid smile curved his lips, and a devilish gleam appeared in his eye. He simply put his hand out for hers. Possessively. As if he had a right.

Inexplicably, Lizzie put her hand in his.

He slowly drew her toward him as something palpable flowed between them. Lizzie had felt it before with

Jack; it left her feeling light-headed and strangely liquid in her bones. The sensation caused her to panic slightly. "What is it, Jack?" she asked breathlessly. "Feeling a wee bit excluded?"

"No, *leannan*," he said again, using the Gaelic endearment that had the power to rile her blood. "I feel a wee bit sorry for you."

"For *me*?" she scoffed, trying to disengage from him, but his grip on her only tightened as he put his other hand on her shoulder and caressed her earlobe with his finger. "That's absurd. I am happy! I will be proud to be his wife while *you* run from someone or something!"

"You may be proud to be his wife, lass, but if you marry him, you will never know what it is to be with a man who desires you more than the air he breathes."

"You are unbearably glib," she said heatedly. "He desires me!"

Jack smiled as if he knew something she did not. "Aye, he desires you, Lizzie. Who could not desire a woman as fresh and alluring as you? But he does no' know what to *do* with you. He offers you a home and hearth instead of passion. I saw that kiss. Your man desires to be a husband above a lover."

It was true, it was *true*. Lizzie suddenly realized that Mr. Gordon's kiss had lacked the same passion, the heat, the *strength* that she felt from Jack each time he touched her. It lacked the knowledge of his ability to rouse her to anything more than a wifely duty. That Jack knew it, too, appalled and alarmed her both. "You think you know so much," she said angrily, "but you know *nothing*!"

"I know that a woman like you deserves the passion and love she wants. Lizzie, *leannan*—" He caught her chin in his hand, forced her to look at him. "You deserve to be *kissed*."

"And I suppose you think you are the one to do it! *You*, who flit about instructing women on the proper way to be kissed, only to leave at dawn's first light?"

"*Me*. Donna deny it, Lizzie—you *want* me to kiss you again. You *want* to know true, gut-aching passion. You donna want only love, you want it in all her untidy forms. You want to feel the thrill of it coursing through your veins and filling you up and making you cry out in ecstasy. I can give that to you before you bind yourself to the likes of him for all your days."

"*No*," she whispered, but he stopped her weak protest with a kiss.

Lizzie's mind cried out at her to stop him, but her heart was on another plane entirely. Her yearning to be kissed precisely as Jack described it, precisely as he was kissing her now, seemed to overtake all her common sense and decency and batter them into nothingness.

He caught her up in one arm at her waist and whirled her around, putting her back to the wall. He paused, bracing his arms on either side of her head. "You deserve to know what it is to be wholly seduced," he said roughly as his gaze moved over the crown of her head. He caressed her hair, tangled his fingers in loose curls. "You deserve to know what it feels like to be aroused to the point of weeping, to be released from that arousal in a manner that leaves you weak and short of breath. You deserve to know the raw intimacy that only a man and a woman can share," he said, and let his hand drift down her shoulder, to the swell of her breast.

Lizzie could hardly seem to catch her breath. "I think you are mad," she whispered breathlessly.

"Aye, if I'm mad, then half the world is mad with me," he said low as his gaze raked over the features of her face, lingering on her lips, sliding to the flesh of her bosom. "I think you want to know what I can teach you, Lizzie. I think you want it more than you are willing to admit even to yourself," he said, and caressed the swell of her breast with his knuckles.

She was angry, but she was astoundingly aroused by his words. Aye, aye, she did want to know his touch! She wanted it so badly that her body was quivering with a single caress! But how could she succumb to blatant seduction? She was not that sort of woman who would ruin herself for the mere pleasure of it, not when Mr. Gordon had been so good and kind to come and rescue her.

But Jack's gray gaze seared her with his intent to arouse, seduce, and make love to her, and it was her undoing. A heady feeling swirled inside her, pulsed through every vein, into every finger and every toe, pooling in her groin. Her gaze landed on his moist lips, and Lizzie felt a stirring unlike anything she'd ever felt. She wanted to feel those lips on her mouth, on her body.

Jack leaned in, so that his mouth was almost touching her cheek, his breath warm on Lizzie's skin, inflaming her even more. "I think you want to be completely and utterly seduced," he whispered, and brushed his lips across hers.

It sent her reeling. Her skin began to tingle, her breath grew even shorter. Jack kissed her again, nipping at her bottom lip, then splaying his fingers along her jaw, tilting her head back just so, he swept his tongue inside her mouth.

He dropped his arm from the wall and pressed his body against hers, so that she could feel his hard desire against her abdomen, could feel the restrained power of his arms, his torso, his legs. He moved a hand to her hip, squeezing and boldly pushing her into his body to make certain she felt it.

A dangerous conflagration erupted deep inside Lizzie and began to lick at all those places in her that weakened her resolve. She'd never experienced such desperate longing, and never as urgently as this. She felt hot inside her gown, wanted to take it off, to peel it from her body and lay herself bare to his delicious touch.

Aye, she wanted to know what he could teach her, the desire for it as strong as the desire to eat or drink, and she realized that she was pushing into him, wanting to feel every inch of him, every muscle, every hard angle, every hard ridge.

He dug his fingers into her cleavage, pushing deep into her gown until he had freed her breast. Lizzie gasped with apprehension and delight; Jack pressed his mouth against her neck at the same moment he took the tip of her breast in between his thumb and forefinger, rolling it.

She looked wildly at the open door. "*The door,*" she hissed.

But Jack did not stop. He lifted her off her feet and moved her down the wall, to the corner of the room, where they could not be seen from the corridor. He lowered her until her feet touched the ground, dipped down so that he was eye level with her, and with a sensual smile put a finger to his lips, indicating she should be quiet. How could she possibly? He was moving down her body and brazenly taking her breast into his mouth, nibbling at the peak, lashing across it with his tongue.

She gulped down a sob of pleasure and pressed the back of her head against the wall, holding his head at her breast, submerging herself in the sensation of the damp pressure of his mouth and tongue, the arousing sensation of the stubble of his beard on her tender skin, his hands touching her.

Jack dipped again, sliding his palm down to her ankle, and grabbing the hem of her gown. His hand slipped beneath her gown and moved up her leg, to her knee. Lizzie bent her knee and put her foot against the wall, so that he could easily reach the most intimate part of her.

He made a sound deep in his throat and slowly rose up again, his hand riding up her leg as he sought her mouth with his. He kissed her, pushed her gown up and moved his fingers along the inside of her thigh, brushed against the curls between her legs, then slipped one finger into her flesh.

"*Oh,*" Lizzie said aloud.

"*Sssh,*" he warned her and slid down her body again, going down on his haunches before her.

Lizzie watched his dark head with disbelief. She knew instinctively what he was about to do, knew that she should stop this *now,* but when he touched his tongue to her, the heart-stopping burst of sensual pleasure caught her by surprise. She groaned with pleasure; he reached up, put one hand over her mouth, and began to lick her.

She couldn't breathe. Lizzie put her head back against the wall, splayed her arms wide, and bit her lip as Jack moved his tongue and lips over her, slipping in deeper yet, sliding over sensitive flesh, moving softly but urgently and sending staggering shocks of pleasure rippling through her, over and over again.

It felt as if her body somehow coiled around him. With each stroke of his tongue, she simmered, until she was boiling and could not endure even his soft breath on her skin without it reverberating almost painfully through her.

At last the coil in her sprang, pitching her into ecstasy. She slid off into bliss, her chest heaving with the force of the pleasure, the sensation so powerful that she could not contain the sob of fulfillment that flooded through her.

She collapsed over his head, her arms sliding down his back, her fingers raking up again.

Jack shifted and rose up, enfolding her in his arms as he did so, bearing her weight, for she scarcely had the strength to stand.

Lizzie sagged in his arms and into the incredible, mystical thing he'd just done to her. But as the fog of her physical abandon began to lift, she began to realize what had happened. Uncertainty filled her heart and mind, and she slowly disengaged from his arms and awkwardly returned her breasts to the bodice of her gown.

His gray eyes were blazing, his hair mussed where she'd clawed at his head. His lips were set and swollen, and he, too, was breathing hard. But it was the intensity of his gaze again, the feeling that he was seeing through her and into the truth of her heart that made her shiver.

Something was wrong. Something was terribly askew inside her, for Lizzie was feeling ragged, wild feelings of . . . of *affection* for this rogue. Pure, undiluted affection.

"*Lizzie,*" he whispered.

"I donna know what to say," she whispered. "I donna know what is happening to me."

"Lizzie—"

"I am no' this woman," she said, more to herself than to him, and looked at his gray eyes, searching them for something—a promise? Hope? "I've been brought quite low," she whispered, confused. She'd felt such grand desire and passion, such incredible things, yet she felt cheapened by them somehow.

Jack brushed his fingers across her cheek. "Lass, you are . . . you are a treasure, do you know it?"

His tone was tender, almost reverent, and it confused Lizzie even further.

"A beautiful, unique treasure."

Was it possible he was feeling the same things for her that she was for him? If he were, what could it ever mean? It didn't change anything: a man like Jack would never settle for life at Thorntree, and Lizzie could never leave it because of Charlotte. "I donna know who I am any longer," she said as she slipped away from him.

"An alluring, sensual woman," he said earnestly.

"Am I that, indeed?" she whispered, more to herself than to him. "Or did you make me that? I am a woman with far too many responsibilities to risk . . . *this*, aye?"

"Would you deny all pleasure in life?" he asked her.

"Would you risk all for it?" she returned.

He did not answer. Lizzie started to move.

"Donna go, Lizzie," he said, but she was already walking with Red on her heels, through the open door she had so brazenly disregarded, an open door that had somehow titillated only minutes before.

Who *was* she?

She could feel his gaze on her as she walked away from a most extraordinary experience, from a man who held an extraordinary power over her that Lizzie had no idea how to withstand.

Chapter Twenty-nine

Jack did not need Lizzie or anyone else to tell him that the powerfully stirring encounter in the library was a mistake. He knew it. He knew it the moment he kissed her, the same moment he knew he couldn't—or wouldn't—turn back.

He'd spent the night rebuking himself for it. There was no supportable excuse for it and it had done nothing but rile every fiber of his being.

She had infected him, she was in his blood now. Lizzie Drummond Beal was flowing through his veins, spreading through him, and circulating back through his heart over and over again.

Jack could not recall a time in his life a woman had altered his thoughts, his reference, or his ability to breathe properly. He pondered how this provincial Scottish lass had captured his imagination in the way that she had. She was pretty, refreshingly so. She had a zest about her and a fierce streak of independence that Jack understood completely, for it was entrenched in him. And she was not, no matter what he tried, easily seduced. Aye, she was work, this one.

Perhaps it was the sum of those things that attracted him; the only thing he knew was that he'd never been moved so by a woman and it disturbed him as much as it captivated him.

But there was nothing to be done for his extraordinary feelings. In spite of Jack's randy reputation—which, aye, he'd earned fairly enough—he'd never been one to toy with the emotions of a woman. He'd done it once or twice in his youth and despised himself for it. He despised men who made a practice of it. His father had been a bloody master of degradation and manipulation. The bastard would seduce Jack's mother with gifts and small declarations of love, promise that things would be different between them, but would soon lash out again over some perceived slight, belittling her, humiliating her, striking her.

In his own young way, Jack had tried to make up for his father's shortcomings, but he'd never been able to remove the shattered look in his mother's eyes. Jack realized, sometime after he heard the hall clock chime twice, that as a grown man he'd never been able to see hope in a woman's eyes and believe it could last. Something would come along to shatter it, even if he did not intend it.

He didn't know if he could bear to see that in Lizzie's eyes. It was best he leave Thorntree before an attachment between him and Lizzie became impossible to quit.

And if he were going to leave, he had to enlist Gordon's help to do it.

That burned him.

He didn't know much these days but that this affair with Lizzie was making him unusually irritable and out of sorts.

The next morning Jack remained in the kitchen after he'd had a bit of food to break his fast, working to repair a window that Mrs. Kincade had pointed out was not closing properly. She had not exaggerated—Jack muttered an expletive beneath his breath and gave the window a yank. It did not budge. Its crank was misaligned, and after studying it for a time, Jack determined he needed a hammer to knock it into alignment.

As he rummaged through a box of tools Mr. Kincade had given him for the job, Dougal and Gordon appeared, the latter looking pressed and rested in spite of having spent the night in the old nursery with Newton just outside.

"Good morning, Mr. Gordon!" Mrs. Kincade trilled when she saw him. "I'll pour you a wee bit of coffee, aye?"

"That would be most appreciated," Gordon said. With his legs braced apart, he stood in the middle of the kitchen floor glaring at Jack as Mrs. Kincade bustled about the cups and saucers, and brought him a cup of coffee.

"Sleep well, did you, Mr. Gordon?" Jack asked snidely as he withdrew a large hammer from the box.

"Exceedingly," Gordon said, and glanced darkly at the hammer in Jack's hand. "You donna need it, milord. I'd no' harm ye before Mrs. Kincade."

Jack forced a smile and lifted the hammer. "And I'd no' threaten a humorless man. I am repairing a window for Mrs. Kincade."

That had Gordon's attention. He peered at the window in question. "Extraordinary. If I did no' know you were an earl, I'd think you a tradesman, repairing roofs and windows and the like."

"He's quite good," Dougal said, unhelpfully.

"I am an earl of many talents," Jack said, a bit tetchily. "I can claim at least as many as you, Gordon."

Gordon scowled at that and strolled closer to the window. "What's gone wrong with it, then?"

"The crank is broken," Jack said, and in a bit of pique, hit the crank with the hammer so hard that a pane of glass shattered, startling them both. He growled at the window, but Gordon gave him a superior smile.

Jack sighed irritably and turned round. Mrs. Kincade had frozen in her task of stirring something, her gray brows almost as high as her gray hairline. "Dougal, we have need of another pane of glass, aye?"

"Aye, milord," Dougal said, and went out as Mrs. Kincade tried very hard not to smile.

Jack brushed away the chunks of leaded glass as Gordon moved closer and peered over his shoulder. After a moment or two, Jack glared at him. "Do you mind, then?"

Gordon ignored him. "Seems rather odd work for an earl. Are you certain you're an earl?"

Jack leveled a withering look on him. "The help is desperately needed, and as I am a virtual prisoner here, I am thankful for the occupation." He gave Gordon a once-over. "You may prefer to be idle, sir, but I am no' an idle man."

"What would make you less a prisoner," Gordon said, putting aside his cup, "and perhaps more a traveler, on his way?" He glanced over his shoulder at Mrs. Kincade, who was busy kneading bread, and moved closer.

Jack did not like this brash young Highlander. "A clear path, first and foremost."

Gordon's smile faded. "Perhaps I should say it another way. What will make you leave?" he asked flatly.

Jack stopped his work on the window and assessed Gordon. He seemed serious in wanting to know what he might offer to make Jack take his leave of Lizzie. "I am no' at liberty to leave, you might recall. And even if I were, I signed an oath."

"What if that oath was set aside?" Gordon asked quietly.

"How?"

"If you disappear, the oath will be abandoned, aye? And when the magistrate comes in the spring, I will see that it is set to rights."

Jack hesitated.

"I will no' allow this to continue. Either you go, sir, or I will turn you in to the authorities."

"I will leave Thorntree when I know it is safe for the sisters."

"And how will *you* determine it is safe for them?" Gordon persisted.

Jack picked up a cloth and wiped his hands, then tossed it aside. "An excellent question. Perhaps you might help me with the answer, Mr. Gordon." He proceeded to tell him again that there was something here Carson wanted. He told him about the trail, and the activity of horses and men around it. He said he needed to discover what it was, for he felt certain once they discovered it, they would know how to keep Carson from it.

Gordon studied him, clearly mulling over what he'd said. A moment later, he gave Jack a curt nod. "If that's what it takes to make you abandon the handfasting."

"That is what it will take, aye."

"What will take?"

Lizzie's voice startled them both; the two men turned toward the door where Lizzie had appeared, looking as damnably beautiful as she had last night. She had to be the only woman in all of Scotland who could wear a drab brown gown and make it seem lovely. She walked into the kitchen and paused by the long wooden table.

"Take what?" she asked again.

"The window," Mr. Gordon said calmly, surprising the hell out of Jack. "It will take another pane of glass before it is properly repaired," he added as he walked to where Lizzie stood. "I am glad to see you, *leannan*," he said, and the endearment sliced across Jack like a scythe. "Shall we break our fast together?"

"Aye. I am famished," she said, and with a quick glance at Jack, she took the arm Gordon offered her.

Jack watched the lovebirds walk out of the kitchen.

Unfortunately, Mrs. Kincade's bones proved right once again; a heavy snow began to fall that morning and continued throughout much of the day. They all watched from various windows about the house. The higher the snow piled, the more restless and tense everyone grew, particularly the four men. They traded barbs and insults, remarks that left Charlotte cross and Lizzie exhausted.

It felt as if they were all waiting for something.

For several days they endured the tensions as snow fell on and off. It seemed to Lizzie that Jack intentionally put himself everywhere Mr. Gordon might be, and vice versa. On the first day the sun shone bright and clear, Lizzie sent up a silent prayer of thanks.

It did not relieve the tensions, however, and if anything made them worse. The men wanted out of doors, but the snow was too thick to navigate.

Over the course of the next two days, Lizzie spent as much time as she could in the hothouse, wishing and praying the snow would melt faster. On the third day, a row over a game of cards almost came to blows, and Lizzie retreated once more.

She was moving pots around when she noticed Jack standing in the door, watching her. Lizzie reacted from frustration of the last several days. "What are you doing, then?" she asked curtly. "Have you nothing better to do than hover about and wreak havoc?"

"Oh, aye, there are diversions aplenty," he answered peevishly. "What in the blazes do you suggest I do, then?"

"You might find a rag and polish candlesticks. I donna care, just as long as you stop arguing with Mr. Gordon at every opportunity!"

"*Ach*," he said, looking heavenward. "He is the most disagreeable man I've ever had the misfortune to meet!"

"I think he might say the same about you," Lizzie said. She saw a movement through the small window. Mr. Kincade was hurrying toward the hothouse.

Jack frowned at her admonishment and leaned up against the wall. "Lizzie, I—"

"Miss Lizzie, riders are coming," Mr. Kincade said as he poked his head into the hothouse. "Five of them."

Her first thought was bounty hunters. She quickly removed her apron and hurried past Jack. Jack was right behind her.

When she reached the house, she heard the banging at the front door and reacted without thinking. She ran to the umbrella stand in the foyer. She kept a shotgun there that she used to ward off debt collectors.

"*Diah*, Lizzie!" Jack shouted when she hauled the heavy shotgun from its container.

But Lizzie ignored him and marched to the front door, throwing it open at the same moment she heaved the shotgun to her shoulder.

But she lowered it again when she saw who was standing there. "Oh," she said. "You again, is it?"

"And a jolly good day to you, Lizzie," Carson snapped as he pushed past her and walked into the foyer. Behind him trailed four Highland thugs who carried their own guns.

"That's one way to gain entrance," Jack drawled as the men crowded into the small foyer. "You might consider a battering ram next time."

"What do you want?" Lizzie demanded.

Carson nodded at the men, who instantly moved into the house.

"What are you about? Who are they?" she cried.

"Men who are loyal to me," Carson snapped. "I've heard a rumor, lass. I've heard it mentioned that Gordon is here. Is that true?"

Lizzie blanched. A gust of cold wind lifted the hem of her skirt.

Carson's face mottled with rage. "And put that gun away before you hurt someone!" he snapped.

Lizzie knew precisely whom she wanted to hurt, but she put the gun into the umbrella stand and shut the front door.

"It would seem that the news is true, then," Carson said as his men trooped through the house. "A *Gordon* is in our midst."

"No," Lizzie said. They were searching each room, she realized. She could hear doors opening and slamming shut.

"Honestly, Beal," Jack said. "Would a Gordon be at Thorntree knowing that I occupy Lizzie's bed? If so, he is no' a man you should fear as much as you seem to do."

"I donna fear him, Lambourne," Carson sneered.

"He's no' about. You may as well call off your men," Jack said calmly.

"You speak as if you are lord of this manor, Lambourne," Carson snapped.

"In a manner of speaking, I suppose I am," Jack said

with a grin. He lifted his fist to Carson. "A handfasting gives me certain rights, aye?"

"Really, Uncle, must you always come to Thorntree threatening and making demands?" Lizzie interrupted. "How could Mr. Gordon be here with three feet of snow on the ground and your men about? We scarcely take a step that is no' reported to you! If Mr. Gordon were here, you may rest assured I would have escaped with him by now."

One of the men appeared from the corridor, looked at Carson, and shook his head. Another one followed, pushing Newton into the foyer ahead of him.

"Would you have escaped indeed, Lizzie?" Carson snapped. "And what of the oath you made and the vow you signed? You're so bloody quick to turn back on your word! The Beals have been enemies of the Gordons for nigh on five hundred years, and we'd no' give them an *inch* of our land. Thorntree has been Beal property for three centuries. *Three* centuries," he repeated, as if she didn't quite appreciate how long that was.

"Thorntree is *no'* your land, Carson!" she cried angrily. "Thorntree belongs to *me* and to Charlotte! Papa didna think to leave us any means on which to live, but he left us Thorntree, and it's all we have to make a betrothal bargain! On my word, I canna think what difference it should make to you! It is a mere one hundred acres and it canna support as much as a pair of ewes! I ask you again, Carson, what honest and true objection can you possibly have to our using the only asset we have to provide for ourselves?"

"He is a *Gordon*!" Carson shouted.

"That is enough!" Jack snapped, and strode forward, putting himself between Lizzie and Carson, with her at his back.

But Carson was too intent on Lizzie and moved to see around him. "My brother is but a year in his grave and already you think of giving Thorntree to the Gordons!" he shouted at her.

"That is *enough*, Beal," Jack said icily. "Leave her be."

Carson looked as if he might explode, but he whirled around and punched his fist into the wall. "By the *saints*, you leave me no choice! I should beat my point into your empty head!"

Lizzie flinched, but Jack's gaze turned murderous and he clenched his fists at his sides, as if he had to fight to keep himself from hitting Carson. "Now will you stoop to making physical threats, Beal? Do it again, and I'll put my fist in your gullet."

His threat was enough to move one of Carson's men to his side.

"You owe me two thousand pounds, Lizzie, or have you forgotten?" Carson continued heedlessly.

"Come now, sir, that's no' very sporting of you, is it? But then again, I should like a reason to shut you up," Jack snarled.

"You know very well I canna repay you," Lizzie said, her heart beating so wildly she could scarcely catch her breath.

"Oh no? Perhaps you might sell another cow, aye? For if you donna repay me and you disavow this handfasting, it will be debtor's prison for you. Or worse—a Glasgow workhouse," he added menacingly.

"That is *enough!*" Jack bellowed, and shoved Carson up against the wall with such force that the umbrella stand with Lizzie's gun fell over. "Say one more word. Just *one*. Give me a reason to break your neck!" Jack cried as Carson's men descended on him. One grabbed him from behind, but Jack was too strong for him. He clung to Carson, his arm across his throat, pushing him against the wall and cutting off the air to his lungs.

One of the henchman raised his gun and pointed it at Jack's head; Lizzie cried out with fear. Newton suddenly moved, pulling Jack off Carson.

Carson faltered, sputtering and gasping for breath. He looked at Jack with hatred as he put his hand to his throat. "You'll bloody well hang for that," he said hoarsely.

"If you think *that* threat will keep me from your throat, you are a fool!" Jack shouted as Newton pushed him aside.

"You're fortunate I donna have my man put a bullet in you now!"

"You'd no' do that, laird," Newton said, holding up his hand to the other Highlanders. "He's all that stands between you and Gordon now. Gordon is no' here. I'd have sent word straightaway if he'd come."

Carson shifted his gaze to Newton, eyeing him suspiciously. Newton stood calmly and stoically, steadily returning his gaze. A moment later, Carson nodded to his men, all four of whom had returned to the foyer. He gestured for them to leave and followed them to the door. But he paused there and glared daggers at Jack. "Mind yourself, Lambourne. I can send for the prince's men before you can even saddle a horse."

"Then send for them, by God!" Jack said angrily.

Carson whirled around and stalked out behind his men, slamming the door behind him.

Lizzie sagged, her heart pounding, her palms dampened by her fear. But Jack turned his murderous gaze to Newton. "Where in hell is he?"

Newton pointed down the hall, to the drawing room.

Chapter Thirty

Black, blinding, impotent anger surged through Jack like a poison. He could not bear to see a man treat a woman so abominably—he'd witnessed his father doing it enough to last an eternity. His father had a penchant for making Jack's mother cower like a child when he was displeased, and he'd been displeased quite a lot.

Jack marched into the drawing room and glared at Gordon, who had appeared from the adjoining door. His shoulders were dusty—he'd obviously hidden in some small cranny. Lizzie rushed to Charlotte, who, astoundingly, did not look the least bit ruffled.

"Do you see what your presence has caused here?" Jack said.

"One might argue *your* presence is what has caused it," Gordon said curtly.

"Think of *them*," Jack said, sweeping his arm in the direction of Lizzie and Charlotte.

"Really, milord, what did you expect he'd do?" Charlotte asked.

Surprised, Jack looked at Charlotte.

But Gordon shook his head. "He's right," he said, surprising everyone.

Jack swung his startled gaze to Gordon. "I'm *right*?"

"He's mad, Lambourne. Whatever it is about this

paltry estate that he wants, it must be something grand indeed, for I can think of nothing that would move a man to behave so abominably."

"Aye, but as we've discussed, precisely *what* is the mystery," Jack said angrily, and looked again at Newton. "Unless there is one among us who might have an answer?"

Gordon also twisted around to face Newton. "What do you know?" he demanded of Newton.

Newton laughed derisively. "Do ye honestly think he entrusts such information to me? No, sirs, he does no'."

"Will you stand there and deny you know what Carson Beal wants with Thorntree?" Gordon demanded.

"Aye." Newton said. "But if I wanted to know, I'd have a look at the parish land rolls."

Four pairs of eyes turned toward him, and Newton shrugged. "If there is anything to be learned about the land, it would be there," he said.

"The parish rolls!" Lizzie exclaimed. "Where would they be? In Crieff?"

"I'd suspect that whatever is in the parish rolls concerning Thorntree is surely in your father's study," Newton said. "In fact," he added as he strolled to Charlotte's side, "I'd wager yer father might very well have had an inkling of what it is Carson wants."

Jack, Lizzie, and Gordon looked at one another as the realization dawned. "I never thought . . ."

"But of course," Jack responded to Lizzie's unfinished thought.

"Let us have a look," Lizzie said to Jack and Gordon.

The three of them moved without hesitation, leaving Charlotte and Newton in the drawing room.

At the door of her father's study, Lizzie withdrew a ring of household keys she carried in her pocket and unlocked the door. She pushed it open and a cold sweep of air met them.

Lizzie marched across the room to one precarious stack of papers and began to look at them, discarding them one by one. Gordon stepped in behind Jack and looked around, wearing an expression of incredulity. Jack knew what Gordon was thinking, for he was thinking the very same thing: it would be an impossible task to go through all the papers and ledgers and books and God knew what else. But what else could they do? The three of them spread out and began to search in the sea of paper.

Gordon found what it was Carson wanted at the bottom of a stack of old bills of services and goods. He almost missed it, tossing the bills aside one after the other, convinced he'd never find anything worth the effort in this chaos. But this document had seemed different and out of place, and he'd paused before tossing it aside and had looked at it.

"*Mi Diah*," he muttered as he reviewed the paper. This was it—he was slightly abashed he'd not thought of something like this earlier, given the conversations he'd had with his father about profitable ventures in which they might engage. "This is it," he said.

"What?" Lizzie asked, and hurried forward to have a look at the paper he held.

Gordon looked at Jack over her head. " 'Tis slate."

"Slate?" Lizzie repeated.

"Slate," he said. "*Slate.*"

"I donna understand," Lizzie said, turning away from Gordon to hold the paper to the light.

"That is a property survey," he said, pointing to the paper she held. "It references the slate mine on this very land."

At Jack's blank look, Gordon said, "Do you no' understand, then? The slate is at the core of this matter. Slate has become quite profitable for many Highlanders, as it is being used in construction all across England. If one can transport it, one stands to profit handsomely."

"Seven miles," Lizzie muttered.

At Gordon's look, she quickly explained: "We—Jack and I," she said, looking at Lambourne, "heard some men talking. They said seven miles. But when we looked at the atlas, we could find nothing within of Thorntree but Loch Tay. Of course!" she exclaimed, her face brightening with understanding. "That is how they would transport it!"

"How profitable is slate?" Lambourne asked, taking the paper from Lizzie.

"If Lizzie were to use Thorntree as a dowry, she would give my family a substantial income for generations to come," Gavin said. He knew this was true, for his father had told him as much. Not about Lizzie's mine specifically, but Gavin was beginning to understand that somehow his father knew of the slate mine at Thorntree. He knew his father was interested in expanding their estate into new ventures but Gavin had been so caught up in the wool export he'd not really thought of anything else. Was it possible his father had looked at the parish land rolls and knew what was at Thorntree? That was the only thing that made sense, the only reason he would have overlooked the handfasting and urged Gavin to come for her. It wasn't for any particular fondness of Lizzie—his father hardly knew her.

"And if the Beals of Glenalmond face dwindling profits as the land their cattle graze are giving way to sheep," Lizzie said, "it must be the only thing that will save them. That is why Carson must have it."

"Aye, it is that precisely," Gavin said. "And as a Beal man can no' own the property, he has no choice but to keep you on the land to keep the profit."

"But why the handfasting?" Jack asked. "Why would he no' just explain to Lizzie that the lands must stay in Beal hands?"

"And dictate whom I should marry, then?" Lizzie asked defiantly. "To choose among the Beals of Glenalmond? *Ach*," she said, throwing up a hand.

"You may have your answer there," Gordon said with a smile for Lizzie. "Only women may inherit land in the Beal family by royal decree, aye? If she were to marry outside of the clan, then the land would go with her."

"That does no' explain why he was happy to handfast her to me," Jack said.

"Because he assumed, rightly so, that you'd never consent to marry her and would cry off, and even if by some miracle you did marry her, you are partly a Beal. I rather imagine he thought he might strike a deal with you if it came to that."

"Or if I discovered his scheme," Jack said.

"Precisely," Gordon agreed.

"Be that as it may," Lizzie said, her face curiously flushed now, "we are no closer to a resolution now than we were moments ago."

"Aye, but perhaps we are," Gavin said. "First, we must determine that there is indeed a slate mine at Thorntree."

"How can we possibly do that without a map?" Lizzie asked.

"I have an idea how," Jack said, and looked at Gordon. "There is a man who lives deep in the glen and sells slate and other odds and ends. McIntosh is his name. I'd wager he knows precisely where the mine is. Shall we have a look about on the morrow, Mr. Gordon?"

As much as Gavin wished Lambourne would disappear, he was the only real ally he had. "Aye," he said, reluctantly.

"And me!" Lizzie exclaimed excitedly. "You'll no' go off without me!"

Chapter Thirty-one

They went off without her.

Lizzie was furious when she discovered it, and let loose a string of Gaelic that would have made her father cringe. Newton, however, did not seem the least bit disturbed by it when she encountered him in the barn. She'd gone to milk the cow, having fed the old pig they couldn't bring themselves to slaughter and the few remaining chickens.

In fact, Newton had the audacity to tell her it wasn't proper for her to go along.

"*Proper?* And what would you know of proper?" she'd scoffed.

"Only that a lass is no' welcome among men when trouble is brewing," Newton said. "She'll do naugh' but talk when she ought no' and slow things down."

Lizzie gasped with outrage, but Newton handed her a bucket for the milking. Lizzie snapped up the bucket as she stomped away, hitting her leg with it in her haste.

She'd stewed all day, for the two men did not return until late afternoon, their boots covered in mud, and the shoulder of Mr. Gordon's greatcoat torn.

Lizzie could scarcely contain her anxiety as they removed their coats, gloves, and hats. "Well?" she blurted. "Did you find it, then?"

"Aye, we did," Mr. Gordon said solemnly. "Just as Lambourne suspected, McIntosh knew precisely where the mine was."

"Slate?" she asked excitedly as Mr. Gordon began to walk toward the drawing room. "It's true, then? Thorntree has a slate mine?"

"It is true," Jack said, and caught her elbow, wheeling her about and propelling her to walk behind Mr. Gordon to the drawing room.

Inside the drawing room, Charlotte and Newton were playing a game of backgammon. Charlotte scarcely looked up as they entered. "Look here, Mr. Newton," she asked cheerfully. "The merry men have returned from their trek."

"What news?" Newton asked as Charlotte moved her pieces around the board.

"Aye, there is slate," Jack said curtly, his gaze narrowing on Newton. "But I suspect you know it."

Newton did not deny it.

"It was difficult to find the opening, but once we found it, it seemed as if some preparation to mine has already begun," Mr. Gordon said.

"Impossible!" Lizzie cried angrily. "What right has he? It is *ours!*"

"Aye, but who will stop him, lass?" Jack asked. "Even if you went before a magistrate, it would be spring before you might have an inquest, aye?" he said angrily as he moved to the fire to warm his hands.

"Nevertheless, he canna mine. The land belongs to us!"

Jack and Mr. Gordon exchanged a look.

"What? What are you no' saying?" Lizzie demanded.

"That Carson will never let it go," Charlotte sighed, as

if they'd been around this topic before. "He'll find a way to have it."

"She's right, Lizzie," Jack said at Lizzie's frown. "He could ask for an injunction until the matter could be brought to a higher court. He might even take it to Parliament if pressed, as it was a royal decree that forbids him from land that should be his by all rights. With the current sentiment against the monarchy, he might be successful. Leaving land to women and disallowing men to inherit goes against every primogeniture law ever penned."

"He has the power to make things very difficult for us, Lizzie," Mr. Gordon said.

"We shall call a constable if he persists."

"I'd no' call the constable when he answers to the laird," Newton mentioned as he took his turn at the board.

Mr. Gordon took Lizzie's hands in his and dipped down to look her in the eyes. "I *will* think of something, lass. You must trust that I will."

She wanted to trust that he would, but she did not believe that he could. She wanted to look at Jack, to see the reassurance in *his* eyes. She stole a quick look at Jack; he was standing with his arm propped on the mantel, staring into the fire. He did not offer her any reassurance.

Nor did he later, when the five of them debated the situation over leek soup. Lizzie posed the possibility of finding someone to mine the slate on their behalf, but Mr. Gordon assured them that would not succeed. No one, he said, would do business with them, not with Carson working against them.

So Lizzie posed the unthinkable: Could Jack, by virtue of being handfasted to her, seek redress on her behalf?

The question was met with stunned silence.

"I believe," Jack said, "that law does no' exist in Scotland as it does in England. I think Carson would see me dead first. Or at least in the hands of the prince's men. He'd see to it that the handfasting was voided by abandonment or death before he'd face me in a court of law."

Lizzie knew he was right. Carson wouldn't allow honor or decency to stop him. That meant, she thought silently, that she and Charlotte would never leave Thorntree if Carson had his way, and would only be more and more indebted to him.

The absence of any easy solution left Lizzie feeling exhausted.

Jack saw things the same way as Lizzie, but he saw a solution she did not see. The only problem was that it would cost him his freedom and possibly his life. Quite simply, Jack knew the king. He could ask the king to settle the matter, to ensure that Carson could not circumvent the decree in any way. But it was not something he could simply write and hope would reach the king in the time Lizzie needed it to occur. No, making that request of King George would necessitate putting himself in the king's presence. And if he did that, the king would have no alternative but to hand Jack over to his son, Prince George. What else could His Majesty do? Anything less would only add to a growing scandal.

Naturally, Jack was far more interested in finding another solution, one that did not include stretching his neck, and he spent the better part of the meal mulling it over. He was so preoccupied by the growing thought that he excused himself after supper, retiring in a sour mood.

He was seated in a chair at the hearth of Lizzie's room with his feet propped before a weak fire, Red curled up on the rug beside him—the dog had become quite

attached—and nursing a stout dram of whisky courtesy
of Mrs. Kincade. He'd mulled over the options until his
head hurt.

His eyes closed, he was attempting to will away the
pain in his head away when he heard a strange thumping
noise behind the wall at his back.

Jack sat up and peered at the wall that separated
the sitting room from the bedroom. He heard nothing
but silence and assumed he'd imagined it. He turned
round and settled in his chair again to sip the last of his
whisky.

The thumping noise startled him once again, and
it was followed by a scraping noise that sounded as if
someone was trying to dig through to this room.

Jack gained his feet, took care to step over Red, and
started for the door that adjoined the room to the dressing room. He put his hand on the door handle and
yanked it open.

On the other side of the door, Lizzie cried out
with shock and dropped a box she was holding. The
contents—yellowed papers, some coins, and a bit of
jewelry—scattered across the floor.

"You gave me a fright!" she said breathlessly as she
knelt down to retrieve her things. "You might have
knocked!"

"I am no' the one stumbling about in the dark,
Lizzie."

"It is no' dark—I have a candle," she said, pointing to
it. She began to scrape up the things that had spilled.

"What is this?" Jack asked, squatting down to help
her.

"Nothing. I only just remembered it," she said, peering at one paper. "These were my mother's things. I
found the box after she died and put it away in the bu-

reau." She smiled wryly. "I remembered there were some papers. . . ." Her voice trailed off. She looked at the things she'd gathered up.

Jack silently watched her examining the things one by one. She opened a brittle piece of foolscap and frowned lightly. "I thought perhaps there was something she'd left behind, something that might be of use to us now, or perhaps something of value," she added, holding a bauble in the palm of her hand. "But there is no value here. Only sentiment." Lizzie dropped the bauble and looked up at Jack, her blue eyes full of helplessness. "I am drowning and grasping at straws, for there is nothing that can help me now."

"Lizzie . . ."

"I *know* it is hopeless, Jack. I know it very well! I am destined to be a prisoner of my uncle's and Charlotte and I will rot here in a rotting house with rotting food and rotting animals—"

He caught her face in his hand. "Stop."

"The stench of two spinsters in the glen will waft—"

Jack stopped her by pulling her into a protective embrace. She pressed her face to the lapel of his coat, her body shaking from her failed effort to keep her tears from falling. But only a moment, for Lizzie Beal was not one to cry in her porridge. She abruptly lifted her head and her wet eyes glittered with impotent fury.

"I hate him. He would keep Charlotte and me from ever knowing the happiness of looking into our children's faces, or the comfort of passing a winter's night in the warmth of our husband's bed. We'll be alone and beholden, and there is nothing worse!"

"It will no' be so," Jack tried to soothe her.

"I am no' blind!" she cried. "Who will no' require a dowry? Even Mr. Gordon, as dear as he is to us, will no' marry without a dowry—his family would never allow it, aye? So who will come along to love me, Jack? Who will take my sister as she is? Who will make me *feel*," she said on a gulp, pressing her fist to her breast, "as you have made me feel?"

Jack's heart leapt. "How have you felt?"

She responded by lifting up on her knees and kissing him. It was an incongruently shy kiss, but the kiss of an innocent full of untapped passion, and it detonated within Jack. He raked his hands through her curls, cupped her face. His kiss was full of a man's constant thirst for a woman's mouth, for a woman's body, for Lizzie's legs to be wrapped around his waist.

He began to caress her, his hand gliding over the swell of her breast, to her ribs and the curve of her waist. He fell back against the wall, pulling Lizzie with him, and she lay across him, her shyness evaporating, her kiss deepening in response to him. With his hands he stroked every curve, sought every bit of warm flesh. He buried his face in her neck and ran his tongue inside her ear as he inhaled her scent.

Lizzie was transformed; her hands and lips moved feverishly as she untied the knot of his neckcloth, pulling at the ends of it, seeking his flesh.

Jack could not say how his clothing fell away, article by article, until his chest was bared. He could not say when her breasts had been freed from the bodice of her gown, but only that there had been a mutually blind, mutually furious need to hold each other. His mouth filled with succulent flesh, and his heart filled his chest.

Lizzie seemed lost in her own desire, caressing him, her mouth warm and wet. He guided her to straddle his lap; her dark curls spilled around her bare shoulders, and her eyes glittered with anticipation. She slowly moved down his body. Jack caught a breath in his throat when her tongue flicked across a nipple and her hands fumbled with his trousers to free his arousal.

He was mad to have her. Her hand surrounded his rigid erection and she pressed her open mouth to the hollow of his belly, sending a violent shiver through him. Jack had been with courtesans and experienced women, but none had ever seduced him so utterly as this. Raw emotions chafed beneath the surface of his skin, making him entirely vulnerable to her.

He couldn't think clearly. His body, his heart, stormed to be inside her, and when he shifted her, moving her above the erection she had stroked, her lips landed softly on his, and she thrust her tongue into his mouth.

He understood her. He knew she wanted him as badly as he wanted her. There were shallow, distant thoughts of impropriety, of consequences, but Jack's hunger for Lizzie was so voracious he shoved those thoughts aside. He fought her skirts until they were hiked above her hips, then slipped his hand between her legs. Lizzie gasped against his lips and he breathed a silent moan of ecstasy into her body at finding her so wet with desire for him. His fingers slipped inside her; his thumb stroked her mindlessly until she made a little cry and began to move against him, sliding and wiggling on his lap, making restraint unbearable for him.

With his hands on her hips and himself, Jack guided her onto his cock, slipping slowly inside her, using one hand to stroke her and open her to him. But when he reached her barrier, she tensed.

"I'll stop," he whispered, surprised by how quickly those words had come, how earnestly he meant it. "Give me but one word, and I will stop," he added breathlessly.

But Lizzie, her lips swollen from their passionate kissing, shook her head. Rich, auburn curls danced around her face, and she seemed like an angel to Jack in that moment. "*Mi Diah,* forgive me, but I . . . I want it to be you, Jack. Please."

Those words held an almost preternatural power over Jack; he lifted up, caught her mouth with his at the same moment he slid completely in. There was a moment in which she shuddered and her whole body stilled, but then he felt the release of her breath, the relaxing of her thighs. He eased in deeper still, and began to move slowly and carefully inside her.

Lizzie understood the rhythm and began to move with him. The more she moved, the more Jack was aroused. He was quickly lost in the heart-binding sensation of it all, the warmth of her body and her breath and new, unknown emotions swirling inside him. "You've driven me to a madness I've never known, lass," he said roughly. "I canna resist you."

"Donna say more, Jack. Donna say what you can no' mean," she begged him.

"Lizzie . . . *leannan* . . ." He buried his face in the valley of her breasts, taking them into his mouth as her body took him in. Over and over again he slid into her, stroking her with his hand, and restraining the beast within him as he sought to help her find her release. "I want you to feel what I am feeling, aye?" With every stroke he came closer, and when he felt her tighten around him, he was unable to contain the powerful need to release himself into her.

Lizzie dropped her head back at the moment of fulfillment, digging her fingers into his shoulder and stifling the cry on her tongue by biting her lip. But her body reverberated, contracting tightly around him, and with a strangled sob of his own, unfathomable ecstasy, Jack let go with a powerful thrust.

She collapsed against him, her body heavy after her passion had been spent, her moist face in the crook of his neck, her breath hot and ragged.

Jack wrapped his arms around her and slowly eased back. He was drained. He believed his heart had erupted along with his body; he felt extraordinarily tender toward her. For a man who generally took nothing from a woman but pleasure, that was almost inconceivable to him.

Her breathing began to slow and soften; Jack curled one corkscrew lock of hair around his finger.

"What have we done?" Lizzie whispered.

He had no acceptable answer for that, other than that it had been stunning.

She suddenly propped her chin on his chest and looked up at him with eyes still warm with the glow of lovemaking. "I think I've lost my fool mind, aye?"

"If you have, it has gone the way of mine," he said, stroking her cheek.

"What are we to do now? Go on as if nothing has happened between us?"

"Go on," he said, aware of how incredibly alive he was feeling, how impossibly tender his heart. "But without forgetting this moment." He really had no idea what he was saying. He could not look in her blue eyes and recall them in the throes of passion and imagine walking away from them.

No, no, he could not think of that now. He could not play a boyish game of imagining it could be any other way, because he knew it could not. In reality, they were on two different ships and there was an entire ocean between them.

Jack turned his head slightly, so that he wasn't looking into her eyes, and stroked her back. He could not think of more than the immediate future, an incredible, startlingly clear thought in and of itself. Making love had taken the fog from his brain and Jack realized what he must have known all along: he would speak to the king on Lizzie's behalf. Only he could do it, and there was no other answer.

It hardly mattered that he was sacrificing himself to do it. Incredible though it seemed, for the first time in his adult life, he had come to care about someone else's happiness more than his own. He had . . . he had fallen in love.

It was a remarkable moment of awareness, one that shook him to his core.

Jack suddenly maneuvered to his knees.

When he did, Lizzie slid from his lap and onto her back. She still felt as if she were dreaming as he bent over her. He was frowning down at her, his gray eyes shining with a deep and distant light, his brow wrinkled in thought. His fingers trailed down her abdomen like a whisper of a summer breeze on her skin. The sensation made her feel drowsy and confused; she shifted slightly, but he put both hands to her rib cage and murmured, "Lizzie . . . listen to me, lass."

"*Mmm,*" she said softly.

"I know how to put your predicament to rights. I will put this all to rights," he said low as he traced a line down her belly.

Her heart fluttered wildly with the promise in that statement. She caught his hand as the other drifted to her thigh. "How?" It was the only word she could manage; her body was drifting down another sensual path.

"It will require that we go to London," he murmured

as his gaze slipped to her breasts and his hand methodically moved from her thigh to her ankle and slowly up again.

"I canna go to London," she said with a seductive smile. "You are mad as an old hen even to suggest it."

His hand brushed over the spring of curls, to the hollow of her abdomen. "I am mad, there is not doubt of it. We are to London," he said, and paused to kiss the peak of her breast.

"Who is 'we'?" she asked breathlessly.

He smiled a little and kissed the peak of her other breast. "You. Me," he said, pausing once more to kiss the plane of her abdomen, "and bloody Gordon." He moved his mouth over the juncture of her thighs again.

"That's ridiculous," Lizzie sighed while he slipped his hand between her legs, heating flesh that was still inflamed. "The three of us will up and hie ourselves to London, then? As if we are merry friends?"

A slow, lazy smile curved his mouth, and Jack easily straddled her. He pressed his hand to her cheek and neck and shook his head. "I donna tease you, Lizzie. I am quite earnest in this. We will go to London and I will speak to the king on your behalf."

She blinked. Then laughed. "What, and see yourself hang?"

But instead of laughing as she expected, Jack dropped his gaze so that she could not see the truth in his eyes. He tilted her head back and kissed the hollow of her throat.

"Jack," she said as his hands began to move on her again, slowly caressing and gliding and moving her to feel the burn of wanting him all over again. "*Jack*," she tried again, but it was no use. She was lost the moment his mouth claimed hers.

He made love to her with great deliberation, touching

every part of her with his hands and mouth, stroking and tasting her skin, his lips and tongue everywhere, in places and ways that she was certain would sentence her directly to hell, but Lizzie didn't care. It was madness, but it was divine.

When he entered her again, and began to move her toward ethereal fulfillment once more, he whispered her name over and over as he found his.

It wasn't until later—much later—when she heard the deep and steady breath of his sleep that she forced herself to return to earth, to the reality of her life. She'd only added to her troubles tonight. She'd only confused her thinking even more, and in giving herself to him so completely, she would be marked forever by a man she could not have. But no matter what, she would have this night to remember and cling to all her days.

Nevertheless, she would not go to London and Jack would not hang.

Chapter Thirty-two

The morning after that extraordinary night, Lizzie found she was not able to think clearly. Charlotte asked her where Fingal and Tavish had gone off to, and Lizzie thought of those frantic moments in Jack's arms. Mrs. Kincade said they were low on flour, and she fought the despair and disappointment that she could not be with him always.

Later, Mr. Kincade found her milking a cow that had already been milked and told her Charlotte had summoned her to the drawing room. When Lizzie entered, still wearing her milking apron, her eyes saw only Jack.

He was standing tall and handsome and his eyes—*his eyes, eyes that had hovered over her, watching her, going so dark with desire when she'd found her release*—avoided her gaze as he calmly set forth his plan.

They—Mr. Gordon, Lizzie, and Jack—would travel to London, where Jack would seek the king's audience and ask His Majesty to set aside the handfasting and bless the engagement of Lizzie and Mr. Gordon. Once he had that, Jack would request that the king confirm the decree that left Thorntree and its slate to Lizzie and Charlotte.

It all seemed so simple when he said it, and Charlotte

had almost levitated from her chair with joy. "There, you see, Lizzie? He's proved himself quite useful after all!"

"Has he?" Lizzie demanded crossly. "And how will we go with bounty hunters on every road?"

"We'll go north," Mr. Gordon said. "Over the hills. I know how to do it."

"Then do you agree, milord," she said, her eyes on Jack, "to hang?"

"Lizzie!" Charlotte cried.

"That is precisely what he proposes, Charlotte! He will hand himself to the king on our behalf, and he will hang!"

"I will no' hang," Jack said dismissively.

"What makes you so certain of it?" Lizzie cried.

Jack looked directly at her. There was a smile on his lips but a dangerously dark look in his eye. "Why, Miss Lizzie Beal," he said with a mocking bow, "you'll have me believe you esteem me after all." And he laughed in that damnably insouciant, supercilious, charming way he had.

"Donna flatter yourself," she'd said, her anger rising— at what, precisely, she wasn't certain, "but I'll no' have your neck on my conscience." And with that, she whirled about, striding from the room.

She did not see Mr. Gordon's sharp gaze. She didn't see it until he came looking for her. He found her in the kitchen hacking carrots to bits. He sent Mrs. Kincade on a fool's errand, turned around, then stared at Lizzie until she put her knife down.

"What is the matter with you, then?" he demanded. "He offers us a plausible path out of this debacle, and you flatly refuse it and insult him as well?"

Lizzie had hardly spared him a glance as she gathered

her carrots and put them in a bowl. "Honestly, Mr. Gordon, you canna expect me to . . . to pick up and be off to London!" she insisted, waving her hand in the direction of London.

Mr. Gordon surprised her by suddenly advancing on her. Lizzie let out a sound of surprise and moved back, butting up against the table. He caught her by the shoulders and said, "*Gavin*. Say my name, Lizzie."

"Pardon?" she asked, confused.

"*Gavin*," he said again. "Say *Gavin*, Lizzie, no' Mr. Gordon. You call him Jack, yet you rarely speak my name at all and refer to me as Mr. Gordon. Why is that?"

His sudden interest in what she called him flustered her. "What do you mean? It is out of respect." She could see he did not accept that explanation. "Gavin, then," she said, and tried to move away, but he held her tight.

"No, no mere *Gavin, then*. No, Lizzie. Donna pretend there is no cause for my concern."

Lizzie's heart began to pound guiltily.

"I've been quite honest, have I no'?" he demanded. "I want to marry you, but frankly, I am no' certain you want to marry me."

"That is no' true. You know I do," she said warily, even though a voice inside her shouted *no, no, no*. She'd betrayed him horribly, she'd betrayed her own heart. What was she to do now? Try and fill her heart with a love she did not have?

"Then *say* it. Say aye, *Gavin*, I want you above all others."

"Aye, Gavin," she said. "I want to marry you above all others." Her lips were moving, but Lizzie's heart was breaking. How could she be so wretchedly confused?

"Do you, indeed? Because we canna marry until this business with your bloody handfasting is done, aye?"

"Aye, aye," she said disagreeably, wanting to be anywhere but here now. She couldn't think. She couldn't *think*. She stared at the carrots over Gavin's shoulder.

"*A chiall*, Lizzie! We must do as Lambourne suggests, do you no' understand it? If you intend to be my wife, then we must do as he suggests, and if you donna agree to it, then we shall never be with one another, and I will believe that is what you prefer! Do me the honor of telling me truthfully—have you come to love him?"

Lizzie sputtered guiltily at that suggestion. "*Gavin!* No, no, of course no'! Love *him*?" she cried, shaking her head and catching Gavin's arms, which, she noticed madly, were not as thick as Jack's. "Can you honestly believe I'd come to love a . . . *rake*? A wanted man? A scoundrel?" *Oh, but she had come to love him, had come to love him deeply.* "Of course no'! How can you question me like this?"

"Because I must know," he said firmly. "He is a charmer, aye, and it seems to me you've been charmed—"

"*Mi Diah!* I've no' been charmed!" she cried, and tried to wrench free of his grasp, but he held her tightly, forcing her to look at him.

"Then you want to marry me yet?" he insisted. "For God knows I want to marry you, Lizzie. I've been entirely too fond of you since the day we met. I've stood by you through this scandal and I will stand by you forever—but I will no' stand to be made a fool of."

Her heart warned her, *pleaded* with her not to lie, but Lizzie could not look at the man who had pledged himself to her, who had ignored the worst of scandals and promised to be with her yet and say otherwise. She could not ignore the fact that whatever she might feel for

Jack—raw, unshaped feelings so strong they made her slightly ill—Gavin was her future. Gavin was the one who would be steadfast and keep her and Charlotte safe. Gavin would be at her side, in Scotland. He'd be steadfast and true.

And while Jack stirred her blood like no man ever had, he would never—*never*—remain at Thorntree or want a provincial lass in London. He wanted to leave so badly he was willing to sacrifice his freedom, if not his life. How could she hope that he'd suddenly change his perspective on life and settle for a bucolic existence far from the glamour of the king's court?

"Lizzie?" Gavin asked, looking a bit alarmed.

"Aye, Gavin," she said softly, and forced her smile. "I'll say it again. I want nothing more than to marry you."

He stared hard at her for a long moment, but a slow smile finally appeared on his lips. He kissed her. It was not the tender kiss he'd shown her days ago, but one that clearly conveyed his hunger for her. When he lifted his head, he stroked her cheek with the back of his hand. "You must face what is true, Lizzie. You canna mistake this opportunity: if we are to be together, and no' beholden to Carson Beal in any way, we must do as the earl suggests."

"But what of Charlotte?" Lizzie had protested. "I canna go off and leave her!"

"Newton has said he'll stay on to keep an eye on things."

"Newton!"

"And Mr. and Mrs. Kincade are here."

"Aye, and what about me? I am to travel to London with two gentlemen?"

"Lizzie—*leannan*—you are handfasted to the earl. It

is perfectly acceptable. And think of it, lass," he said, his eyes beginning to gleam. "It is *London*. It is a chance we might never have again, aye?"

She looked into Gavin's brown eyes and saw genuine affection for her, as well as his eagerness to see the brightest city in the world. Lizzie did the only she could do after all Gavin had done for her. She nodded.

Chapter Thirty-three

A new report from Dougal's brother that more men had joined in the hunt for Jack, enticed by the higher bounty, forced the trio to slip of out Thorntree sooner than they might have liked.

Jack regretted that they had to ride north, over a steep mountainous path and through a forest so thick that his greatcoat was torn in several places. He regretted that he had to abandon his mare in the small hamlet of Ardtalnaig and buy passage on a rickety old river barge guided by an old man whose face was creased with the deep grooves of his life. The old man carried two bags of wool to Perth, but if he was happy with what Jack considered an exorbitant fee, he gave no indication.

Jack regretted that slow river trip seated next to Lizzie and Gordon, hearing their low, intimate conversations.

He regretted it, too, when they disembarked from that old boat and made their way to Callendar, where they hired a carriage and the three of them stuffed themselves into it—Lizzie and Gordon on one bench, Jack directly across from them—and made do all the way to Glasgow.

In Glasgow they met Dougal, who had brought a fresh team of horses. Jack had thought it best to send Dougal with the horses on a different path, so as not to arouse suspicion in Glenalmond. It was a futile hope, he discovered, for Dougal was full of news. Carson had come to call shortly after they'd departed, and while Newton had done a fine job of denying any knowledge—Miss Charlotte, too—Carson had sent men in search of them.

Jack regretted mightily that he was a fugitive once more, for nothing was quite as bothersome as having to hide. On the other hand, he was something of a veteran now, and quickly assembled Lizzie and Gordon into action. The three of them started out, Jack on his horse, the happy couple in the carriage.

He regretted that, as well.

And he regretted the dodgy public houses they were forced to sample on the weeklong journey, and the old carriage he'd felt compelled to purchase at a thievishly high cost when the driver refused to take them further than Glasgow. He regretted the long stretches of rutted road after Glasgow, where he rode silently alongside Gordon, who had taken up the reins of the carriage.

He regretted that, having reached the outskirts of London, they were forced to wait, as Jack believed they must enter the city at night, if for no other reason than not to be seen, and thereby delay his hanging as long as was possible. And when they did cross into London in the dead of night, abandoning the old carriage in Southwark and riding into Mayfair on horseback, Jack regretted having Lizzie seated in front of him, her body pressed against his, her scent filling his senses.

But Jack did not regret returning to London.

Aye, he was surprisingly thrilled to be in the one place he felt he truly belonged, particularly after a long absence. He could feel the city's rhythm in his veins, and even though they entered the city in the early morning hours, the sight of a pair of well-dressed, foxed gentlemen stumbling past massive town homes and a single, ornate coach gliding down a cobbled street made Jack feel quite at home.

What he regretted most of all and to his very marrow was making love to Lizzie, because now he could not purge the sensation from his blood. He could not erase the memories or wash away the feel of her skin, or drink away the taste of her in his mouth. And he could not be so near her as he'd been during the interminable journey from Scotland and not touch her. It was as if bits of her were entwined in bits of him—she was impossible to let go.

He watched the looks that flowed between her and Gordon and wished it were he. He bristled when Gordon called her *leannan,* and felt a dull pain when Lizzie smiled sweetly in return. He could not reveal his feelings; doing so would jeopardize her one chance to be happily married.

The entire journey had been so bloody uncomfortable for Jack that he was uncharacteristically cross when they arrived at his town home on Audley Street and his butler was not awake to receive them.

When Winston finally appeared at the door with his nightcap askew, a pair of footmen similarly dressed and scurrying about to light candles behind him, Jack stalked into the entrance hall. "We've guests, Winston," he said, as if he'd been gone days instead of months. "We'll need a pair of rooms for them."

Winston blinked at Jack, then at Lizzie as she walked in, her eyes wide as tea saucers as she took in Lambourne House. Gordon followed closely behind her, his eyes gleaming as he surveyed the entrance hall.

Frankly, after several weeks in the Highlands, it all looked a wee bit ostentatious to Jack.

"My lord?" Winston said.

Jack glared at him, warning him away from asking any questions. Winston knew him well. "Welcome home," the butler said without further ado. "If I may, I will show the lady to her rooms?"

"You may," Jack said curtly.

Winston bowed to Lizzie as if he were dressed in his full butler regalia. "If you will follow me, Miss . . . ?"

"Beal," she said. "Miss Elizabeth Beal. Thank you, sir."

Jack pretended to be busy with his gloves and hat as Lizzie followed along behind Winston, but he glanced sidelong at her as she began to climb the curving staircase after the butler. She looked uncertain, almost cowed by his home. Her plain muslin gown seemed out of place in this city.

"What is this, then, marble?" Gordon said behind him, tapping his foot on the floor.

Jack reluctantly shifted his gaze to the younger man. "Aye," he said.

"Very fine marble it is," Gordon said. "Very fine indeed." He took one of the candles the footman had left on a console and wandered across the entrance hall, to a pair of Rococo paintings that hung side by side, perusing them as if he were standing in a museum somewhere. "Quite grand," he muttered. "A sound investment, I understand."

Jack hardly cared what Gordon understood. He wished he'd never laid eyes on the man.

"Winston will see to you, Gordon," he said curtly. "I should like to retire if you donna mind."

Gordon did not respond but continued to admire the paintings as Jack strode to the stairs, almost colliding with a footman, who hurried to give him a candle.

Aye, he was glad to be in London! This is where

he would come to his senses! This is where he would welcome a private moment in his suite with his things around him and a fine Scots whisky to dull his memory. *This* was his life, not repairing some ramshackle roof in Scotland!

Lizzie had understood Jack was a wealthy man—he was an earl, after all—but she'd had no idea he was *this* wealthy. Sumptuous surroundings such as this were beyond her ability to fathom.

Mr. Winston, poor man, in his dressing gown and nightcap, had quickly turned down a bed stuffed with feathers and covered with a silk coverlet so fine Lizzie would very much have liked to have made a gown of it, and had promised her a lady's maid to attend her first thing on the morrow. Lizzie had attempted to assure him she did not require a lady's maid, but Mr. Winston seemed fairly determined that she would have one. "All of His Lordship's lady guests have them," he'd said firmly.

When Winston had left her, and a footman had built a roaring fire—with wood, she noticed—Lizzie wandered around the room, her fingers trailing over the rich brocade fabric of the furniture, admiring the delicate carving of the vanity. There were three rooms: a bedroom, a dressing room, and the sort of enclosed privy closet she'd read about but had never seen. The rugs beneath her feet were so thick it was almost like walking on pillows, and the draperies' woolen weave thick enough to keep out all drafts.

Lizzie sat on the edge of the bed, then lay back. Above her head was a painting of heaven. Little wonder; this room seemed like heaven. She ached with exhaustion, but sleep had eluded her for days now. Her heart had warred constantly with her mind, and now, to see how he lived! The riches he was accustomed to, the servants who had risen in the middle of the night to do his bidding! Lizzie had not even a feather to fly with, but here she lay, a country woman who had had the grand misfortune to fall hopelessly in love with him!

She could not possibly have fallen in love with a man more ill suited to her, and this beautiful room made that painfully obvious. She no more belonged in this house than an old cow, and he no more belonged at Thorntree than a fine piece of china.

The next morning, Lizzie was awakened by a soft knock on the door. That was followed by the forceful opening of the door, and in scurried a young woman dressed in a maid's uniform, followed by a woman who looked to be about Lizzie's age, her brows furrowed in a disapproving vee.

The maid quickly dipped a curtsey. The other woman—who looked vaguely familiar—folded her arms across her middle and eyed Lizzie critically. "Who have we here, if I may ask?"

"I . . ." Lizzie wasn't quite certain what to say.

The pretty woman, with dark hair and lovely amber eyes, stepped closer. She was wearing a beautiful white and gold day gown that fit her superbly. From her lobes dangled marquis-cut ambers to match those that hung around her neck. She was the sort of woman Charlotte had dreamed of being—refined, sophisticated. She was lovely. And angry.

"Lucy informs me that Winston instructed her in the *middle of the night* to tend to the earl's guest, but, lassie, the earl is *no' here.* I know what you are about, aye? You'd best gather your things and be on your way," she said coldly.

It dawned on Lizzie that this woman thought she was an intruder, an interloper. Or *worse*. "I beg your pardon!" Lizzie exclaimed, and quickly came up, throwing her arisaidh around her. "If I am to be sent home, it will be the earl who does it, aye? Did you speak to Mr. Winston? Did he tell you that the earl is the one who brought me here?"

The young woman opened her mouth to speak, then closed it. She squinted at Lizzie. "You're a *Scot*," she said, perplexed.

"*Aye*," Lizzie said proudly.

"A Scot! What do you mean, he brought you here? He is no' *here*, is he? He best *no'* be here! He is in Scotland!"

"Either he is in London or his ghost escorted me here," Lizzie retorted.

"Oh no," the young woman said, shaking her head. "Oh no, no, *no*, he canna be in London! Does the bloody fool wish to hang?" She whirled around and fled for the door, leaving it open as she hurried down the hall calling Jack's name.

Lizzie put a hand to her heart and looked at the maid. "*Who* was that?"

"Lady Fiona," the maid said, dipping another curtsey. "The earl's sister. I'm Lucy, mu'um. I'm to be your lady's maid."

A maid *and* a sister? Jack Haines had failed to mention a sister in London, and for that, Lizzie would very much like to kick him.

Jack didn't mention his sister because he was not aware Fiona was in London. The last he'd seen her, she'd announced her unlikely and very surprising engagement to Duncan Buchanan, the Laird of Blackwood, and then gave Jack the news that the prince's men were looking for him. She sent Jack into the hills with a warning that he'd hang if he lingered, and Jack had been on the run since.

When Fiona burst into his room, she startled him so badly that he almost cut his own throat with the razor.

"*Jack!*" she cried. "*Mi Diah*, what have you done? Are you mad? Do you have a secret wish to die?"

"Good morning, Fiona," Jack said, and took a deep breath, put down his razor, and dabbed at his face with a towel before turning to face her.

His sister's eyes were blazing.

"What in the devil are you doing in London?" he asked. "Please tell me you've come to your senses and cried off from Buchanan."

"*No*, you wretched man," she said, frowning at him. "Duncan and I are to be married on May Day! I have come to London to be fitted for a dress."

"Is Buchanan with you?"

"No, of course no'! He's got quite a lot to do in the rebuilding of Blackwood, but that is neither here nor there, Jack! You should no' be in London! You could be hanged!"

"No one will hang me," he said, and opened his arms with a grin. "Come here, Fi."

She sailed into his arms, throwing her arms around his neck and kissing his cheek. "They will indeed hang you—they hanged Sir Wilkes last month."

Jack suddenly grabbed her shoulders and pushed her back. "Then it is true? I thought . . ." He'd thought perhaps Carson had been lying in an effort to intimidate him.

"Aye, it's true," Fiona said. "He did something awful that I canna even bear to repeat. You *must* leave! Things have only gone worse between the prince and princess, and no one is safe from accusation!"

"Bloody hell," he muttered. "You must tell me everything," he said, and grabbed up his neckcloth. "I'll have every last word of all that's happened."

"Aye, you will," she said, pushing his hands away to tie his neckcloth for him. "But first you will tell me what *she* is doing here."

Damn it all to hell, but Jack felt himself flush slightly.

"Jack?" Fiona said, peering up at him. "Who is she? *A chiall*, she's wearing an arisaidh like a country woman! Where did you find her? *Mi Diah*, tell me she's no' someone's daughter and you've done something you ought no' to have done—"

"Fiona! Mind your tongue. The woman is . . . She's . . . I've never met . . ." Words utterly failed him.

Fiona's hands stilled. She gaped at him. "Heaven as my witness, you've risked your life for a *woman*."

"*Diah*, donna be so bloody dramatic."

"Do you love her?" Fiona asked, pulling the neckcloth a bit too tightly.

"For God's sake, Fi!" he rumbled, slapping her hands away and turning to the mirror to tie his own bloody neckcloth. "Still as mad as a March hare, are you? Lizzie is naugh' to me, but only one more problem with which I must contend!"

His sister did not speak. When Jack had finished tying his neckcloth, he turned round again. She was standing with her arms folded, one brow cocked high above the other. "*Lizzie*," she said, drawing the name out.

"Donna do that," he said, pointing at her.

"Whatever do you mean?" she asked innocently.

"You know very well what. You've wrapped your silly imagination around some fantastic notion," he said, fluttering his fingers at his head. "I owe the woman a small debt. She's come with her fiancé, and he is most decidedly *no'* me. Come, then. I'll have the news about Wilkes." He began striding out of the room.

"You may no' be her fiancé," Fiona said smartly. "But you wish you were."

"Fiona!"

"I may be as mad as a March hare, but you're still as stubborn as an old goat!" she cried, and swept out before him.

Fiona gave Jack only sketchy details about Sir Oliver Wilkes. Apparently Wilkes had tried to kill the Countess of Lindsey. It was impossible to believe . . . Jack knew that Wilkes was disgruntled, but he'd never believed him capable of murder.

He had too many questions that Fiona could not answer. Jack decided his first point of business would be to ask Grayson Christopher—Christie, one of his closest friends—what had happened, and more.

Christie could always be counted on to give sound advice.

Chapter Thirty-four

It was almost one o'clock when Lizzie finally found the nerve to venture out of the room she'd occupied. The house was so large she got lost looking for a kitchen or some place she might find a bite to eat. She wandered several corridors, taking in the luxury. His house was spectacular. He was, obviously, extraordinarily wealthy. Thorntree seemed almost a hovel compared to this, and she felt more and more like an intruder.

Her one wish was that Charlotte could see this finery. This is what her sister had urged to her to seek when Jack had come to them, but Lizzie was glad she had not. She was overwhelmed and inadequate for a house like this.

When she found the foyer, she also found Mr. Winston, wearing a suit of clothes as fine as any her father had ever owned. He handed her a note, told her that Gavin had gone out, and indeed, the note was from Gavin, telling her he'd accepted an invitation to see a bit of London.

From whom, Lizzie wondered idly, but didn't care enough to inquire. She really didn't care about anything at all except one thing: Jack. She had to see him. But how did she find him in a house as big as Castle Beal?

She recalled that once, when she and Charlotte were girls, their mother had taken them to visit her cousin, Lady MacDavid. Lady MacDavid lived in a fine old mansion near Aberdeen, and in that house, the study and library and drawing rooms were all on the first floor, the family's private rooms above. Lizzie went on the assumption that all fine mansions were designed that way, and made her way to the first floor.

She wandered down the corridor. The only sign of life was the occasional chambermaid who hurried past, her head down. At last a footman emerged from a room carrying a silver tray with several folded letters. Once he'd passed, Lizzie hurried to the very door he'd come out of. Thankfully, it was still open, and she saw Jack sitting behind a mahogany desk with heads of lions carved from the top of its legs and sweeping down into clawed feet.

He was bent over correspondence, his brow furrowed in thought. A lone footman stood to one side, his back against the wall, his gaze pointed at something on the opposite wall. As Lizzie debated making her presence known, Jack said, "Here, then, Beauchamp." He lifted the paper and waved it impatiently to dry. He put the paper down, folded it haphazardly, then sealed it with wax and a signet. He looked up again, held out the letter to the footman. "Take it straightaway to Lindsey."

"Yes, milord," the footman said, and turned toward the door.

Jack saw Lizzie then, and surely thought she was spying on him. What else could he think with her peeking through the open door? A look—perturbation?—glanced across his features, but he was quickly on his feet. "Lizzie," he said. "Come, come."

He didn't seem at all happy to see her. There was no charming grin, no shining gray eyes, and Lizzie suddenly felt even more at sea, bobbing about with no anchor, as it were. She entered the room cautiously as the footman went out, and tried not to ogle her surroundings. It was impossible to do—this was obviously a private study, as richly appointed as the rest of the house. Her feet sank into thick carpet, and the fire was built up to the point her shawl felt too warm. Lizzie had noticed that about every room: the hearth was always lit, there was warmth and light everywhere, and she was keenly aware that no one here wore gloves with the tips of the fingers cut off.

"I ah . . . I trust you found the accommodations to your liking?" Jack asked.

So formal! So stiff! "You've seen Thorntree, aye?" Lizzie said, in a feeble attempt at levity. He did not smile. "I find the accommodations very fine, indeed, I do."

"Good." He nodded. He looked down at his desk.

"Jack—"

"You should avail yourself of the town," he said quickly. "See a bit of London while you are here. You might no' have the opportunity again, aye?"

See a bit of London, as if she were a casual visitor, as if this were all very frivolous and gay.

"There are many fine museums and some rather exquisite gardens the likes of which I've no' seen in Scotland," he continued. "Or, if you prefer, I have box seats at the opera. Obviously, given my situation, I can no' attend. But you and Mr. Gordon should."

Lizzie gaped at him. "I'm . . . I'm no' attending the opera, Jack."

"Why no'?"

"Why *no'*? For the love of Scotland, do you hear what you are saying? I can no' go to the opera! I can no' flit about as if I am a tourist! I've come only to attend to some very ill business, or have you forgotten?"

"I assure you, I could no' forget it, for Lord knows I have tried," he said tightly. "But if you'd rather no' . . ." He shrugged indifferently.

Why was he acting so strangely, so distant? "What I wish has little to do with my reason for being here."

"It is unfortunate," Jack agreed. "If there is anything we might do to make your stay more pleasant, you must no' hesitate to tell Winston." With that he sat and resumed his review of correspondence, effectively dismissing her.

"Jack!" she cried.

"Lizzie, if you please," he said calmly. "I've been gone quite a long time and have a lot of business to tend to."

"Why are you speaking to me as if . . . as if you hardly know me, as if you have better things to occupy your time than a civil conversation?"

"Perhaps because I do," he said, and looked up. At seeing her pained expression, he sighed. "Come now, Lizzie. What we shared at Thorntree was nice, I'll grant you—"

"Nice!"

"But we have run the course of our handfasting, aye? We have come to London, where I have my life. I will see the king on your behalf, and you will return to Thorntree, where you have your life. We both knew it would eventually be so. What is the point of protracting our acquaintance?"

He could not have stunned her more if he had slapped her. "You donna mean that," she said shakily.

His expression did not change. It was cold. Hard. "You knew what I was the moment you met me, Lizzie. Donna imagine I am anything more," he said brusquely. "If you will excuse me, I've quite a lot to accomplish before I face the prince's allegations. Which, by the bye, may take a few days. You may as well spend your leisure in pursuit of the town's many diversions. I can offer you my home, Lizzie, but that is all."

Her heart was sinking to her knees and she felt ill. It seemed impossibly close in that cavernous room. "That's all you would say?" she said, her voice shaking. "After the last few weeks—"

"I beg your pardon, but you once sought to keep me in a barn, aye? It is no' as if we ever shared a great affection."

"Clearly you did no'," she said, her voice breaking. "But please do no' speak for me."

Jack glanced down and swallowed hard. "If you are in need of a carriage, you need only inquire of Winston." He looked back at the papers on his desk, silently dismissing her as he might a servant.

"Bastard," she said softly.

She could see him tense, could see his hand tighten around the pen.

"You are a *bastard*, Jack, the worst sort of monster. You took advantage of my feelings—"

"Did I?" he snapped, pinning her with a cold gaze. "You understood that there was no future in our liaison," he said evenly. "Will you play the part of the wounded miss now?"

She hated him. In that moment, she hated him with all her heart. "I hope they do hang you," she said. "You deserve no less." She turned abruptly, desperate to be away from him and his black heart.

"Lizzie!" he called after her.

Against her better judgment, she stopped. She clenched her hands into fists and forced herself to look at him.

His blistering gaze swept over her. "I am having guests this evening. You and your Gordon might be more comfortable dining out."

Lizzie's fury soared to such heights that she could not draw breath. She concentrated on fleeing the room without stumbling, for her knees felt weak. She ran so quickly that she almost collided with a tall man who was in the company of Mr. Winston.

"I beg your pardon," he said, bowing his head and stepping out of her way.

Lizzie didn't answer but walked as quickly as she might down that beautifully carpeted corridor. The hairline crack his words had put in her poor heart had begun its ugly and rapid spread. She felt as fragile as glass, as if the slightest nudge would shatter her completely.

Christie, the Duke of Darlington, looked puzzled as he entered the study behind Winston, and glanced over his shoulder once.

Jack looked down at his hand and the line of blood across his palm where the quill had cut into his flesh. He hadn't realized he was gripping it so tightly.

Jack pressed a handkerchief to the cut as Christie crossed the room to him.

"Lambourne! I am surprised to see you alive. And in London, of all places."

Jack smiled a little and took the hand Christie offered. "Your surprise is eclipsed only by my own, Christie. How are you?"

"Very well," he said. "And you look well. A fugitive's life agrees with you. You look a bit thicker."

"Thicker?" Jack asked.

Christie looked at his arms. "Yes. Thicker and weathered."

That much Jack had recognized too. His face had tanned during his time on the run. He smiled wryly. "I've come to appreciate my life in London."

Christie laughed and glanced over his shoulder to the door. "Who . . . ?"

"A rather long tale," Jack said dismissively. "Whisky?"

Christie waved him off. Jack poured a tot for himself and gestured for Christie to sit in one of three chairs grouped around the hearth. "I heard of Wilkes," Jack said with a wince. "I can no' express how it pained me."

"Yes." Christie sighed sadly and filled him in on the sordid tale, repeating much of what Fiona had told him, but explaining the awful conspiracy around the prince to unseat the king. The prince had not known of it before Nathan, the Earl of Lindsey, brought it to light.

"Then the scandal goes on?" Jack asked, hoping against hope that it had begun to fade.

"It's even worse," Christie said, and told him about the men who, suspected of adultery with the Princess of Wales, had been rounded up, and how the king was famously indecisive as to what to do about the wretched affair. In the absence of any guidance from the throne, the scandal seemed to mushroom.

"And *you*, sir," Christie said, "are in quite a lot of trouble. You would have done well to stay in Scotland."

"Aye, that I know," Jack said, frowning. "That is why I asked for you, old friend. I must have an audience with the king."

Christie laughed roundly.

Jack did not.

"Are you mad?" Christie sputtered. "An audience with the king will be your undoing, Lambourne! He can scarcely protect you from George if you are standing in his privy chamber!"

"I am aware," Jack said wearily.

Christie looked at him as if he believed Jack was indeed mad, which, Jack feared, he may very well be. "But why?" Christie demanded. "Why risk all that you have, and possibly your life?"

"I have no choice," Jack said simply. "It . . . it is no' on my account, but for someone else."

Christie glared at him, then slowly sank back against his chair. "By all that is holy, this is about the pretty one in the hall, I take it?"

Jack nodded but said quickly, "It's no' what you think. It is the least I can do for her, given what has befallen her." He proceeded to tell Christie the contemptible tale of the handfasting, the slate, and the certain ruin of a woman and her crippled sister. He did not tell Christie of his affection for Lizzie, or how it had almost killed him to turn her away so cruelly, and how he was still feeling that awful pain in his gut.

Nor did he tell Christie about the many thoughts he'd had of his father of late, and his father's streak of cruelty, his affairs and his disrespect of Jack's mother, and how Jack feared himself capable of that too, as he'd never been in love before now.

He just said that he felt strongly he must see the king on Lizzie's behalf.

Christie listened, his eyes intent on Jack, his mouth in a tight line. When Jack had finished, Christie sighed, stood up, and poured them each a whisky. He tapped his tot against Jack's and tossed it back. "You know doing this might very well ruin you?"

"Or kill me, aye," Jack said.

"I've never understood a man who would disregard his title, his responsibilities, his estate, his family, all for a woman. It defies logic."

"I could no' agree more," Jack said morosely.

"Very well, then," Christie said stiffly. "I will see to it. But the scandal is brewing and it is the eve of the parliamentary session. It will take a bit of doing to gain an audience."

'Thank you, Christie," Jack said. "I am in your debt."

"Bloody bad business asking a friend to see to your hanging," Christie grumbled as he stood to leave.

Bloody bad business being hanged, Jack thought.

When Gavin returned late that afternoon, he encountered a pretty young woman who bore a resemblance to Lambourne in the foyer. He bowed.

"How do you do, sir?" she said. "You must be Mr. Gordon, then. I am Lady Fiona Haines, the earl's sister."

"Lady Fiona, it is my great pleasure to make your acquaintance," Gavin said. Aye, this one was quite pretty, with a lovely figure.

"You've been out," she said, smiling. "Is it your first time to London?"

Aye, he'd been out, all right. "It is indeed. I've seen many wondrous things today."

"Indeed? What have you seen?" she asked, and seemed to be interested.

Gavin smiled and gestured to the corridor. "Perhaps I might tell you about it over tea. That is, if you are no' engaged elsewhere?"

Lady Fiona looked at the clock in the foyer. "I suppose I have a few moments," she said and, smiling, walked with Gavin to one of the many sitting rooms.

Chapter Thirty-five

❧

I f she'd had a rope, Lizzie might have bound Gavin and tossed him in a closet. What cheek, to go into London society as if they were part of it! Did he not understand they would be ridiculed?

Somehow he'd managed to wrangle an invitation from Lady Fiona to attend a supper party as her guests. Lizzie had balked, but Gavin had been insistent and demanded that she attend.

Lizzie was hardly in the mood for anyone's society, much less that of anyone even remotely attached to Jack. She had alternately fumed and despaired all afternoon over Jack's treatment of her. She supposed she ought to be thankful that the moment they arrived in London, he had indeed shown his true colors. He was quite right—he was *precisely* what she'd suspected from the beginning, a man with no moral compass, a reprehensible rake!

Jack had used her ill, and the clench in Lizzie's belly made her weak. *She loved him.* She loved him, and she was devastated to discover that she'd given herself to a man who held such little regard for her in return. He'd made a game of her, a fool, and worse, she'd made herself a wanton. The pain was almost more than she could bear.

What hurt most of all was that she did want love, a

soul-searing, breathless love. She wanted it above the security Gavin offered her. She wanted it above life, and all the hope she'd put into the one man who could give that to her had been crushed.

Now, to have to go out into London society, broken and used, was not to be borne.

She readied herself woodenly, her arms and hands performing the motions of her toilette. She remained dressed in her teal gown, for it was the only gown she owned that was suitable for such an evening. The very gown she'd once believed so beautiful now seemed so plain.

She couldn't help but stare in the mirror as Lucy gamely attempted to dress her hair. Lizzie had cut it several months ago, for she had no one to dress it at Thorntree, and she could hardly contend with it, what with everything else she had to do in a day's time.

But as Lucy bit her lower lip and cocked her head, studying the curls, Lizzie very much regretted the decision now. She unclasped the string of pearls she'd wrapped around her neck, hoping to spruce up the dull gown a bit. "Perhaps this might help, then," she said.

"Ah!" Lucy smiled brightly and wrapped the pearls through her hair, tucking up the curls, leaving two or three to hang gracefully down her neck. "That will do very well, mu'um," Lucy said, smiling at her handiwork. "Shall I fetch you a wrap?"

She had nothing for warmth but the thick wool shawls she wore about Thorntree. "No, thank you," Lizzie said on a sigh. "I shall wear a cloak."

"Very good, mu'um," Lucy said.

It wasn't very good at all, Lizzie thought as she made her way down to the entrance hall. She felt entirely conspicuous, an obvious rustic in an unfashionable gown, a woman who had given her heart to a man who had smashed it into bits. She was fairly certain that was all quite noticeable to the sophisticated townspeople of London.

There was no one in the entrance hall, Lizzie noted irritably, and glanced at the tall grandfather clock. It read ten past seven, which she supposed meant the clock on the mantel in her room was fast. Lizzie sighed; twenty minutes of waiting meant twenty minutes of moping, and she absently wandered the length of the entrance hall, her fingers trailing along the wainscoting, her mind's eye filled with Jack.

Jack.

Jack was walking across the house on his way to the red salon, where he would meet Christie and Lord Lindsey, who was up from the country. His footfall was silent on the carpet that lined his halls and, he realized, as he neared the entrance hall and caught sight of her, that Lizzie had not heard him. He paused just inside the corridor and watched her wandering aimlessly about, glancing up at the paintings he'd had sent back from Italy and mindlessly touching an empty, hand-painted porcelain vase.

How was it that she seemed lovelier to him each time? She dressed plainly, nothing to adorn her gown but her eyes. Her hair was prettily bound up with a string of pearls. But as she turned slightly to look up at another painting, he noticed a sadness about her eyes, a pain, he imagined, like that he felt rather deep in himself.

But his pain came from knowing he'd put the sadness in her eyes. He'd hurt her in a way he'd hoped himself incapable of, yet it had seemed the only way. How else could he make her understand him? He'd made a horrible, cruel mistake with Lizzie. He'd given a woman he loved a hope he could not fulfill. It was little wonder the entire populace of Scotland had found him so untrustworthy at first glance. They'd seen something in him he hadn't seen in himself.

She suddenly turned, as if sensing his presence, blinking those clear blue eyes that haunted his every moment. "Jack," she said, her voice soft and uncertain.

"Lizzie." He bowed politely.

They stood only feet apart, but the breach between them seemed so wide that he was mildly surprised he could see her at all. She moved forward a step or two, as if she believed he would speak. Hardly aware of it, Jack moved too, his gaze taking in every lovely curving inch. When his gaze reached her eyes, his chest tightened painfully. "You are going out," he remarked flatly.

"Aye. With Mr. Gordon and your sister," she said. "She insisted."

And she had protested, but Jack had been firm with Fiona—remove this woman from his sight. He had not told Fiona that he could not bear to be near Lizzie and not touch her, that he could not breathe the same air as her and not feel as if he were gasping for breath. "My sister is the consummate hostess."

"That is rather surprising, really, given that her brother is no'."

"*Touché*," he muttered. *Walk on*, he told himself. *The damage is done. Just go.*

"You look . . ." She clasped her hands behind her back and let her gaze wander over him. He was dressed in a new suit of clothing, one that had arrived from the tailor shortly after he departed England. "Very handsome. London obviously agrees with you."

Jack hesitated. He wanted to tell her she looked beautiful in any location, that he could scarcely take his eyes from her, that the glimmer in her eye alone made his heart beat a thousand times faster. "Thank you," he said simply.

"I beg your pardon, but I have no' had the opportunity to tell you how . . ." She glanced around her. "How beautiful is your home. I've never even dreamed of something so fine. It's little wonder you were anxious to come back, even with your troubles."

The band around Jack's chest tightened. His home seemed like an opulent monstrosity. He was beginning to think that a home was a wee bit more like Lizzie's house.

"I thank you, Jack," she said. "You've done me an enormous favor, really. I fooled myself into believing I could trust you, but, as you pointed out, my instincts about you were quite right. You would no' have changed for me and Thorntree. My only true regret is that I was . . . I was foolish enough to have fallen in *love*," she said, gasping a little with the word.

"Lizzie—"

"But that I did, and I only have myself to blame. So thank you," she said, inclining her head, "for so clearly disabusing me of the notion that you might have returned that affection. Surely one day I shall look back and know that in your cruelty, you spared me immeasurable sorrow. And how odd it is yet, that I can no' thank you enough for it, for you have saved my life while stealing my heart."

"*Diah*, Lizzie—"

"Please, please, donna say a word," she said, throwing up her hand to stop him at the same moment someone knocked on the front door. "I canna bear to hear another word but that you've arranged to see the king so that I might go," she said, her voice breaking. "Go home to Thorntree, where I belong."

A footman opened the door behind her.

"No' as yet," he said.

Christie swept in, Lindsey in tow. "Lambourne!" Lindsey said jovially. "Christ be to saints, I was certain I'd never see you again!"

Lizzie walked forward, away from the door and passing so close to Jack that she brushed his arm, sending a charge through him. By the time Christie and Lindsey had handed over their cloaks and gloves, she had disappeared.

"There is much to tell you," Lindsey said as he greeted Jack with a handshake. "It would seem the entire world has gone mad, lad."

Lindsey had no idea just how mad.

Jack spent the better part of the night hearing the news from Lindsey and Christie. His shock over Wilkes was not diminished when Lindsey told him all who had been involved in the failed plot to murder Princess Caroline so that when George ascended the throne, he did so without the haze of the awful scandal hanging over his head. Evelyn, Lady Lindsey, had been targeted when they suspected her purported lover might have told her about the plot.

The men—they called themselves the prince's coterie—included some of the most prominent men in England. It was shocking, unbelievable.

Jack found himself missing his own little Highland scandal, which seemed almost laughably sedate in comparison to what he was hearing.

They talked quite a lot about Jack's fate. Neither Christie nor Lindsey seemed to think it mattered if Jack was guilty of bedding the princess or not. "What matters is that His Grace believes it to be true," Christie said. But neither man thought Jack would hang. However, they were not confident he'd emerge unscathed, either.

"A repossession of lands," Christie suggested. "That would be a fitting punishment."

Jack cringed. "But I never touched her!"

"No," Lindsey said, shaking his head. "The prince doesn't have the funds for the upkeep of a castle in the middle of bloody Scotland. Prison is more likely."

"That hardly eases me," Jack groused.

"You mustn't fret, old chum," Lindsey said solemnly. "We shall visit you."

"What of an audience with the king?" Jack asked Christie.

"Bloody hell, Lambourne, *why*?" Lindsey insisted. "Is there no other way you might help the lass?"

Jack shook his head.

Lindsey suddenly surged forward. "You need not see the king. We can help you, band together—"

"Can you void a handfasting vow?" Jack asked angrily. "Can you keep her land safe from her uncle? Rein in a Highland laird?"

Lindsey and Christie looked at each other.

"Believe me when I tell you that if there were any other way, I'd be quite pleased to do it, for I do no' relish twisting at the end of a rope." Jack slowly leaned back. "Have you requested the audience?" he asked, his voice calmer.

"I am waiting," Christie said solemnly. "It is not the easy matter it might once have been."

"How long might it take?" Jack demanded impatiently.

Christie shrugged. "A day. A week. A month. One cannot predict."

"I canna remain trapped like an animal in this house!" Jack said testily, thinking of his close proximity to Lizzie. "I've told Winston no one may mention I am in residence, but how long might I expect before someone slips?"

"That is the risk," Lindsey said. "You may leave London yet, Jack. No one knows you are here."

That was sorely tempting, but the image that popped into Jack's head was the one of Lizzie standing in the entrance hall tonight, and the unbearable hurt in her eyes. "I can no'," he said shortly, and tossed back a tot of whisky.

The gentlemen left well after midnight, but Jack remained in the red salon, nursing a whisky and mulling over the many changes his life had undergone in the last three months and the many changes he was facing.

Fiona found him ruminating when she returned from the supper party to which she'd dragged Lizzie and Gordon. She entered in grand fashion, tossing her shawl onto the settee and helping herself to a bit of whisky before bending at the waist to peck Jack on the cheek.

"Your guests have gone so soon?" she asked with some surprise. "I fully expected to see you with cards in hand."

A game of cards seemed an empty and frivolous activity to Jack now, but that is precisely what he might have done three months ago. "I've little patience for card games, given the circumstances. Lindsey informs me I shall have quite a lot of time for it in Newgate."

"Jack! You will no' go to prison! I suspect they will banish you from England. That seems far more likely, aye?"

Only in the fairy tales Fiona had read as a girl, but he had no desire to frighten his sister with the truth. "How was your evening, then?"

"Oh!" she exclaimed with a roll of her eyes. "Lady Gilbert had her awful little mongrel in tow. *Diah,* but that thing is incorrigible, and Lady Gilbert completely blind to it! Oh, and did you know, then, that Mrs. Kirkland has been having an illicit association with Lord Howard?" she asked excitedly.

"No," Jack drawled. He hardly cared. There were such weightier matters at hand.

Fiona nodded eagerly. "They've been scandalously open about it, too. I heard from Victoria Runsgate that they attended the opera! Can you imagine it, attending the opera with your lover, in plain view of your husband?"

"No," he said again. How did people fill their days with such prattle? "How did our guests find the evening?"

"Oh, very well, I suppose. Mr. Gordon was quite animated and engaging. I do believe Lady Gilbert's sister, Miss Handlesman, was *quite* taken with him. And he with her. He's handsome, which puts him in good stead in London. Has he any fortune?"

As if fortune were the true measure of a man. He could hardly fault Fiona—that was the *ton*'s way of thinking. Certainly that had been his measure all these years. "I would no' know," Jack said. "And Miss Beal?"

"She was rather subdued. But honestly, Jack, you canna expect her to go out in the same gown night after night."

"Pardon?"

"Her *gown*," Fiona said impatiently. "I should think it a lovely summer frock, but it is no' suitable for London, and it is so plain."

"I am sure she will wear another one," he said, chafing at this bit of shallow conversation.

"Another one! She does no' possess another one. She's purse-pinched and her best gown is the teal one. She needs a proper wardrobe to go into society."

Of course. Why hadn't he thought of it? "Then you

must get her one, Fiona. You must find proper gowns
that she might wear. And a bonnet."

"A bonnet?"

"Aye, aye," he said, and suddenly sat up. "You must
find her the best bonnet London has to offer. And . . . and
gowns, and shoes, and that sort of thing. But a *bonnet*, Fi.
The best bonnet."

"A bonnet." Fiona's eyes narrowed on him. "If you
love her, why do you no' admit it, then?"

"I donna love her," Jack said gruffly.

"Jack." Fiona gave him a look that told him she knew
him quite well.

He sighed, slumped in his chair, and ran a hand
through his hair. "It's all very complicated, Fi."

"Rubbish."

"She is a provincial woman, and I . . . I am . . ."

"A man? A man in need of a wife, a wife he could love
desperately and completely, and one who might very
well love him just the same?"

"I am a man bound for prison. Or worse."

"You're no' in the least!"

"And besides . . . she'd never consent to life in London. She has a crippled sister in the Highlands who
needs her."

"Then you must consent to life in Scotland. I have, and
I am right glad of it."

Jack chuckled.

Fiona slapped him on the knee. "I have! And so might
you! Have you even considered it?"

"No," he said. Strangely, he never had. He'd always
thought of Scotland as lacking any proper society. But
he'd not missed society at Thorntree. Perhaps society was
of one's own making? "There is something else," Jack
said. "Our father."

"Father! He's dead, God rest his soul!"

"No, no," Jack said, trying to verbalize his very vague fears. "Do you remember him, Fi? Do you remember how hard he was on Mother?"

"How could I forget it?" she said, slumping into her chair.

Jack couldn't forget it either. One night, when he was only fourteen years, he'd found his mother with a bruised cheek and black eye. He'd taken up a gun, intent on killing his father. But he'd been just a boy, and his father had taken the gun from him easily, then slapped Jack so hard he'd been knocked to the ground.

He could remember lying there, stunned, and his father looming over him, his eyes so wide they seemed almost completely white. "One day you will understand what misery a woman can cause a man, lad," he'd said. "One day you will understand the only way to manage them is the same way you'd manage your dog, aye?"

The memory of it made Jack shudder to this day.

"What is it, then?" Fiona asked him.

Jack glanced at her sidelong. "I have often wondered if I might be driven to . . . to harm as Father was."

Fiona surprised him with a laugh. "Jankin Haines, you are no more like him than I am! There is no' a cruel bone in your body!" She laughed again, but when Jack did not laugh with her, she quickly sobered. She reached out to put her hand on his knee. "*Mi Diah!* You are no' like him! You could never *be* like him. You are the kindest, most generous man I've ever known, and I donna tell you that because you are my brother. You have taken care of me all these years and never so much as raised your voice. You are a gentle rogue, darling."

Jack squeezed her hand in gratitude.

"Have you truly feared it? Is that what keeps you from her?"

"No' all of it," he said, shaking his head with a wry smile. "Her sister has lost the use of her legs and has no one on which to depend but Miss Beal. And she has a small estate from which a few derive their livelihood and only her to manage it. And I . . . I am better suited to life in town, I am. I've no' lived in Scotland since I was a young man. Lambourne is an empty shell—"

"Of your own volition. It could be quite nice."

He shook his head. "I can scarcely abide it."

"Because when you are there, you are alone with your memories, Jack. But what if it were filled with light? And laughter and love and children? And I shall be close by."

That was something. But Jack shook his head again. "No, Fi, my life is here now. And what does it matter, really? She will marry Mr. Gordon."

Fiona made such a sound of laughing surprise that she startled Jack.

"*Marry* him?" she cried gleefully and fell back in her chair with a laugh. "She will no' marry Mr. Gordon."

"What do you mean?" Jack demanded.

"Darling, if she marries him, I am English. Oh, donna look so shocked! She certainly would no' be the first woman to settle for the best match of fortune instead of the heart. I suppose she's done the best she might, aye? But she loves you, Jack. It is perfectly obvious and she strikes me as the sort who would follow her heart."

"She has no choice," Jack said.

"We *all* have a choice," Fiona said sagely. "It is precisely what I told Lady Gilbert about Francesca Boudin. Are you acquainted?"

"No," Jack said, his mind already wandering.

"Francesca Boudin is *hopelessly* in love with Lord

Babington, but she'll no' admit it, no' to a single soul, for Lord Maberly is a better match for her in terms of fortune and position in society, aye? Lady Gilbert, who can be contrary when presented with facts, argued with me. She said . . ."

Jack did not hear the rest of his sister's long and rather convoluted tale. He was feeling too perplexed. Everything seemed so different now. *He* was different now. And London's high society suddenly seemed meaningless and vapid to him. All he could seem to think about since he'd arrived in this town was Lizzie or his own wretched future.

"Jack! You are no' listening to me at all!" Fiona complained.

"No," he said, and stood up. "I am no'." He leaned over and kissed his sister on the top of her head. "Bring round some suitable gowns for our guest. And the bonnet. Donna forget the bonnet, Fiona. Good night, *leannan*."

"A bonnet! When did you become so particular about your bonnets, then? I shall write Duncan straightaway and tell him you've gone quite soft in the course of becoming a fugitive."

Jack smiled to himself as he went out. If there was a constant in his life, it was Fiona. And Lizzie in his blood.

Chapter Thirty-six

L izzie was so miserable in London that the next day, she kept to her rooms, save the few moments at breakfast when Gavin reviewed his itinerary for the day. "Vauxhall Gardens," he began. "Miss Handlesman told me they were spectacular and offered to show them to me. Will you join us, Lizzie?"

Lizzie smiled thinly. "You'll pardon me, will you? I am feeling a wee bit unwell."

"Nothing serious, I hope?" he asked as gained his feet.

"No' at all. You should go without me."

"You're certain you willna mind?" he asked, looking at his pocket watch.

"Of course no'. I think I shall rest."

"Aye, that will do you a bit of good." He looked up from his watch and smiled. "Good day, lass," he said, and leaned down to peck her cheek.

The day was interminably long. Lizzie pined alternately for Jack and for home. She worried constantly about Charlotte and fretted that Carson was so angry, that he'd done something awful to her or Thorntree. She wrote two letters, one to Charlotte, and one to Carson begging him to leave Charlotte be, promising that she'd return to Thorntree to resolve their differences.

That evening, when Gavin returned much later than he'd promised, Lizzie sent word that she'd gone to bed early. She had no heart for him.

The next morning, Gavin was gone by the time she appeared for breakfast. Winston informed her he'd been invited to attend an auction for horseflesh in the village of Kilburn with Lord and Lady Montrose.

It seemed to Lizzie as if Gavin had forgotten the reason they were in London. To that end, she asked Winston if he might inquire of His Lordship how much longer they might be forced to wait. Winston returned with his answer a half hour later. "Indefinitely, madam," he said with a bow of his gray head.

With a groan, Lizzie returned to the suite that had become almost as confining as the little turret room Carson had forced them into. At least there she'd had a bit of company. Exasperating, exciting, charming company.

Here she had nothing to do but wander about and think. She despised thinking! There were only dark, painful thoughts wandering about her head, and one small thought that would not stop biting at her.

She'd been over and over it, and frankly, she didn't believe Jack. She didn't believe he was as cold as she'd shown her. But why, then, would he have done it? There were no promises between them, nothing he couldn't have said to her.

Lizzie would be happy if she never had to think again. What she wouldn't give for a list of chores to occupy her!

But midafternoon, she was surprised by Lady Fiona and a family friend, Lady Lindsey. They knocked on the door of the sitting room, and when Lizzie answered, they swept in, directing two footmen whose arms were laden with gowns. They deposited them over the back of a settee, and Fiona shooed them away, then made the introductions.

Lady Lindsey—"You must call me Evelyn," she said with genuine warmth—was even prettier than Lady Fiona. "You poor dear, thrust into London with no introduction! I could scarcely believe it when Fiona told me. I came to London years ago, just as alone as you, but at least I knew a person here or there."

"Aye," Lizzie said weakly.

"We must have you properly outfitted," Fiona said. "Lady Lindsey has kindly offered to share her lovely gowns."

Lizzie blanched at the mere suggestion. "No!" she exclaimed. "Oh no, no, I could no' possibly!"

"It is quite all right, Miss Beal," Lady Lindsey said kindly. "I cannot button a single one." She grinned. "I'm with child."

It was obvious. She was glowing with her pleasure.

"I should kick Jack for no' giving you time to assemble a full wardrobe, aye?" Lady Fiona said. "It was terribly thoughtless of him. But when I told him, he said I should make it right, straightaway."

"No, no, no— He did?"

Evelyn held up a gown, eyeing Lizzie against it. "You must choose one for the ball tonight."

Lizzie's heart dropped to her toes. "A *ball!*" Panic filled her chest. "No! I canna attend a ball. I—"

"Miss Beal, we will be by your side," Fiona assured her. "We'd no' dare abandon you. And it is a very small ball. A mere one hundred guests."

One hundred guests! Lizzie's gasped as Evelyn held up another gown, this one a deep claret silk. She shook her head and tossed it aside as if it were paper, and then picked up one made of gold velvet. It was beautiful.

It looked like what Lizzie imagined a princess would wear.

Evelyn smiled as she held it up to Lizzie. "It is perfect, isn't it, Fiona? It suits her coloring perfectly."

Fiona stood back and nodded. "Aye," she said. "It is perfect."

"I will no' attend a ball," Lizzie insisted.

"You will have a change of heart once you've seen yourself in this," Evelyn said. "This was designed and sewn by Mrs. Olive, one of the most exclusive modistes in London. She typically confines her work to the royal family, but she owed me a small favor. And now, you will be the envy of every woman at the ball."

But Lizzie did not want to be the envy of anyone. She just wanted to go back to Thorntree, where life was simple and her society known to her. She could not attend a ball in a gown made for a princess!

Yet even she had to admit to a moment of pleasant surprise when she was dressed in the gown and standing before a full-length mirror. She wouldn't have thought she could look so . . . so lovely. So *regal*. When Fiona put a necklace of gold on her, she felt like a queen. She turned one way, then the other, admiring herself, wishing Charlotte could see her.

"It is breath taking," she said softly. She wondered how much a gown like this might cost, what things she might buy for Thorntree with the money Lady Lindsey had certainly spent on this gown.

"Have you ever been to a ball?" Fiona asked.

"No," Lizzie said laughingly. "In Glenalmond, we've only country dances."

"Mmm," Fiona said, admiring the fit of the gown on her. "A country ball in Scotland is the poor cousin of a London society ball. There is dancing, my dear, and"—

she leaned in to whisper—"there is *dancing*. You and Mr. Gordon will be properly scandalized by it."

Lizzie had already been scandalized by it. And she would never dance a waltz with anyone, lest she ruin that perfect memory.

"But I've no reason to attend," Lizzie said. "I willna be in London long."

"Why should you no' have a diversion?" Fiona asked cheerily. "If you attend, you might return to Scotland and amuse them all with what you've seen and done, aye? Come, then, Evelyn," she said. "Let us find our own costumes for the evening."

They left Lizzie dressed in the gold velvet gown, staring at herself in the mirror. The gown was exquisite, it was, but . . . but she was not a debutante. She was not the sort of woman to chat idly as they had the night she'd dined with Lady Fiona's friends. The things they'd talked about had seemed so trifling to Lizzie—who might marry whom, what fortune did this or that gentleman have, and so forth. Lizzie had a crippled sister at home and worries these women would never have. Their main concern was social position; hers was survival.

And there was something wholly lacking from last night's supper table and the ball this evening: Jack.

Lizzie did not want Jack's world, but Lord, she wanted him. Two days of mourning him had done nothing to dampen her love for him. And their last meeting, in the entrance hall, had only confused her more. He'd said the words without emotion, but she had seen the look in his eyes. It was the same look she'd seen the night they'd made love—a look of gnawing hunger, of a desire that ran through to the marrow.

Lizzie had not been able to shake that image. In her heart of hearts, all she wanted was Jack, and everything else seemed small and inconsequential compared to that overwhelming desire. To be in the same house as he—even a house as big as this—to be so close and not with him was excruciating. How would she survive such pain?

When Lucy appeared, carrying a large millinery box, Lizzie assumed it was another bit of borrowed clothing from Fiona and Evelyn. "It came from Mrs. Olive's dress shop," Lucy said. "Lady Fiona said His Lordship purchased it for you."

"Pardon?" Lizzie asked, looking up from the book at which she'd stared blindly for an hour.

"From His Lordship," Lucy said uncertainly. "She said I was to tell you he purchased it for you."

Lizzie took the box from Lucy. She quickly untied the ribbons, pulled the lid from the box, and withdrew a straw bonnet. A beautiful, perfectly trimmed straw bonnet. The ribbons were made of velvet, the floral trim of velvet and silk, and the flowers delicate and small. It was exquisitely made. "It . . . it is the finest bonnet in all of Britain," Lizzie murmured.

"Oh, it is *very* nice," Lucy said. "The latest fashion—that is Mrs. Olive for you."

"Aye," Lizzie murmured.

"They are waiting for you mu'um," Lucy said.

"Pardon?" Lizzie asked, distracted.

"Lady Fiona and Mr. Gordon. They are waiting for you in the gold salon."

Lizzie gasped and looked at the clock on the mantel. She'd tried to reset it, but it was now an hour slow. "I'll be there straightaway," she said, and stood up, still holding the bonnet, holding it out from her body, staring at it as her mind whirled. "I'll . . . I'll be right along, then," she said.

Lucy curtsied and went out, leaving Lizzie with the gorgeous bonnet. She finally put it back in its box but took the hatpin from its crown and turned around to the mirror. She looked at herself in that beautiful gold gown, bit her bottom lip, and said, "I beg your pardon, Lady Lindsey." She dragged the hatpin along the seam, creating a slight tear.

Several minutes later, she hurried into the gold salon, where Gavin and Lady Fiona were waiting. Gavin was prattling on about something, but was interrupted by the sight of Lizzie. He smiled broadly. "*Leannan*, you are beautiful," he said admiringly. "I shall be right proud to have you on my arm, I will."

"Thank you," she said, smiling self-consciously. "Un-unfortunately, I've run into a wee bit of a problem," Lizzie said. Gavin and Lady Fiona looked at her. She pointed to her side. "A wee tear in the fabric. I suppose I am a bit bigger than Lady Lindsey. I must repair it before we go."

Gavin looked slightly disconsolate. "Well. We shall wait."

"No, no, you must go on without me!"

"I'd no' think of it," he said, looking at her gown.

"Of course we will wait," Lady Fiona said, her gaze fixed on Lizzie. "I'll send Lucy to you."

Lucy, who had just left her, and who would be surprised to learn of a tear in Lizzie's seam. "Please," Lizzie said as evenly as she could. "I can repair it, and then . . . then His Lordship said I need only ask for a carriage. I'll just ask one to be brought round. You donna want to be tardy, aye? And . . . and I must remove the gown and stitch it, then dress again, and . . ."

"I see," Lady Fiona said, her gaze as clear as a hawk's. "We should take our leave, Mr. Gordon. I will tell the Brant butler to expect Miss Beal a bit later, shall I?"

Gavin looked almost relieved. "A perfect solution, milady," he said, and offered his arm.

Lady Fiona put her hand on his proffered arm and the two paraded to the door. But Lady Fiona paused to look at Lizzie once more.

"I shall be along as soon as possible," Lizzie said.

"Donna fret about the time, Miss Beal," Lady Fiona added. "The Brants are famously lax about social engagements."

And, if Lizzie wasn't mistaken, Lady Fiona gave her a slight wink.

She watched the pair walk out. She waited until she was certain they had gone, until she heard the front door close and the clip of the footman's shoes on the marble floor.

Jack.

She had no idea where to find him, but she was prepared to go door to door if she must. And she was going now, before she lost her courage. Lizzie marched from the gold salon and turned right, down the carpeted corridor, pausing at each door, timidly opening them, and finding dark rooms. There seemed to be at least a dozen, and she was beginning to lose hope and bravado when she opened a door and startled the occupants.

Jack and two other gentlemen came quickly and awkwardly to their feet.

"I beg your pardon," Lizzie said as the two men turned to look curiously at her.

Jack, on the other hand, looked stunned. His gaze swept over her, and from where she stood, she saw him swallow. "Miss Beal?"

If she didn't gain his attention now, she'd never have the courage again. "Lizzie," she said. "You call me Lizzie. You've always called me Lizzie."

Jack's eyes widened slightly and he exchanged a look with his companions.

"A pleasure, Lizzie," the tall one said with a smile for Jack.

"Excuse me," Jack said low, and strode quickly across the room to catch Lizzie by the elbow. "What are you doing?" he whispered hotly.

"When did you stop saying my name?" she whispered just as hotly.

"This is no' the time, lass."

Lizzie swallowed. "Jack, I know the truth."

"The *truth*?"

"You've been dissembling these last few days."

"*Diah*," he muttered. His gray eyes narrowed on her for a moment, and then he glanced over his shoulder. "I beg your pardon, gentlemen. Please, avail yourself of the wine, and I shall return momentarily."

He grasped Lizzie's elbow tightly and wheeled her about, marching her from the room and propelling her into the hall. "What are you doing, Lizzie?" he asked curtly. "I donna know what you think you have discovered—"

"I received the bonnet."

"The what?"

"The bonnet! The best bonnet in all of Britain! *You* sent it to me."

"Aye, Lizzie, but it is a *bonnet*. It hardly means anything at all."

"That's no' the least bit true and well you know it, Jack Haines. You *do* esteem me, but for some foolish reason, you've determined that you must pretend you do no'."

"I donna esteem you," he snapped, and threw open the door of his study. The hearth was still lit from the day, casting a low light over the room. He pushed her inside, shut the door, and leaned against it with his arms folded tightly over his chest, his head lowered. He glared at her. "What in heavens is the matter with you? What more must I say to convince you that there is naugh' between us?"

"If that is true, then what of the bonnet?"

"Lizzie, honestly—"

"You remembered, Jack. You remembered your promise. When I saw that bonnet in the box, I knew this . . . this wretchedly cold and heartless side of you was a hoax. A cruel one, aye, and one I donna understand *why*, but I knew that you esteem me yet."

"For God's sake!" Jack cried. He pushed both hands through his hair, then sighed heavenward. "Lizzie . . . Lizzie, lass, listen to me now," he said, pushing away from the door and moving toward her. "You will return to Thorntree with your fiancé and you will marry and you will have love and wee bairns and your family around you. What more could you want?"

"*You*," she said. "I could have you. You esteem me, Jack. Admit it!" she said, smiling broadly.

"No, no," he said, pointing at her. "Donna smile at me like that. I am the worst sort of man for you. You were right about me, Lizzie. I am a scoundrel, a rogue. I come from bad stock."

"Bad stock!"

"Aye! Bad stock! You are a fool if you donna take the promise Mr. Gordon gives you. He's a good man. He will do right by you, he will. He'll provide as he ought and he'll honor you, and he'll no' waste money on prime horseflesh or gambling debts or the like," he said with disgust.

Lizzie's grin widened. "He will be my husband and no' my lover. Jack . . . I love you. I have loved you since you kissed me in my room. That searing, *lovely* kiss," she said breathlessly.

Jack caught her hand. "There, do you see? I was trying quite desperately to take advantage of you. Donna do this, Lizzie. Donna pretend. You are expected at a lovely ball, and you are ... you are astoundingly beautiful this evening. You must go, aye? Do you remember what I taught you?"

"I will no' go."

He slipped his other arm around her waist. "*One* two three, *one* two three," he murmured, pulling her into a waltz, moving her in a tight circle as his gaze drifted over her face, her décolletage, her hair. She watched the warmth return to his eyes, could see the shine return to them, and she was sinking into hope and love—

"*Lambourne! Where are you, Lambourne, come at once!*" someone called from the corridor.

"Jack—"

"Bloody hell," he moaned, and stopped dancing. He lifted his head, brushed his hand against her cheek, ran his thumb along her bottom lip.

"*Lambourne! The king!*"

"Donna answer them," she said desperately, and gripped his hand tightly. "Donna go."

He smiled softly. "Go to your ball, Lizzie Beal. Dazzle all of London society. Enjoy yourself. Be happy." He pulled his hand from hers and stepped back.

"No! Jack, wait!"

But he was already to the door, was walking through, was leaving her behind, her body tingling, her heart soaring.

And just like that he was gone, having been called to an audience with the king.

Chapter Thirty-seven

Jack considered himself rather lucky that the prince had him put away in the Tower of London as opposed to Newgate, where he'd heard conditions were decidedly uncivilized, even for a man who could afford to pay for his accommodations.

The Tower was rather sparse, and the guards rather rude and not as careful with Jack's person as he would have liked. Nor was the Tower as comfortable as Lindsey had led Jack to believe, either, but he had a hearth, a desk and chair, and a serviceable bed. And a view of the Tower green, where, George reportedly said, in a fit of fury at learning Jack was in London, "Lambourne can gaze upon the spot his bonny Prince Charlie was beheaded."

He'd been a prisoner since the night he'd gone to the king. Just as Jack suspected, the king was right angry with him for returning to London, particularly when he'd gone to such great lengths to warn Jack to stay away.

Frankly, Jack had not known until that very night that His Majesty had given his own personal chaise to Fiona to run ahead of George's men and warn him. That seemed like something Fiona might have mentioned.

The king was in a very cross mood with a gouty foot and bad knee inflamed. He demanded an explanation for Jack's return.

Jack told him as simply as he could. "There is a lass in Scotland who is on the verge of losing what is rightly hers, and it would seem that I am the only one who might help her."

The king had glared at him, waiting for something more. When he didn't receive it, he'd said, "Then it seems proven that, indeed, the Earl of Lambourne will do anything to find his way under a skirt, including risking his own fool neck!"

Jack had bristled at that. Lizzie was different. He'd not risk his neck for just anyone. But he'd smiled, bowed his head and said, "Aye, Your Majesty, I risk my own liberty to help her, for she has been terribly wronged. She needs her king."

The king had stopped rubbing his knee to study Jack a moment. "Remarkable," he'd said thoughtfully. "What do you seek?"

Jack had quickly explained the situation. An old royal decree prohibiting the Beal men from owning land. The vein of slate that would keep Thorntree and its inhabitants for generations to come, and the struggle to possess the slate.

But Jack could see he was losing the king, who began to rub his knee with vigor, tossing aside the poultice that obviously did nothing and drawing the worried looks of two doctors who hovered nearby. "Your Majesty, I'd no' ask it of you did I no' believe this woman is the most deserving of your subjects."

The king snorted.

"She has been badly treated by the men of her family, but she remains cheerful in the face of adversity and determined to right those wrongs, even though she is merely a woman."

"Women should listen to their men if you ask me!"

the king said testily. "The Prince of Wales and his wife have made a mockery of marriage, for the simple fact she would not do as he bid her!"

"This woman did as her family bid her, Your Grace," Jack carefully continued. "And still they would do her harm."

The king grunted and waved Jack away.

But Jack did not intend to leave without the thing he needed. "She . . . she has a heart as deep as an ocean and a countenance as bright as a starry night, Your Majesty. Moreover, she possesses a determination that would put most men to shame. She is the essence of Scotland," he said.

That drew the king's attention. "You speak so eloquently, Lambourne. It is unlike you."

Jack smiled and bowed. "Even I can be moved when justice is denied."

The king began rubbing his knee again as he studied Jack. "What precisely is it you want?"

"That in your infinite wisdom, Your Grace, you set aside the handfasting that was done between us, and bless the engagement of Miss Beal and Mr. Gavin Gordon."

"You came for that?"

"And that the royal decree prohibiting Beal men from possessing property be somehow strengthened so that Mr. Gordon might protect it on behalf of Miss Beal, and Carson Beal be excluded from ever possessing the land or the slate, or disposing of the same."

"Carson Beal?" the king echoed.

"A Jacobite, Your Majesty," Jack said. Jack didn't think there were really Jacobites in Scotland any longer, but in the king's mind there were. "A Jacobite who would steal the land that is rightfully hers, given to her by His Majesty, your father."

"No," the king said, shaking his head. "Traitors, the lot of them! They made my father a most unhappy man! He had ulcers, were you aware?"

"I was no'."

"Why should I grant them land? No, no, I shall make it quite clear that this . . . this woman owns it and any minerals, et cetera, found on the land. The laird shall owe her a tax of—what do you think, one hundred pounds per annum?"

"That would do nicely, Your Majesty."

"To this woman—"

"Miss Elizabeth Drummond Beal and her sister, Miss Charlotte Drummond Beal—"

"And furthermore, will submit to the Crown twenty five pounds per annum for the trouble he's put us all to! Where is my scribe! I should like a scribe!" the king bellowed at one of the footmen, who scurried out to find a scribe at that late hour.

"I am forever in your debt, Your Majesty," Jack had said, bowing low.

"You are forever in my son's clutches," the king said. "Submit yourself for questioning, my lord."

Jack had been brought to the Tower that night. Each day, royal guards took him by way of Traitor's Gate to the home of Lord Mulgrave, where a privy council questioned him endlessly about his association with Caroline, Princess of Wales. Had he ever been intimate with her? Could he name men he believed had been intimate with her? Had he ever seen Captain Manby emerging from the princess's rooms?

Jack denied it all, but the men who questioned him—lords, like him—found his refusal hard to believe. The Earl of Lambourne, who had a notorious taste for women, had not sampled the princess's delights?

He was returned and tossed into his pair of rooms in the Tower each night without regard for his person, exhausted from the questioning and left to ponder his fate and what was left of his apparently ghastly reputation. He thought of Scotland, of the days of his childhood spent hunting the hills around Lambourne Castle.

When he wasn't mulling over his fate, Jack was pining for Lizzie. He thought of her, dreamed of her, summoned the image of her as she had appeared that last night, dressed exquisitely in the finest gown he'd ever seen, her eyes glistening with happiness. She was, he had no doubt, the most beautiful woman in London. In *Britain*.

He imagined Gordon offering her comfort when it was learned their host had been arrested, and her turning to Gordon and the security he offered. *Love*—what was love when the world was pounding at one's door? She needed someone like Gordon and she was far too clever not to realize it.

Jack spent countless hours imagining her return to Scotland bearing papers that confirmed Thorntree was hers, free and clear of any interference from Carson Beal. He imagined her bearing Gordon wee bairns, lots of chubby, happy bairns.

And Jack . . . he would be locked away for God only knew how long, rotting in this putrid cell. He had occasional visitors—the guards seemed disinclined to respond to requests to call on him except when pressed. But Christie, Lindsey, and now O'Conner, who had recently returned from Ireland with several fine horses to sell, would come when they were allowed, and they told him that the scandal was coming to a head, that decisions would be made very soon.

One day Jack met another prisoner at the Tower. Sir Richard Newlingale had just been brought up from Newgate, where he'd bartered his way into better accommodations at the Tower, and told Jack that the Crown was in a hanging mood, and several men were scheduled to hang on Wednesday next.

That was when Jack began to imagine his own hanging. He imagined the noose around his neck, the moment when the executioner put the black bag over his head and the floor fell out beneath him.

When royal guards roused him Wednesday afternoon with the very cryptic, "It is time to go, gov'na," and shoved him out the door, Jack assumed the worst. They told him to gather his things and did not respond when he asked where they were taking him as they dragged him across the Tower green to Traitor's Gate.

This was it, then, Jack thought. They would take him to his public trial, where he'd be found guilty of high treason and would hang, perhaps even today. He'd not see Fiona, but that was just as well. He did not want his sister's last memory of him to be his execution. He was thankful he'd written his farewell letters after all. He had not finished the letter to Lizzie, but there was so much he really didn't know how to say.

At Traitor's Gate they put him on a royal barge and moved him upstream, to Whitehall Stairs. Jack concluded the trial was to be held before Parliament. He really had no idea how trials for treason were carried out, but thought that made sense. He imagined his old friend, the traitor Wilkes, walking the same path before him, and wondered if he'd known he was going to die, if he'd imagined it as vividly as Jack had.

At Whitehall Stairs, he was surprised to see Christie, Lindsey, and O'Conner standing about, as if they were waiting for a water transport. He assumed that they, as gentlemen and lords, were duty bound to escort him to trial. "So this is it, then, aye?" Jack said as he moved heavily up the steps, the guards flanking him.

"One might say," Christie said solemnly.

"Well," Jack said with a sigh as one of the guards handed a bag of Jack's things to O'Conner, "no one can say I did no' have a good life, aye? I've enjoyed almost all of it, I have. Granted, there were times when my father lived that I thought it rather bleak, and I donna take any fond memories from this last fortnight," he said with a withering look for his guards. "But all and all, I've no complaints."

The three men exchanged a look but said nothing. The guards escorted the four of them to a royal coach. It seemed fitting somehow that George would provide a coach to see Jack to his end.

Lindsey was the first to enter. Christie and O'Conner followed him. "Milord," one of the guards said, and held open the door of the coach.

Jack climbed in and took his seat and looked around at his closest friends. They seemed rather relaxed, given the gravity of the day. Jack was a bit exasperated with them, in truth. It was possibly his final day, and a wee bit of ceremony did not seem out of the question.

"I've thought quite a lot about my estate," he said, and nodded to the bag O'Conner held. "There are papers within, but the sum of it is, as I leave no male heirs, the estate will naturally go to Fiona and," he added with a grimace, "*Buchanan.*"

Lindsey cocked a brow.

Jack frowned. "Here's a bit of parting advice, lads: never trust a Buchanan. Now then, there is the matter of some shares I hold in the three percents. I should like them to be divided among some charities. I donna know the precise charities, as regrettably, I've no' become as familiar with them as I ought to have done, but Lindsey, the countess will know, will she no'?"

"Ah . . . yes. Yes, she will," he said, exchanging a look with Christie.

"There are other papers there," Jack said. "Official documents and whatnot," he added, and patiently explained them all as the coach pulled away from Whitehall Stairs.

They rode in silence for a few minutes, Jack ruminating about how precious was this last glimpse of London. Funny, what he wished he could see now was Scotland. He wished for one last look at the hills and the pines, and those things that reminded him of who he was. He wished he could see Thorntree one last time, for that small manor had come to symbolize Scotland to him in a way Lambourne Castle never had. It was rather sobering to know that he'd not realized until his last day how much a Scot he truly was. At Thorntree he'd rediscovered it, and it would be his dying regret that he'd not had a chance to redeem himself in that regard.

The coach turned onto a major thoroughfare, and Jack realized his time was growing short. "There is one last thing I'd say."

His companions looked at him expectantly

"Miss Beal. Miss Elizabeth Drummond Beal, to be precise. She's . . . she's undoubtedly gone back to Scotland, aye? *Ach,* I can scarcely blame her. I've put a letter to her in the package, Christie, but it is unfinished. If you would, please, do tell her that I . . . I did indeed love her. M-more than life, apparently, for I am here on her behalf. No, donna tell her that, for I'd no' have this on her good conscience. But I should like her to know that I did indeed love her, more than I could find the words to say."

"Lambourne—"

"I never loved a woman ere this, you know I have

no'," he continued earnestly. "But Lizzie . . ." He shook his head. "Lizzie lit something inside me that I was no' even aware could fire, and I believe I will miss knowing her most of all."

Lindsey, seated next to him, turned his face away from Jack and looked out the window. Across from him, O'Conner had pulled his hat low over his brow so that Jack could not see his eyes. Only Christie looked directly at him, his gaze completely shuttered. "You were saying?" he prompted Jack.

Lindsey coughed.

"Only that if there was one thing about my life I would change, it would have been that I had married Lizzie and sired quite a lot of wee bouncing bairns with her. Scores of them. I think I might have liked children underfoot." -

Lindsey coughed again and sank into his seat. O'Conner surged forward, propping his arms on his knees and dipping his head between his shoulders. Christie covered his mouth as he quietly contemplated what Jack had said.

"What is it, do you suppose? What is that thing women have that can slip under your skin and anchor there? The thing that will no' let you go, night or day, that makes you do things you never thought yourself capable of doing? What do you name it?"

Christie shook his head.

"Aye, she filled my heart to the point of bursting," he said, tapping himself on the chest, "and it is my dearest wish that the lot of you might know that sort of love one day. *That*, gentlemen, is what makes this life worth living. Pity I discovered it far too late, aye?"

"Indeed it is," Lindsey said in a strangled voice. And as Jack turned to look at him, he noticed they were pulling up at Jack's house on Audley Street. Lambourne House!

"What the devil?" he asked, confused.

Lindsey and O'Conner dissolved into fits of laughter. Grinning, Christie leaned across the coach and clapped Jack on the shoulder. "My friend, you will not hang today. You've been released for lack of evidence. The prince has forgiven you."

Dumbfounded, he stared at the lot of them. "Do you mean . . ."

"Yes," Lindsey said, and spasmed with another fit of laughter.

"Bloody hell, do you think you might have said so a wee bit sooner?" he exclaimed crossly, his ire soaring. But the realization that he was free suddenly began to register. "Lizzie!" he cried. "Has she—"

"She's inside," Christie said, opening the coach door.

Chapter Thirty-eight

Lizzie had finally given in to Fiona's desire to dress her. Today she was wearing a beautiful green and white day gown, overlaid in organza and embroidered with tiny butterflies around the hem and sleeves. She might not have warmed to London, but she had warmed to fine ladies' clothing.

Her hair was knotted at her nape and she wore pearl earrings to match her necklace, likewise borrowed from Fiona. Fiona was leaving on the morrow, returning to Scotland to prepare for her wedding. Lizzie was going to miss her. They'd become good friends in this long fortnight.

She would not miss Gavin, who had accepted the news of a change in her heart with élan. When she'd discovered what Jack had done for her with the king, she'd found the courage to cry off, and told Gavin truthfully that while she would always hold a fond place in her heart for him, she'd fallen hopelessly in love with Jack.

"Lambourne?" he said. "He's locked away."

"And my heart with him," she said sincerely.

Gavin smiled. "I can hardly claim no' to have noticed it," he said with a weary sigh. "I am sorry for it, for I've always been right fond of you, Lizzie, I have indeed. But I will wish you the best." He shook his head, looked at his hands. "Perhaps this is just as well, aye? For I think I have fallen in love with London and the friends I have met here."

The *ladies* he'd met here—Lizzie knew very well what Gavin had been up to, thanks to Fiona.

Gavin spent the fortnight of Jack's captivity taking a lease on a smaller but suitably situated town home. He intended to stay on in London indefinitely, and wrote his father, asking him to look after the Gordon estate in his absence.

Lizzie had written Charlotte, too, telling her she'd be home just as soon as she could. But she would not leave London without speaking to Jack, and now that he'd been freed . . .

She was quite nervous. He was coming home today, and she didn't know how he'd feel about finding her here. She checked her reflection one last time in the mirror and was tucking up a curl when she heard him.

"*Lizzie!*" he shouted.

She whirled around and put a hand to her heart to still it. It would not be stilled. She flew out of the suite, down the hall to the curving stairs, her feet flying down the marble steps to the entrance hall.

Jack was standing there, his hat swept off his head and clutched in his hand. His gaze raked over her. "You're here yet."

"Aye," she said uncertainly.

He suddenly strode forward, cupped her elbow, and marched her into the gold salon. Just inside the door he paused, and the two of them looked at each other. How long they stood there just gazing at one another, Lizzie could not guess. A world of meaning and understanding seemed to flow between them in the silence.

At last Jack spoke. "Gordon, he's . . . ?"

"Gone," she said quickly. "Our understanding has come to an end."

His eyes narrowed. "And what of our understanding?" he demanded. "The handfasting?"

Lizzie's heart skipped a beat. She swallowed down her fear and lifted her chin. "I've no' cried off if that is what you mean. You sent me a bonnet—"

"Woman, I've never in my life imagined one could attach so much meaning to a bloody *bonnet*. It was a hat! No' a jewel, no' a horse—"

"And I am still waiting to hear you say that you esteem me," she said stubbornly. "If ye donna, I will return to Thorntree today and you have my vow I shall never bother you again."

"I donna *esteem* you!" he cried heavenward, and Lizzie's heart lurched. "What is in that head of yours, lass? I *love* you!"

Lizzie gasped. Desire began to flow in her like a living, breathing thing.

"Do you think I've thought of anything else these long weeks? There, then, you have it—I love you, Lizzie Beal! I have loved you I think since the moment you jumped from the window at Castle Beal! I have loved your spirit and your determination, and how you've cared for your sister and done your best to keep Thorntree from ruin, and I . . . I *love* you," he said, taking a small step forward. "I love you more than I have a right to, for I've done some bloody awful things. But I love you more than I thought possible."

"*Jack*," she whispered.

He reached for her the same moment she leapt into his arms. He enveloped her in his arms and kissed her deeply, kissed her like a man who had thirsted for love and had faced his own mortality and who would never let her go, not ever.

She returned his kiss just as passionately. He felt as hard and strong and secure as he ever had. He pushed her up against the door, and lifted his head. "By the bye, you could no' be more beautiful, but today you take my breath away."

"Say it again," she sighed longingly as his gaze began to drift down her body. "Say you love me, Jack."

"Please, *leannan* . . . donna make me say how much I love you, for you will faint with astonishment," he said as his hands followed his gaze, painting a path down her body, sending delicious shivers through her. "You remained here. You waited for me," he said, as if he could not quite believe it.

"I would have waited through eternity," she said, and clasped his head in her hands, made him look at her. "I love you, Jack, with all my heart. I will never love another." She moved her hands to his chest.

Her warmth radiated through his skin like sunshine, and as he gathered her in his arms, he felt himself rising up, hard and eager to make love to her.

"Allow me this truth, Lizzie," he said, sobering. "I've never been in love in my sorry life until now. I donna want to be the sort of man my father was, but there are times that I fear it—"

She stopped him put her hand across his mouth. "Fiona told me. But you . . . you are far superior to him in every way. Jack, you were willing to sacrifice your life for who you love. You are your own man—you are no' him. On that, I would stake my own life."

No one had ever said words like that to Jack, and it made him feel as tall as a mountain. "*Diah*, I love you, lass!" he said, and put his mouth to her neck at the same moment he picked her up. He carried her across the room and put her down on the settee, determined to show her just how much he loved her then and there. He went down on knee beside the settee, his hands already working at the fastenings of her gown. The need to be with her, to hold her, was suddenly overwhelming. "*Alainne*," he said, using the Gaelic word for *beautiful*. "You can no' know just how beautiful you are to me."

"Show me," she said, and sat up, drawing her legs under her so that she was on her knees. She took his head in her hands once more, and said, "Please, Jack. Please, I beg of you, show me how much you adore me."

He grinned. "Are you *begging* me?"

"I am begging you," she whispered, and kissed his temple, then his cheek.

"Well, then, as you've asked me in such a pleasing manner," he said, lifting her breast from the bodice of her gown, "I am very happy to oblige." He took her into his mouth as Lizzie bent over him with a giggle.

Jack showed Lizzie that afternoon that he'd never desired anyone or anything so completely in his life. He'd found the purest form of love in the most unlikely place, and Jack realized, as he and Lizzie reached new heights of ecstasy, that he had, at long last, come home.

Epilogue

There were many in Glenalmond who predicted Carson Beal would not go willingly to the authorities when it was discovered he was poaching slate from the Thorntree mine. It was Newton who discovered it and it was Newton who convinced Carson that he should surrender.

Newton was a loyal man, but his loyalties had shifted to his wife, Charlotte, and the baby she carried in her belly.

In an ironic twist of fate, the Beal clan voted Newton laird and put Carson on the wee bit of arable land Newton had farmed for several years.

Neither Charlotte nor Newton cared for Castle Beal, however, and they gave it to the clan. Tours of the castle brought some much-needed revenue to the clan's coffers. Lizzie gave Thorntree to Charlotte and Newton free and clear after she and Jack married. She and Jack took up residence in the abandoned Lambourne Castle, much to the delight of a small clan of Haines people, whom Jack had never really known, but among whom he found his society, and he ruled over it with the same joie de vivre he'd had in London.

He kept in touch with his old friends, and occasionally one would come to Scotland to call. The summer past,

Lindsey had come for a fortnight with his wife, Evelyn, and their wee daughter.

Jack was happy to present his young son to the Lindseys. He and Lizzie had named him James, in honor of Newton, who, they discovered, had a given name after all.

At Lambourne, Lizzie was determined to erase Jack's painful childhood memories from that forbidding old castle, and with Jack's blessing she enlisted Fiona's help to refurbish all the rooms. That meant Fiona and Duncan Buchanan were around quite a lot, and Jack, in turn, grudgingly came to admire Buchanan, his old nemesis. The two of them liked to hunt together, although neither would admit the other was much of a hunter.

Lambourne Castle slowly became a different place than it had been in Jack and Fiona's youth. It was a happy place now.

That summer, however, Jack and Lizzie had returned to Thorntree, as Charlotte was fearful of facing her first lying-in alone. One lazy Sunday afternoon, they sat on the newly constructed terrace Newton had built. Dougal, who had determined he liked working in the service of the laird of Lambourne, was James's nurse, and he carried around the wooden rocking pony James liked to ride.

Lizzie poured her husband a tot of whisky and handed it to him as they watched James ride his pony. Jack took the whisky with a frown and ignored his companions on the terrace, looking out over the gardens, which were much cleaner and brighter than he remembered. Mr. Kincade had a helper now, he'd heard. The lad Lachlan from Castle Beal was learning the art of gardening under Mr. Kincade's tutelage.

"Still cross, are you?" Lizzie asked, putting her hand on Jack's shoulder and squeezing fondly.

"Donna goad me, *leannan*," Jack warned her.

"As petulant as a child," Charlotte sighed.

"I'm no'," Jack insisted. "But you must admit that my bows were as good as hers. I can hardly help the wind that kicked up!"

"There was a wee breeze," Newton said. "No' enough to put an arrow off course."

Lizzie laughed roundly. "Admit it! You canna bear being bested by a woman in a game of archery!"

"Or racing," Dougal helpfully added. "She's a better horsewoman than you, too, milord."

"Thank you, Dougal, for pointing that out," Jack said tersely. "I suppose you all think she is a better fisherman than me, too, aye?"

Charlotte snorted; Dougal exchanged a look with Lizzie, then shrugged noncommittally. "Come then, me fine young lad," he said to the baby James. "Let us walk among the flowers your Uncle Newton has seen fit to bring back to life." He picked up James in one beefy arm, and strolled down the stone steps, into the garden.

"Really, Jack, it's no' uncommon for a Highlander to be good at such diversions as archery and fishing and riding," Lizzie said. "We live off the land here, aye?"

"Lizzie, my love, you are no' helping matters in the least," he groused.

"Think of it this way," Charlotte offered. "You are very good at cooking. Mrs. Kincade still speaks of the day her back ailed her and you made the bread as she instructed you."

Jack shot his sister-in-law a look. "I thought we all agreed *that* was an emergency. One loaf of bread does no' make me a cook."

"Aye, but you clearly have a talent for it."

"And making fires," Newton added. "Quite handy when it comes to lighting peat."

"Is that all?" Jack drawled.

"Embroidery," Lizzie said.

With a growl, Jack abruptly leapt up and lunged for her, but she jumped out of his reach and picking up her skirts, began to run.

"You best run, Lady Lambourne!" he called after her.

Lizzie loved the sound of *Lady Lambourne*. She glanced over her shoulder—he was already on her heels. With a squeal, she flew through the pair of French doors, but Jack caught her by the waist and dragged her up against his chest. "You've gone and done it, lass, have you no'? For now I must exact my punishment."

She laughed and twisted in his arms, tilting her head back to see him. "Punish me, Jack. Make me weep."

He kissed her hard on the mouth, then lifted his head, brushed the rogue curls from her face. "If only I could make you weep with happiness as I do every day."

Oh, but Lizzie wept. She wept with angels and her tears were drops of pure joy.

Jack slipped his arm around her waist and glanced over his shoulder. "Come, then, let us find a moment of privacy before Newton determines it is time I light a bit of peat," he said. "The man goes about as if he is the bloody laird here."

Lizzie laughed; Jack kissed her, then slipped his arm around her waist and the two of them hurried along to steal another moment of bliss before it came time to do the evening chores.

ENJOY THE FOLLOWING PREVIEW OF

A Courtesan's Scandal

THE NEXT PASSIONATE NOVEL IN
JULIA LONDON'S CAPTIVATING
SCANDALOUS SERIES

COMING FROM POCKET BOOKS IN
NOVEMBER 2009.

❦

LONDON, ENGLAND
CHRISTMAS, 1806

On a snowy Christmas Eve, as the most elite ranks of the *haut ton* gathered at Darlington House in London's Mayfair district to usher in the twelve days of Christmas, an annoyed Duke of Darlington was across town, striding purposefully down King Street through a light dusting of snow, studying the light fans above the town house doors in search of the entertwined letters *G* and *K*.

He passed a group of revelers who called out "Happy Christmas" to him, but it irritated the duke, as they blocked the walkway. He curtly tipped his hat, stepped around them, and continued on, looking at every fan above every door in the line of tidy, respectable townhomes.

He found his *G* and *K* on the last town house, a large red brick. Quite nice, actually. The duke could not help but wonder what salacious little act the resident had performed to earn a house of this quality.

He stepped up to the door, lifted the brass knocker, rapped three times, and stepped back. His hands clasped behind his back, he waited impatiently. He was in a very cross mood to be sure. He'd never been so exploited, so ill-used—

The door swung open and a swarthy-looking gentleman in a rumpled suit stood before him. He looked the duke directly in the eye and offered no greeting.

"The Duke of Darlington." His voice was gruff as he reached into his coat pocket and withdrew a calling card. "I have come to call on Miss Bergeron. She is expecting me."

The man held out a silver tray. Darlington tossed his card onto it. "I'll inform her you're here," the man said, and moved to shut the door.

But Darlington had been vexed past all civility; he quickly threw up his hand and blocked the door to prevent it from shutting. "I'll wait inside, if you please."

The man said nothing, but shoved the door shut, leaving Darlington standing on the stoop.

"Bloody outrageous," he muttered, and glanced up the street. It was Christmas Eve, and in spite of the inclement weather, people had set out to various gatherings. He himself was expected on the other side of Green Park a half hour ago to preside over the annual soiree held for one hundred and fifty of the family's closest friends.

The door abruptly opened, startling Darlington. The man said, "Come."

Darlington swept inside and removed his beaver hat, which he thrust at the man. "What is your name?" he demanded.

"Butler."

"I do not mean your occupation," he said shortly, "but your name."

"*Butler*," the man responded just as gruffly. "This way," he added, and carelessly tossed the duke's hat onto a console. He walked on, lifting a candelabra high to light the way.

He led Darlington up a flight of stairs, then down a corridor that was lined with paintings and expensive china vases stuffed with hothouse flowers. The floor covering, he noted, was the finest Belgian carpet that could be had in London.

Miss Bergeron had done very well for herself.

Butler paused before a pair of red pocket doors and knocked. A muffled woman's voice bid him enter. He looked at Darlington. "Wait," he said, and walked in through the doors, leaving them slightly open.

Darlington sighed impatiently and glanced at his pocket watch again.

"Here now, darling," he heard a feminine voice say silkily. "Tell me, how do you like this?"

"*Mmm*," a male answered.

Darlington jerked his gaze to the pair of doors and stared in disbelief.

"And *this*?" she asked with a bit of a chuckle. "Do you like it?"

Her response, from what the duke could gather, was a sigh of pleasure.

"Ah, but wait, for you've not lived until you've—"

"Caller," Butler said.

"Not *now*, Kate," the man objected painfully. "Please! You leave me with such hunger."

"Please show him in, Aldous," the woman said. "Digby! Keep your hands away!"

Darlington started when Butler pushed the doors wide open. He quickly glanced down, almost afraid to look into the room, afraid of what lewd act he was interrupting.

"Your Grace?"

Darlington looked up. Whatever he might have expected, it was not what greeted him. Yes, the room looked a bit like a French boudoir with peach-colored walls, silken draperies, and overstuffed furnishings upholstered in chintz. There were magazines, hats, and a cloak carelessly draped over a chair. But the woman inside was not lying on a daybed with a man on top of her as he suspected.

He was surprised to see her standing at a table piled high with pastries and sweetmeats. Moreover, there were Christmas boughs and hollies adorning the walls and the mantel, a dozen candles lit the room, and a fire was blazing in the hearth.

There was indeed a man, as well, a portly fellow who weighed eighteen stone if he weighed one, but he was holding nothing more lurid than a teacup. On his lip was a white substance, which, judging by the look of things, was the remnants of a pastry.

Darlington was stunned, first and foremost because he had supposed something entirely different was occurring in this room. But perhaps even more so because the woman, Miss Katherine Bergeron, was breathtaking.

Darlington had known this woman was unusually beautiful. He'd heard it from more than one quarter and he'd seen it with his own eyes not two nights past at the King's Opera House, when he'd attended the first London performance of Mozart's *La clemenza di Tito* at the behest of his friend George, the Prince of Wales. He'd sat with George in the royal box, and it was George who had pointed her out, seated two boxes away. She was in the company of Mr. Cousineau, a Frenchman who had made a respectable fortune from selling fabrics to wealthy London society. Miss Bergeron was infamously his model and his mistress.

As he observed her that evening, she'd leaned slightly forward in her seat, enraptured by the music. She'd worn a milky white silk gown trimmed in pink velvet that seemed to shimmer in the low light of the opera house. Pearls had dripped from her ears, her wrist, and, more notably, her throat. Her hair, pale blond, was bound up with yet another string of pearls. She did not wear a plume as so many ladies seemed to prefer, but instead allowed wisps of curls to drape the nape of her long, slender neck.

She'd seemed to sense his gaze, for she'd turned her

head slightly and looked at him. She did not glance shyly away when she discovered him observing her, but calmly returned his gaze a long moment before turning her attention to the stage once more.

The duke had found her boldness mildly interesting. Nevertheless, he had not anticipated seeing her again . . . until George had summoned him. Now he was standing in her private salon.

But she looked nothing like she had the night at the opera. She was beautiful, astonishingly so, but a simpler, natural beauty, free of cosmetic. She wore a rather plain blue gown with a shawl wrapped demurely around her shoulders. Her hair was not dressed, but hung long and full down her back.

"Your Grace," she said again, smiling warmly. She picked up a plate of muffins. "May I entice you with a Chrismas treat? I just made them," she added proudly.

"They are divine, Your Grace," the portly man said, coming to a pair of small feet and bowing his head.

"*No,*" Darlington said incredulously. Did they think he'd come for tea? He looked at Miss Bergeron. "A word, madam?"

"Of course," she said, and handed the plate of muffins to her companion. "Please do go with Aldous, Digby, and mind you don't eat them all."

"I shall endeavour to be good," he said jovially, "but you know how wretched I can be." He patted his enormous belly. He took the plate from her, gave the duke another curt bow, and followed Butler out.

When they had left the room, Darlington looked at Miss Bergeron. "I regret that we've not had the courtesy of a proper introduction, but it would seem the situation does not lend itself to that."

"Yes," she said, eyeing the rest of the food on the table, "I had not expected you so soon."

"Your patron was rather insistent."

She gave him a wry look and gestured to a chair near at the table. "Are you certain I cannot tempt you to taste a muffin? I confess, I am just learning the art of baking and I am not certain of the quality."

No, she could not; Darlington did not move.

"Please," she said again, gesturing to the chair. "I hope you will be at ease here."

"Miss Bergeron, I do not find the circumstances the least bit easy."

"*Oh,*" she said, lifting a fine brow. "I *see.*"

He rather doubted she did. She was a courtesan, hardly accustomed to the pressures of propriety he faced every day. "I have come as the prince has demanded to make your acquaintance and to mutually agree on an appearance or two that will serve his . . . purpose," he said with distaste.

She smiled then, and Darlington knew in that moment how she had captivated the prince. "Very well." She folded her arms across her middle and moved away from the table, that lovely, captivating smile still on her face.

If she thought that he could be so easily seduced, she was very much mistaken. And pray tell, what was that just above the dimple on her cheek? A bit of flour? "There is the Carlton House Twelfth Night ball," he said, a bit distracted by the flour.

"That would do," she agreed. "Shall I meet you there?"

"I will come for you."

Her smile seemed to grow even more enticing.

"There is an opera scheduled shortly thereafter. Will that suit?"

"I adore opera," she said smoothly.

"Very well," Darlington said. "That should suffice for the time being. Furthermore, I will remind you that in the course of this *ruse,*" he said with an angry flick of his wrist, "I expect you to defer to me as one would defer to a peer. We are merely to be seen in public together and rely on the usual wagging tongues to do the rest. Therefore, I see no reason to touch or otherwise engage in any untoward behavior that might be remarked upon by my family or close acquaintances. When these public events have concluded, I will see to it that you are escorted safely home, but I see no point in prolonging our contact any more than is required. Are we are agreed?"

She smiled curiously. "Are you always so officious?"

Officious. If only she knew what sacrifice he was making at the prince's behest. "Do not mistake me, Miss Bergeron. I have been coerced into this . . . charade," he bit out. "I take no pleasure in it. I would not give you the slightest cause for false hope of any sort. Now then—if we are agreed, I shall take my leave," he concluded, and turned toward the door.

"If by false hope you mean that you will not taste my muffin and pronounce it very good, you must not fret, Your Grace," she said, drawing his attention back to her. "I had no hope of it, I was merely being civil." She picked up a delicacy and walked toward him, her gaze unabashedly taking him in. "There is just one small matter," she said, pausing to bite into the delicacy. Her brows rose, and she smiled. "*Mmm.* Very good, if I do say so myself," she pronounced, tilting her head back to look up at him, her pale green eyes softened by the length of her dark lashes.

The duke frowned suspiciously. He had an insane urge to wipe the flour from her cheek. She was delicate, her height slightly below average. She had a softly regal bearing, an elegance that set her apart from most women. And her hair . . . her hair looked like spun silk.

"I should not like to give you cause for false hope, either. Therefore, I should like to make it perfectly clear that this arrangement is not *my* preference any more than, apparently, it is yours. I am not yours to use, Your

Grace. You may not touch me, or otherwise take liberty with my person."

The duke cocked one dark brow above the other and smiled wryly, his gaze on her lush lips. He certainly understood what pleasure a man would find in kissing that mouth. "You may rest assured, Miss Bergeron, that is neither my desire nor my intent. I find the suggestion quite distasteful."

Something flickered in her eyes, and she smiled with relish. "*Really?* No man has ever said that to me." She popped the last little bite into her mouth.

Did this chit not know who he was? What power he wielded in the House of Lords? In *London*? He shifted slightly so that he was towering over her. She did not seem the least bit cowed.

"*I* am saying it, Miss Bergeron. I am not the prince. I am not bowled over by your beauty or your apparent bedroom charms."

"Splendid! We should get on quite nicely then, Your Grace, for I am not a debutante yearning for your attention or a match."

For once, the duke was speechless. "Is there anything else?" he asked curtly as she calmly—and provocatively—used the tip of her finger to wipe the corner of her mouth.

"Yes. You may call me Kate," she said pertly. "What may I call you?"

"Your Grace," he snapped, and strode out of that French boudoir with an uncharacteristically hot temper.

BONUS PREVIEW!

READ AN EXCERPT FROM JULIA LONDON'S
EMOTIONALLY CHARGED, PAGE-TURNING
CONTEMPORARY ROMANTIC NOVEL

Summer of Two Wishes

AVAILABLE FROM POCKET BOOKS IN
SEPTEMBER 2009.

The first time a U.S. Army Casualty Notification Officer came looking for Macy, it was to tell her that her husband Finn had died in Afghanistan.

Suicide bomber, the officer had said. Nothing left but a half-burned dog tag.

Macy didn't remember much after that, except that she was getting groceries out of the car when the officer arrived, and his eyes were the exact shade of the head of iceberg lettuce that had rolled away when she'd dropped them.

Three years later, when the second Casualty Notification Officer came to see Macy, she would remember Finn's black Lab, Milo, racing through the tables they'd set up on the lawn, pausing to shake the river water from his coat and spraying the pristine white linen table cloths with dirty brown spots. She'd remember thinking *don't panic, don't panic,* over and over again as she stared at those spots.

Everything else would be a blur.

The officer found Macy at her Aunt Laru's limestone ranch house just outside of Cedar Springs, Texas, in the Hill Country west of Austin. It was a beautiful spread, forty acres of rolling hills covered in live oaks and cedar on the banks of the Pedernales River.

Laru Harper had married and divorced three times before the age of forty-five. The marriages had left her a little bit jaded and a little bit wealthy, and when Laru learned Macy was hosting a luncheon fund-raiser, she'd insisted that Macy host it at her house. "I didn't put up with Randy King for six years to sit and look at this view by myself," she'd said with a flip of her strawberry blond hair over her shoulder. "Have the luncheon here, Macy."

Even though it was June, it was not yet miserably hot, so Macy had decided to have it on the grassy riverbank and had set up three large round tables beneath the oddly twisting limbs of the live oaks. She'd dressed the tables in linen, littered them with rose petals and rose centerpieces, and set them with fine china from Laru's second marriage. She'd enlisted her aunt to make batches of her signature white and red sangria, and had food catered from Three Sisters, which specialized in "discriminating palates."

"If by *discriminating* they refer to folks who won't pass over a single morsel that isn't nailed down, then I think we've got the right caterer," Laru quipped.

The day was overcast and a slight breeze was coming up off the river. An hour before the guests were due to arrive, Laru insisted on tightening the halter of the pink sundress Macy had found on sale for the occasion. "You look so cute!" she said at last, he hands on her waist. "Very hostessy. Has Wyatt seen you in that?"

"Not yet," Macy said as she donned the pearl earrings and necklace he'd given her. He was always giving her gifts. Pearls, an iPhone. A boat.

"Best make sure he doesn't see you until after the luncheon. He's likely to tear it right off your body."

"Laru!" Macy said with a laugh.

"What?" Laru asked innocently. "It's no secret that every time that man looks at you his eyes get as shiny as new pennies."

"Well, he's not invited. It's ladies only. *Rich* ladies,

and as we both know, that's not his type," Macy said, and Laru laughed. "Besides, he's in San Antonio today. I won't see him until tonight."

Satisfied with her appearance, Macy walked outside to check on everything once more. Ernesto, Laru's handyman, was out front, sweeping the stone porch. "If you see women in floppy hats, send them on around, will you?" she asked, indicating the flagstone walkway around the side of the house. *"Gracias!"*

The setting was lovely, Macy thought as she rounded the corner of the house. Everything looked perfect. But as she stood there admiring her work, Milo, Finn's dog, shot past.

"Hey," Macy muttered. Milo was not the sort of dog to run. Generally, he was much happier lying around in the shade. But when he emerged through the tables, she saw that he had a grungy rope toy in his mouth. Out from beneath another table shot a beagle in hot pursuit.

"Hey!" Macy shouted as Milo headed for the river. "Milo, *no!*" But Milo dove heedlessly into the river, paddled around, then climbed up on the bank again, taunted the beagle with his toy, and dashed up through the tables, where he paused to shake the water off his coat.

"No!" Macy cried.

The beagle barked, and Milo was off again.

"Ms. Macy Clark?"

Startled by the sound of a male voice, Macy whirled around and came face-to-face with an officer standing before her in full dress uniform. She knew instantly what sort of officer he was, and her heart skipped in her chest. What was he doing here? Finn was dead, dead three miserable, long years. Dead for three years of waking up every single morning to face the heartache of him being gone all over again, of her sun and moon missing, of realizing she wasn't living in a dream, that he wasn't going to come through the door with his tanned arms and his straw hat pulled low over his eyes, grinning like he wanted her with syrup for breakfast.

"Beg your pardon, ma'am—I am Lieutenant Colonel Dan Freeman with the United States Army," he said, dabbing at the perspiration on his forehead with a handkerchief. The bags under his eyes made him look like a sad old hound dog. "I need to speak with you, please."

"Me?" she said as Milo and the beagle dashed in between them. "Is it the fund-raiser?" she said, thinking wildly that perhaps the Army didn't approve. "It's the fund-raiser, isn't it?"

"The fund-raiser?"

"The Lifeline Project," she said. "My friend Samantha and I—I met her in a support group, and we wanted to help the families of fallen soldiers because they really need more than just the death gratuity. Not that the gratuity isn't generous, it is! But there is all this . . . this emotional stuff that money can't fix. So we started the Lifeline Project. That's okay, isn't it?"

She realized she was beginning to ramble, but there was something about the officer's demeanor that made her strangely anxious. He was looking at her blankly. He clearly hadn't come to talk about the Lifeline Project fund-raiser, and butterflies started to flit around Macy's belly. "You've never heard of us, have you?"

He shook his head.

What was the matter with her, why did she have such a bad feeling? There was nothing this officer could tell her that could hurt her, not anymore.

A barking dog, a sound of a car's wheels crunching on the gravel drive in front filtered into her consciousness somehow. Someone shouted, *"Damn dog!"*

"What is it?" Macy asked softly. "What has happened?"

"Would you like to sit down?" he asked, carefully returning his handkerchief to his pocket.

Macy's belly swooned. "I am about to host a fund-raiser."

"It can't wait, ma'am," he said sympathetically, and smiled. "Maybe we can sit at one of those tables."

"How did you find me?" she asked, ignoring his gesture toward her tables.

"Your neighbor told me you were here and was kind enough to give me directions."

"Okay," she said resolutely, in spite of the rubbery feeling in her legs. "Okay, Lieutenant Colonel Freeman, you can't tell me anything worse than the Army has already told me, right? So please, whatever it is, just say it."

"Yes, ma'am," Lieutenant Colonel Freeman said. He kept his dog eyes steady on her as he reached into his coat pocket. "Ms. Clark, I bring you some startling news." He held out an envelope to her.

Her heart pounding, Macy stared at it. She didn't want to touch that envelope. It was impossible that it could say anything—*Finn is dead! He's dead, he's dead!* The officer shifted slightly, moving the envelope closer to her, and Macy reluctantly took it. Her hands were shaking so badly she could hardly open it; the envelope fluttered to the ground as she unfolded the letter.

"Ma'am, if I may," the officer said. "The secretary of defense regrets to inform you that we have made a gross error in concluding Sergeant Finn was killed in action because he has indeed been found alive. On June twenty, at oh two hundred hours . . ."

Macy never heard the rest of what he said. She couldn't breathe, she couldn't speak, and everything began to swirl in an emotional vortex. The last thing Macy saw was Lt. Col. Dan Freeman lurching forward to catch her as she melted.

Delve into a passion from the past with a romance from Pocket Books!

Delve into a timeless passion...
Pick up a bestselling historical romance from Pocket Books!

Karen Hawkins
To Catch a Highlander
In this game of hearts, love is the only prize.

Johanna Lindsey
The Devil Who Tamed Her
He loves a challenge...and she is an irresistible one.

Jane Feather
To Wed a Wicked Prince
This prince has more than marriage on his mind...

Sabrina Jeffries
Let Sleeping Rogues Lie
Enroll in the School for Heiresses, and discover that desire
has its own rules...and temptations its own rewards.

Meredith Duran
The Duke of Shadows
Born an outcast. Raised to nobility. Only one dangerous
passion can unlock his heart.

Ana Leigh
One Night With a Sweet-Talking Man
He talked his way into her heart.
Can he do the same with her bed?

Available wherever books are sold or at www.simonsayslove.com.